D1327743

700039738527

ROCK CREEK PARK

ROCK CREEK PARK

SIMON CONWAY

HODDER &
STOUGHTON

First published in Great Britain in 2012 by Hodder & Stoughton
An Hachette UK company

1

Copyright © Simon Conway 2012

The right of Simon Conway to be identified as the Author of the Work
has been asserted by him in accordance with the Copyright,
Designs and Patents Act 1988.

A CIP catalogue record for this title is available from the British Library

Hardback ISBN 978 1 444 72776 0
Trade Paperback ISBN 978 1 444 72777 7

Map Illustrations © Rosie Collins

Typeset in Plantin by Hewer Text UK Ltd, Edinburgh

Printed and bound by Clays Ltd, St Ives plc

Hodder & Stoughton policy is to use papers that are natural,
renewable and recyclable products and made from wood grown
in sustainable forests. The logging and manufacturing processes
are expected to conform to the environmental regulations
of the country of origin.

Hodder & Stoughton Ltd
338 Euston Road
London NW1 3BH

www.hodder.co.uk

For Sarah

Thanks: Nick Sayers, Alicia Koundakjian, Walter Shapiro, Justin Moyers, Joel Garreau, Jon Snow, Phil Robertson, David Smith, Wendell Steavenson, Robert Draper, Laura Macdougall, Dai Baker, Tom McGuire, TK Mehlhaff, Gordon Conway, Victoria Monroe, Iain Hutchison, Morag Lyall, Adrianne Threatt, Paul McAuley, Nerina Cevra, Paddy Nicoll, Misha Glenny, Vicky Charles and Portia Stratton.

It seems feasible that over the coming century human nature will be scientifically remodelled. If so, it will be done haphazardly, as an upshot of struggles in the murky realm where big business, organised crime and the hidden parts of government vie for control.

John Gray, *Straw Dogs*

PART ONE

THE DISTRICT

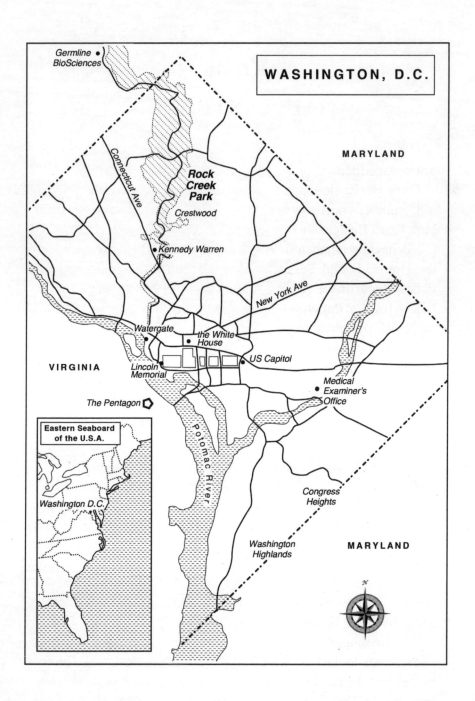

WASHINGTON, D.C.

Germline BioSciences

MARYLAND

Rock Creek Park

Crestwood

Connecticut Ave

Kennedy Warren

New York Ave

Watergate

the White House

Lincoln Memorial

US Capitol

VIRGINIA

Medical Examiner's Office

The Pentagon

Eastern Seaboard of the U.S.A.

Washington D.C.

Potomac River

Congress Heights

Washington Highlands

MARYLAND

N

ONE

Snowmageddon.

Dirty glacial clouds hammered the city's anvil. On the District of Columbia's north-western edge, gusts of snow rolled across the Park Road Bridge like volcanic ash.

Michael Freeman, a detective lieutenant on the up and up with the Homicide and Sexual Offenses Branch of the Metropolitan Police Department (MPD), climbed out of his unmarked white Chevy Impala, impetuously hurdled the crash barrier and skidded across the pavement into a railing built to deter suicides. The sidewalk was slick with ice as brittle as glass. He patted the pockets of his down-insulated jacket, checking for a notebook and flashlight. He felt for the reassurance of the Glock 17 in a holster in the small of his back. He blew on his fingers and peered at his watch. It was Tuesday, just after four in the morning and the temperature was well below freezing.

Three and a half hours until sunrise.

Parked in the icy slush on the north end of the bridge there were two other vehicles. One was a patrol car from Third Police District, its revolving red and blue lights lighting up the skeletal latticework of trees beside the road. There was a uniformed officer huddled miserably inside and through the patrol car's open window came the crackle of static punctuated by short bursts of speech. The other car was the Medical Examiner's, a black Chevy Suburban with blacked-out windows.

The harbinger of death.

Freeman looked down through the cage-like railings of the bridge and the swirling snow at the road beneath. Forty feet below him, on the Piney Branch Driveway, there were two patrol cars from the Park Police. He looked up again at the hillside. He could see the lights of more patrol cars, parked on the reverse slope of the hill, reflected like distant searchlights in the cloud cover.

A policeman with a flashlight approached through the trees and ducked under the yellow incident tape. He was overweight, his belly struggling against his uniform pants and fully loaded leather belt, and his face was flushed despite the freezing cold.

'Lieutenant Freeman?' he asked, breathing heavily.

'Yes,' Freeman acknowledged.

'We expected you sooner than this.'

'I'm here now,' he said. 'What's your name?'

'I'm Kelly. Park Police.'

'Well, Kelly, what time was she found?'

'Just over an hour ago. I took the call.'

Freeman looked at his watch again. She was found at around 3 a.m.

They were on the boundary of Third and Fourth Police Districts, on a narrow spur of Rock Creek Park insinuated between the two and therefore under Park Police jurisdiction. That was DC for you, a mish-mash of competing jurisdictions. Behind him at the south end of the bridge was the residential area Mount Pleasant, and ahead of him at the top of the hill, on the far side of the trees, was Crestwood, a small exclusive neighbourhood.

'Who found her?'

The policeman jerked his fleshy thumb back up the hillside. 'A young woman out running.'

Freeman frowned. 'At this time of night?'

Kelly shrugged as if nothing would surprise him. 'She says she couldn't sleep. She's up there waiting for you. I'll take you there now.'

Freeman followed along a footpath that struck out diagonally from the bridge and then curved around to the left, alongside a narrow, steep-sided ravine thick with snow. Ahead of him Kelly climbed over a fallen tree blocking the pathway. If anything, it was snowing harder now. Kelly slipped and landed on his back. He cursed. Freeman helped him to his feet.

'This is fucked up,' Kelly groaned.

'Come on,' Freeman said, chivvying him along.

They continued. Abruptly the path forked to left and right.

'Where does this go?' Freeman asked.

Kelly pointed into the darkness to his left with the flashlight. Trees etched in snow. 'That way leads down to Beech Drive. We have another patrol car down there. The other way leads up to Crestwood.' As he turned with the flashlight in his hand, Kelly lit up a steel chain-link fence about ten feet away, running parallel to the path. A sign said: PRIVATE PROPERTY, NO TRESPASSING.

'Who lives the other side of that?' Freeman asked.

'Senator Cannon.'

'You're serious?'

Kelly grinned maliciously. 'They threw you a red ball, Lieutenant.'

A red ball: twenty-four-hour days and all other cases on indefinite hold. Now he understood what Walter Streeks had meant when he'd said down the phone, 'You're going to have to tread carefully.'

The call hadn't woken Freeman. He had been lying awake in the darkness of his apartment and it hadn't rung more than once before he'd snatched the cell off the nightstand.

'The body of a young white woman has been found in Rock Creek Park,' Assistant Chief of Police Streeks had told him. Streeks was head of the Criminal Investigation Division, and the most senior black police officer in the District. 'I'm making you the primary. You need to get over there right now.'

Freeman wasn't on duty. He was on dayshift and down three members of his squad but there was no way he was going to raise that.

Michael Freeman was thirty-five years old – a former Special Forces soldier turned policeman. He was a tall and slim black man, with grey-flecked hair and dark almond-shaped eyes. His smile was tight-lipped – half knowing and half strategic. It hid a mouthful of craggy teeth. A childhood in Detroit's East Side with an aggressive, alcoholic father had taught him to play things close to his chest, to look and listen. His colleagues knew him as a patient thinker, sedulous, missing nothing given time. Intellectually savvy and emotionally guarded, he exuded certitude. In Afghanistan, in the immediate aftermath of 9/11, he spent several weeks as a mounted outlier with the Northern Alliance in the Alma Tak Mountains, beyond the range of reinforcement or rescue – drinking filtered ditchwater and eating nuts scavenged from corpses – and calling down massive airstrikes on Taliban positions. He gained a certain reputation. Word spread the length of the Darya Suf River valley, through the Tiangi Gap to the stronghold at Mazar-i-Sharif that there was a monster loose in the mountains and the Taliban called him '*bor-buka*', which seemed to mean black or devil or whirlwind, and, at times, all of these things.

Freeman continued along the path through the trees. The ground fell away steeply to the right and down in the ravine there were hushed voices and then the sudden flash from a camera. Freeman got a brief glimpse of something shocking: a woman's naked body sprawled in the snow. His heart missed a beat. Wait, he told himself, resisting the urge to move directly there. The body would be there for as long as it took to process the crime scene. It wasn't going anywhere without his authorisation. Do what you were taught back in the academy, he told himself: begin at the periphery; establish a perimeter and then move in an ever-decreasing circle towards the corpse.

'When did the Mobile Crime Lab Unit arrive?' he asked.

'About ten minutes before you. Their truck is parked up on Quincy.'

'And the Medical Examiner?'

'Twenty minutes ago. He was wrapping up a shooting in North-East. He came straight over.'

'Have you got a map of the area?'

'In the car.'

'Come on, then.'

At the top of the hill there was a flat area of woodland, a clearing of sorts with several fallen trees and beyond it the lights of houses and more police cars. The neighbourhood had been jolted awake. There was a woman standing shivering beside a log with a space blanket wrapped around her. By the beam from Kelly's flashlight he studied her. He judged that she was in her late twenties or early thirties, maybe five foot seven, and a hundred and twenty pounds. She was wearing dark sweatpants and a pale sweatshirt with bloodstains on it. Shoulder-length blonde hair poked out from beneath her knit cap.

'My name is Harriet Armstrong,' she said calmly, with her hands interlocked in front of her. He caught the flash of a substantial engagement ring on her left hand. 'I called nine-one-one.'

A strange accent. 'You're Australian?' he ventured.

'Scottish, actually.'

'Well, Harriet, maybe you can tell me what you were doing in Rock Creek Park after dark?'

'I was taking a short cut to Crestwood,' she explained, unruffled. 'It's safer to run here after dark than in Mount Pleasant where I live.'

Washington was full of joggers, it was one of many things that distinguished the District in Freeman's mind – lobbyists, lawyers and journalists all pounding the pavement like hamsters on a wheel – they were everywhere and at all times of day and night.

'So what happened?'

'I was on the path near the fence when I heard someone in the trees. He was coming towards me, carrying something over his shoulder wrapped in a blanket or a tarpaulin, something like that. I was alarmed. I got down behind a tree and he went past me, within a few feet. He fell and that's when I first got a glimpse of what I thought was a body. I didn't move. I didn't do anything to give myself away. The man started swearing and cursing and crying. Then he went quiet for a while and then he ran off. I heard him splashing through the river at the bottom of the hill. After that I went to have a look. That's when I found the body. I turned her over. I checked for a pulse. Her airway was completely blocked. I tried to clear it. I scooped out what I could with my fingers. Then I performed CPR, but it was too late – she was dead. That was just over an hour ago.'

'Would you recognise the man if you saw him again?'

7

She shook her head emphatically. 'I never got a clear look at him.'

'Then what happened?'

'I ran up the hill and knocked on the door of the nearest house. I woke up the owner and, once I'd told him what had happened, he agreed to let me in. I dialled nine-one-one and then came back here to wait for the police to arrive. That's it.'

'You're going to need to go to Police Headquarters and give a statement.'

'Of course,' she agreed. 'Right now?'

'Officer Kelly will take you.' He glanced across at Kelly who gave him a grateful look for delivering him from the snow. 'Bring me that map.'

'Sure.'

Kelly led the woman away. Freeman followed them to the edge of the tree line and stepped out onto the road. Facing the park there were several Federal-era double-fronted houses with exposed brick and painted shutters. Gaslights flickered on half-acre lots with snow-covered lawns and flagstone walkways. Kelly's patrol car was parked outside the nearest house, the address that the 911 call was made from.

The lights were on. There was a Jaguar in the driveway.

Freeman watched Kelly help the young woman into the back of the patrol car and then he turned back and looked in the direction of the woods. At the edge of the trees, there was a National Park Service boundary post and a sign that said: CLOSED AT DARK.

Kelly produced the map and then retreated to the warmth of the driver's seat. Freeman blew on his fingers and spread the map out on the car's hood, searching for the boundaries of an outer perimeter. To the west there was Rock Creek with Beach Drive running alongside it, to the south the Piney Branch River, to the east the busy thoroughfare that was 16th Street that ran straight to the White House, and to the north, jutting into the park like an inquisitive nose, there was Crestwood. He located the senator's house with its long, curving driveway that led up from Beach Drive.

He was aware of the witness watching him from the back of the car.

'Michael.'

A woman in a grey wool duffel coat with the hood thrown back, a laptop bag like a mailman's pouch slung cross her chest, a pair of black-framed glasses and a black crocheted hat was walking towards him from the direction of the police cordon. Detective Maja Hadžiosmanagič was also a cop, the youngest though not the newest member of the Homicide and Sexual Offenses Branch of DC MPD. Like Freeman she was from Michigan, though not from Detroit. She was from Grand Rapids where her family settled after fleeing Mostar in Bosnia in the mid-nineties. She was something of an oddity in the department. She had arrived in Washington with a political science degree from Grand Valley State University and a freshly issued US passport. She had completed a year of American University law school and then dropped out and joined the DC police. After two years in a patrol car in Seventh District, two years in the Prostitution Enforcement Unit, and a further two years on the mayor's security detail, she had transferred to Homicide.

There was no point asking her why she'd chosen the police over the law. Freeman had tried several times in the last year and got answers ranging from 'What would you do without me?' to 'Why walk among giants when I can tower over you pygmies?' It was one of the things that he liked about her. For all that she gave the impression of being open, there was another side to her, an elusive quality that was not readily apparent, some feature of being a refugee, he thought. There were questions she wouldn't answer, topics she wouldn't discuss; try to pin her down and she would skip away laughing, her pale blue eyes flashing.

'You got lucky today, handsome,' she greeted him.

The irony was not lost on him. 'Looks like I did.'

'It's a mess back there,' Maja told him. 'There's already a police reporter from the *Post* and three or four photographers on the cordon and there are satellite truck crews from NBC4 and ABC7 parked outside the mayor's house. I bet you more are on their way.'

'The mayor's house . . . ?'

'Oh yes! He lives a block away. They're only there because they can't get any closer to the senator's house. Let me show you.' She joined him at the map, touched his shoulder and then pointed to the intersections with an index finger that stuck out of fingerless woollen mitts. 'I've told uniform to shift the cordon back to 17th Street there and push it up to Varnum Street to the north there. That should give you the room you need.'

And now he had an inner perimeter. 'We'll be knocking on these doors first,' he said, looking up and down the street. 'We're going to need some help.'

'Stan and Olly are on the way,' Maja told him. Stan and Olly was what she called her fellow detectives Hector Menendez and Kari Marschalk, which Freeman knew to mean that they had been judged competent and therefore worthy of her barbed, teasing affection. He'd once asked her if she had a name for him and she'd replied, 'Don't even go there, Michael.'

Standing at the edge of the woods in the biting cold, she was staring at him.

'Earth to Michael?'

'Can we get some lights in the woods?' Freeman asked, once he'd collected his thoughts.

'For that, I'll have to talk to the National Guard.' She hesitated. They both knew why. It would be daylight before they could coax any lights out of the National Guard.

'What about an area search?'

'We can get cadets from the Police Academy here in the morning.'

'Good.'

'Are you OK?' Her hand rested briefly on his forearm as it often did when she was talking to him.

'I'm fine,' he said and folded the map carefully before tucking it into his jacket's inside pocket. Maja was the closest thing to a friend that Freeman had in Homicide, or anywhere for that matter. Freeman was the newcomer. He'd transferred in from the Detroit Police Department just after the President's inauguration. He'd loyally followed his better paid, better connected and fiercely ambitious wife Shawna who had spent 2008 campaigning for Obama and now worked in the Office of Counsel to the President at the White House.

'I'll tell you what,' Freeman told Maja, 'let's go take a look at the body.'

'Let's do that,' she agreed.

Freeman nodded to Kelly who drove away with the witness in the back and he and Maja walked together into the trees, snapping on latex gloves.

TWO

Freeman often dreamed that he was back in the Tiangi Gap in Afghanistan with smoke seeping from the earth and powdered dust rising at every footfall, turning his clothes white, his face to a mask of dust.

The further he walked into the ravine the greater the damage.

Provided that he had line-of-sight to an enemy position, Freeman found the mechanics of calling in an airstrike were relatively simple. He was equipped with a commercial GPS with a projection function, a prismatic compass, a set of binoculars with a laser rangefinder good out to three and a half kilometres (distance and terrain are metric in war) and a 40 MHz radio to communicate with the B-52 bombers that were circling above, their contrails leaving twenty-mile-wide ovals in the sky. He fixed his own location, and then, using the compass and rangefinder, fed the bearing and distance to the enemy into the GPS. It gave him back the enemy's grid coordinates. He sent the grid to the bomber.

In the bomb bay the smart-bombs (JDAMs) came awake.

The pilot said, 'Pickle, pickle, pickle.'

As the bomb fell, the GPS unit in its tail sent signals to the fins, which feathered the breeze and ruddered the projectile on course.

'Thirty seconds . . . twenty seconds . . . ten seconds.'

You saw it before you heard it: the mushroom cloud and then the boom that rolled up the hills and over the ridgelines like a freight train.

If the mechanics were simple, Freeman's response to seeing the devastation first hand was more complex. The value of n may be different for each of us but by the time you have seen the nth victim or nth dismembered part of a victim in the nth pile of rubble it has ceased to be personal. Sooner or later fatigue sets in. You withdraw. For Freeman, alumnus of Afghanistan, his first experience of death at first hand was on such a massive scale and so clearly by his own hand that the sense of withdrawal was almost immediate. In the face of numberless and nameless dead in stove-in bunkers and collapsed trenches he simply shut down. If that was true in Afghanistan, then the opposite was true now. He had felt a deep compulsion ever since to find his way back to the personal, to recover his sense of outrage. With each murder solved, with each story fully told, he was a step closer to what was so abruptly lost.

But even now, almost a decade later, unidentified bodies provoked the fiercest emotions in him. He repeated his mantra: *I will find out who you are. I will determine who killed you. I will bring them to justice.*

He was not a religious man. His wife was the one who owned a bedside Bible. But there was a piece of scripture that he regarded as his own. Luke 8,17: *For nothing is secret, that shall not be made manifest; neither anything hid, that shall not be known and come abroad.*

Kaplan, the Medical Examiner, was straddling the corpse with his feet planted either side of her waist and his aluminium scene case open beside him. He looked up as Freeman and Maja slid down the bank towards him, their torches making goggles of his spectacles. He was a small, round man with a bald head and tufts of hair sprinkled with snowflakes that stuck out horizontally from just above his ears.

Kneeling on the ground beside Kaplan, a female Mobile Crime Lab tech wearing a head torch and an all-weather suit was picking up fragments of teeth with a pair of tweezers and depositing them in a clear plastic bag. If the witness was to be believed she had scooped them out of the victim's mouth before giving CPR. Another tech was standing by holding a camera and beside him, squatting on the bank, there was a uniform taking notes for the top sheet of an incident report.

'Y'all are the primary?' Kaplan asked.

'I am,' Freeman replied.

Kaplan was from Louisiana. 'I'm just a poor Coonass Jew from the Bayou, trying to make my way through this thorny world and into the next,' he would often say by way of introduction. He was known across the city for a probing intellect and a disconcerting stare.

'So I guess they're either getting set to build you up or knock you down,' he said.

'We'll find out soon enough,' Freeman agreed, squatting on his haunches beside the body. She was lying sprawled on her back with her arms partly extended and her face a bloody pulp. He had thought that he was veteran of such things but he had never seen a face so completely and deliberately smashed in. It provoked a strong sense of moral outrage in him.

'Your President came up here,' Kaplan said.

The rest of her body was dead white; even her nipples were pale as alabaster. Here and there twigs and leaves adhered to her skin.

Freeman retrieved a pencil from his pocket. He frowned, half listening. 'My President . . . ?'

'Abraham Lincoln. He rode up the Piney Branch Road to Fort Stevens in 1864, about a year after he freed the slaves.'

Freeman's wife Shawna, who was more strident in these matters, might have taken exception to this. She refused to accept the idea of the slaves as passive recipients of freedom. She claimed with some justification that Lincoln was initially ambivalent about abolition and that it was only the hundreds of thousands of blacks, Northerners and escaped Southerners, who fought in the Union Army that brought home to the President the necessity of emancipation. But Freeman was not a preacher. He didn't have any kind of axe to grind.

'I thought that you were referring to our cigarette-smoking Kenyan-born President,' he replied.

Carefully, he lifted the dead woman's hair away from an ear with the tip of the pencil. There was a row of silver rings that followed the delicate curve of her ear. The hair was blonde, with dark roots.

'Lincoln came under fire from Confederate forces that were looking to capture the city,' Kaplan blithely continued. 'He's the only sitting President to have come under enemy fire; this is hallowed ground, Lieutenant, ground that the Union would not yield.'

'Thanks for the history lesson,' Freeman told him. 'Perhaps you could direct your brain to the matter at hand.'

'I'm just getting started,' Kaplan said. 'We're less than a mile from where the bones of Chandra Levy were found.'

Chandra Levy was the twenty-four-year-old intern who'd gone missing in the spring of 2001, and whose skeletal remains were discovered in the park a year later. After she went missing, Chandra's family – white middle-class Jews from Modesto, California – had revealed that she was having an extramarital affair with a congressman from the 18th District by the name of Gary Condit. It was an instant sensation, a round-the-clock news story that gripped the nation's attention in a way it had not been gripped since Monica Lewinsky talked on prime-time television about her affair with President Bill Clinton. Writing in the *New York Times*, the commentator Maureen Dowd had described it as *the oldest Washington story, one part romance, and two parts droit de seigneur. The powerful man who thrives on adoration and adoring young women he meets in his office.* It remained DC's most famous unsolved crime. Although Condit was never a suspect, the months of relentless media scrutiny destroyed his political career and almost did the same for those responsible for the hapless police investigation. Only the national cataclysm that was 9/11 caused the cable news networks to switch their attention from the case.

'What can you tell us about the deceased?' Freeman persisted, knowing that patience would win through in the end.

There was a pause while Kaplan's eyes swam behind his spectacles. He resembled a mole, a subterranean creature.

'Very well, Lieutenant, she's a well-nourished white female measuring five foot seven inches. A hundred pounds or so. I'd say in her mid-twenties . . .'

'And the cause of death?' Freeman insisted.

'We'll have to wait and see what toxicology reveals but I'd say the most likely cause is that her tongue lost its attachment to the lower jaw and fell back.'

'She asphyxiated?'

'We'll know for sure after the autopsy.'

Freeman glanced across at the technician with the gruesome bag of teeth. 'Any sign of the murder weapon?'

The tech shook her head. 'Not yet.'

'Was she raped?'

'There is no apparent evidence of genital or extra-genital injury,' Kaplan replied, in a tone that suggested that he was not completely happy with the answer. It was easy to see why. The woman's hairless vulva was visibly swollen, the furls of flesh engorged with blood. There was something shocking about it, pornographic even, and if it were not for the systematic destruction of her face it might be the most shocking thing about her. The dark marks on her inner thighs that Freeman had mistaken for blood were in fact earth.

'But she's had sex?'

'I think so,' Kaplan replied. 'We'll know for sure back at the lab.'

Freeman lifted the woman's head slightly. There was no pooling of blood on the ground beneath her. 'She was dumped here,' he said. 'She was killed elsewhere and carried into the park.'

No wonder the techs were so disconsolate. The transportation of the body away from the murder site meant that there would be few forensic clues. The male tech's torch lit up a bloody tarpaulin, curled like a discarded rag on the slope of the ravine. 'She was dumped there and rolled here.'

'The witness spoke the truth,' added Maja.

'There are lesions on her wrists and ankles consistent with her being restrained,' Kaplan said. 'Probably with some kind of rope or strap.'

Freeman's cell phone rang. It was Assistant Chief of Police Streeks. He said, 'When you're done with the body, head up to the senator's house. Chief Thielen is waiting.'

'Yes, sir.'

Streeks cut the connection.

'You can tell the morgue wagon to pull up down there on the bridge,' Kaplan said. 'We'll take her out that way. It's more discreet. Do I have your permission for that?'

Ignoring the question, Freeman turned the woman's left upper forearm.

'Are you OK with us moving her?' Kaplan repeated in his strange obsessive-compulsive way.

Freeman's latex-covered thumb rubbed a patch of dirt, which turned out not to be dirt.

'What's that?' he asked.

'It's a barcode tattoo,' Kaplan replied. 'Personally, I find it offensive.'

Freeman glanced up at him. 'Because they used to tattoo your people there when they arrived at the camps?'

'You're not wholly ignorant, Lieutenant Freeman. Though tattooing was particular to Auschwitz.'

'You have enough photos of the body?' Freeman asked the male tech.

'Yes.'

'I have to go,' Freeman said, abruptly standing up.

'You've been summoned?'

'I've been summoned,' Freeman agreed. He glanced at Maja. 'Can you take charge of the crime scene and the door-to-door?'

'Sure. What do you want me to tell the media?'

'Nothing.'

'Mark my words, Lieutenant, you'll be writing reports to the entire chain of command until this case is solved,' Kaplan told him. 'White girls aren't supposed to die in DC. When they do there's hell to pay . . .'

Freeman had few illusions about his work. Sure, it was a kind of expiation for the airstrikes but Homicide in DC was rarely complicated. Nine times out of ten it began with a gunshot and a corpse on a pavement or in a stairwell. The victims and the perpetrators were invariably black or Latino and the location was either the south-east or north-east quadrant of the District. The current average was just over ten killings a month; a hundred and forty homicides in the district in the previous year. For the detectives of Homicide it was straightforward work: there were shell casings to examine, motives to explore, witnesses to cajole. Maybe a thug cut a deal and snitched on the killer. But in most cases it was the killer's incompetence that led to their arrest. Cases were swiftly closed.

Not this time.

'You can remove the body now,' he said.

THREE

Freeman unpeeled the latex gloves from his hands as he stepped out of the woods, and discarded them in the gutter at the park's edge. The media crowd beyond the cordon had grown larger and louder. There were now several satellite trucks with news crews, and the barricade was lit up by the unreal glare of television lights that were much stronger than anything the cash-strapped DC police could muster. Several reporters called out his name but he would not talk to them now. Instead he walked up Argyle Terrace in the company of a skinny white officer named Newell from Fourth District. They turned left on Shepherd and after five or six hundred feet arrived at the discreet rear entrance to Senator Cannon's estate. Two brick pillars with stone finials stood either side of an electronically operated steel gate.

There were two routes to the house: the first the sweeping tree-lined driveway that ran up from Beach Drive in the park and the second, this one, which did not appear on the map, a short cut that fed into the main drive. Two routes in and out. Back and front. Newell pressed a button on a stainless-steel console and spoke his name. After a minute or so the gate slid silently open on freshly greased wheels.

The senator's DC residence was a three-storey mansion capped by a roof of blue slate. It was said to be the largest private home in the District. In front of it was a paved circular driveway with a raised bed at its centre that was currently piled with snow.

'The senator isn't short of guest rooms,' Newell said.

Freeman counted seventeen windows across the front of the house. It was not the first time he had visited the house, though the last time the raised bed had been full of flowers. He recalled what his wife Shawna said to him, close to this very spot, on a warm spring evening in 2008: *Just remember that long before Bill Gates or Warren Buffett there was old man Tyrone Cannon, who bequeathed successive generations of descendants a truly astonishing boodle of money.*

That was Freeman's first trip to Washington. It had seemed like a world away from his previous experience: Afghanistan and Detroit's East Side. He had given evidence to a hearing of the Armed Services Committee and after the hearing the senator had invited Freeman and his wife to a drinks party at his home. Shawna had jumped at the chance. Looking back, he supposed that she already had her eyes set on a career in the capital.

Now, standing and staring up at the mansion's impressive facade, he remembered something that she said to him just before they entered the house. She had straightened his tie and said, *Just don't leave me alone in a room with him.*

He regretted it now that he had failed to ask her what she meant.

There were three cars arranged around the mound of snow at the centre of the forecourt. The cars included Newell's police cruiser, the Chief of Police's Town Car and a black Lincoln Navigator with a large man inside who Freeman recognised as the mayor's bodyguard and controversial business partner, Jay Albo. The mayor had been there that spring night also.

It was shaping up to be quite a reunion.

Freeman climbed the marble steps and walked between the white Ionic columns that framed the doorway. He noted the camera mounted above the door. He gripped the brass door-knocker that was shaped like a woman's hand.

He knocked four times.

A tall, striking brunette opened the door. She was wearing a short-sleeved black silk dress that ended just above the knees, and exuded an opulent smell of perfume.

Freeman stood at the door and showed her his badge. 'I'm Lieutenant Freeman, Homicide.'

'Of course,' she said, smoothing a stray hair from her cheek. Her face was free of make-up, which he suspected was not usually the case. He judged that she was probably forty-five but on most other occasions could pass for ten years younger. 'They are expecting you.'

He stepped into the hallway and stamped his boots on the mat to dislodge the snow. It was as he remembered. Ahead of him there was a broad, sweeping staircase that rose to a landing midway to the next floor, and divided to the left and right. There was an oak table with a huge display of fresh flowers and paintings that he remembered that his wife had told him were originals by John Singer Sargent and Mary Cassatt.

'This way . . .'

He followed the woman down a wood-panelled hallway, trailing in her cloud of scent. She had noticeably great legs. She showed him into a book-lined study. The senator was there with three others, two men and a woman. Two of them he knew. Police Chief Michelle Thielen was in uniform, standing stiffly with her cap tucked under her arm and her grey hair swept back behind her ears, a stern and Presbyterian expression on her face. Beside her, sprawled in a leather armchair and looking like he'd risen from his bed in a hurry, was her benefactor, the mayor – a black man in an overwhelmingly Democratic, overwhelmingly black city. He was wearing a pair of sweatpants and a sweatshirt with HOWARD UNIVERSITY printed on it. He acknowledged Freeman's arrival with a swift nod of the head and returned to the BlackBerries that he was holding in both hands.

Senator James D. Cannon, son of the industrialist John T. Cannon and grandson of the railway magnate Tyrone Cannon, rose from the other armchair like a king from his throne. He was a big man, at least six foot two, with tanned skin, a broad leonine forehead and swept-back white hair without a single strand out of place. He was wearing pyjamas and a monogrammed dressing gown and navy blue velvet slippers; a massive gold signet ring. There was something profoundly alien about him. Even his eyebrows looked expertly groomed. Freeman remembered the shock the first time he met the senator in the flesh; up until then he'd only ever seen people of power like this on TV and he'd always thought that their gloss was a quality of lighting or make-up, not of themselves. Cannon's gloss was real. The sheer physical presence was intimidating.

'Well,' Cannon said, in a slow, gruff voice. 'This is a terrible thing.'

Freeman could have sworn there were tears in his warm, oleaginous eyes and for a moment he thought that the senator might embrace him as he stepped forward. Instinctively Freeman drew back, thrusting out his hand to block him, offering him a handshake instead. Cannon's eyes appeared to turn from green to grey and his face went cold.

'A truly terrible thing,' he said. His handshake was bone-crushing.

He looked around. 'Forgive me,' he said and made the introductions. 'This is my chief of staff Larry Lumpe.'

Lumpe was a short pudgy man with a child's face. Freeman recognised the type; Capitol Hill was awash with them – young, bright and fiercely ambitious men and women making their way in politics. Lumpe's shirt was creased and his tie was poking out of the pocket of his pants. He fixed Freeman with a slightly manic look and pumped his hand. 'We're here to help, Lieutenant.'

'And you've met my Director of Communications, Sonia Rojas.'

The tall brunette who had answered the door to him bowed her head. Sonia Rojas was more difficult to read, she held herself slightly apart from the others. Her mouth was set in a hard, thin line.

'And you know the mayor?'

'I met you here once before,' Freeman said.

The mayor nodded in his direction.

'Of course you did,' the senator said. 'I was telling Larry and Sonia about it just now. I said Lieutenant Freeman is just the kind of man we need at a time like this: a son of Detroit, a former Special Forces soldier and a decorated hero of the Afghan war.' He turned to Chief Thielen. 'We were in the same unit, Michelle. We wore the same Green Beret. Fifth Special Forces Group. Different wars, sure: mine was Vietnam and his was Afghanistan.

But we're made of the same stuff.' He returned his attention to Freeman. 'Michael is a committed public servant and a reluctant cavalryman. Am I wrong?'

'No, sir.'

In November 2001 Freeman and his Special Forces team had ridden with the victorious Northern Alliance into Mazar-i-Sharif, vanquishing the Taliban in what a euphoric media dubbed *the first mounted charge of the twenty-first century*. He'd never been on a horse before his deployment to Afghanistan and he hoped never to have to get on one again.

'I had lunch with Crusty Buchanan last week,' the senator told him. Representative Crusty Buchanan of the state of Texas had been Freeman's team leader in Afghanistan. Described in his *Yale Banner* yearbook as a 'wild and profligate man', Buchanan had distinguished himself in Special Forces before making a fortune selling car alarms and standing for office as a Republican. He was generally regarded as one of the more colourful members of the one hundred and eleventh Congress. 'Crusty is a big fan of yours, Michael.'

That seemed unlikely. The last time Freeman had seen Crusty Buchanan he'd punched him. They'd almost court-martialled him for that.

'And I was telling them that your wife is an operator,' the senator continued, 'an adviser to the President, a woman of substance. You're a lucky man, Lieutenant.'

'Yes, I am, sir,' he agreed.

A telephone rang and Sonia Rojas immediately answered it. 'It's the Secretary.'

'I'll take it in the other room.'

The moment that Cannon was gone, the mayor looked up from his BlackBerries and said, 'You better ask your questions, Lieutenant.'

Freeman looked at Lumpe, the senator's chief of staff, who stared back expectantly.

'The body of a young woman has been found in the woods adjacent to this property,' Freeman told him. 'I'd like to know who

23

was here this evening and if you heard anything or saw anything that might help me with the investigation.'

'Of course, Lieutenant,' Lumpe replied eagerly. 'I'll tell you what I told Chief Thielen. The senator worked late tonight, preparing for the hearings the day after tomorrow. As you may know the senator is a member of the Armed Services Committee. I can't emphasise enough the importance of his work. If we don't do the work our end then our soldiers on the front line go without bullets. I'm sure that as a war veteran you understand what I'm talking about.'

'The senator worked late, you've made that point.'

'I have been with him all evening. We were in his office on the Hill until about 9 p.m. Then a car service brought us here. The senator's housekeeper has the night off but she left out some food. We had dinner. The senator freshened up and then we got back to work. That's it until the police showed up. Sonia joined us just before the mayor did; that must have been about half an hour after Officer Newell informed us that the body had been found.'

'And did you see anything or hear anything suspicious?'

'Not a thing, Lieutenant. I'm sorry that we can't be more helpful.'

'Was there anyone else in the house?'

'Like I said, his housekeeper has the night off and she's visiting relatives down in Richmond. The senator's car is in the shop so his driver is also off and away visiting relatives, and his wife is at their home in Tennessee. To be frank, it's one of the reasons I was happy to come back home with him, to make sure he was OK.'

'I'll need both you and the senator to give a statement.'

'I don't think there's any requirement for the senator or Mr Lumpe to attend Police Headquarters at this time,' the mayor cut in. 'Can you arrange for an officer to take their statements here?'

'Of course,' Freeman replied. 'I'll ask Detective Hadžiosmanagič to come straight over.'

The mayor's eyes narrowed. 'You got Maja Hadžiosmanagič working for you?'

'Yes,' Freeman replied. The mayor had pronounced Maja's

surname correctly, with what she called her secret *Hs* – 'zh' for the 'z', 'sh' for 's' and 'tch' for the 'c' at the end. Of course, he thought, she'd worked on the mayor's security detail.

Cannon returned. 'It was Bob,' he told the mayor.

To Freeman it seemed credible that the senator had been speaking to Robert Gates, the President's workaholic Secretary of Defense, who, it was said, rarely slept. 'He told me to tell you that you can expect any assistance you need to solve this case.'

'I was just telling the lieutenant that we didn't hear or see anything suspicious,' Lumpe said.

'Have you identified the woman yet?' the senator asked.

'Not at this early stage, sir,' Freeman replied.

'Somewhere she has a family, Michael, a mother and father.' Cannon gripped him by the upper arm. 'They will be worrying about her. We must not prolong their pain. What about missing persons?'

'We'll check that out.'

'What about the FBI? You want me to call Bob?' Freeman assumed that this time he meant Robert Mueller, the Director of the FBI. 'I'll get him out of bed. If you don't think you can handle it?'

'We can handle it,' Chief Thielen said.

Cannon nodded. 'And I've already told the mayor here that you need men and overtime, isn't that right? So don't you worry, Michael, you'll get the help you need.'

'Thank you, sir.'

'Good man.' The senator tapped Freeman on the back. 'I told them you were the one for the job.'

'There is something that you can do for me, sir.'

'Anything. You ask, you'll get.'

'I need you to hand over the footage from the security cameras.'

Cannon raised his eyebrows as if the request was unexpected and looked across at Lumpe, who intervened smoothly: 'Of course, I'll have them sent over to you at Homicide straight away.'

'Excuse me,' said Cannon and left the room once more. Lumpe followed him out.

'Well, I'd better be going,' the mayor announced.

'He'll be upset if you are not here when he gets back,' Sonia Rojas told him.

'You know him well, do you?'

After a moment's awkwardness, when Sonia Rojas didn't look like she cared for his implication, she said, 'Only Mrs Cannon knows Senator Cannon well.'

Once she was gone, the mayor frowned at his BlackBerries and said, 'You want to make captain, Freeman?'

'Sure,' Freeman replied.

'Make sure you clear this up swiftly.'

'I understand.'

Chief Thielen went to the French windows and after giving Freeman a significant look, she opened them and stepped out onto the terrace. If he hesitated for a moment, it was only because it was so damned cold outside.

'Excuse me,' he said to the mayor.

The terrace was as long as the house and maybe twenty feet deep and the forested hillside fell away steeply from it. Thielen walked to the end of it and looked out over the parapet. Freeman joined her. In silence they watched the play of torches and shadowy figures in the trees beneath them. The girl's body was being moved down to the bridge where the morgue wagon was waiting, well away from the cameras.

'Identification may be difficult,' Freeman explained. 'Her face is damaged beyond recognition.'

'Do your best and do it quickly. You pick up any leads you report them directly to me.'

'Of course.'

'We have a downtick in killings. Last year the District logged the fewest number for nearly fifty years. I don't want anything messing with that.'

'OK.'

'The mayor is up for re-election later this year. As soon as the snow clears, the yard signs will go up with his name on. We have good school test scores and a growing population. There are new parks and recreational areas for kids to play in. Nobody wants a homicide to become a campaign issue.'

'OK.'

'I don't mind telling you, Michael, I was sceptical when the senator suggested you for this case. You can only ride so far on your wife's coat tails. And as for that maverick war hero bullshit, forget it. I have no tolerance for heroics.'

So the senator had made his call and the mayor and the Chief of Police had come running, and when the senator had told them who to put in charge of the investigation they'd gone along with that too.

'I understand,' he said.

'Do you? Just remember you're not in Detroit now.'

Freeman opened his mouth and closed it again. He felt his face flush with anger.

FOUR

They didn't need war toys. Any old stick or length of rebar became a weapon in their hands, and lumps of concrete were grenades. It was always war. They fought, block by block, through the abandoned factories, yelling, 'I gotcha!' and 'Yo' dead!'

As a child, you didn't take a piss without choosing a target and bombing it.

Sometimes, drawn by the smell, they'd come upon a real body in Motor City, the massive abandoned complex, spread over thirty-five acres that had once housed Packard Motors and closed down in 1957. The body of some hapless foot soldier in the drug wars, his limbs at crooked angles among the swaying grasses in the gaps between buildings, or perhaps in a pool of oily goo beneath a shattered warehouse ceiling. They'd gather around and stare in reverential silence at the bloating corpse. Somebody might say something: 'He died on his feet like a warrior,' or 'He went down fighting.'

You were on a war footing from the very start.

That was Detroit: the arsenal of democracy against the Nazis and the incubator of the American dream. The city that taught the rest of the world mass production, now reduced to block after block and mile after mile of abandoned and rotting factories, office buildings, storefronts, apartment blocks and houses.

It wasn't easy to be a stand-up cop in Detroit. Some people, Chief Thielen for instance, seemed to think it was impossible. Freeman joined the Detroit Police Department in a year when more than a dozen cops were indicted for concocting false reports, planting guns and drugs, assaulting citizens and lying under oath. Each passing year had brought more investigations – Internal Affairs, Justice Department, FBI – and with them more indictments. There were times when he almost regretted having returned to Detroit. The army was the perfect escape tunnel. He'd got out. He'd witnessed the wider world. Why go back? But he had gone back, drawn by a sense of responsibility – a calling, perhaps – a commitment to return something to the community that had produced him.

And if he hadn't gone back? He wouldn't have met Shawna.

He drummed his palms on the steering wheel.

Detroit: sometimes it felt like you just couldn't get out from under it.

At Dupont Circle Freeman took the exit for Massachusetts Avenue. It was still dark and the streets were quiet. Only the snow-ploughs were out.

Metropolitan Police Headquarters was downtown in the Henry J. Daly building on Indiana Avenue. It was an ugly place – a heavy, bunker-like building, six storeys high, located midway between the White House and the Capitol building. Henry 'Hank' Daly had been a homicide detective with twenty-eight years' service with the Metro PD. In November 1994 an enraged suspect had walked into the building, entered the cold case squad of Homicide Branch and shot Daly and two FBI agents with an assault weapon. The building was later renamed in Daly's honour.

About twenty minutes after leaving the Park Road Bridge, Freeman backed the Impala into a parking space on the lower tier of the basement garage, strode grim-faced through a metal bulk-head door and sprinted up the stairs to the fifth floor.

The Joint Operations Command Centre (JOCC) was routinely described by Chief Thielen as the nerve centre of the nation's capital, ready to respond within seconds to any incident or crime in the most powerful city on the planet. To access it Freeman had to swipe a card and press his palm against a biometric recognition pad.

The room was cavernous. One wall was an enormous real-time

three-dimensional map of the District of Columbia, 'the District', looking like a diamond with a chunk bitten out of its south-west corner. It was subdivided into seven police districts and marked with seven police stations and five substations. Most of it was grey, a grid of numbered streets and long diagonal avenues named after the states of the Union: Connecticut, Pennsylvania and New York, etc. There were also several splashes of colour: the jagged blue fork of the Potomac and Anacostia rivers; the horizontal green rectangle of the National Mall stretching from the Lincoln Memorial to the Capitol building; and, running north to south, an irregular vertical wedge like a lightning flash: Rock Creek Park.

Either side of the map more than forty video screens relayed live feeds over a secure, wireless network from ruggedised police cameras dotted around the city, as well as from cameras located in schools, subways and parks. The network was expanding all the time: private cameras in banks and shops, and the lobbies and elevators of apartment buildings and hotels were being added to the system daily. More than five thousand were already connected. Standing before it you could watch travellers, drivers, residents and pedestrians going about their business. A zoom lens enabled the watchers to focus on the face of someone walking towards the White House or the Capitol building. Digital images of the captured faces could be flashed around the world in an instant on the Internet. Married to face-recognition technology and tied in to public and private agencies around the world, an electronic library of hundreds of millions of faces was being created.

The JOCC was a facility jointly staffed by Metro PD, US Secret Service and the Federal Bureau of Investigation, sitting at about fifty computer consoles. The wall behind them was inscribed with President George W. Bush's pledge, delivered soon after the September 11th attacks: *We will not tire. We will not falter. We will not fail.*

At that hour the JOCC was relatively quiet. Freeman sat at one of the empty consoles, put on a headset and one of the dispatchers routed the 911 call through to him. He leaned back in his seat, closed his eyes and listened. He imagined the young woman, who identified herself as Harriet Armstrong, standing in a stranger's hallway with the handset pressed to her ear and the dead woman's blood on her hands and her sweatshirt. She sounded calm on the tape, her voice evenly modulated. She described how she had found the body, its location and the life-saving actions that she had performed. Freeman remembered the Crime Lab technician recovering tooth fragments from beside the corpse with tweezers. As he had done at the crime scene, he again imagined Harriet scooping the woman's shattered teeth out of her throat to clear the airway. She did not seem to have hesitated.

'I tried,' she said, and for the first time he heard a hint of emotion in her voice, 'but it was too late.'

It occurred to him that she was a woman who did not like to fail.

When he found her, Harriet was lying curled up on the floor of an interview room, with her hands squeezed between her thighs and her head resting on her folded sweat-top; Freeman watched her for a minute or so from the corridor outside, his face pressed to the wire-cored glass of the viewing pane. She appeared to be sleeping.

Under normal circumstances he might have found this suspicious; the innocent were usually the most nervous. In the homicide lexicon, it was taken as read that an innocent person left alone in a room would remain awake, staring nervously at the cubicle walls. And statistically speaking, there was a significant probability that the person who found the body also committed the murder, but there was something about this young woman that he hadn't yet figured out. He decided to wait for Maja to return before waking her up and questioning her further.

Instead he sat at a government-issue metal desk beneath the washed-out glare of overhead strip lights and leaned back in the chair. He picked up a remote and switched on a wall-mounted television. MSNBC was running the breaking news strapline: 'Body of unknown woman found in Rock Creek Park' and Fox 5: 'Hill link puzzles in hunt for woman's killer'.

The Fox anchor was saying: 'Associated Press are reporting that DC Police Chief Michelle Thielen met with Senator James D.

Cannon in their investigation of a woman's body found adjacent to his property in Rock Creek Park. Both a police spokesman and a spokesman for Senator Cannon refused to confirm that investigators talked to the senator. Police also refused to confirm reports that investigators expect to interview Senator Cannon in the future. Let's go to our reporter on the scene.'

The screen split in two. A woman in ear muffs was speaking to the camera: 'Hi, Gwen, I'm in Crestwood, a small, prosperous neighbourhood of Washington, DC, that is tucked away inside a thickly wooded area of Rock Creek Park. Behind me is the DC mayor's house and just a few hundred yards from where I am standing is the estate of the veteran Republican Senator James D. Cannon. According to the police, at about 3 a.m. this morning a passing jogger observed the naked body of a dead woman, lying in a ravine close to the perimeter fence that surrounds the senator's property.'

The anchor raised an immaculate eyebrow. 'What was a jogger doing in the park at that hour, Brandy?'

'It's pretty strange. The police are saying the jogger claims she had insomnia.'

'So what do we know about the dead woman?'

'Not much. The police are hoping that the public can help identify her. They are saying she is a white female in her early twenties. She's five foot seven and weighs a hundred and eight pounds. I understand that because of the horrendous nature of her injuries, the police will not be releasing a photo.'

Freeman switched off the television.

He sat for a while and watched the dark outline of the city through the squad room's sixth-floor windows.

It was all so normal.

Maja returned after about an hour with the results of door-to-door canvassing: no one saw or heard anything. She was also carrying bland, unrevealing witness statements from Senator Cannon and his chief of staff and the news that only three out of six cameras at the residence were functional.

'All we've got is the front door, the terrace and the main drive,' she explained, pulling off her crocheted hat and flinging it on the nearest desk. She sat down and removed her glasses. She yawned.

Freeman was incredulous. 'What?'

'The other three cameras are on a separate circuit. The main switch for that circuit was tripped sometime yesterday morning. One of the three cameras covers the Crestwood entrance to the property and the other two cover the kitchen door to the main house and the kitchen gardens. The circuit also includes the lights and sockets in the garage and the attic space of the main house. At the time of the murder the back of the house was in total darkness.'

'Are you serious?' Freeman exhaled loudly.

'The senator speculated that contract workers clearing snow from the driveway yesterday morning may have used the sockets in the garage and overloaded the system, tripping the switch.'

'You better check if that's true,' Freeman told her.

'It stinks.'

'Be careful what you say,' Freeman cautioned.

FIVE

It was 5.45 a.m. The light over the door of the interview room was green, indicating that a tape was rolling. Inside, Harriet sat on one side of a metal table that was bolted to the floor and Freeman and Hadžiosmanagič sat on the other. There was a black hemisphere mounted on the ceiling, with a camera inside feeding images to the adjacent video monitor room.

'Can you identify yourself for the recorder, please?'

'My name is Harriet Armstrong. I'm known as Harry. I'm thirty-five years old. I'm a British national.' If she had been a citizen Freeman might have cynically referred to her as all-American – clean-cut, blonde with innocent blue eyes, like a corn-fed farm girl from the Midwest. 'I live with my husband on Park Road, between 18th and 19th Streets,' she said with her unusual accent. 'He's a journalist. He writes for a magazine.'

'How long have you been here in the United States?'

'Since the spring of 2008; my husband came to cover the primaries. I came with him.'

'Are you employed?' Maja demanded.

'I'm trying to get a green card so I can work here.'

'What did you do back home?'

She hesitated. Then she said, 'I was an officer in London's Metropolitan Police Service.'

Freeman sat forward in his chair. 'You're police?'

She nodded. 'I was. I left.'

'Why?'

She shrugged. 'I wanted to try a different life.'

'What did you do in the police?'

34

'I worked for the Specialist Protection unit of SO1, that's Protection Command.'

'You were a bodyguard?'

'Yes. The correct term is protection officer.'

Freeman and Maja exchanged glances.

'Did you guard anybody famous?' Maja asked.

'I protected politicians and diplomats, mostly.'

'What about the princes?'

'No. I was Specialist Protection not Royalty Protection.'

Freeman thought he could detect a hint of impatience in her tone. He reached across the table for her metallic-blue iPod. She'd been listening to Thievery Corporation.

'So you know how to look after yourself?'

'If pushed, yes . . .'

'Is that what happened? Did she push you too far?'

'I don't know what you are talking about.'

'The dead woman. I mean you must have hit her pretty hard.'

'I didn't hit anybody.'

'It's better that you tell us the truth now than we find out for ourselves later.'

'I've told you what happened,' she replied, meeting his gaze. 'The first time that I set eyes on the woman she was lying face down on the ground. I turned her over. She wasn't breathing. I tried to revive her. I was not successful.'

'How long have you been married?' Maja asked.

Harry glanced across at her. 'Just over two years. Why?'

'Not long then?'

'Not long,' she admitted.

'Is your husband faithful to you?' Maja asked.

'I believe so,' she said.

'Are you aware that the park is closed at night?' Freeman asked.

'Yes. I know that I shouldn't have been there.'

'What were you doing there?'

'I don't sleep very well. I often wake up in the middle of the night. So I go running. I run for an hour or so and it helps me get back to sleep. Plus I'm supposed to be in training for the National

Marathon in March. Usually it's quiet but there have been a couple of muggings in Mount Pleasant during the last few weeks so I decided to run around Crestwood instead – it's safer up there, less urban. To do that I had to take a short cut through the park and up to Quincy Street.'

'Crestwood has a large black population, including the mayor,' Freeman told her.

'I'm sorry?'

'You said it was less urban. In this town when people use the term urban they sometimes mean black? Less urban, less black.'

'That's not what I meant,' she said emphatically.

'Go on,' Maja said.

Freeman listened to her describe again how she heard someone come crashing through the trees towards her and she crouched down, hiding herself in the shadows. She watched while a man staggering beneath the weight of a heavy bundle passed her, just a few feet away. When he fell Harry got her first look at the body, nude and shockingly white, as the tarpaulin unravelled and it rolled down into the ravine. The man started shouting, cursing in a foreign language. And then he whimpered for a while. After that he climbed to his feet and staggered away. Once she heard him splashing through the river, she approached the body. She tried her best. There were no slip-ups and no contradictions. Her body language suggested that she was telling the truth.

'Honestly, I couldn't tell you what he looked like, beyond that he was kind of skinny.'

'What language do you think he was speaking?'

'I'm not absolutely sure but it sounded a lot like Russian to me.'

Maja glanced across at Freeman. There had been several memos from the Homeland Security Bureau's intelligence unit in the past year warning of a possible influx of Russian mobsters into the District, but no actual evidence of it as yet.

'You said that he was carrying the body down the hill?' Freeman asked.

'That's right.'

'So he was coming from the direction of Crestwood.'

'That's right.'

'You're sure about that?'

'Absolutely.'

'And he ran down to the Piney Branch Driveway. That was his route of escape.'

'Yes.'

'And you went to take a look at what he'd dropped.'

'Yes.'

'Do you work for a foreign government?'

'No.'

'Are you a spy?'

In Washington spies were almost as common as joggers.

'No.'

'Are you prepared to voluntarily submit a DNA sample?'

'Of course.'

'And a polygraph?'

'A lie detector?'

'Yes.'

'Absolutely.'

Freeman leaned against the dirty beige wall in the corridor outside the interrogation room. They had taken a five-minute break. Maja was staring at him.

'What do you think?'

'I think she's telling the truth,' Freeman replied, 'or she's an accomplished liar.'

'You want me to make some calls and check her background?'

'Yes. Find out why she left the police. And make her do the polygraph. I'm going to pull together some of the paperwork and then I'm heading back to the crime scene. I want to walk the ground again.'

'And if she passes the polygraph?'

'Send her home. Be sure to tell her that we're not finished with her.'

In the interview room, Harry Armstrong did not appear to have moved. She was sitting calmly with her hands folded in her lap.

SIX

Half an hour later, Freeman parked at a metered space on 16th Street, and walked west along Shepherd past the logjam of satellite trucks and news crews. Thankfully nobody recognised him this time. He showed his badge at the police barrier and entered Crestwood. He walked parallel to the edge of the park, stopping every now and then to look around. Dawn wasn't far off and the cloud cover was lightening. He didn't have a clear idea of what he was looking for or why he had returned to the scene before daylight when it would surely reveal more clues. In the military he had been taught to regard ground as both an obstacle and a source of protection. He had carried a dog-eared copy of Clausewitz's *On War* in his chest-rig: *in a thickly wooded country the obstacle to sight preponderates*. At Fort Bragg he had been taught to look through the obstacle: s*tudy the ground; see it as your enemy sees it*. He had carried the interest in ground with him from the army to the police, and it had stood him in good stead in the study of crime scenes, though as a homicide detective he was more used to walking the back alleys of row houses than wooded hillsides. There were clumps of blackened ice in the gutter and he spotted a discarded Christmas tree just inside the woods. He crossed to the opposite side of the road. He glanced back the way he had come. The initial excitement was over and the houses were mostly dark again, except for a lamp here and there in a living room or behind an upstairs curtain. There was a long wooden-clad house on the corner of 18th Street and Shepherd. There was something about it. It took him a few seconds to recognise the distinctive metal shoebox of a security camera above the back door.

He immediately returned to the junction to look at the front of the house. As he had hoped, there was another camera, this one in the eaves on the corner of the building. It was pointed at the carport and the street beyond. Standing underneath it, facing in the direction that it was pointing, he realised that any car entering Crestwood along Shepherd should be visible on the footage. He hurried back to the police barrier and told the uniform to get another patrol car down to the scene and wake up the inhabitants of the house.

'Get me everything recorded by those cameras for the last twenty-four hours,' he said. 'Don't take no for an answer.'

Freeman entered the woods and followed a path towards the clearing, climbing over the fallen trees. Firm snow crackled underfoot. There was no other sound. The city had not yet woken. The buses carrying cadets from the Police Academy had not yet arrived.

When they first arrived in DC, Freeman and his wife had explored Rock Creek Park – hiking and jogging – ranging as far north as the Boundary Bridge and south to the Potomac. Freeman loved the park for its wildness – the thick brush, deadfall and jumbled rocks. You didn't have to step far from the main trails and it was like you were swallowed up. He didn't know of any other city that had such a wilderness at its heart. His wife Shawna was less keen. She preferred to run on a machine at the gym of the Ritz-Carlton Sports Club, presumably because it allowed her to rub shoulders with those persons who she viewed as essential to her future success. His wife's fierce determination to succeed manifested itself in many different ways, from the late nights at the office to their membership of a fashionable African-American congregation, from the tickets for the ballet at the Kennedy Center to volunteering for the DC-based charity Coalition for the Homeless.

She'd had a meteoric rise, from local campaign manager in Detroit, to national campaign coordinator and finally as a special adviser in the Office of Counsel to the President. It was understandable if she felt a little anxious about her new-found status, if she was, on occasion, a little too eager to fit in.

Such things did not bother Freeman. Yes, he was a joiner – he'd joined the military and later joined the police. You could even describe him as institutionalised, but he had always viewed these institutions with a dose of scepticism. If he had largely managed to avoid controversy in his career it was because he mostly kept his opinions to himself. He wondered if that was why he had been chosen for this case. He may not have been a politician but he was by necessity a political animal, or at least an animal with radar attuned to politics.

Freeman paused for a moment on the far edge of the clearing and looked down into the ravine at the site where the body was discovered. Dawn's pale light had not yet reached that far and it took a few seconds for his eyes to grow accustomed to the gloom. He saw a dark shape: a shadow of a figure. At first he thought it was an animal from the way it was crouching close to the ground and then he caught a glimpse of a hooded face raised to the air as if sniffing; a ski mask, glistening eyes in round holes, a knife slash of a mouth, bright white teeth, the lips curled back from a snarl.

'Who's there?' Freeman called. He stepped forward.

The figure in the mask froze for a moment and then, with startling speed, jumped to one side.

Freeman followed, skidding down the hillside with his arms out. He crashed through the trees, branches whipping at his face and hands. There was no time to reach for his gun.

'Stop! Police!' he shouted.

There was still a police car down by the river; some hope that someone inside it would hear him shouting. Ahead of him, the masked fugitive moved with an effortless, loping stride, swiftly reaching the river and scrambling across the jumble of rocks and shallow pools. Freeman felt a moment's elation – at the top of the far bank, a uniform had got out of his car and was holding his torch aloft. Then the man smacked into him. The impact flung the police officer against his patrol car and a flurry of blows knocked him to the ground.

As Freeman reached the river, he leapt and plunged into freezing waist-deep water. He struggled forward, pulling himself across

the slick rocks and pushing aside a tangle of brush. At the roadside, the police officer was being hammered with fists.

Freeman scrambled up the bank and threw himself forward but
a startlingly fast kick to the groin dropped him to his knees.

'Police . . .' he tried to shout, but it came out as a humiliating
whisper. Then a fist to the chest struck him like a hammer blow
and knocked him back into the river, his ass taking the punishment of a violent landing on the rocks. He picked himself up
and staggered, gasping and clutching his chest. Then he climbed
the bank again. The police officer was lying face down on the
tarmac. He was breathing raggedly. The gun was missing from
his holster. The masked man had snatched it – seventeen rounds
if the clip was full. He had crossed the road and was scrambling
up the rocky embankment towards Mount Pleasant and the
south end of the Park Road Bridge. A dark shape, about halfway
to the top.

Freeman started running.

At the top the masked man stopped and raised both hands
together, pointing in the direction of the police car. Freeman saw
the muzzle flash and dropped to the ground. He heard the crack
of the shot and the sound of glass shattering on the police car and
then seven more shots and the sound of tearing metal and explosively deflating tyres.

In the silence that followed the eighth shot, Freeman sprang to
his feet. He scrambled up the hillside, reaching the top in time to
see a dark shape disappear up a back alley at the edge of Mount
Pleasant. Freeman sprinted into the alleyway. He turned a corner,
skidded across an icy space, and dived behind a row of garbage
cans as he was fired at again, three shots, one of the bullets nicking
the brickwork of a garage wall just above his head.

Eleven expended. Six more in the magazine.

Freeman drew his own weapon and pulled back the slide,
loading a round in the chamber. He risked a look. His quarry was
running, dodging between garbage cans and had almost reached
the top of the alley. Freeman resumed his pursuit. Ahead of him,
the man skidded on the ice and crashed into a pile of snow.

Freeman sprinted harder. His opponent was up in an instant and fired again, the rounds kicking up snow at Freeman's feet.

Twelve. Thirteen. Fourteen.

The man ran out onto the street with Freeman following, sprinting diagonally across a four-way junction and rolling over the hood of a braking car. Reaching the pavement he turned and fired, just as Freeman rolled into a ball behind the front wheel of the car. The bullets punched through the hood.

Fifteen. Sixteen. One left.

Freeman jumped to his feet and charged. He saw the man dash up another alleyway. Freeman turned the corner sprinting flat out.

Seventeen.

The bullet so close he could feel the displaced air like wind on his face. Head down, charging like a bull.

And something struck him square in the forehead and knocked him to the ground.

SEVEN

Harry let herself in and ran to the top of the house, taking the stairs two at a time. From the bottom drawer of the desk in Jack's messy attic study, she retrieved her passport and carried it downstairs with her. Passing the bedroom, she heard the looped bass line of Jack's habitual shower music. Back out on the porch, she handed the passport to the policeman who had driven her home. He flicked through the pages and compared her with her likeness on the photo page.

'That's you,' he said.

He made her sign a carbon-copy receipt and gave her the pink sheet from the middle.

'Take care now, miss,' he said. 'And stay out of the park after dark.'

'I will,' she told him with a rueful smile and closed the door.

In the kitchen, she kicked off her running shoes and drank grapefruit juice from a carton straight out of the fridge. She spotted a new cartoon, cut from a newspaper, fixed to the fridge door: below the headline *Billy wasn't too excited about his new action figure* was a picture of two young boys; one of them was holding up a doll in the likeness of the President and saying, 'He just calmly analyses the situation.'

The fridge door was Jack's work: a mish-mash of garish magnets, rarely completed to-do lists, cocktail recipes cut from the *Post* and the *Times* and satirical cartoons.

Again, she took the stairs two at a time.

Their bedroom was dominated by a super-king-size teak four-poster bed that Jack had acquired from a Cambodian general, who ran a lucrative logging business up on the Thai border. Jack was investigating rumours of a former Khmer Rouge cadre, an interrogator from the notorious Tuol Sleng prison, who was said to be hiding out in the forest. He hadn't managed to find the interrogator, another journalist had beaten him to it, but he had won the bed from the general in a night-long game of poker in a karaoke hut beside one of Pol Pot's misbegotten dams.

Jack was in the shower. Massive Attack was playing on the docking station. He'd been listening to Massive Attack in the shower every morning for ten years, or so he claimed; she'd known him for less than three. He said he was fascinated by the gloomy, beguiling beauty of the music. She thought it was spooky, as spooky as his description of the alabaster trunks of dead trees standing in the dark waters of Pol Pot's dams. She stripped naked, discarding her clothes on the bathroom rug and stepped into the shower behind him. He gave a satisfied murmur when she ran her hands up his back and across his chest. Her fingers traced the lines of the shrapnel scars that he gained while camped out on the Northern Alliance lines in the Shomali Valley in Afghanistan in late 2001.

'Good morning,' he said sleepily. He often spent ten minutes or so in the shower, waking up in stages, vertebra by vertebra, beginning with his head down under the showerhead and his hands splayed on the white tiles and then gradually straightening up. Unlike Harry, Jack could sleep for hours and hours. He could pull a twelve-hour stretch, no problem. Watching him wake was a bit like watching a bear emerge from hibernation.

'What's the news?' she asked, knowing that he might be half-asleep but he would already have squinted at his BlackBerry.

'The panda recall,' Jack replied and yawned. 'The end of the unipolar American moment. Did you know that every panda in the world is owned by China?'

'You talk of nothing else,' she said dryly.

'Tai Shan is going home to be with his people.'

Tai Shan was the four-year-old giant panda born at the National Zoo in DC that was due to be repatriated to China in accordance with the operating agreement between the two countries. Commentators had gleefully seized on the return of the panda as a metaphor for the leaching away of American power and the rise of China.

'What about you? What are you up to today?' Jack asked.

She cupped his meaty balls in her hand. 'I thought I might go to the range, blast away at my demons.'

'You know I love a girl with a gun in her hand!'

She had a brief flash of the dead girl's smashed face, as she had done several times, waiting in the clearing and in the interrogation room, since turning over the body. She shuddered. She'd been running on adrenalin since finding the body. It couldn't last. At some point she knew that she would come crashing down. She must keep herself busy to keep depression at bay.

'Maybe I'll go running again this afternoon,' she said. 'In daylight this time.'

'I didn't hear you come in last night,' Jack said. 'Come to think of it, I didn't hear you go out again this morning either.'

'I didn't,' she said.

'I don't understand?'

'I've just passed a polygraph test.'

'Polygraphs aren't worth shit,' he said, yawning again. 'Where have you been?'

'Police Headquarters. I found a body.'

Naked, Harry sat at her glass-topped dressing table and blow-dried her hair. She studied herself in the tri-fold mirror; her broad face that she had been told was designed for a smile. She thought that she didn't look particularly tired for someone who had been up all night.

There were two small photographs Blu-tacked to the mirror's right-hand panel. One was of her as a young girl presenting a bouquet of flowers to the ballet dancer Margot Fonteyn after a production of *Swan Lake* at the Edinburgh Playhouse; the other was of her playing the girl in the *Nutcracker* a year later, again at the Playhouse. She'd competed against girls from ballet schools across Scotland to land the role. There had been a time when all she had wanted was to be a ballet dancer. These days her dreams were more prosaic; two years after resigning from Protection Command she was still dreaming about blocked exits, flash-mobs, suicide bombers and the magazine ejecting from her pistol as she raised it to fire.

She was aware of Jack staring at her and drinking his coffee on his ridiculously large and spooky bed. She knew that he was exasperated with her because she hadn't called him from Police Headquarters and annoyed with himself that he hadn't noticed her absence. He had chided her for letting him ramble on in the shower before telling him.

She switched off the dryer. 'You're just jealous because you didn't find the body,' she said. 'Believe me, it wasn't a pretty sight.'

'That's not it,' he said emphatically. 'They haven't ruled you out as a suspect. You should get a lawyer.'

'I don't need a lawyer,' she said and reached for her mug of tea. Jack drank coffee and she drank tea, otherwise she thought they agreed on most things.

'This is America,' Jack said, 'everybody needs a lawyer. An attorney.'

'Do you know any attorneys?'

'Only disreputable ones.'

'I'll have one of them.' She switched on the dryer again. He pulled a face.

He was so transparently concerned for her welfare. But she was aware of the sub-text. Jack was committed to the idea of being a father. As impetuously as she had agreed to marry him and move with him to the US, she had agreed that she would do her best to get pregnant. They had gone at it with zeal. Around the time of the Presidential Inauguration she had learned that their efforts had been successful. Harry was pregnant! Jack had been ecstatic, full of talk of how he was going to be a better father than his own, of how he was going to stop the endless travelling, and stay at home and write that damn book he'd been threatening to write for a decade or so.

When she began to cramp early one evening at Easter, after a day visiting the cherry blossom in the Tidal Basin, neither of them had known what it was or what it meant. She passed it off as an upset stomach. At midnight he had rushed her to George Washington Hospital and within two hours she had learned that she had lost the baby.

The doctor, a Lebanese émigré with meticulously combed hair, had told her that it was just something that happened. There would be opportunities to have other children. She had been brave that evening, or at least that's what everyone had told her. She had behaved with dignity. It was the first real crisis of their marriage and she had been great. Jack, who had been made to sit in a waiting room for two hours with no word from anyone, had listened to the doctor in stunned silence. She had felt sorry for him, he was so out of his depth. He didn't know what to ask and he did not want to seem a fool.

She had cried only once, when Jack arrived in her room the next morning with a bunch of lilies. She had spent the night lying in her bed, staring at the ceiling. There had been some pain but by morning it was merely discomfort. She had looked at him and wondered if she was not the slightest bit relieved. Not relieved, exactly. But they had been married for such a short time and hardly knew each other. And children were such a responsibility. Everyone said that children would change their lives forever and possibly not for the better. She had no idea how he would deal with nappies, night-time feeding, colic, tantrums . . .

Yes, she wanted a family but they were happy as they were. She was terrified of losing that.

'My father is coming to DC next week,' Jack told Harry. 'We are supposed to be having lunch with him.'

'I hadn't forgotten,' she replied. In fact she'd been looking forward to it. It was Jack's father who had brought them together. She had him to thank.

She remembered the first time that she met Douglas. It was just after 7 a.m. and she was sitting in the front passenger seat of his Jaguar XJ Saloon beside Ron, the detachment commander. Ron was giving her the benefit of his wisdom and insight.

'In my team I value loyalty, intelligence and calm – in that order. We're an elite. Not as elite, mind you, as we used to be but an elite nonetheless. I want you to follow my lead in all things. I expect you always to be cautious and firm.'

Harry remembered wondering whether the recent diminution of the team's elite status in Ron's mind might be linked to the addition of a woman, namely Harry herself, when the minister came hurrying out of the doorway of a house, not his own, on a side street near the King's Road in London. It was raining and he was holding a folded newspaper over his head.

'People usually are their own worst enemies,' Ron told her, watching the minister approach. 'Sometimes we have to protect them from themselves. Sometimes we just have to sit and watch. A lot of people think the worse of him.'

It was less than a month since one of the tabloids had broken the story of the minister's affair and his security detail had been playing a game of cat and mouse with photographers on motorbikes ever since. Harry had been drafted in at short notice after one of the minister's usual protection officers broke his ankle in an impromptu football match against a fire station crew in the minister's constituency. The attrition rate among the minister's protection officers was notoriously high.

'You'll find this a challenging job,' Ron had told her. 'Now open the door for him, there's a good girl.'

She'd got out of the car and opened the door just as the minister skidded to a halt at the edge of the pavement. He looked her up and down. Then he smiled, the same ever youthful and impish smile that it was said the voters loved and that she would soon discover he'd passed to his beloved only son.

'Hello,' he'd said. 'I'm Douglas.'

'Hello, Home Secretary, I'm Harriet. Call me Harry.'

From the back of the car he'd called out, 'To the Lubyanka,' which was his name for the Home Office, 'and don't spare the horses.'

It was another two years before she met Jack. It was at the wedding of Jack's younger sister Mary to the son of a former Foreign

Secretary now elevated to the House of Lords, an event that was being described in the national papers as the merging of two powerful Scottish political clans. Harry had received the invitation back when she was still a protection officer and she'd accepted without hesitation. Six months later and recently resigned from the police she had considered backing out, but then Douglas had sent her a handwritten note encouraging her to attend: *Make an old man happy, Douglas x*

What the hell, she'd thought.

Later she'd describe it as the moment that the Old Her became the New Her.

The service was held in the ancient abbey on the Hebridean island of Iona, where Christianity had first made landfall in Britain a thousand years before. Douglas was newly reunited with his wife, and his son Jack had flown in for the wedding from Kabul. She remembered that it was Douglas who had told her that his son had moved overseas on his promotion to the Cabinet. 'My son considers my career to be an impediment to his own,' he'd told her in a pensive tone one afternoon. 'He's sworn to stay out of Britain until presumably I'm of no further use to the Prime Minister.'

She remembered their first encounter with almost preternatural clarity. The Prime Minister was due to arrive for the reception by helicopter within the next thirty minutes and Harry, who was still burdened with a need to feel useful, was attempting to shoo a large and curious bull out of the village hall before the wedding party arrived. She'd been standing flapping her arms at the recalcitrant animal when Jack had appeared at her side, holding a broom.

'Need a hand?' he'd said and smiled that same smile and she'd recognised him immediately.

The bull was standing broadside to them with his back arched and his head down, which Harry had decided was a bad sign. Jack dashed forward with the broom-head out in front of him and jabbed it at the bull's head. 'Get out!' he yelled and the astonished animal skittered away, backing out through the open doorway and fleeing across the adjacent field. She remembered feeling a lurch in the pit of her stomach followed by a warm glow in her cheeks.

49

Against her better judgement, Harry kissed him later that night in a narrow lane on the way back to the Argyll Hotel. She couldn't help herself. They'd been dancing together all night. The Prime Minister had departed and Jack's repentant father was safely returned to his marital bed. She was without job or purpose. It couldn't be described as a conflict of interest – but what could it be described as? she'd wondered as his hands traced a line down her spine.

Certainly a lack of caution.

Six weeks later Jack asked the New Her to marry him. She'd surprised herself by saying yes without hesitation. She'd been even more surprised by the warmth with which Jack's family had greeted the news. Her soon-to-be father-in-law Douglas had given her a huge hug and said, 'Welcome to the clan.'

Jack turned to her on the stoop with a plastic-wrapped paper in each hand. '*Post* or *Times*?'

'Either,' she replied. She was standing at the front door in a bathrobe.

He threw her the *Washington Post*.

'Pussy,' he demanded, with a boyish pout.

She loved this benignly smutty side of him and obligingly parted the leaves of her robe. He made as if to swoon at the sight.

'Don't forget we're at the embassy tonight,' he told her. 'I've got to run.'

She could hear the sound of the airbrakes on the Metro bus as it came down Park Road. She watched him sprint across the road and along the pavement to keep up with it, his long legs pumping like Basil Fawlty's. She felt almost overwhelmed with love for him and she told herself that as long as they were together nothing else mattered.

It didn't matter that she didn't have a child. It didn't matter that she didn't have any money. That she threw away her police career in a fit of anger.

Who was she trying to kid?

She knew it was because she'd been up all night and that she was euphoric one moment and despondent the next, but she couldn't help it. It was like scratching a mosquito bite – a tour of the worst parts of her life. She was there on the stoop but her mind was spooling backwards: first to the food depot in Pakistan in the split second before she squeezed the trigger of her firearm and killed a man with two carefully aimed shots to the chest; and then several weeks later, in the dimly lit hallway outside the interview room, when the chairman of the fatal shooting investigation panel had taken her to one side and told her, 'It's OK to be angry, Harry.'

'No, it's not,' Harry had replied, through gritted teeth.

She didn't think of herself as an angry person. It wasn't in her nature. After the shooting they'd made her see a shrink who'd asked her how she thought of herself. She'd told her that she saw herself as someone with a warm and sunny disposition. An optimist.

She couldn't help the things that life threw in her way.

EIGHT

Thwock-thwock-thwock.

Freeman was sitting on a log with a paramedic stitching his forehead when a Sea King helicopter from the Marine One fleet flew overhead with its thudding rotors echoing in the ravine. There were so many decoy flights it was impossible to know whether the President or his family were on board – given the flight path it was most likely returning from a re-fuelling stop at Quantico – but every time he saw one of the helicopters pass over-head Freeman couldn't help but feel the same shiver of excitement that he felt on the day of the inauguration. A black man in the White House. *Anything was possible.* His wife Shawna had nothing but scorn for such sentiments. 'It's the same tired story, every time,' she'd say, 'the first general, the first senator, the first Supreme Court judge. It's not about the first anything! It's about the plight of the average man and woman.' It seemed strange to Freeman that she spoke that way, given how much work she put in to get the candidate elected.

'You're lucky you're not concussed,' the paramedic told him.

'I have a thick skull,' he said. Shawna had told him that too, on several occasions that he could recall.

Below them at the bottom of the Piney Branch Driveway police cadets carrying sticks spilled out of a bus and spread out along the road verge with the river before them. His colleague Maja approached from further up the hill.

'What are you doing here?' Freeman demanded.

Maja looked at him with the kind of expression that she usually reserved for kids playing hooky. 'I heard you got injured.'

'I'm fine.' He ventured a smile, regretting his tone. 'The Park policeman is in worse shape.'

'What happened?'

'Asshole threw his gun at me.'

Maja snorted. 'I guess you're lucky he didn't shoot you.'

'He ran out of bullets,' Freeman replied wryly. 'It's what we were taught to do, when you're out of ammo and before you close and grapple with the enemy you throw your gun.'

'You think he had the same training as you?'

Freeman shrugged. 'It's kind of a leap.'

Below them the cadets were beginning to climb the hill, poking at the snow with their sticks.

'Where did you get with the witness?' Freeman asked.

'Her story checks out. Word is she was good police.'

'So why did she quit?'

'She was involved in a fatal shooting incident in a food distribution centre in Pakistan. She was there providing security for a politician, the head of the British equivalent of AID. They came under attack and she shot and killed a Taliban who she claimed was wearing a suicide vest. The investigation cleared her of wrongdoing but she quit all the same.'

'She didn't have the stomach for it?'

'I spoke to her former boss in the London Metropolitan Police. He said it wasn't so much the shooting but that she felt they shouldn't have been there in the first place. She blamed the politician for the incident.'

A Crime Lab tech approached. 'We've found a hole in the senator's fence,' he told them. 'It's not far.'

'Let's go,' Freeman said.

They followed the tech up the path, retracing Freeman's steps from the night before. By daylight it was easier to identify the trees, the smooth grey trunks of beech trees and the corrugated bark of oaks. They stopped briefly at the fork in the path where Freeman first set eyes on the perimeter fence of the senator's property but instead of turning right and climbing towards Crestwood as he had done the night before, the tech turned left and headed down the hill into a steeper ravine where the fence ran close to the path. After a hundred feet or so, the ground levelled briefly before dropping down to the stream.

A mature tree had fallen across the fence, flattening a section of it. A second Crime Lab tech was kneeling by the tangled wreckage, taking photographs. You could just see the distant outline of the senator's house through the trees.

'From the look of it the weight of the snow brought it down,' the tech said. 'It's too wet for fingerprints.'

'Do what you can,' Freeman said, looking around, surveying the melting snow and slush. There weren't going to be any recognisable footprints either. The techs had a saying that when it was snowing the killer was laughing.

'You think he carried her out this way?' Maja asked.

He looked up towards the house.

'Maybe,' Freeman mused. If she were killed on the senator's property then getting her off site without a car would have been a problem. Larry Lumpe had told him that the senator's car was in the shop. Hand-carrying the body out through the back drive and into Crestwood and the busy 16th Street area beyond risked being seen. The front drive, which led directly into Rock Creek Park, was the obvious route but it had a working camera. On foot, this was the safest route, or at least it might have seemed that way viewed from the house.

It was a tempting theory.

'Except why not just flip the switch on the main circuit, cut the remaining cameras and walk the body out down the front drive?' he said.

'Because the main circuit of the senator's house supplies power to the panic room and is directly linked to Homeland Security and the Joint Operations Command Center,' Maja replied. 'It's a deterrent to home invasions. We would have had a patrol car on the scene within minutes.'

'They couldn't risk it,' Freeman mused.

'So this was the only route out,' Maja finished for him.

He looked back into the ravine. About twenty feet further down it was blocked by deadfall – fallen trees as densely packed as a beaver dam. The snow was probably waist-deep. If the man carrying the body had come from the senator's property and crossed the fence here, he wouldn't have got far down the ravine before finding his way blocked. He would have had to turn back and climb upwards in search of an alternative route out.

Freeman started back up the way he came, grabbing at branches to steady him as he climbed. He slipped several times. He imagined how difficult it must have been while carrying a body, how strong the temptation to dump it and run. When he reached the top he looked down to see the line of cadets advancing towards him from where the body was found. A couple of minutes later one of the cadets called out and another blew on a whistle and the line came to a stop right in front of him. A cadet lifted his stick; hanging off the end of it was a shoe.

A black alligator loafer with a brass bridle-bit. A luxury shoe, not a casual discard.

You weren't dressed for it, Freeman thought, they wouldn't let you use the road, you were stumbling around in the woods, weighed down by the body, looking for a way out, and then you lost your shoe. It was too much. Just a few steps and your foot was wet and cold, the sock clotted with snow.

You dumped the body.

'Yes,' he said, 'I think he carried her out this way.'

NINE

The Assistant Chief's wall was a measure of his success and of his ambition.

There were framed Bachelor's and Master's Degrees in Management from Johns Hopkins University, and a Master's Degree in National Security Studies from the Naval Postgraduate School in Monterey, California. There were graduate diplomas from the FBI National Academy and the federal DEA's Drug Unit Commander's Academy. There were also framed photos of him beaming, lantern-jawed, at the camera in the company of three presidents, two mayors (crack-smoking Marion Barry not included), a clutch of senators and congressmen, as well as with those symbols of black rectitude Bill Cosby and Ben Ali of Ben's Chili Bowl.

Freeman took a step forward to deposit his hastily written single-page preliminary report on the Assistant Chief's desk and then retreated deferentially. He waited while Streeks read it. He had a splitting headache.

'You don't mention that Chief Thielen or the mayor were at Senator Cannon's house,' Streeks said without looking up.

'Should I have done?'

Streeks raised his eyes to Freeman, taking in his torn and soiled clothing and the stitches on his forehead. Melting snow from his boots and trouser cuffs was creating a pool of water on the floor. 'Your work for the Criminal Investigation Division has been exemplary. I expect you to demonstrate the same high standards in the investigation of this case.'

'Are you suggesting that I investigate the senator?'

'I'm not telling you how to do your job. However, I aim to make sure you have the resources to give it your best shot. I've spoken to the FBI and we've agreed to set up a joint task force.'

'I got the impression that the Chief was keen to keep the FBI out of this.'

'Under the terms of our Memorandum of Agreement, the FBI has the right to take control of this investigation. I have spoken to the DC Field Office of the FBI and they have agreed that for now MPD will remain as lead agency in the joint task force. They have agreed to expedite DNA analysis and they will be assigning a special agent named McCafferty from the Behavioural Science Unit as liaison.'

'Behavioural Science? They think we've got a serial killer?'

'That's for you to find out, Michael.'

'And what if the victim was killed on the senator's property?'

Streeks raised his bushy eyebrows. 'No one is above the law, Michael.'

Freeman couldn't believe that Streeks was so unruffled. 'This will turn into a shit storm,' he protested. 'With healthcare stalled on the Hill the TV networks are desperate for a story.'

'Just be careful that you don't make any unsubstantiated accusations.'

Freeman opened his mouth to speak but found that, taken by surprise, he had nothing else to say.

'Given the level of media interest that is likely to attend this case,' Streeks continued, 'I believe that Police Headquarters is too insecure an environment for the conduct of the investigation. This morning when I spoke to the FBI they offered to make a suitable alternative immediately available. As for personnel, as well as Sergeant Menendez, you've got Detectives Hadžiosmanagič and Marschalk and you're being assigned Detective Wrath from Narcotics and Officer Diggs from the Delinquency Section.

'If you require further resources you can come back to me. If there are any leads in the case you report them directly to me. I will then brief the Chief of Police. Do I need to give you a lecture on the chain of command?'

'No, sir.'

'Thank you,' Streeks said. Freeman was dismissed

TEN

'So you're a city cop?'

Freeman remembered the look on the realtor's face the day that he showed up for the viewing, the hint of condescension. The suggestion left hanging in the air that a condo in the Yale Steam Laundry development in the newly gentrified Mount Vernon Triangle was way beyond what a humble MPD cop could afford. She was right of course; most of his colleagues in Homicide lived in much more modest accommodation further out of town.

She was also right when she said it was an impressive view. From the living room looking south, you could see the white dome of the Capitol. Until 1976 the building had operated as a laundry, washing linens for many of DC's hotels and government buildings including the Congress and White House.

'Does your wife work?' the realtor asked.

She'd spotted the wedding band. 'Yes,' he said.

'Two incomes?' she said, seeking reassurance.

'That's right.'

The second time he'd brought Shawna. She fell in love with it at first sight. The yellow brick walls, high ceilings, semi-circular warehouse windows and modern blond wood fittings.

The iconic view.

Shawna, who was raised in a tiny apartment on Chicago's South Side with an invalid mother, loved the space and status that it conveyed. Freeman, with a similarly hardscrabble upbringing, was less sure. He had a nagging sense that there was something inauthentic about it post-makeover.

It was all gleaming new surfaces, devoid of soul.

★ ★ ★

He let himself in the door, discarded his clothes and his gun and phone on the polished wood floor and headed straight for the walk-in shower. He spun the dial until the water was as hot as he could bear and stood there for ten minutes or so. His whole body ached from the blows that he had taken by the river. You couldn't describe it as a fight. He'd been kicked, punched and then repeatedly shot at. He hadn't been knocked around like this since the grappling room in the Isolation Facility at Fort Campbell in his Special Forces days.

He thought that he understood why Assistant Chief Streeks would go against Chief Thielen's wish to keep out the FBI. It was widely known within the Criminal Investigation Division that Streeks coveted Thielen's job and that a change of mayor would increase the likelihood of him getting it. If it turned out that the victim was killed on the senator's property it would cause grave embarrassment to both the mayor and the Chief who had rushed to the house at the senator's behest.

As Freeman towelled himself he wandered into the kitchen in search of something to eat. Shawna's weekly schedule was stuck to the stainless-steel door of the fridge. He glanced at it with his hand on the fridge door. Last night had 'Chicago' printed on it, tonight's entry was blank, which meant she might be around or not. Tomorrow night she was due to attend a fundraiser out in Prince George's County where the incumbent congressman was standing for re-election in the midterms. Freeman had attended many such fundraisers during the election campaign, fulfilling a role as his wife's supportive and civic-minded husband, the wartime hero and tenacious police detective.

He carried a spoon and a yogurt carton through into the living room and sat on the sofa, still wrapped in a towel. It was tempting to lie back and close his eyes, to allow the fatigue to overcome him but instead he switched on the television. Fox 5 was running the strapline 'Killer on the rampage'. The Fox anchor was saying, 'Police have now confirmed that investigators at the murder scene came under fire from an unidentified assailant. Let's now go live to the scene. What's the latest, Brandy?'

'Extraordinary scenes here, Gwen. I'm in Mount Pleasant, just across the Piney Branch Driveway from Crestwood where the young woman's naked body was found in the early hours of this morning.'

It was the same reporter with black earmuffs on the screen as he'd seen on the squad room TV a couple of hours before. She must be pretty cold by now, he thought.

'Behind me crime scene investigators are collecting evidence from an alleyway where an as yet unidentified person wearing a ski mask traded shots with police. I can tell you, there's a lot of local speculation here that it must have been the killer, returned to the crime scene for reasons unknown.'

'Were there any casualties?'

'Gwen, we understand that one police officer from the Park Police was hospitalised and another suffered minor injuries. The unidentified person got away. We are waiting for the police to issue a description.'

Good luck with that, Freeman thought. There was almost nothing of use he could say about his attacker other than that he was strong and nimble.

'Brandy, I'm going to have to interrupt you. We're now going live to the Capitol where Senator Cannon is holding a press conference . . .'

The senator was standing on a podium flanked by his blonde and attractive wife on one side and a similarly blonde and attractive young woman, probably his daughter, on the other. He'd obviously got them back from Tennessee in a hurry. The senator confirmed that a murdered woman's body had been found in the early hours of the morning in the woods alongside his property and called on anyone with any knowledge of the crime to come forward with information so that the young woman could be identified and her parents notified.

'Our thoughts and our prayers are with the dead woman's family,' Cannon said. 'The focus should now be on finding out who she is and why she was so brutally killed.'

It is an adroit move, Freeman acknowledged, for the senator to intervene now to try to get ahead of the news cycle and head off any speculation that he might have been involved. Also smart to be framed by two supportive women. He wondered if it was Sonia Rojas's idea. He imagined her standing in the wings with her unreadable expression.

The senator left the podium without answering any questions.

Freeman's cell was ringing. He hurried through to the hallway and scooped the phone off the floor. It was Maja. 'You've got to come and check out this place,' she said. 'It's awesome.'

'Where are you?' he asked.

'At the Watergate.'

ELEVEN

Maja's ass was the talk of Criminal Investigation Division.

You could see why. She was on tiptoe on top of a stool, pinning photos to an incident board that she had rigged up from a felt room divider. Like Freeman, she had changed her clothes and each time she reached upwards the material of her black knee-length skirt stretched across her taut well-formed buttocks. Watching from a few feet away, there was a young man perched on a desk and sipping at a sixteen-ounce cup of coffee. At the sight of him so obviously ogling her, Freeman felt a flicker of sudden irritation. He cleared his throat. The man in the suit jumped to his feet.

'You must be Special Agent McCafferty?' Freeman guessed.

'That's right, Lieutenant. Like the cat, only spelled differently.' He winked. His grip was firm and as they shook hands, McCafferty leaned forward and told the old joke: 'I'm from the federal government and I'm here to help.'

He stepped back and wiped the foam off his upper lip with the back of his hand. He was wearing a dark suit and crisp white shirt with a Burberry check tie, and a pair of brightly polished lace-up shoes. He looked like he'd stepped out of a catalogue. 'We'll get this cracked in no time, am I right?'

'We'll see,' Freeman said stiffly, staring over his shoulder.

Close by, Officer Winnie Love Diggs was sitting at a desk with a carton of Krispy Kreme doughnuts, projecting an aura of professional boredom. She was a massive woman with jet-black braids that reached down her back and gaudily decorated acrylic nails. It was rumoured to have been several years since she was able to fit behind the wheel of a patrol car.

She scrunched up her face in a kind of scowl which was as

animated an expression as Winnie ever wore. 'What the fuck am I doing here, Michael?'

'Investigating a murder, Winnie.'

'Shit! With these crackers?'

Behind her, Detectives Hector Menendez and Kari Marschalk, 'Stan and Olly' in Maja's lexicon, were making themselves at home in an open-plan cubicle fitted with brand-new-looking desktop computers. Hector Menendez was a blunt, tenacious Mexican from Columbia Heights. Squat and big-bellied, he had heavily stubbled jowls, a punch-flattened nose and a black moustache. He was wearing a brown nylon suit and he was struggling with meaty fingers to pin photographs of his four daughters to the dividing wall. Kari Marschalk, by contrast, was a tall, lean and stooping man with thinning sandy hair and a wistful expression on his face. He wore a brown corduroy suit with leather patches and frayed cuffs that made him look like a grade school teacher.

'Isn't this great?' Maja pirouetted on the stool and spread her arms.

'Everything works,' Kari agreed, and shook his head as if such a thing was barely credible.

Detective Eli Wrath was sitting on his hands on a desk at the back of the room, shooting furtive glances at his colleagues. He was a slight man in his mid-twenties, pale-skinned with a pinched face, shiny eyes and a bushy reddish-brown beard that gave him a prophetic look; his family was from Brush Mountain in western Virginia and happily called themselves hill folk. He was wearing a pair of baggy stonewashed jeans, a faded blue LURAY CAVERNS ball cap and a bulletproof vest with POLICE stencilled on it in large white letters. He was not known for his conversation.

'It's the *Marie Celeste* all over,' McCafferty said.

'What do you know about this place?' Freeman asked, looking around. There was a poster of the new F-22 fighter jet on the wall behind Eli's head. The view through the windows was of the Potomac River, and beyond it the office blocks on the west bank in Rosslyn, Virginia. The Heights of Buildings Act ensured that no building in the District was higher than the dome of the Capitol but over in Virginia there were no such restrictions, and a cluster of tower blocks, mostly occupied by large defence contractors, had sprung up as if clamouring for attention.

McCafferty shrugged. 'Some lobbying firm that had its assets seized as part of a public corruption investigation.'

'This girl must be *muy importante*, eh?' Hector observed.

'If she was important,' Winnie snapped, 'she sure as shit wouldn't have a sorry-ass motherfucker like you on her case.'

Hector offered her an upright finger. 'I love you too, *puta*.'

'There was nothing on the corpse to identify her,' Freeman said.

'Everybody is frightened that we've got another Chandra Levy on our hands,' Maja said.

'Gather round, people,' Freeman told them.

He sat on a desk with the incident board behind him and stared at their expectant faces. It reminded him of the excited buzz in a theatre before the curtains go up. He was the centre of attention. This was his investigation and they were his people, his responsibility. They were a competent team, Streeks had made sure of that, and he was confident that given the right direction they would rise to the occasion. The problem was that there were no leads to speak of, not yet at least.

'We don't know her name,' he told them, 'we don't know where she's from and we don't know what she looked like.'

There was a collective groan.

'Well, Michael, what do you know?' demanded Winnie.

Freeman explained the details of the case so far, the location including the park and the adjacent neighbourhoods; the broken-down fence; Harriet Armstrong's witness statement and the extensive background checks on her undertaken by Maja; the statements of the senator and his chief of staff; the tarpaulin and the shoe recovered from the scene; the victim's race, age and height as well as Freeman's initial assessment of her injuries; and finally, the man whom Freeman had interrupted at the crime scene, who had hospitalised a police officer, shot up a Park Police cruiser and given Freeman a nasty gash on his forehead.

'You're saying the victim's face was completely destroyed, all features deliberately erased?' McCafferty asked.

'That was the result,' Freeman said. 'I can't say yet whether it was deliberate.'

'If it was deliberate then it is classic de-personisation: the killer erases key features that we take to be indications of personality. He is reducing her to sub-human status. It may also indicate that he knew her.'

'You need to look back at cold cases and victims with similar injuries.'

McCafferty nodded. 'I can access the database at Quantico.'

'Are we hunting a serial killer here?' Eli asked.

Winnie swivelled around to look at him, the air suspension on her chair sighing beneath her weight. 'Shit . . .'

McCafferty raised a hand to speak and Freeman nodded.

'Setting aside the fact that we only have one body,' McCafferty replied, 'and at this stage no established connection to a previous homicide, we do know that serial killers will often go back to a crime scene, either because they've an interest in police procedure and they're studying you, or because they're asocial, and they're there to re-live the experience.'

'We have only one body,' Freeman cut in, 'and we have no confirmation as yet that the person that I disturbed at the scene is responsible for the murder. I am waiting on prints from the gun that was used. In the meantime, given the sensitivity involved in this case, I don't want to hear any more talk of serial killers. Is that clear?'

'Sure,' Eli replied with a shrug.

Freeman looked at each one of them in turn to make sure that they understood. McCafferty sipped his coffee.

'This is the missing persons list.' Freeman handed Hector a printout from the National Missing and Unidentified Persons System (NamUS) with names, dates of birth and other physical and circumstantial details including time and date of disappearance. 'According to Kaplan, she died sometime last night. So it's possible that no one will miss her until this morning. She may not even be on the system yet. But we have to consider the possibility that she went missing before she died. Hector, Kari, Eli, I want you to cross-reference what we know about her against what's in the NamUS system. There're currently about two and a half thousand open cases. I want a short list based on the information that we have.'

They groaned in unison.

'Kaplan will enter her in the unidentified decedents database. I'll be a lot happier when we have a name for her.'

'What are we gonna call her in the meantime?' Hector asked, stroking his moustache.

'Suggestions?' Freeman asked.

'The girl with the barcode tattoo?' McCafferty suggested.

'Absolutely not,' Maja snapped.

'That's nice,' Hector said, shaking his head. 'You disrespect the dead, man.'

'Then come up with something better,' Freeman told them. 'Until then we stick with Jane Doe.' He turned to Winnie: 'I want you to review the security camera footage from the house on 18th and Shepherd. Any vehicles coming or going, private cars, cabs, etc. I want them all checked out.'

'I'm on it,' Winnie replied.

'Maja, you come with me to the Medical Examiner's office.'

He looked at McCafferty who stared expectantly back.

'You want more than cold cases?' Freeman asked him.

'Sure.'

Freeman thought for a moment. 'OK. Write me a profile of Senator Cannon, all the salient facts.' And because that might not sound controversial enough, Freeman added, 'And any dirt.'

Maja put on her hat and buttoned her coat. She followed him out into the cold Washington morning.

'What are you playing at?' she demanded. 'They'll think you want to make the senator into a suspect.'

'I'm just trying to find out where my boundaries are,' Freeman told her.

TWELVE

The Maryland Small Arms Range was situated on a neglected stretch of the Old Marlboro Pike adjacent to Andrews Air Force Base.

To get there, Harry drove through Anacostia and out along the Suitland Parkway. In the lot outside the long, low building that housed the range were the usual collection of loudly decaled law enforcement vehicles: US Marshall Service, Maryland State Troopers, Federal Protective Police, MPD. Except for the weekends, when off-duty cops brought their spouses along to teach them to shoot, Harry rarely had to wait long for a lane. She handed over her driver's licence and rented a Glock 24. She liked the 24 for its low trigger pull weight and the long sight radius; it was the same size as the Glock 17L, which she was used to using back in the UK, but chambered for the larger American 0.40 Smith and Wesson cartridge. She bought a carton of ammunition and chose six standard shooting targets from a selection displayed on the wall that also included charging Nazi zombies, turbanned skeletons and Osama Bin Laden.

She fired three strings of five shots at a target at twenty-five metres. She re-set the alarm on her watch between each string: she fired the first string in eight seconds; the second in six seconds and the third in four seconds. She did it again: thirty shots in all, what was known in competition shooting as a 'stage'. She fired another stage. Two stages made a course. She scored 594, four short of the maximum. She was satisfied.

She was walking across the parking lot to her car when her mother called. 'Harriet? Are you all right? Is there an emergency?'

67

Harry pointed at her Jeep with the key fob and the hazard lights flashed as the locks clicked open. 'No. Why?'

'The police called Clive at work. The American police.'

Clive Mackenzie was Harry's stepfather. He was a Professor of History at the Centre for Medieval and Renaissance Studies at the University of Edinburgh. 'I bet that made his day,' she said dryly, opening the car door and throwing her bag across to the passenger seat. She slid into the driver's seat. Clive liked American crime fiction, preferably hardboiled.

'What's going on?'

'I was witness to a crime,' Harry explained. 'They were just checking up on me. It's nothing to worry about.'

'Where are you? What are you doing?'

'I'm at the range.'

'Oh, Harriet!'

Julia Mackenzie had never made any effort to hide her exasperation at her daughter's life choices – her hobbies, her police career and her husband – which she regarded as evidence of a wilful contrariness. Like her second husband, Julia was also an academic at the University of Edinburgh, a lecturer in the Department of Linguistics and English Language. She taught Old English – the *Anglo-Saxon Chronicles* – to undergraduates.

'I'd have thought that you would have given that up by now,' her mother said. She had a particular horror of guns. It was hardly surprising. Her family were originally from Dunblane, the small Scottish town where in 1996 a former Scout leader walked into a primary school armed with four handguns and killed sixteen children and one adult. In the wake of the massacre the government had passed legislation banning handguns. Like drink-driving or pornography, an interest in guns had become socially unacceptable in Britain.

'Are you pregnant again yet?' her mother demanded.

'You know I'm not.'

'I don't. You don't call. Your brother does.'

'I've been busy.' She bit back her anger. She glanced out of the car window and watched a US marshall crossing the lot. She often reflected that she had had the misfortune of being the younger sister of a brighter star – a louder, more talented, more intelligent sibling. She had become to some extent the opposite of these things: where her brother was cerebral she was physical; where he was talkative she was watchful. Sometimes it felt as if her character had grown to occupy her brother's vacancies.

'We're all busy,' her mother said, 'but I like to know that you're alive and well. I think I deserve that much. And I want to be a grandmother before you hit forty.'

There were times when it didn't seem like the Atlantic was wide enough.

'Harriet? Sweetheart?'

'I'm here.'

'Is Jack at home or is he off on a story?'

'He's here.'

'Is he looking after you?'

'Yes.'

'His terrible father is in the news again.'

'What's he done now?'

Her phone beeped. She looked at the screen. It was her friend Gary calling.

'Look, I've got someone else on the line.'

'Don't you hang up on me.'

'I'll call you later,' she said. 'Bye for now.'

'Harriet!'

'Bye.'

She cut the connection.

'Harry?'

'Hi, Gary.'

Gary Sinstadt and Harry had worked together during several visits by the UK Foreign Secretary to DC and the US Secretary of State to London. He was a former Secret Service agent and one of the few people she knew in Washington that she had not met through her husband. He now ran a private consultancy based out at Annapolis and on occasion offered Harry work.

'What's going on, Harry?'

'I've been shooting.'

'Score well?'

'Not bad for someone who was up all night.'

'Yes,' he said. 'I had a visit from the police this morning. They were very interested to learn about you.'

'I'm sorry about that. They've been thoroughly checking me out.'

'Hey, no problem. I told them they were lucky to have you at the scene.'

'I don't know about that.'

'Look, can you come and see me? I may have something for you.'

Annapolis was roughly forty-five minutes' drive away on Route 50. She glanced at her watch. She could be there by midday.

'I'm not going back to Boulder,' she told him, a little too fiercely.

'Hey. It's a local job. Better than the last one, I give you my word.'

Harry sat in the car park behind the wheel of her beaten-up Cherokee Jeep that Jack liked to call the 'bumper car' and stared through the windshield at a row of pines on the perimeter of the airbase. If she had been hoping that a morning at the range would take her mind off the body she had found, then the calls from her mother and Gary had effectively dashed that hope. She felt out of sorts as if she might weep. She considered phoning Jack but she knew that at this time of day he would be up against a deadline and inevitably distracted. She should have called him from Police HQ.

She wasn't sure that she could do another job for Gary if it was like the last one. As a female Protection Officer with a reputation for discretion there were certain jobs that inevitably came your way, whether you liked it or not. The key was to concentrate on the task of securing the client and ignore the circumstances. But it was difficult sometimes and her most recent job had left her deeply dismayed.

Six weeks before, she had accompanied a congressman's

sixteen-year-old daughter to an abortionist's clinic in Boulder, Colorado. Gary had persuaded her to take the job with the assurance that it would be a cakewalk, a simple to-and-from escort job, but it had proved to be anything but that.

The congressman was a Republican firebrand from Ohio and a well-known supporter of the Right to Life movement. His daughter was twenty-four weeks pregnant and her foetus had been diagnosed with anencephaly – it was missing a major portion of the brain, skull and scalp. Doctors had agreed that failure to abort would put the mother at risk of substantial and irreversible harm. Harry would never forget the barely concealed expression of distaste on the congressman's face when he'd opened the door of his Georgetown mansion to her or his daughter's fury and disgust as she sat in her airplane seat, with her fists clawing at her belly.

On the first of three meetings with him before the procedure, the abortionist, an elderly, severe-looking man in surgical scrubs, had said to the sixteen-year-old, 'You told the counsellor that we should all be killed.'

'Yes, you should be killed,' she had replied.

It was only a few months since George Tiller, a late-term abortionist in Wichita, had been shot dead while handing out bulletins to worshippers in the lobby of his Lutheran church. There were three US marshalls standing in the corridor outside the room they were in. To reach it, Harry and the girl had passed through four bulletproof doors.

'Why?' the abortionist asked.

'Because you do abortions.'

'Me too?'

'Yes, you should be killed too.'

There was a pause.

'Do you want me to be killed before or after I perform your abortion?'

'Before,' she hissed.

On the next visit a nurse escorted them into an examining room and told the girl to undress from the waist down. As well as requiring the strictest confidence, the terms of Harry's contract stipulated that she stay with the girl at all times and she had remained through the examination and the subsequent procedure. She stood inside the operating room in surgical scrubs while just a few feet away the abortionist used forceps, scissors and a suction tube to break up the foetus. She had found all of it – the shock, the girl's anger, the violence of the procedure, the unspeakable sorrow of her own miscarriage welling up – threatening a composure that she desperately needed to maintain. She had bargained with herself. She would not do any more jobs that pushed at the limits of her tolerance. She would not be so easily persuaded.

Just say no, she told herself.

THIRTEEN

There were protesters on the National Mall.

Slowing for a set of lights on Constitution Avenue, Freeman spotted a placard of the President as Heath Ledger's Joker, his face smeared with clownish make-up; another of the President with a daubed-on moustache as Hitler; and another of a pile of bodies at Auschwitz with the slogan: NATIONAL SOCIALIST HEALTH-CARE. The demonstrations against the congressional healthcare bill had been going on across the country since the previous summer, when the former vice-presidential candidate Sarah Palin used Facebook to accuse the new administration of seeking to create death panels that would ration healthcare, dividing those who would live from those who would die. To Maja it was clear evidence of the truth of Godwin's Law (also known as Godwin's Rule of Nazi Analogies) that the longer an Internet debate goes on, the greater the probability of a comparison to Nazis or Hitler.

'Look,' she said, pointing angrily at a man wearing a T-shirt with PRAY FOR OBAMA written on it and beneath it PSALM 109.9. 'They should lock them up.'

After the first few times Freeman had observed the message on T-shirts and bumper stickers, he'd looked it up in his wife's Bible and realised that it was effectively a death threat: *May his children be fatherless, and his wife a widow.*

It wasn't lost on Freeman that the protesters were white. Like many people he had succumbed for a while to the heady notion of a post-racial America, that with the election of Obama America had moved on, but he soon realised that it was nonsense – the mixture of white anxiety, anti-communism and sex was too volatile to subdue. The image that really brought it home to Freeman was of Obama as witch doctor. It was forwarded to him by a colleague from Afghanistan, who was now with the FBI's Hate Crime Unit. The image had been uploaded to a Tea Party listserv by a Florida neurosurgeon; in it Obama's head was grafted onto a picture of a savage in nothing but a loincloth and bead necklaces, his legs spread wide and a club in his hands. There was a bone through his nose and a confection of feathers and flowers on his head. Under the picture was the slogan OBAMA CARE, with the red, white and blue 'new dawn' campaign symbol as the O and a hammer and sickle as the C.

The message was clear: Obama was foreign and strange, a communist, seductive perhaps for his magic – his promise of cures – but ultimately loathsome, not someone that a white man should leave alone with his wife or daughters.

The Office of the Chief Medical Examiner, the chop shop, was a low red-brick building on the far side of a sprawling complex of older grey municipal buildings and parking lots jammed full of cars on the DC Health Campus at the south-east end of Massachusetts Avenue. All the police reserved spaces were taken and Freeman parked on icy waste ground alongside the Anacostia River.

They checked in at reception at 11.30 a.m. and walked down a corridor with waxed linoleum floors to the autopsy suite. In the changing room they put on double gowns, gloves, sleeve protectors, shoe covers, surgical caps and masks. Looking through the glass partition into the lab, Freeman saw Kaplan, with his back to them, hunched over the body on the table. Only the woman's feet and her maroon-painted toenails were visible.

Together they pushed through the stainless-steel doors, their paper shoe covers swishing across the floor.

The corpse was lying on a stainless-steel table beside a large sink. She was albino-white under the fluorescent strip lights, her skin raised in fat goose bumps, with the only trace of lividity in her swollen genitalia. Kaplan had already cut through her ribs and opened her chest, the incisions leaving a Y-shaped scar on the torso, reaching from both shoulders and her abdomen and meeting at her sternum. Her heart and lungs and the glistening whorls and loops of her intestines were in bowls arranged beside her on the table. But it was her face that Freeman's attention was drawn to; from scalp to chin and from ear to ear, all features had been erased.

'She was cold and stiff on arrival and pronounced dead,' Kaplan told them. He crossed to the far side of the room where X-rays were mounted on viewing boxes on the wall. 'The bones of the skull and the face make up the most complex area of skeletal real estate in the human body.' He flipped a switch and the light flickered on. 'In this case reduced to rubble.'

Skull X-rays, lateral and Waters' views, but these were unlike anything that Freeman had seen before. He scanned the opaque shadows of overlapping bone fragments and the mosaic of fractures like so many broken shards of pottery.

'Her face was methodically destroyed with carefully aimed blows. There is complete craniofacial disruption with multiple fractures of the zygoma, infra-orbital rims and maxilla,' Kaplan explained, pointing to the cheekbones, eye sockets and upper jaw. 'Numerous bone fragments from the fractures penetrated the brain tissue.'

'How many blows?' Freeman asked.

'It is impossible to say for sure. Twenty or thirty blows maybe. It took time and the blows were applied with great force ante mortem – while she was still breathing. The chest X-rays show evidence of aspirated tooth fragments in her lungs. He hit her so hard she inhaled her own teeth.'

'Damn!' Maja muttered.

'Apart from her face and the lesions on her wrists and ankles from being restrained, her body is otherwise unmarked. For the killer, the manner in which she was killed had some kind of specific, possibly ritual, meaning. Which means he's probably done it before. You need to be looking for homicides exhibiting similar injuries.'

'We've got the FBI helping us with that,' Freeman told him. 'What about cause of death?'

'The symphyseal region of the lower jaw fractured so that the tongue lost its attachment and dropped back. Hence she asphyxiated.'

'The murder weapon?' Freeman asked.

'If you look here at the anterior wall of the frontal sinus you can see the coin-shaped imprint of what looks like a hammer. Not a very large hammer. One pound in weight perhaps. The weapon may have had some meaning to the killer.'

'Toxicology?'

'A screen for basic compounds using gas chromatography-mass spectrometry came back negative.'

'What about evidence of recent sexual activity?'

'Vaginal fluid samples were removed for analysis and an acid phosphatase spot test confirmed the presence of motile sperm cells in the vaginal fluid. She had sex before she was killed, Lieutenant, possibly with several different people. The samples have been submitted to the FBI for DNA analysis. The outer labia are visibly swollen but not especially bruised. She may not have been raped.'

Maja frowned. 'What do you mean?'

'If she had been raped I would have expected vaginal and rectal tears and defensive injuries to her forearms consistent with a struggle against her attacker or attackers. There are none. That said, there are lesions on her wrists and ankles consistent with her being tied down.'

'If she was tied down it would have been difficult for her to struggle,' Maja said. 'It's still rape.'

'Of course. But it seems possible that she allowed herself to be tied down. That this started out as a consensual sexual encounter and at some stage it turned violent. There's something else.'

'What?'

'She's sterile. There is no uterus and no ovaries.'

'You're saying she's had them removed?' Maja asks.

'No,' Kaplan replied. 'They never developed. It's interesting. My guess is that DNA analysis will reveal that she has an unusual chromosome pattern.'

'Does it have any bearing on our case?' Freeman asked.

Kaplan looked at him. 'I don't know, Lieutenant. Do you?'

'What about time of death?' Freeman asked.

'Body temperature, rigor and livor mortis, and stomach contents approximate the time of death between 11.30 p.m. and 1.30 a.m. last night, somewhere between ten and twelve hours ago.'

'So she was killed close to where she was found?'

'In my experience, close is an elastic concept. It depends on the mode of transport used by the perpetrator.'

'According to our witness the man carrying her body fled the scene on foot.'

'But did he arrive on foot, Lieutenant?'

'We're following up on that. What about the tattoo?'

Kaplan crossed back to the body and lifted her left forearm for them to see.

'Over time, skin tissue loses moisture and elasticity. In a tattoo, this produces a softening of both colour and line. I'd say this tattoo is at least ten years old.'

'Is it a real barcode?' Freeman asked.

'We tried running a standard barcode scanner over it without success. That doesn't mean to say that it wasn't machine-readable once. I suppose y'all might be able to find someone who can visually read a barcode.'

'I'll get on it,' Maja said.

'I'll send you the preliminary summary report as soon as I've typed it up,' Kaplan told them. He stripped off his gloves and threw them in a bin. 'I'd like to speak to you alone, if I may.'

Freeman glanced at Maja who shrugged and rolled her eyes. 'I'll wait in reception.'

They went to Kaplan's office, where, to Freeman's surprise, the Medical Examiner retrieved a bottle of bourbon and two glasses from a filing cabinet. He poured two generous measures. 'Even for a Homicide detective, you look terrible,' he said.

'It looks worse than it is.'

Kaplan raised his glass. 'To Michael Freeman, war hero.'

The bourbon performed a slow burn down Freeman's throat. 'I was never a hero,' he said.

'How much weight have you lost recently?' Kaplan asked.

'Some.'

'How much sleep have you had?'

'Not enough.'

'Problems at home?'

'What is this?' Freeman demanded.

'You're in no fit state to undertake this investigation.' Kaplan leaned forward and inspected Freeman's wound. He touched the tender swelling on Freeman's forehead. 'I heard that they moved you into new offices at the Watergate.'

'News travels fast.'

'Why do you think they did that?'

'I don't know.'

'And I heard Streeks got you a twink from Behavioural Science Unit.'

'He's a good-looking boy,' Freeman agreed. 'He's got that Celtic thing going, kind of like Colin Farrell.'

Kaplan paused. 'You know there's a saying, if you've been playing poker for half an hour and you don't know who the patsy at the table is, you're the patsy.'

FOURTEEN

Harry came bearing lunch: a six-pack and pizza.

She drove through the narrow streets of Eastport, between the clapboard houses with their screened porches and American flags and parked the Jeep outside the Maritime Museum. Gary lived on a forty-foot wooden-hulled yacht called *Nancy* that was moored at the Yacht Center opposite the museum. She walked across the tarmac lot, past yachts in dry dock undergoing repairs and out along the wooden jetty to the boat.

'I brought you the essentials,' she called to him from the jetty, six-pack in one hand and pizza in the other.

'Come aboard,' he said, ducking under a stay. Gary was a large man, but he was agile and sure-footed on his boat. His father had been a commodore in the US Navy and he'd grown up on naval bases in Europe and the Far East. He liked to tell people, in his easy-going way, 'I was born to mess about on boats.' Jack and Harry had spent several weekends with Gary on the boat, exploring the islands, anchorages and deserted hideaways of Chesapeake Bay.

They cast off the ropes and Gary eased *Nancy* out of the marina into Back Creek using the engine and headed for open water. They passed the Annapolis Sailing School, and a channel marker topped with an osprey's nest. They unfurled the main sail and sailed north out past the naval academy and 'Ego Alley' – known for the expensive yachts that regularly paraded up and down.

Harry opened a beer. The further they got from shore the more relaxed she felt, as if she was finally putting the night's events behind her. She sipped her beer and stared at the passing coastline.

On the far side of the Severn River were the three 800-foot-high radio towers at Greenbury Point that had always reminded her of the old film studio logo of the RKO Radio transmitter beaming its signal out to a revolving black and white world. The towers were all that remained of the old DC transmitter that the US Navy had put up in 1918 and used to communicate with surface ships and submarines since then through to the late nineties when satellites took over the function. Gary had told her that right up until the main umbrella antenna was demolished the transmitter fed a million watts of energy to the array. He said that when it was idle the antenna transmitted a standard string of letters in Morse code and the power was so high and the frequency so low you could feel the signal in your dental work.

Once they were well out on the water, Gary said, 'I've got a job interview for you if you're interested.'

Harry paused, beer in hand. 'Go on.'

'It's a babysitting job in DC. The client's a Russian by the name of Markoff. Dr Alexander Ilyanovich Markoff.'

'I don't do oligarchs.'

'Don't worry he's not an oligarch. He's a scientist. He works for a biotech company out on the Rockville Pike near the National Institutes of Health. He came over here with his family in 2008, during the Russia-Georgia war.'

'Why me?' Harry asked.

'Dr Markoff is looking for a woman to provide companionship for his niece and he's adamant that he won't accept an American. He wants a Brit. An old client of mine put him in touch with me. I thought of you.'

'How old is the niece?'

Gary helped himself to a slice of pizza. 'Eighteen or nineteen, maybe. Her name is Eva Markoff. I'm told her English is pretty good. She's a gymnast. I think you'd get on.'

Harry sipped her beer thoughtfully.

'How long does the job last?' she asked.

'A few days, a few weeks, it's up to you and the girl. It depends how you get on. Look, it's a cakewalk, a nine to five with no downside. I know the job in Boulder, the whole abortion thing, left a bad taste in your mouth. I understand that.'

'What's the threat?' Harry cut him off, not wanting to go there.

'Nothing specific. Animal rights people, anti-vivisectionists, you know. Dr Markoff experiments on monkeys and there are protesters outside the company offices. But there's no need for you to go anywhere near them.'

'What are the current security arrangements?'

'The family is living in a secure house in Chevy Chase with a static guard force provided by a Tennessee security company called Raeburn. In addition Dr Markoff brought one of his own security people over when he came. And the neighbourhood is crawling with embassy police.'

'Does he know I don't have a firearms permit?'

'Come on, Harry. Of course he does. You're there as a companion and someone who can make intelligent assessments about risk so that, as far as possible, Dr Markoff's niece can lead an ordinary life. She's surrounded by goons; she just wants someone to go shopping with.'

'Shopping?'

'Hey, the money is good. Five hundred dollars a day in your pocket. No reason to mention it to the IRS.'

'I could do with the money,' she acknowledged. Five hundred dollars a day was very tempting. She was tired of being dependent on Jack for money and his birthday was coming up. She wanted to get him something paid for with money that she had earned and not withdrawn from his account. Besides, it would be good to work. After all, it was what she was trained to do.

'Just as long as the girl's not pregnant.'

'Not as far as I'm aware,' Gary replied.

'Who would I answer to?'

'You'd talk directly to Dr Markoff. In matters relating to the girl's security his people will follow your lead. You'd have the final say. Any issues arise you know you call me, day or night. I can draw up a contract with Dr Markoff's legal people. What do you say?'

'OK.'

'So you'll take the interview?'

'I'll do it.'

'Good girl.' He finished his beer and opened another. 'There's something I should let you know. I had to talk to Dr Markoff about the business with the body you found.'

Harry was incredulous. 'You've spoken to him about me already?'

'I had to,' Gary protested. 'In something like this you have to have full disclosure. I mean what if the media get hold of your name and start following you around? This could be a big story.'

'Great,' she muttered.

'Listen, it's a good gig. You're made for the job.'

She had a sense that something wasn't quite right with what Gary was telling her. 'Let me get this straight: you told the client that I found a body this morning, that I'm a witness in a homicide case, and he still wants to employ me?'

Gary shrugged. 'Dr Markoff's intrigued. He wants to meet you.'

'When?'

'Straight away. I told him that you'd be there to meet him at five this afternoon.'

'I can't believe you.'

'It's paid work, honey . . .'

He reached for another slice of pizza.

There were times when Harry wanted to shout in exasperation. Instead she finished her beer and crushed the can. Once again, she had allowed herself to be persuaded. So much for *just say no*.

FIFTEEN

They were on Massachusetts Avenue heading north-west when Freeman first got the feeling that something was different. It was just after 1 p.m.

Front and follow.

There was a hint of constancy to what showed up ahead of him and in his mirrors, no specific colour or model that he could identify for certain, and the falling snow made it difficult to be sure, but he found himself checking out the cars around him as he drove. If they were being tailed then whoever was doing it was using several cars and knew what they were doing. He glanced at Maja. If she'd realised she wasn't letting on.

Winnie called. Freeman put her on loudspeaker. 'I've got a lead on a black Lincoln Town Car pictured on the video footage from the house on Shepherd Street,' she said. 'It's filmed heading west on Shepherd at 10.12 p.m. and then leaving again in a crazy hurry three hours later at 1.15 a.m. We've got two further photos of it running red lights on 16th Street and New York Avenue. The car belongs to a company called Cardinal Limousine Services based down at Buzzard Point in South-West. I spoke to them. The car was on a contract job for a company called Potomac Global Strategies. It's a limited liability corporation registered in Delaware. I'm checking with the Secretary of State's office.'

There was nothing unusual in that. More than half the USA's publicly traded companies were incorporated in the state of Delaware. It was cheap to incorporate, there was no residency requirement and provided that you didn't conduct any business in Delaware you were not obligated to pay corporation taxes.

'What about the limousine driver?' Maja asked, drumming her fingers on her knees.

'His name is Byron Bastian. I ran him for sheet and it came back for manslaughter. He was released from prison in 2007 after serving seven and a half years on a conviction related to a 1999 shooting in Prince George's County. It turns out that the owner of Cardinal Limousines also did some time, found God and now he offers employment to ex-offenders who are willing to clean up their act. Bastian's been working for him for about two years. He's described as hard-working and discreet. He lives with his sister Renee Bastian in Congress Heights.'

'Where is he now?' Maja asked.

'He hasn't returned the car as scheduled and they can't reach him on his cell.'

'Put out a BOLO on the car,' Freeman said.

BOLO – Be On the Look Out.

'It's done. There's more. Cardinal Limousine Services had a break-in early this morning. Somebody left the safe but rifled through their personnel records.'

Freeman glanced left, spun the wheel and made a U-turn. He flipped on the blue and red lights mounted on the dashboard.

Follow this, he thought.

'Give us that address in Congress Heights,' Maja said.

It was one of several semi-detached red-brick cubes on the south side of Savannah Street.

They parked alongside a snow-bank out front and Freeman bounded up the steps with Maja just a few feet behind. The lock had been forced, the jamb was splintered and the door was slightly ajar. Freeman and Maja exchanged a look and drew their fire-arms. Freeman pushed the door slowly open; it was like opening an oven; the heating was cranked right up.

'Hello?' Maja called. 'Police . . .'

Freeman eased himself inside, gun in one hand and the other shrugging off his jacket. He switched hands, right to left, and discarded the jacket on the mat. Switched back. He was always happiest with his gun in his right hand.

There was blood all the way down the hall – signs of struggle and blood splatter arcing high onto the walls. The victim's heart was still beating, still generating a blood pressure as she fell back before her attacker. There was a bloody handprint by a light-switch and an open clamshell phone lying by the skirting board. Then she fell. A glossy pool of blood on the linoleum in the kitchen. Beyond that, drag marks.

Freeman stepped out through the back door and into the freezing air again.

The killer dragged her out onto the porch and finished her there, plunged a kitchen knife through her sternum and into her heart.

Freeman knelt down beside the body. Exsanguination had drained her skin to the colour of ash: a heavy-set, middle-aged black woman wearing a pink terry-cloth bathrobe; naked underneath it. Her hair was wet from the shower and her dark brown eyes were fixed wide. The palms of her hands and the ulnar side of her forearms were covered in stabs, cuts and slices. Defensive injuries. Several of her fingers had been hacked off and littered the floor. A kitchen knife with a dimpled-steel handle and a six-inch blade lay discarded beside her.

The murder weapon.

Freeman looked up. There was another handprint on the screen door: a splayed hand shockingly red against the white paintwork. So fresh it seemed to gleam.

Freeman stood up again and pushed open the screen door. Maja followed. Bloody footprints in the snow led across the yard and into the alley, where they petered out in the icy slush. Freeman ran to the end of the alley and looked left and right down the street.

Nothing. No one.

'I'll call it in,' Maja said, grim-faced, holstering her gun.

There were five missed calls from her brother Byron on Renee Bastian's clamshell, the most recent less than an hour ago. Using her cell, Freeman called him back. Byron answered on the second ring. He sounded breathless as if he had been running.

'Renee? Renee? Where the hell you been at, girl? I been worried sick.'

'Byron,' Freeman said, in a calm and unhurried tone.

Silence at the other end and then, cautiously, 'Who's that?'

'Lieutenant Freeman, MPD. I have some bad news for you.'

'What you talkin' about?'

'Your sister is dead, Byron.'

'What the fuck?'

'Somebody came into your house and killed Renee. Why'd they do that, Byron?'

'Renee dun' nuttin' wrong.'

'She's dead.'

'Damn.'

There was a pause while Byron let out a strangled gasp. Freeman heard the Doppler shift of an ambulance siren in the background.

'Where are you, Byron?'

'Why they done that?' Byron asked. 'I'll answer fo' what I done. I know that. I'll answer aw'ite. But why they done that?'

'What happened last night, Byron?'

'I ain't killed that girl,' he said in a soft voice.

'Who did, Byron?'

'I can't talk to you.'

'Yes you can. You say you didn't kill her, well, you come in and give me a statement to that effect. I can help you.'

Byron snorted contemptuously. 'You think you gonna keep me safe?'

'I know it, Byron.'

'You know jack shit. Only thing is gonna keep me safe is my chrome.'

Byron cut the connection. Freeman called him back but it went straight to voicemail. He left a message.

'You call me, Byron,' he said. 'Day or night. I've got Renee's cell here. You call me and we'll work something out.'

* * *

Freeman sat shivering on the back steps while techs from the Mobile Crime Lab worked the scene, brushing aluminium powder and spraying for fingerprints with autistic concentration, and Kaplan examined the body in his own compulsive way.

The sense of outrage provoked in him by the discovery of the first body had deepened with the discovery of the second body.

His cobbled-together squad were working the case and periodically reporting in: Hector and Kari were interviewing the owner of Cardinal Limousine Services at Buzzard Point; Eli Wrath was at the Seventh District station talking to the local uniform; Maja Hadžiosmanagič had driven the Impala over to Perfect Nails IV at the Park Village Shops to interview Renee's work colleagues and Winnie Love Diggs was scouring databases and social networking sites for references to Potomac Global Strategies.

Hector reported in first. 'We got shit. Potomac Global Strategies has had an account with Cardinal Limousine Services since November 2008 and according to the owner he has had absolutely no interaction with anyone from the company in all that time. The bill is paid by company cheque the first of each month. Delaware-based bank. Illegible signature. Byron is the only driver ever to have been assigned to the account. The owner says Byron would ride the bus to Buzzard Point, sign out the Town Car and wait on a call telling him where to go. There's no way of knowing where he went or at what time unless we find the current vehicle log-book. And forget about historical records. Logs are kept until the client pays and then destroyed.'

'Give the bank details to Winnie,' Freeman told him.

Maja called next. 'Renee Bastian spoke to a co-worker named Vilma Simms at seven forty-five this morning. That must have been just before she was killed. According to Vilma, Renee mentioned that her bother Byron had not yet returned from a job and she was worried. It wasn't like him to come in late without calling. Then her doorbell rang and she ended the call.'

The killer did not wait for her to answer the door, Freeman thought. He kicked it in. She staggered backwards down the hall while he attacked her with a knife. He killed her on the porch and then he exited via the alley to the rear of the house.

It was not a robbery. Nothing was stolen. Cash and cards remained in Renee's handbag on the dressing table in her bedroom.

'What about next of kin?' Freeman asked.

'There's a father. He lives locally in sheltered housing. You want me to go tell him?'

'No. I'll get Hector on it. He can escort the father to the morgue to identify the body. Maybe the father knows something about where his son might be. I don't think a guy like Byron is gonna go far. He's probably holed up here, somewhere in the city.'

Freeman called Winnie and told her to apply to the duty judge for a 2703(d) order that would oblige the cell phone company to release its tracking records for both Byron and Renee's cell phones.

Kaplan pushed through the screen door. 'Aren't you cold?'

'I'm from Detroit.'

'So you are, Michael.'

'What happened?'

'He attacked her straight off; the moment he was through the door he started slashing at her with the knife, which suggests he brought it with him. Defensive injuries on her hands and forearms are consistent with her retreating down the hallway and attempting to deflect the blows. Then she fell, maybe she tripped. She continued to struggle and he hacked off several of her fingers. Then he stabbed her in the heart.'

'Is it the same killer?' Freeman asked.

'Not necessarily.'

'What does that mean?'

'The transportation of the first victim's body away from the murder site makes it difficult to be sure, but the manner in which she was killed is in stark contrast to the manner in which this woman was killed. I mean the killer took his time over the first victim, each blow was considered. Violent but precise. Like I told you before, it may have had some kind of ritual meaning personal to the killer, particularly the destruction of the facial features. By contrast, this was a homicide committed in haste with no attempt to obscure the evidence or move the body. We have the murder weapon. We have prints and hair. It's a lot messier. I'm talking about the distinction between an organised killing and a disorganised one. I'm not saying there isn't a connection but don't assume it's the same killer. In fact you may be looking for two killers. The second killing could be a response to the first. An act of revenge perhaps.'

Eli called.

'I think we got the car.'

The cable strained and the water seemed to boil, chunks of fractured ice bobbing to the surface. The Town Car emerged from the Anacostia River, rear bumper first with its wheels up. The air in the tyres must have caused it to flip over when it sank. The licence plate was clearly visible.

'That's it,' Freeman said. He was standing beside Eli in the encampment beneath the bridge. All around them the homeless and dispossessed squatted among blankets and cardboard and shopping trolleys piled with cans and plastic bottles.

'Description matches Byron,' Eli said. 'He must have come straight down here and dumped the car.'

The fire engine revved and winched the car out of the river, the metal of the roof screeching as it was dragged up onto the snow-covered concrete apron. A fireman released the cable. Water streamed from the vehicle, staining the snow a dirty brown.

For a moment no one approached. Then Freeman trudged over to the upside-down vehicle. He squatted down by the driver's side and peered in. He noticed the keys in the ignition and the automatic shift in drive. The windows had been left open so that it would sink more quickly. He lifted the sunshade. Nothing. He circled around, squatting down now on the passenger side. He reached in and opened the glove compartment, releasing a sudden rush of water. The driver's log-book was there; its pages reduced to mush.

Freeman shook his head. 'There's nothing usable here.'

He was walking back to his car when Winnie called.

'Go ahead,' Freeman told her.

'Potomac Global Strategies is a one-man outfit, all corporate officer positions are held by one Olivier Davide. No such name in the DC phone book or in the wider metro area. I found him on Facebook though. I got him tagged alongside a 2007 Pontiac Solstice GXP. I checked with DMV. It's registered in his name to an apartment in the Kennedy-Warren on Connecticut.'

SIXTEEN

They arrived at the Kennedy-Warren at 3.47 p.m. with a search and seizure warrant signed by a District Court judge. Two Impalas and two patrol cars from Second District rolled to a halt in the forecourt and the police tumbled out and charged into the lobby past an open-mouthed doorman. They sprinted up the emergency stairwell, arriving breathless at the fifth floor.

The door to the apartment was intact. There was no sign of forced entry. In accordance with the terms of the warrant they knocked on the door and they issued verbal warnings. They waited. They counted the seconds. They broke the door open with a ram. Freeman was first in, followed by two uniforms. Then Maja and more uniforms.

Inside it was a charnel house. It was difficult to believe that so much blood could come from one person. A startled uniform skidded in it and crashed into a glass-topped coffee table that shattered beneath him.

'Get out!' Freeman yelled. 'Everybody out. Now!'

Maja stripped to her brassiere and panties and Freeman to his boxer shorts. They were alone in the corridor and almost naked. The uniforms had retreated around the corner to give them some privacy. Freeman was pulling off his socks when he glanced upwards. Maja was also bending over and Freeman found himself with an intimate view of her cleavage. He felt a sudden urge to reach out and cup her breasts in his hands. Then she looked up. Their eyes met and they both turned away in embarrassed silence. What was he thinking? They dressed again quickly, this time in semi-translucent white paper suits with hoods, plastic bootees and latex gloves. The Mobile Crime Lab was on its way and so was Kaplan but Freeman was impatient and revved up with adrenalin; it was his third body in twelve hours. He was angry and he wanted answers. He wasn't prepared to wait.

'Ready?'

She nodded. They both took a deep breath. Once again, he was first in.

Olivier Davide knew his killer, or at least felt comfortable enough to let him in the door to his apartment, that much was clear. It was a one-bedroom apartment with wooden floors, north- and east-facing windows with a view of the Klingle Valley. It was full of the sour-sweet metallic smell of freshly spilled blood.

On the wall above the bed there was a four by four-foot framed print, a photograph of a terracotta sculpture of a woman and an alligator copulating. The woman was lying on her stomach with her head raised and her breasts spilling across the floor. The alligator was mounting her from behind, with his mouth wide open, and his lower jaw resting on the crown of her head. It was about the only thing in the bedroom not splattered with blood.

'It's beauty and the beast,' Maja said, deadpan. It was a fitting backdrop to the corpse on the bed. Freeman turned 180 degrees. There were two webcams facing the bed, one in each corner of the ceiling, like eyeballs on inverted pyramids.

He liked to film himself fucking, Freeman thought.

After that there was no excuse not to look: Olivier Davide was spread-eagled on the bed. His face and groin had been savaged, his chest stabbed repeatedly and several fingers had been crudely amputated. A frenzied attack.

Freeman crossed to the walk-in closet and opened the sliding door; inside was a row of tailored suits, a rack of gaudy ties and several neatly arranged pairs of brightly polished shoes. Olivier Davide was clearly a fastidious man, something of a dandy. Freeman went through into the bathroom. A razor, shaving brush, toothbrush all neatly arranged on a glass shelf above the sink. He pulled aside the shower curtain and squatted down. There were two long blonde hairs in the bottom of the stall.

'There's a half-finished packet of cigarettes in the bedside dresser and several condoms,' Maja called out.

Freeman straightened up and walked back through into the living area. There was a large flat screen and on the carpet among the wreckage of the coffee table was what Freeman most hoped to find: a laptop. A wafer-thin MacBook Air. But in the condition that he least hoped to find it in – the case was cracked in several places, the battery had popped out and the ribbon cable holding the keyboard to the logic board had come away. Whether the damage was done by the killer, or the police officer who fell into the table was not clear.

He should send it to the FBI to break into the hard drive.

'Takeout,' said Maja, peering in the flip-top trash-can. 'Noodles. A couple of days old.'

The FBI would probably take weeks. They always did.

'Damn,' he muttered.

'There's a knife missing,' Maja said, pointing to a stainless-steel knife block on the counter with five familiar dimpled-steel handles and six slots. She was right, a knife was missing – Renee's murder weapon. Freeman left the laptop, crossed back to the bed and squatted down beside it. The corpse's back and buttocks had the purplish hue of stagnant blood. *Livor mortis.* He had been dead for several hours, longer than Renee Bastian. They had come at this in the wrong order: Olivier Davide died first and then a few hours later Renee. They had the same stab wound in the chest; the same cause of death and the same weapon. There were differences though: the defensive injuries on Davide's forearms looked like – well, bites.

Freeman looked over his shoulder.

Judging by the blood splatter and the scuffmarks and the distribution of the bitten-off fingers on the living-room floor, Davide was attacked at the door. The killer barged into the apartment. He attacked Davide with his hands and his teeth: he gouged out his eyes and bit off his fingers; and Davide fell back before the onslaught, ending up in the bedroom. Then, by the looks of it, there was a pause. Bloody footprints led from the bed and across the living room to the kitchen counter and back again. The killer went and fetched a knife and came back and cut off his penis, probably while Davide was still alive. Then he plunged the knife several times into Davide's chest. Afterwards, the killer wiped the knife's blade on the blanket and took it with him when he left. He subsequently used it to kill Renee. Assuming it was the same person that he encountered in Rock Creek Park, he must have had it with him when Freeman interrupted him at the crime scene; it occurred to Freeman that he was lucky not to have had it used on him.

'Can you see a cell?' Freeman asked, getting down on his hands and knees to look under the bed.

'No,' Maja answered.

'I have found his penis though,' Freeman said.

From beneath the kitchen sink Maja removed a black garbage sack. Inside it were soiled and bloody clothes and a shoe. A distinctive black alligator-skin loafer with a brass bridle-bit, it looked like a match for the one recovered by the police cadets in the park.

It was Olivier Davide who dumped the girl's body in the ravine, Freeman thought.

His mind made up, Freeman returned to the cracked laptop, reached into its innards and pulled on the white tab to release the hard drive. He handed it to Maja.

'Let me know what's on that,' he said.

'You're the boss,' she said and tucked it in her bra.

There was a knock on the door. It was Kaplan. He was standing in the doorway holding his aluminium scene case. 'Oh, how simple it would all have been,' he declared, looking from Freeman to Maja, 'had I been here before they came like a herd of buffalo and wallowed all over it.'

Maja threw a puzzled glance at Freeman, who ventured a guess: 'Sherlock Holmes?'

'Very good, Michael, "The Boscombe Valley Mystery". You are indeed a surprise.'

'We're done here,' Freeman said, stripping off his gloves and balling them up.

Stepping carefully to avoid the pools of blood, Kaplan approached the bed.

'I'll call the odontologist,' he told them. 'We may be able to get an impression of the killer's bite.'

Door-to-door canvassing yielded a Russian émigré in her sixties who lived with several cats on the same floor and was convinced that Olivier Davide was a Russian spy. She taught Foreign Relations at Georgetown and informed them imperiously that she was the spinster daughter of a high-ranking former member of the Soviet leader Khrushchev's Politburo.

'I can tell you it wasn't worth the money, whoever sent him here,' she explained to Freeman and Maja, after sitting them down and offering them tea from an ornate silver samovar. 'The Soviet Union would have trained him better. He was not convincing as a French Canadian. He had a rather thick Russian accent. His English was perfect, very proper and grammatically correct but I certainly knew he was a Russian. Not judged only by his accent but rather by his distinct Russian personality, that he was always somewhat unhappy about various things . . .'

SEVENTEEN

Because she believed the first appearance of a protection officer to be important, Harry had put on her smartest work-wear, a Jaeger trouser suit over a silk jersey top. The solitaire diamond studs that her father-in-law Douglas gave her as a gift when she got engaged to his only son. Simple shoes though – plain, black Adidas trainers because you can't protect yourself let alone anyone else while wearing heels. She aimed to look smart and capable, sophisticated if you knew what you were looking at, but not at all showy.

She drove west, cutting across Rock Creek Park between canyons of snow, and then turned north towards Chevy Chase. It was one of the most affluent neighbourhoods in the city, with tantalising glimpses of spacious homes in park-like settings behind high walls; a place not in the city but not out of it either.

She pulled up at a closed metal gate as the sun was setting. She was right on time: 5 p.m. She opened the driver's side window and two sullen-faced men in bulky, black jackets and peaked caps with RAEBURN printed on them appeared from a guard hut. She handed over her DC driving licence and one of them checked her name against the list on his clipboard while the other circled the car, checking underneath it with a mirror on a pole.

'Step out of the car please, miss,' said the man with the clipboard.

She stood shivering in the cold while they diligently checked under the hood and in the trunk, in the glove compartment and under the seats. They inspected the contents of her briefcase and ran a hand-held metal detector over her body while she raised her hands in the air.

Her licence was returned to her and the man said, or at least she thought he said – he muttered it under his breath – 'Welcome to Cemetery Lane.'

The gate glided open. She drove along a track between beech trees with branches cross-hatching overhead and listened to the crunch of gravel under the Jeep's wheels, felt the cold air on her face from the open window. There was almost no sound of cars, as if the city had receded, so that there was only a memory of it as muted as the murmur of the sea in a seashell.

She glimpsed something moving between the trees and then something struck the side of her head and exploded in a blizzard of whiteness. Her hands tightened reflexively on the steering wheel. For a few moments, time crawled and the car fish-tailed. *Drive through it!*

A snowball.

She rolled to a halt. Then she undid her seat belt, got out of the car and shook the snow out of her hair and off her shoulders.

A young woman dressed in black was standing just beyond a gap in the trees, in a snow-covered clearing that might be a playing field. She had her hand over her mouth in a parody of surprise. Behind her there was a very large snowman, about six feet tall, with a grossly swollen body and sinewy branches for arms that seemed to be clutching its bulbous, misshapen head. It had two lumps of coal for eyes and a hole excavated in its face in a passable rendition of a scream. When she took her hand from her mouth, Harry saw that the young woman was laughing, though the sounds she was making were not like any laughter she had ever heard.

'I'm fine thanks,' Harry muttered angrily and just as suddenly felt embarrassed that she had let her temper show. 'I'm sorry.'

Without responding, the young woman took a BlackBerry from her pocket and started typing on it. She was a pale and gothic beauty: her skin was milky-white and strands of her jet-black shoulder-length hair were blowing across her face. She was wearing a black down jacket, black skin-tight leggings and black wellington boots and when she looked up Harry saw that her eyes were bright blue. A shard of preternatural colour embedded in monochrome.

She passed the BlackBerry to Harry; it was a shiny black Curve, with a trackpad rather than a ball. The girl had opened a file in MemoPad and written a message.

u had ur window open!

The young woman gestured impatiently and Harry handed her back the Curve. She typed a further message under the first and held up the screen for Harry to see.

r u alrite?

'I'm fine,' Harry replied. 'Absolutely fine.'

u look cold

The young woman had a solemn expression on her face.

'Hold on,' Harry said and ducked back into the Jeep for her winter coat that was folded on the passenger seat. She buttoned it up over her suit. 'That's better.' She smiled to prove it and the young woman with the Curve smiled back.

u HARRY?

'That's right.'

EVA

'Eva. That's a beautiful name.'

Eva shook her head and wrote again before handing the Curve to Harry.

i lip read ENGLISH badly im DEAF

'I'm so sorry,' Harry said and made a note to roast Gary for not forewarning her. Eva was shaking her head and pointing to the Curve. Harry realised that she was being asked to type her response. She held the device in her hands and typed a message with her thumbs. When she had finished – it seemed to take an age – she handed it back.

Sorry for being so slow! Eva is a beautiful name. Are you Russian?

Eva stuck out her lower lip as she read the message. She gave a swift response.

yup sort of wot about u?

They passed the Curve back and forth.

I'm Scottish. That's an interesting snowman.

Eva glanced back at the snowman and giggled.

da monster!

It's scary!

There are monsters here in DC did u know? YURI helped me w/ it

Harry got the feeling that she was missing something.

Yuri?

behind u

She spun around and almost jumped out of her skin. A man had stepped out from behind a tree and for a moment she thought that she was in the presence of something otherworldly. The man was standing between two beech trees with the setting sun behind him. He was taller than Harry, but not by much and he was as broad across the shoulders as he was tall, with the upper body of a Soviet-era weightlifter. He was standing very still with his hands hanging knuckle-down by his sides and he was gazing at a point beyond her shoulder, nothing on the face of it to be afraid of. Eva pulled on Harry's sleeve and passed her the Curve.

sorry if he startled u

Who is he?

Which was a stupid question because Harry already knew his name and she recognised muscle when she saw it.

YURI

Yuri stepped forward and Eva gestured at him with her fingers. It took Harry a few seconds to realise that she was communicating in sign language. In response, Yuri laughed softly and looked away.

cum on

Eva walked around the car to the passenger door and climbed in. After a short pause, Harry got in beside her. She glanced in the rear-view mirror at Yuri who was standing beside the skid marks in the road-verge.

Is he coming with us?

i no im safe with you!!!

Eva smiled playfully, adjusting her seat belt, making herself comfortable.

The Jeep's engine started immediately. Yuri diminished in the mirror. For a while Eva sat beside Harry with the Curve in her hands and Harry felt herself begin to relax, as if nothing had happened, as if the grotesque snowman and the appearance from nowhere of the young deaf woman and her muscle-bound minder Yuri were all acts of her imagination. Except the young woman was beside her in the passenger seat, fiddling with the window and the glove compartment.

They skirted a small duck pond with a frozen surface as smooth as a sheet of steel and Harry had her first glimpse of the Daedalus Mansion and concluded that it was by far the ugliest building that she had ever seen. It was pre-cast concrete, Bauhaus era: a bunker two storeys high with a long, flat roof; a drainage channel that resembled a moat; and windows facing the drive that were as narrow as gun-slits. In what was presumably an attempt to liven up the atmosphere someone had at some point painted it a gaudy pink colour. Time had not been kind. The paintwork was now stained with moss and algae, livid streaks that branched out from the guttering like veins on a pensioner's legs.

Harry drew up alongside a large tulip tree, one of two that stood like sentinels either side of the house. Before she had switched off the engine, the front door had opened and another armed guard in a black down jacket and peaked cap was standing at the entrance, waiting for them. Eva typed another message and passed her the Curve.

u r a better driver than YURI
Do you drive?
no licence & no passport!!!
How did you come here then?
On a special plane :-)

She chuckled.

That's quite a house
uncle SASHA calls it STALINS bunker!

Eva didn't seem to be in any hurry to go in. From somewhere she had produced an unopened packet of cigarettes, a blue packet, Gauloises Blondes. She tore the foil seal and tapped the pack against her finger. Then she opened the passenger door, got out and lit up. She sat back against the car hood and Harry joined her.

When Harry looked at her, Eva was gazing up at the house and the unsmiling guard, the last of the sunlight catching in her eyes, searching out the mottled depths of her irises. Eva exhaled and wrote another message.

do u hav children?

Harry shook her head.

No

can u?

The question floored her. After the miscarriage the doctor had told Harry that it was no barrier to future pregnancy. She was fit and healthy. But nonetheless the fear was there, alongside the fear of having a baby, the more terrible fear of never having one.

Beside her, Eva leaned forward to crush the cigarette and then she smiled at Harry and held up the Curve for her to see.

its special to hav children :-)

Harry nodded.

Cum on uncle SASHA is w8ting

They climbed the steps past the guard, who closed the door behind them and retreated to a glass-walled booth with a stack of monitor screens. Harry looked around. The rectangular entrance hall included an impressively high ceiling and a densely veined marble floor. There was a glass-topped table and on it a crude wooden figure with a giant phallus.

thats BOB

Eva kicked off her wellington boots. Harry thought she meant the security guard, but she wasn't absolutely sure. Eva gestured for her to follow.

Slate steps led up to a gallery on the first floor that ran like a spine the length of the house. The tiled floor was covered with thick *gabbeh* carpets and in carefully lit alcoves in the gallery walls there was a series of bronze busts of apes: chimpanzees, orang-utans and gorillas. Beyond them were busts of primitive men – *Homo erectus* and *Homo neanderthalensis* – Peking man with his sloping forehead and thick protruding brow ridges and the Neanderthal with his elongated skull, long collarbones and wide shoulders. Eva stopped by one of the busts and tapped away at her Curve for longer than usual.

uncle SASHA sez NEANDERTHALS brain was large as yrs & mine BUT they made lousy tools so they died out uncle SASHA sez the same thing happened to USSR! I don't remember USSR would u like a drink?

Harry shook her head.

u sure???

Absolutely. You said your uncle was waiting?

did I?

Yes

I must have! cum on then

Harry followed her to a study. Three walls were lined with books while the fourth was a wall of glass with a view across the dark mass of Rock Creek Park. The air was tinged with the smell of antique leather and wood smoke from the fireplace. A television was showing an American football game with the sound muted, and there was music playing that Harry recognised – *Sleeping Beauty* by Tchaikovsky.

Dr Alexander Markoff was sitting in a worn leather armchair, facing the windows with a pen and a sheaf of papers in his pale, delicate hand. More papers were arranged in order at his feet as if he had been playing a giant game of solitaire. She glimpsed equations and Gaussian curves. Beside him, on a felt-topped folding table, there stood a tray with a glass of champagne. His eyes were closed.

He might be asleep or listening.

EIGHTEEN

'NNNcl . . . Sas'a . . . ?'

It was the first time Harry had heard Eva attempt to speak and the deep tone of each stretched syllable made her think of the lowing of cattle in a field.

Dr Markoff remained motionless. Eva signalled for Harry to remain where she was and moved closer, leaning over her uncle, gently shaking him.

Dr Markoff woke abruptly. Reflexively, Harry stepped back. It was not for her to intrude on the private moments of a prospective client. There was a creak of leather. Dr Markoff reached forward with a remote and the music stopped. He put down the remote and raised his hands to his niece in a gesture that to Harry suggested a question. It prompted a moment or two of energetic signing from Eva and a more leisurely response from her uncle.

When they were done, Dr Markoff looked past Eva to where Harry had retreated into the doorway. He stood and held out his hand in her direction. He was tall, and he would have looked taller without the slight stoop. He had almost translucent blue eyes, pale white skin and grey hair that was swept back from a broad forehead in two carefully combed waves. 'Miss Armstrong, come in. I'm sorry. I was working rather late last night.'

Harry smiled, a cosmetic projection, quicker than lipstick, beaming out professionalism and assurance. I know what I'm doing – *your strangely compelling niece who builds monsters out of snow will be safe with me.* She crossed to where Dr Markoff and Eva were standing. She shook Dr Markoff's hand firmly, but not too firmly. She didn't want to hurt him but she wanted him to know she could break his fingers if necessary.

'Please call me Harry.'

Beside him, Eva had the expression of someone who could not believe her luck, to have come across such entertainment.

'Would you care for a drink?' Dr Markoff asked. He smiled, his thin lips drawn back fully from shiny, pink gums so that he was all teeth, and knife-like wrinkles fanned from the corner of his eyes. He was older than he looked.

'No thank you,' she said.

'You're not thirsty?'

He spoke English with a peculiar, guttural accent, in furtive and conspiratorial bursts.

'I'm fine, thank you,' Harry replied.

'Are you English? Welsh? Scottish?'

'Scottish.'

He nodded. 'Scotland. Dolly the sheep. Those guys used two hundred and seventy-seven embryos to get one lamb – it's a pretty damn good ratio,' he told her, as if delivering the punchline to a joke. He looked at her expectantly. She was unsure how to respond.

'Sit down,' he said.

She sat. She put down her briefcase, opened it and removed the buff folder containing her references. Out of the corner of her eye she was aware of Eva leaning over her uncle and kissing him on the forehead, but by the time she straightened in her seat Eva had gone. There was only Dr Alexander Markoff, sitting, watching her. He had a watchful quality about him that put her in mind of a scavenger, a wild dog or hyena perhaps, an animal forced to live in close proximity to and be reliant upon larger, more dangerous predators.

'What have you got there?' he asked.

'I've brought my references,' she said, reaching forward to hand him the folder.

He took it and, without looking at it, set it down with all the other papers at his feet.

'You are a policewoman?'

'I used to be.'

'Of course. Are you a good shot?'

'I don't have a green card or an Alien Firearm Permit so I'm not authorised to carry a handgun; you should have been made aware of that.'

'But you're a good shot, right?'

'Yes.'

He raised his glass and toasted her. He sipped the champagne and then set the glass down on the tray once more. He sat back and drummed his fingers on his knees.

'Quite a day for you, eh?' Dr Markoff said. 'That body you found. Things are getting ugly in DC, I think.'

Harry stiffened. 'As a witness, I probably shouldn't discuss it.'

'I heard that he smashed her face into pieces?'

'Where did you hear that?'

'It's a very small place, Harry. It's not London or Moscow.' He leaned forward and lowered his voice. 'Who would have thought that the centre of the world's axis would turn out to be a small, provincial town? I can tell you it's not what I expected. Is it what you expected?'

'I try not to have preconceptions about places or people,' she replied. 'I take them as I find them.'

'And how did you feel when you found that young woman?'

Harry felt a flicker of irritation. 'I felt frustrated that there was nothing I could do and angry at whoever had done it. I'm sorry, I don't mean to be rude, but I really don't think that I should discuss it further.'

He waved his hand. 'Of course. Of course. I apologise if I have offended you. Please.' He sat back again. 'Do you like your job, Harry?'

'Most of the time.'

'Not always?'

'It depends whether I trust the client.'

'Perhaps you don't trust Russians?'

'No. I have nothing against Russians.'

'So what are you saying?'

'There is a distinction in my mind between government work, like my career with the police, and private, commercial work. In the police I didn't question what I was doing. In commercial work I feel that I am under an obligation to consider the rights and wrongs of what I do.'

'That sounds like bullshit, Harry.'

'It's not always easy,' she said coldly.

Dr Markoff laughed. 'You made a very funny face just then. Listen to me, Harry. If I have done wrong in my life it is not as a result of my intentions but rather due to the provocation of others. You can tell your government that.'

'I don't work for my government any more.'

'OK, OK,' he said with a knowing smile. 'I understand.'

She got the feeling he didn't. 'Sir, is this a job interview or not?'

'Of course, it is.'

'Well then, what kind of protection services are you looking for?'

Dr Markoff leaned forward in his chair, his scavenger eyes shining brightly. 'You've met Eva. She is a very special, singular young woman. Very valuable! Do you have children, Harry?'

'No.'

'Do you want children?'

'With respect, I don't think that's any of your business.'

'I think it is, Harry,' he replied. 'You see, I want you to take care of Eva as if she was your own child. I want to be able to rely on you completely. I must believe that the maternal instinct is strong in you. Do you understand?'

'I think so.'

'Good,' he said. 'I think you want children, Harry. I can sense it.'

Was she that transparent? Harry wondered. Was it written on her face?

'Therefore, I am happy to trust you with my niece. You will accompany her and protect her. This is during the day. At night she must stay here under curfew. You understand?'

'What exactly is the nature of the threat to you and her?' Harry asked.

Dr Markoff nodded encouragingly, as if he welcomed the question. 'I have a collection of the lost and unhinged outside my office, shouting, waving signs. In America, they have a constitutional right to protest. I've had death threats, letters and messages left on my voicemail.'

'Have you reported the death threats to the police?'

He shook his head emphatically. 'No.'

'You should.'

'I am not an American citizen, Eva is not, none of my family is . . .' He paused and suddenly he was wearing a different face. All the humour had gone out of his eyes. He looked down at his feet and when he looked up again his eyes were wet with tears. 'Our situation is precarious. We came to this country by a back-door route and I made a promise not to draw attention to ourselves. We keep quiet. It is not a satisfactory situation but I do not make the rules. Maybe there is somewhere better for us . . .' For a few moments, he waited as if he was expecting her to say something. Again she was unsure how to respond. When she didn't he reached for the champagne and drained it. He put the empty glass back on the tray. He smiled wryly. 'For sure there is no going home.'

'I was told that this job is temporary.'

He shrugged. 'That depends. It depends how long we stay here and it depends on how you like Eva and how well she likes you.'

'And when would you want me to start?'

'Tomorrow morning – why not? You're available, right?'

'Are you offering me the job?' she asked.

'Go away and think about it for an hour or two, no more. Tell your husband . . .' He paused and gave her a sly, furtive glance. 'Or whoever. If you want the job call me.' He handed her a business card. It was expensive-looking, the colour and texture of parchment with his name embossed in italicised gold lettering – *Alexander Ilyanovich Markoff PhD* – and underneath it Germline BioSciences and underneath that a DC cell phone number.

He shook her hand again only this time there was a folded square of paper hidden in his palm that he transferred to hers.

'It was interesting to meet you, Harry,' he said gravely and looked past her at the doorway where Eva was waiting. 'Eva will show you out.'

Harry wondered if she had been waiting within sight all this time. She wondered who else was watching or perhaps listening. She resisted the urge to re-inspect the room. She waited until she was walking back down the gallery past the bronze busts before discreetly sliding the folded piece of paper into a pocket. In the entrance hall, Eva lingered beside the table with the priapic statue. She ran her fingers along the table's surface as if inspecting it for dust and then she looked at Harry. She smiled. She had a capacity for filling silence with meanings that could only be guessed at.

'I don't know what you're thinking,' Harry said.

Eva shook her head and typed a message on her Curve.

when he was asleep and I woke him, do u know what we were saying?'

I don't know sign language

Eva regarded her sceptically.

he told me that he was dreaming I said was I in it? he said I wouldn't want to be in it! do u have bad dreams???

Sometimes. About my work. What about you?

i dream about fucking

Harry returned the Curve without answering. Eva wrote a swift message and handed it back.

do i shock u?

It's not my job to be shocked

Eva smiled. It was the kind of smile that gave you butterflies in your stomach; that forced you to smile right back.

i like u HARRY

Thank you

I hope u take the job

Five minutes later, safely out of the gate, Harry pulled over to the kerb on Connecticut and read the message on the folded piece of paper.

I, Alexander Ilyanovich Markoff, Chief Scientist at Germline BioSciences of Maryland, former Chief Scientist at Scientific and Experimental Production Base of Stepnogorsk, seek to negotiate a mutually beneficial arrangement with the government of Great

Britain with regard to permanent and secure residence for my family in exchange for valuable scientific data relating to the KGB Directorate S programme known as Progress. Be very careful. The house has microphones and hidden cameras.

Gary Sinstadt, she thought, rootless Gary, formerly of the Secret Service, with your messy yacht and your subterranean links here and God knows where – what have you got me into?

NINETEEN

Back at the Watergate just after 6 p.m., Freeman sat at a computer screen in a side office and fast-forwarded last night's footage from the security camera of the house on Shepherd Street in Crestwood: a few cars came and went, and the sky darkened while in the bottom left of the screen a date/time counter flickered by. Earlier, Winnie had told him that Byron's car was filmed heading west at 10.12 p.m. He stopped at 10.10 p.m. and pressed Play.

Nothing for two minutes. It was snowing. Then the car approached along Shepherd. First he saw its headlights, blurry in the saturated air, a glimpse of the licence plate, and then a brief sidelong view as it turned left onto 18th, heading into Crestwood. It was a black Lincoln Town Car with darkened windows, impossible to see who was inside. He considered what he knew: the car was registered to Cardinal Limousine Services working under contract to Potomac Global Strategies and the driver was Byron Bastian. Was she sitting there in the back, Byron? Who else was in the car? Olivier Davide, the dead lobbyist?

He fast-forwarded to 1.15 a.m. The Town Car reappeared, moving in the opposite direction, fishtailing as it swerved around the corner and accelerated away. The camera briefly captured its rear plates. According to the Medical Examiner Kaplan, the girl was dead by this time. But it was another hour and forty minutes before Harry Armstrong witnessed Olivier Davide dump her body in the ravine. What happened, Byron? The girl was murdered and then you panicked, didn't you? Out of remorse or fear, you fled the scene, leaving Davide behind to deal with the body. He carried her into the woods, fell, lost a shoe, cursed, dumped her and then ran off. Half an hour later Davide was back at his apartment in the Kennedy-Warren. They knew the route – Winnie had accessed footage from the cameras at the Exxon Garage on the corner of Porter and Connecticut. They showed Davide limping up Porter, in the gritty slush at the centre of the road, and then turning south on Connecticut. He was talking into a cell phone. Ten minutes later he was recorded entering the main lobby of the Kennedy-Warren. He took the lift to the fifth floor. He stuffed his bloody clothes in a bag and took a shower. The door-bell rang, he let someone in – someone he knew and trusted, someone who knew how to evade the cameras because there was no record of him entering the building – and that person killed Davide and then left with his cell phone and a kitchen knife.

Who were you communicating with, Freeman wondered, as you were limping up Porter?

Next, Freeman accessed the Office of the Clerk of the House of Representatives website and initiated a lobbying disclosure search entering Potomac Global Strategies and Olivier Davide in the search fields. For the filing year 2009, Potomac Global Strategies listed a single client in the area of defence: Germline BioSciences Laboratories.

Freeman Googled Germline and followed the link to the company's home page with its bland pastel shades and images of good-looking men and women in lab coats and clear protective glasses:

Germline BioSciences, Inc (GBS) is a Maryland biomedical research firm with an established history of serving the biomedical community. It is dedicated to delivering quality services that advance reproductive health research for the public good. GBS conducts research and provides resources to develop and evaluate vaccines, therapeutics and diagnostics for sexual health and contraception.

GBS is a contract research organisation (CRO) that has extensive experience working with government, commercial and other groups. GBS can assist with all aspects of product development including, but not limited to:

· Basic research
· Vaccine or product design
· Animal models for evaluation
· Manufacturing of biologics for phase I and II clinical trials

GBS meets our clients' expectations by solving their most difficult challenges.

GBS has a scientific team with hundreds of publications and decades of experience in the field of reproductive health research. This team can do much more for clients than merely offer products and services. GBS's scientists become an extension of our clients' research staff. They work closely with clients to ensure the client's product development goals are met in a timely and cost-efficient manner.

Freeman sat back in his chair and stared out of the window at the dark expanse of the Potomac River. A question had formed in his mind. What was a biotechnology company specialising in reproductive health doing employing a defence lobbyist?

Freeman wrote three names in his notebook:

Senator Cannon
Potomac Global Strategies
Germline BioSciences

He called Germline BioSciences but was transferred straight to an answering service. The offices had closed for the night. He decided not to leave a message. He would go out there tomorrow.

Alone, he began typing an update to his investigation report.

Half an hour later, Freeman was sitting reading the report through when McCafferty knocked on the doorframe. He was in shirt-sleeves and red braces and was carrying a single sheet of typed paper.

'Is that for me?'

'It is.'

McCafferty slid the sheet of paper across the desk to Freeman and then sat back on a chair with his legs crossed. Freeman glanced down at the paper. It was a series of bullet points. A potted biography of Senator James D. Cannon.

'It's not *Ulysses*,' McCafferty said.

'Run me through it.'

'Two older sisters and no brothers,' McCafferty explained. 'He attended ten different schools by the age of eleven. His father the industrialist was a tyrant and his mother, as far as I can tell, was a drunk. She died in a house fire when he was just ten years old. He was a keen college football player, a strong side linebacker. He saw active service with Fifth Special Forces Group in Vietnam. That's the same unit you were in, right?'

Freeman nodded.

McCafferty continued: 'He was awarded a Distinguished Service Cross for extraordinary heroism.'

The first time Freeman had met the senator in the flesh was in '99. Back before he met Shawna. It was in the main planning room at the Isolation Facility at Fort Campbell; Fifth Special Forces Group had run a briefing programme where veterans of past conflicts had spoken to the teams about their experiences. Cannon was one of the veterans on the speakers' list. He had described how, together with a squad of ethnic-Chinese Nung fighters, he had recaptured a hilltop position in Laos known as Old Rag that had been overrun by the North Vietnamese Army.

'There's a copy of the citation on my desk,' McCafferty told him. 'You want to see it?'

'Maybe later,' Freeman replied, looking down at the sheet of paper. 'Four wives?'

'Divorced, died, divorced, survived.' McCafferty shrugged. 'No beheadings. The current one is credited with stabilising his personal life and helping him to resume a productive career in the Senate after years of drinking and diddling triple Bs.'

'Triple Bs?'

'Bottle-blonde bimbos. I guess you didn't see many of them in Detroit?'

'At the car shows,' Freeman told him.

'Jesus. They still make cars up there?'

'What about domestic violence?' Freeman asked.

'Nothing concrete. Both divorces were settled out of court with substantial settlements for the wives. His aides are loyal to a fault. He runs a tight ship.'

'Kids?'

'None.'

'Who was that at the press conference?'

'Stepdaughter.'

'What about his political career?'

'He's an old-school Republican, fiscally conservative but socially more modulated – he opposes abortion but is in favour of stem cell research. He's a stalwart of the defence industry. He's the longest serving member on the Armed Services Committee and the ranking minority member of the Emerging Threats and Capabilities Subcommittee. Through most of the Bush years and up until 2006 when the Senate changed hands he was chair of the subcommittee and the word is that he ran it as a private fiefdom. The subcommittee has jurisdiction over Department of Defense policies and programmes to counter emerging threats such as proliferation of weapons of mass destruction, terrorism and narcotics. It also covers information warfare and special operations programmes, the Defense Threat Reduction Agency, and Department of Energy non-proliferation programmes. In addition, the subcommittee oversees sales of US military technology to foreign countries, and defence and military research and development through DARPA. It's the director of DARPA who's giving evidence to the subcommittee hearings the day after tomorrow.'

'DARPA?'

'The Defense Advanced Research Projects Agency. It's the research and development agency for the Department of Defense. It was set up back in the fifties after the Soviets launched Sputnik. It was behind Arpanet, the precursor of the Internet. They claim their mission is to prevent technological surprise for us and to create technological surprise for our enemies.'

'What does that mean?'

'It means they're into all the funky sci-fi stuff: genetics, robotics and nanotechnology. They have an annual budget in the region of three billion dollars. I don't need to tell you that that makes the senator a powerful man.'

'A man worth lobbying?'

'Sure.'

'What about enemies?'

'Shit, he's an old-school, Reagan-style Republican. Progressives hate him and so does the Tea Party. His main political rival is Senator Elizabeth Oberstar, the new chair on the Emerging Threats Subcommittee. His opposite number. She's a blue-dog Democrat, fiscally conservative but also modulated on social issues. She's OK with robotics but opposes genetics and nanotech research. It's difficult to see her dumping a body on the senator's doorstep, no matter how welcome the embarrassment caused. Ah, you'll like this, on the subject of enemies, or the lack of them, I found a profile of Cannon in the *Nation* – not exactly flattering; it accuses him of suffering from "enemy deprivation syndrome". Since the Soviets caved he's been feeling at a loss and al-Qaeda doesn't do it for him. They're just rhetoric and roadside bombs. It calls him a man in search of a bogeyman. Apparently the Chinese building stealth weapons in black labs is what puts wood in his pecker.'

'Any specific threats?'

'There's an old man lives in Arlington who has a restraining order on him issued by the Virginia State Court. It prevents him approaching or contacting the senator.'

'Why?'

'Abusive mail. It's not uncommon. You want to know how much hate mail the average politician gets?'

'Any suggestion that this guy has breached the terms of the order?'

McCafferty shook his head. 'None.' He scratched the side of his jaw. 'You know Cannon's moved out of the house?'

Freeman looked up sharply. 'Where's he gone?'

'He's taken a suite at the Mandarin Oriental and he's requested additional protection from the Secret Service. He's hunkering down.'

'Why?'

'No explanation forthcoming,' McCafferty replied. 'He's also employed the services of Abe Proust of the law firm Seabury, Proust and Mashpee. Proust was Democratic counsel during the Clinton impeachment. Watch out for him, he's a snake.'

He hesitated as if there was something further that he wished to say.

'What is it?' Freeman said.

'You really think that the girl was killed in Cannon's house?'

'Don't you?'

'I went out there, you know,' McCafferty replied, 'to the crime scene. I walked the perimeter of the senator's property. I saw the two gates, front and back, and where the fence has come down. Routes of ingress and egress. It's a real shame their cameras were down. If you had the footage you'd be able to rule it out, right? It's kind of suspicious, I agree.'

'I need more than suspicion,' Freeman told him. 'Right now I need the DNA results from the first victim's vaginal fluid samples.'

'I'll push them on it,' McCafferty said. He stood up to leave. 'But you know it can take weeks.'

'I want it tomorrow.'

'You're really gonna *carpe* this, aren't you?'

'Seize it? Sure.'

'That's not what I was led to expect.'

'It's my job,' Freeman told him. 'I do it the best I can.'

Five minutes later, Hector called in with an update.

'I started out by taking Byron's father to the Medical Examiner's office to identify Renee's body. He's elderly and confused. I don't think he has any idea where Byron is at. I also canvassed the neighbours on Savannah Street. None of them have seen 'im since he went to work yesterday. I went down to the Temple of Praise on Southern Avenue and spoke to Byron's sponsor with Narcotics Anonymous. He said Byron didn't show for his regular early evening meeting tonight. That's unusual. He used to come to the meeting before heading over to the lot at Buzzard Point on the Metrobus to pick up the limousine. I also spoke to his third grade teacher, his pastor and his former parole officer.'

Hector was going somewhere with this. 'What did they tell you?' Freeman asked.

'Byron was clean and has been since the day he was released. He's a model citizen. Quiet, hard-working, not exactly devout but certainly a much reformed character.'

'So dig deeper,' Freeman told him, 'former cell-mates, known associates, etc.'

He cut the connection and sat, staring at the desktop until his vision began to blur and then he rested his head on the desktop and closed his eyes.

TWENTY

Freeman jerked awake.

He was not alone. Maja was standing just inside the room with Winnie behind her, filling the doorway. Maja was holding her laptop to her chest.

'Are you all right?' she asked, the concern written large on her face.

'How long have I been asleep?'

'Not long enough,' she said. 'No more than half an hour.'

He looked at his watch. It was 7.30 p.m.

'What is it?'

Maja glanced at Winnie. 'You first.'

'I've been digging around,' Winnie explained. 'It seems the decedent's neighbour was on the money. Olivier Davide wasn't French-Canadian – he was Russian. I tracked him back to an address in Brighton Beach, aka "Little Odessa". I got two names at that address using the same social security number. Olivier Davide and a New York attorney called Oleg Abramovich Davidov who ran an immigration services business up until 2003.'

'It's the same guy?'

Winnie nodded. 'The photo on Olivier Davide's DC driver's licence is more recent but it's the same guy as the photo on Oleg Davidov's NY driving licence.'

'And Davidov was Russian?'

'Yeah, he was a lawyer back in the Soviet Union. A Jew. He came out through Vienna in 1987. It was the route out for a lot of Soviet dissidents, but according to a legal officer at the State Department that I spoke with earlier, the KGB also used it as a way of kicking out other undesirables, criminal elements and such,

Russian mobsters known as the Bratva or Brotherhood. These guys were supposed to go to Israel but some of them moved over here and pretty soon they were up to their usual tricks. Money laundering, prostitution, visa scams, etc., etc. In 2003 Davidov pleaded guilty to multiple immigration offences including submitting false information on visa applications in exchange for a three-year probationary sentence, a fifty-thousand-dollar fine and the suspension of his licence to practise law in the state of New York. He must have changed his name after the court case and relocated down here to DC.'

'Speak to McCafferty,' Freeman told her. 'Maybe someone at the International Organised Crime Directorate has a contact in the Russian MVD and we can find out some more about Davidov. What was he doing in Russia before they kicked him out? Come to think of it, let's turn everything we've got over to Interpol: DNA, fibres, fingerprints, the lot.'

'Sure,' Winnie said.

He glanced at Maja who held up her laptop for Freeman to see. 'Cigarette break?'

Maja didn't smoke.

Freeman nodded and together they went down the stairs to the basement garage. Maja opened her laptop on the hood of a patrol car and powered it up. She connected it with a USB cable to the hard drive recovered from Olivier Davide/Oleg Davidov's apartment.

'We've got the girl on film,' she explained.

'You're sure?'

'Absolutely. You can see her face and the tattoo. She calls herself Katja. There are twenty individual flash files on the hard drive. Each file is no more than a few minutes long. Some of them were recorded by the cameras above Davidov's bed, some of them elsewhere. The last four are of a hotel room. There's no footage of the killing itself but what there is will definitely interest you. I was going to upload them to the shared folder on the network so everybody could take a look. Then I thought better of it. You need to watch them. A friend of yours makes an appearance.'

'A friend of mine?'

'Yeah, one of your Special Forces buddies – the politician. What do they call him? I remember, *Obama's annoyer-in-chief.*'

'Crusty Buchanan?'

'The very same.'

TWENTY-ONE

The files were numbered 1 through 20.

Twenty fragments. Of what? A work in progress?

He clicked on the icon.

The opening of the first file was another threshold moment. As startling as when he first saw the woman's naked body lying in the ravine. There was a moment of absolute cinematic darkness and then a flicker of interference on the monitor screen that resolved itself into light and shadow. A cinderblock wall. The camera panned back. There was a plastic chair above a drain in the rough concrete floor.

A man's voice issued a command off-camera: 'Sit.'

There was something disturbingly familiar about the scene that sent a shudder down Freeman's spine. He was half-expecting someone to shuffle on in an orange jumpsuit and plead for their life. Instead a woman stepped into the frame, quite casually but with a certain elegance. She was wearing impossibly high black-lacquered stilettos and a long, dark coat to her ankles. With each step, her heels rang out on the concrete like a spoon tapped on a wall.

The woman slid onto the chair and her unbuttoned coat gaped. She was naked beneath it. She remained still for a moment with her head hanging and her face obscured by her dishevelled blonde hair. There was something gawky and adolescent about her posture, with her pale knees pressed together and her feet apart but pointing inwards. There was nothing adolescent about her body though.

'Tell me again about Progress,' said the man. He had an accent. It might have been Russian.

Her voice when she spoke was slow and husky. 'Every day the lights came on at six and we got up. It was very cold. We showered and dressed. We made our beds and cleaned the dormitory. Then we waited in line for inspection.'

'And if you failed the inspection?'

'Then we were punished.'

'Were you often punished?'

'Yes. Our instructors punished every mistake.'

'How many of you were there?'

'At the beginning of the programme there were many. My earliest memory is of the sound of hundreds of metal spoons on metal bowls in the refectory.'

'But by the end?'

'Just a few.'

'What happened to the others?'

'Most died of complications. A few escaped.'

'How did they escape?'

She laughed. 'How do you think, Oleg?'

The screen faded to black.

Freeman stood in the basement garage with Maja at his side. They waited while a couple of uniforms emerged from the stairwell, crossed the lot without noticing them, and got in a Second District cruiser. They drove off.

Freeman clicked on the next file. The woman was sitting on a leather seat in the back of a car, her face turned away from the camera and her forehead pressed to the windowpane. It was dark outside; droplets of rain ran diagonally down the glass.

'What did they teach you?' Oleg asked.

'Byron doesn't want to hear this, do you, Byron?'

'I don't mind,' said a deep voice off-camera.

Byron Bastian, Freeman thought. The missing driver.

'Shut up and concentrate on the road,' Oleg snarled. 'Tell me what they taught you.'

'If you insist. They taught us theoretical lessons in the morning and practical lessons in the afternoon and evening. On Mondays,

Wednesdays and Fridays we were taught economics, psychology and erotological theory; the rest of the week it was politics, cosmetology and languages. Sometimes the practical classes were visited by an elderly man. The instructors treated him with a deference that they showed no one else and were quick to answer his questions. Usually he said nothing at all, watching us work for a few minutes before walking out of the gymnasium. We called him Uncle.'

'What was the purpose of your training?'

She looked across at the camera. There are certain looks that grab your attention and shake it fiercely. It was as if the cameraman had anticipated Freeman's interest and as he leaned forward in his chair the camera zoomed in on the woman's face, revealing high cheekbones, arched eyebrows and long lashes, wide-open eyes with blue-green irises, a narrow nose and bee-stung lips. Beautiful enough to take your breath away. The expression on her face was knowing and provocative, playful, overtly sexual, inviting . . .

She said, 'My name is Katja. Unit 20105700. I can fuck like a goddess.'

Film 3. Freeman didn't hesitate.

He pressed Play as soon as 2 was finished. He was already hooked. This time the woman was staring up at the camera with only her head and shoulders visible, her blonde hair spread out across a pillow.

'Tell me about it?' Oleg whispered, aroused, off-camera.

'What it's like to be me?'

'Yes.'

'It's like the craving for chocolate or sugar, only more intense, much more intense. It's like an itch that must be scratched.' She laughed. 'You think I'm a girl. I'm not. It would be better to think of me as a monster.'

The screen faded to black.

The concrete cell again. Film 4. The camera zoomed on her face.

'There were two distinct groups within Progress, Clade A and Clade B. We were strictly segregated but sometimes we might catch a glimpse of them in a fenced enclosure on the training area. They were surrounded at all times by armed men. They had different instructors. It was rumoured that Clade B was more experimental, that they had a higher failure rate. We were warned never to approach them.'

Film 5. She pushed back her sleeve and revealed the barcode tattoo. For a moment it filled the screen. Then the camera panned out again.

'Progress wasn't officially shut down, it just fell apart. The instructors and the guards hadn't been paid for months. There was no food. They just abandoned us. Before they left, a small group of instructors set fire to the locked facility where the Clade B students were kept. Some of them escaped into the forest though. Uncle let them out a side exit. He went with them. After that, we were all alone and forced to fend for ourselves. Soon we were close to starvation. Then the men of the Bratva, the Brotherhood, came. We were loaded onto cattle trucks and transported west to Tiraspol, in Transnistria.'

'What happened there?'

The camera recorded no change in her expression. 'We were tattooed and we were made to work.'

The files numbered 6 to 12 were pieces in a jigsaw – a map of her anatomy. Static shots, each one no longer than ninety seconds: 6 was a close-up of a nipple, 7 the stubble in the shadow of her armpit, 8 the barcode tattoo, 9 the furl of her labia, 10 the curve of her ear, 11 the hollow at the base of her neck, 12 her outstretched palm.

In 13, she was sitting on the edge of the bed, putting on black stockings, otherwise naked, rolling the sheer nylon up her legs. They were in Davidov's apartment, the copulating alligator and girl visible on the wall behind her head.

'In 2002 I escaped along with one of my sisters.'

'Where did you go?'

'We made our way to the Caucasus, following a rumour, and there in the mountains we met up with Uncle and the remnants of Clade B. For a while we were safe, hidden from all. Then war came. This was 2008. The Russians sent a small army into the mountains and our hideout was discovered.'

'What happened?'

'Some ran and some stayed, pledging to fight. I don't know what happened to them. All I know is, Uncle brought me here to America.'

Film 14. Oleg Davidov's bedroom again. She was on the bed, masturbating.

'Why did you come to America?' Oleg asked, off-camera.

'Why does anybody come to America?' Each phrase coming out between gasps. 'To escape persecution . . . to start a new life.'

'How's that working out for you?'

'Oh, my God!' she said, her pale body arching up from the bed.

Film 15. She was fucking with Byron Bastian beneath her, his face turned towards the camera, moaning with pleasure, 'Oh my God, oh my God, oh my God . . .'

She was laughing exultantly, sweat running off her forehead.

'Da!' she yelled, 'Da! Da! Da! Da!'

In 16, she was lying outstretched on a bed, a different bed, staring at the ceiling. There was a languor in her pose that suggested the aftermath of strenuous activity.

'At Progress, we were taught to make them think that they were unique: make each one of them believe that he is the only one; that your one task, your only task, was to make yourself available to the target. Your hands were not your own, neither were your breasts, neither was your mouth, your cunt or your ass. They were exclusively his to explore and constantly at his disposal. They are Americans, we were told, they believe that anything is possible.'

'Anything is possible in America,' Davidov said, crossing naked in front of the camera with a bottle of Grey Goose vodka in his hand.

'You poor fool,' she told him.

'You don't have to do this,' he said, 'we could run away.'

'Where would we go?'

'California. You can fuck beautiful people instead.'

The files numbered 17 to 20 contained footage from multiple concealed cameras located in a single hotel room on four different occasions with four different men – victims or 'marks'.

Events followed the same pattern on each occasion. The 'mark' was waiting, often sitting on the bed or fretting, pacing the room. There was a knock. He opened the door. Oleg Davidov, Byron Bastian and the woman who called herself Katja entered. She was wearing a white raincoat and heels, the suggestion of nakedness beneath. Byron was carrying a black holdall.

Davidov and the 'mark' stepped outside into the corridor while Byron and Katja made preparations. She stripped naked and Byron tied her to the bed with black nylon straps. He poured oil onto her skin and massaged it in so that her whole body shimmered. He paid particular attention to her vulva.

'Are you ready?' he asked when he was finished, wiping his hands on a towel.

'I'm ready,' she replied.

Byron opened the door. Davidov and the 'mark' stepped back in. Davidov then waited for a moment or two before warning him that he and Byron would be waiting outside the door throughout. They withdrew.

The 'mark' stood on the carpet, his hands clasping and unclasping while in front of him Katja rose up from the bed, straining against her restraints. Her body a perfect bow.

It was at this point that she spoke. What she said was different each time, presumably in accordance with the man's particular fetish. But whatever it meant it seemed to have the same effect. The 'mark' fell upon her like a man possessed.

They fucked. A camera in the bed's headboard ensured that the viewer got a clear look at the participants. For Freeman's benefit, Maja named the first three. Two commentators and a politician:

the conservative pastor of a Baptist mega-church, a liberal columnist for the *Washington Post* and the Democratic chairman of the
House Rules Committee.

The fourth needed no introduction.

In 20, Katja writhed and strained against her bonds and snarled,
'I'll fuck you back to Texas, Tonto!'

There followed a loud and exclamatory groan. The man who
mounted her was a third term Republican congressman for the
state of Texas, a former Special Forces officer, Afghan veteran and
car-alarm magnate, a tireless self-publicist with a Colgate smile
and hair that seemed glued in place, Representative Samuel
'Crusty' Buchanan.

It was Captain Crusty Buchanan who had taught First Sergeant
Michael Freeman and his fellow Special Forces team members
the rudiments of horsemanship on their first day in Afghanistan.
They'd been inserted at night by helicopter, on a SOAR Chinook
Night Stalker flying at fifteen thousand feet, with a hypoxic pilot
and an instrument console flashing BAD DATA, BAD DATA because
the radar system shut down every time they went over five thousand feet. It was terrifying, ridge after ridge, with the radar system
shutting on and off; one moment they were flying over the void
and the next the helicopter was barely a hundred feet over the
knife-like edge of a mountaintop. Freeman had thought he was
going to die.

The following morning, faced with the prospect of riding a
horse for the first time in his life, and into battle to boot, he was
convinced of it. It was dawn and the team was gathered in the
packed-dirt courtyard of a mud-walled fort that looked like something out of the American Old West. They'd already dubbed it the
Alamo. It was serving as the headquarters of the warlord General
Dostum's faction of the Northern Alliance and they were about to
ride out to the Taliban front lines.

Crusty, their team leader, was the only one of them to have
ridden before. He was sitting astride one of the tiny Afghan horses
with his knees bent up to his ears. 'Listen up,' he'd hollered, in his

folksy tone, 'here's how you make this thing go.' He heeled it in the ribs and it walked a few steps. 'And here's how you turn.' He pulled on a rein and drew the muzzle around. 'And here's how you stop.' He yanked back on the reins. 'Got it?'

Freeman and the rest of the team, who were nursing excruciating headaches brought on by altitude sickness, nodded dumbly.

'If it runs off,' Crusty said, with customary relish, 'and your boot gets stuck and you get thrown you'll get dragged after it and you'll die, for sure. So if that happens you gotta shoot the horse. Reach up and shoot it in the head.'

Freeman had read somewhere that every Congress produces at least one designated pest, adept at drawing attention to nuisance issues and making trouble for the White House; Henry Waxman played that role during the Bush administration and Dan Burton before him in the Clinton years. Now there was Crusty Buchanan. Like Waxman and Burton before him, Buchanan was the ranking member on the House Oversight and Government Reform Committee, a perch that gave him the status of a gadfly and a grandstander. Crusty was widely credited with having first coined the phrase, popular on Capitol Hill, 'Don't ever get between a member and a camera'.

'Crusty,' Freeman said, standing beside Maja in the parking lot, 'what have you got yourself into now?'

TWENTY-TWO

The ambassador's residence was a monumental red-brick mansion on Massachusetts Avenue with stone dressings and high roofs crowned with tall chimneys. It was a copy of an English country house of the Queen Anne period by the British architect Sir Edwin Landseer Lutyens who also designed the Viceroy's House in New Delhi and the Whitehall Cenotaph in London. The residence was joined to the original Chancery offices by a bridge forming a porte cochère, a covered entrance leading to a courtyard, and there was a time in her professional life when Harry had been glad of the concealment that it offered to visiting dignitaries.

She gave her name to the polite young man at reception and he ticked her name off against a printout. She checked her coat and climbed the stairs to the public rooms, joining a line of people waiting to be greeted by the ambassador and his wife. She did not envy them the task. When her turn came, the ambassador's eyes glided across her without visible interest, his smile suggesting that he knew her but wasn't sure where from. That was fine with Harry. After all it wasn't her role to be recognised, or at least it wasn't back when she was a protection officer. She remembered him from when he was working in No 10 as a foreign policy adviser to Prime Minister Tony Blair; her father-in-law Douglas had once described him to her as an 'oily drama queen'. The ambassador's wife offered Harry an even more perfunctory smile.

Beyond them there was a wood-panelled hall with an Andy Warhol screen-print of Queen Elizabeth above the fireplace and a hubbub of clashing voices that she associated with crowded termini and elevated threat. She stood for a while, just inside the hall, surveying the crowd, force of habit, really. It was in Harry's nature to enjoy watching without being watched. In the past she had stood close to this very spot with a loaded Glock neatly concealed in a holster in the small of her back so that there was no telltale bulge in the hang of her suit. She knew that if she closed her eyes she could still visualise the exits. Those days were over and she was usually happy that they were. She accepted a glass of champagne from a passing waiter and listened to snatches of conversations around her.

'If he can't pass his signature bill what hope is there for a second term . . .'

'Did you read the article on the Chilcot Inquiry in the *New Yorker*? It was truly scathing . . .'

She recognised a vampish red-haired columnist for the *New York Times*, and beside her a blonde BBC anchor.

'They say he won't move back until his father retires from politics . . .'

With a start she realised that a nearby woman was talking about Jack. She followed the woman's eyes and found him. There he was, in the flesh. Her husband. He was smiling at something someone beside him was saying.

There was something extraordinary about Jack, charisma she supposed (though she'd heard it dismissed as rock star quality). It drew people to him and often made him the centre of attention even in a crowded room. People jumped over themselves to feed him stories. In the last few months he had written about the spiralling violence between Mexican drug cartels in Ciudad Juarez and the spill-over into the US; he had written about the rise of home-grown jihadists in Midwestern towns and their connection to al-Qaeda on the Arabian peninsula; he had interviewed the former President Bill Clinton and the Facebook founder Mark Zuckerberg; and he had written about the exploding population of Burmese pythons and Minotaur lizards, escaped from zoos and private collections, in the Florida Everglades. Not for the first time she wondered what it was that drew him to her. They were so outwardly different. And yet it worked – intimacy came easily to them – they were at ease in each other's company. She felt a hankering to get up close to him, to cup his firm buttock in her hand, maybe run a sly finger between his legs.

She moved nearer. She could hear his voice. He was talking to three men, one of whom she recognised as a regular commentator for one of the cable networks.

She almost made it.

'There you are,' said a voice at her shoulder. With a sinking feeling, she turned. Neil Trefoil had put on weight since she first met him, several years ago at the British Embassy in Islamabad and, not for the first time, she thought that he resembled an over-fed cat. His handshake was as soft as dough.

'I vouched for you to the police today,' he said.

'I found a body.'

He was watching her closely. 'So I heard.'

Harry had known as soon as Dr Markoff made his offer that she was going to have to report it to Trefoil but she had hoped to talk it over with Jack first. That was no longer possible. If she didn't mention the offer now it would appear as if she was holding something back.

'I've been looking for you,' she said.

He raised a sceptical eyebrow. 'Really?'

'There's something that I have to tell you. In private.'

'Shall we step outside?' he said. He took her by the upper arm and steered her across the hall to the French windows that opened out onto a terrace overlooking the formal gardens.

'Well?' Trefoil said, in a world-weary tone.

'I got a job offer today,' Harry explained. 'It's a babysitting job, straightforward really, looking after the niece of a Russian scientist. His name is Alexander Markoff. He works for a company called Germline BioSciences. I think he may be a defector. Does that name ring any bells?'

If it did, Trefoil wasn't letting on. 'Go on,' he said.

'The family is living in a heavily fortified compound out at Chevy Chase.'

'OK.'

'The thing is I'm pretty sure he made me the job offer knowing that I was involved in this police investigation. It's likely that he made me the offer because of the investigation. I think he believes I'm a spy. He slipped me this.' She handed him the folded piece of paper and watched as he read it.

'I see,' Trefoil said, after a lengthy pause, his face not giving anything away. 'Thank you for showing me this. Can I keep it?'

'Yes.'

Harry watched as he pocketed the slip of paper.

'Now I have to decide whether or not to take the job,' she told him. 'What do you think?'

Trefoil grimaced. 'You're asking me whether you should take the job?'

'Yes.'

'I have to talk to some people in London.'

She couldn't understand his reticence. 'I'm pressed for time, Neil. I need to decide in the next half-hour.'

'Harry, I don't mean to disappoint you but it's not uncommon for defectors to become depressed and disillusioned on arrival here. They miss their families, their status. Sometimes they go home. They may even decide that they would prefer to live in Europe. But we don't sneak people out of the US under the noses of our counterparts in the intelligence services.'

'I understand that, Neil,' she said defensively. 'It's a straightforward job and I'm not putting myself in any immediate danger.'

'I think you're missing the point.'

'No, I'm not missing the point!'

And so it was that an ebullient Harry Armstrong, who was not normally known for impulsive decisions (if you didn't count just about every decision she had made since she became the New Her), decided to accept a job as a bodyguard to the teenage niece of the Russian scientist Dr Alexander Ilyanovich Markoff on little more than a whim and for no other good reason than as a fuck you to Neil Trefoil and all of his ilk. And when, a few minutes later, Dr Markoff asked her over the phone if she had consulted the relevant authorities she assured him that she certainly had.

'Very good,' Dr Markoff told her. 'See you tomorrow. Come at nine o'clock.'

'OK.'

'Goodbye, Harry. I like you. Even your ethics bullshit.'

He cut the connection. She walked back to Trefoil.

'It's done,' she told him and treated him to her best shit-eating grin.

TWENTY-THREE

Harry never did get a chance to tell Jack about her new job.

As they spilled out of the ambassador's residence at nine, someone suggested that they go for a drink on U Street, and Harry found herself offering a lift to a raucous crowd of reporters. They crammed into the Jeep and shouted over each other as she drove down Massachusetts and up through Dupont.

They started out at Gibson. Jack knew the doorman and after he'd banged on the unmarked door beside the boarded-up facade, they were shown straight to a table. Harry sat beside Jill Stevens, a reporter from the *Sunday Telegraph* who had covered several wars, and opposite an Irish reporter from the *Independent* called Conal, whose surname she couldn't remember. He had been in DC longer than any other journalist that she knew of, and many regarded him as a kind of sage.

'What is this, pseudo-speakeasy?' Jill asked, looking around at the dark, candlelit decor and the leather-embossed bar.

'We're here for the mortuaries,' Jack announced and ordered half a dozen.

'Are you staying through the summer?' Jill asked Harry.

'I guess so. Until the midterms, maybe longer.'

'Jack's hanging on in there,' said Nick Balden of *The Times*. 'He's waiting for the miracle to happen.' Balden was an embittered former Westminster lobby reporter who it was said had once enjoyed an inside line to Alastair Campbell, Prime Minister Tony Blair's combative Director of Communications. In Washington he was just another alcoholic British hack with no access, butting up against the casual indifference of the Obama administration, and reduced to Cassandra-like rants against

America's political institutions. 'He's waiting for the audacity to come . . .'

'Reagan was being written off as a one-term President after a year in office,' Conal told him. 'It's too early to write off Obama yet.'

'A lot of people are leaving,' Jill said, 'now that the gloss has gone off the man. We're running out of British friends.'

'We're the last rats,' Balden added morosely. He ordered another mortuary. Balden drank unceasingly from about four in the afternoon until after midnight. He was married with children though he was rarely seen in the company of his wife. Harry had heard she spent a lot of time back in London. Balden was said to be fond of children, but had never showed interest in anyone else's.

'To the last rat,' Balden said when his drink came. He drained it.

'Let's eat,' Jack said. 'Before it snows again.'

They left Gibson and walked down U Street. They passed a man slumped on scraps of cardboard in a doorway and two volunteers encouraging him to get in a van.

'OK,' Jill said, 'Dukem or Madjet?'

'Dukem,' Jack decided.

They often ate Ethiopian when they'd been drinking. At the age of thirty, Jack had covered the Eritrean/Ethiopian war of 1998–2000. Jill had been there too and both had had experiences that outraged them. The pointless loss of life, the thousands of corpses abandoned on dusty, flyblown battlefields in a war that Jack had described as 'two bald men fighting over a comb', had made them both deeply angry. A colleague who published an acerbic memoir of life as a war correspondent had once written about Jack, then in his twenties: *he charged in the direction of gunfire like a child chasing gold at the end of a rainbow.* That phase of Jack's life had come to an end in Eritrea. After that he was less likely to charge into the fray – hard-won caution that kept him alive, though not unwounded, in both Afghanistan and Iraq, where others of his trade had fallen.

'Jack and Jill went up the hill,' Balden muttered, 'to cover a piddling sort of war, but Jack fell down and broke his crown, and Jill came tumbling after . . .'

'Fuck off, Nick,' Jill said.

At Dukem they entered merrily, and settled in. It was crowded and there was soccer on the screens. A Premiership game. Balden ordered beer for them all.

'Did you see Trefoil? He was looking for you,' Jill asked Harry.

'Yes, I spoke to him.'

'Are you doing some work for him?'

'No,' she said.

She was aware of Jack watching her. 'Definitely not,' she said.

'Trefoil has tentacles that reach,' Conal said. 'Not just into the Pentagon and into Langley.'

'I refudiate that!' Balden said. 'You have no idea what Trefoil's into.'

When the waitress came over Jill ordered for them all, speaking in Tigrean.

'In three years' time, when the Republicans are back in, somebody should write a book about how they coopted and corrupted the black man in Washington,' Balden said.

'You haven't been here long enough,' Conal told him, 'to talk like that.'

'The way I see it I get to say any fucking thing I want,' Balden replied. 'I almost lost a toe to frostbite in Iowa in January '08. I was in the NBC box at the Pepsi Center when the Republican reptiles were baying for our blood. I bought into the hopey, changey stuff. I got the fucking campaign medals just like you.'

Harry and Jack had also been in the Pepsi Center in Minneapolis at the Republican Convention. Like Balden they had been standing in the NBC box just before Sarah Palin came on stage and gave her *What's the difference between a hockey-mom and a pit-bull – lipstick!* speech, and the crowd had turned on the journalists and shouted and jeered and waved their fists at them. To Harry, it had been strange and disturbing; she remembered backing towards the exit wishing that she had the reassurance of a loaded weapon.

'You're an entertaining sort of fella,' Conal told Balden. 'But in general I object to you.'

The waitress emptied bowls of spicy chicken wat, lamb tibs and barely cooked beef kitfo onto platters of injera.

'I love Obama,' Conal said. 'I don't care what you think. And I love America. In no other country on earth is his story even possible. I was there in Boston in 2004. I heard him describe himself as a skinny kid with a funny name who believed that America had a place for him too. I wrote down every word.'

'Sometimes,' Jill said, 'you act like you invented Obama.'

'You're a pack of vultures,' Conal said. 'Why don't you go somewhere else? Why don't you fuck off to Pakistan?'

'It's too difficult to get a drink,' Jack replied.

They dug into the food with their fingers and ordered more beer.

'I met a girl who made a snowman that looked like a monster,' Harry said. 'She said that there were real monsters in DC.'

'Don't dismiss anything you hear out of hand,' Jill said. 'Check it out.'

'What do you think she meant?' Jack asked.

'She was an exile,' Harry said. 'An illegal, I think.'

'Harry found a body in the park last night,' Jack said.

Harry scowled at him.

'Wait, you were the mystery jogger?' Jill said, looking back and forth between Jack and Harry.

'I never know where she is,' Jack complained.

'I never know where you are,' Harry retorted.

'This is a real-life story,' Jill insisted. 'Do you think Cannon did it?'

'I don't know about that,' Harry told her.

'I hear they still haven't identified her,' Conal said.

'Her face was very badly damaged,' Harry replied.

'They've found two more bodies since,' Jill said.

'What?' Harry says.

'Didn't you know? There's a murderer running loose in the city. You should keep your head down.'

'Whatever fucking happened to fundamental change?' Balden announced. He was swaying drunkenly in his seat. Seconds before, he had been leering at Jill's cleavage. 'I ask you, whatever happened to challenging the broken fucking system in Washington? At least with Bush everyone knew he was an asshole. Now we've got the same wars, the same lawless prisons, the same Washington corruption, but everyone is cheering like the Stepford wives.'

'Give it a rest,' Conal said.

'I'll tell you what fucking happened, his fucking holiness candidate Obama stepped down off the high ground and handed the keys over to a legion of political dwarfs who thought that what America needed most was another Bill Clinton. He's become a defender of the status quo. And in Congress it's corruption as usual; they don't answer to the people, they don't even answer to the President – instead they answer to those interests that feed their pathological dependence on campaign cash. Political policy is transactional. It's bought and sold. These people take money from the insurance and healthcare industries and then oppose the public option, which might actually provide ordinary people with a basic fucking human right. They take money from used car dealers and then exempt the same dealers from financing rules to protect customers. They take money from the banks and the hedge funds that threw the economy over the edge of a cliff last year and then oppose any oversight of financial regulation. And now the Supreme Court has opened the fucking floodgates for corporate campaign cash. The trough is overflowing! The pigs will feed and feed! This city has lost its sense of shame. Stop the hopercoaster, I want off!'

'Shut up, Nick,' Jill said.

'He's right,' Jack said softly from the other end of the table. 'You might not like the way he says it but he's right. The status quo has won the day.'

For Harry, who had joined Jack on the campaign trail, who had stood shoulder to shoulder with eighty thousand people at Invesco Field in Denver to watch candidate Obama accept the Democratic Party nomination, it was depressing to listen to such talk. She hated the idea of herself as naive. She had been profoundly moved by Obama's rhetoric and his promise of change. She had stood in the freezing cold on the National Mall with a crowd millions-strong and watched the inauguration and felt a rushing sensation in her chest. Now, a year later, she clung onto the hope that the President might still bring change, perhaps not radical change, but change of some sort.

All the phones, except Harry's, went off simultaneously. They grabbed their BlackBerries and iPhones off the tabletop and listened in unison.

'There's been an earthquake in the Caribbean,' Jack told her, his ear pressed to the phone. 'It's a big one.'

TWENTY-FOUR

'We're celebrating here, Michael, which makes a beltway cop like you about as welcome here as a skunk at a lawn party.'

Congressman Samuel Crusty Buchanan, representative of a gerrymandered district that stretched like an upright and angry finger all the way from Houston to Dallas, glared up at Freeman. It was 10 p.m. They were in the Palm Restaurant on 19th, a popular haunt of the political class. The congressman was sitting at a table surrounded by his staff and Freeman was standing before him with his badge in his hand. Just moments before he'd walked up to the table and said, in an incredulous tone: 'I'll fuck you back to Texas, Tonto . . . ?'

Crusty pointed a fat finger at him and in his distinctively deep voice said, 'Step away from the table!'

It was a joke of sorts: after Afghanistan and before running for Congress, Crusty made his fortune selling car alarms. His signature product, the Enforcer, featured his voice ordering would-be burglars to 'Step away from the car'.

'You're an asshole,' Freeman told him.

One of the congressman's fresh-faced aides made as if to rise, but Crusty put out a hand to restrain him. He untucked his napkin from his collar, folded it, set it down on the tablecloth beside him and very deliberately looked around. He must have come straight from one of his beloved cable shows: he was wearing a layer of foundation and, as he squinted, the lines etched at the corners of his eyes cracked through the make-up. Freeman followed his pinched gaze. The restaurant was crowded despite what was for Washington a late hour. There was a smattering of politicians, congressmen and senators, and in one corner at a similar-sized table the anchor of CNN's

In the Arena was holding court. No one seemed to have noticed the altercation as yet. Crusty's eyes lingered on the cartoon sketches of well-known politicians, columnists and commentators that adorned the walls and Freeman wondered if Crusty might be reaching the conclusion that how he handled himself in the next few minutes might determine whether he ever made it onto the wall.

'The detective and I are going to step outside. Y'all wait here.'

Crusty rose and lumbered towards the exit, acknowledging the nods and waves of fellow diners as he passed. Freeman followed a few steps behind. Crusty was tall, massively built, a former college lineman, with a neck as wide as his head, and a suit jacket that stretched taut across his shoulders.

Outside, on the pavement, he snarled, 'It's colder than a witch's tit.' He looked Freeman up and down. 'Who sent you? The White House?'

Freeman chose his words carefully. 'I don't speak Texan as a rule, Crusty. I don't care for it. I find the world to be a more complicated place. But I remember a phrase or two from the time I served under you; one of them went something like this: *Lettin' the cat outta the bag is a whole lot easier'n puttin' it back in.* Now in this case, I'll be the one letting the cat out and you'll be the one trying to put it back in. I hope you get my drift?'

'Are you wearing a wire?' Crusty demanded.

'No.'

Crusty reached out and ran his hands under Freeman's coat, around his waist and up his back and along his arms. He turned Freeman's lapels this way and that and then he squatted down on his massive haunches and ran his hands up Freeman's pant legs.

Satisfied, he straightened up. 'What have you got?' he said.

'Film footage of you having sex with a young woman.'

'Shee . . .' He spat and stamped the pavement with the heels of his snakeskin cowboy boot. 'So what? I'm wickeder than Charlie Wilson was, every sumbitch knows that.'

'So the woman in question is dead. Somebody big and power-ful beat her to death with a hammer and dumped her in Rock Creek Park, and now the footage is potential evidence in a homicide. Three homicides in fact. The way this thing is going down there could be more.'

'Shee . . . ! That was her they found in the park? And you think I killed that girl? I haven't set eyes on her for three months at least.'

'You know the other Texan saying I remember, Crusty: *Never miss a good chance to shut the fuck up.* I know you didn't kill her, at least not with your own hands. You flew in from Houston this morning. I checked.'

Crusty's eyes narrowed. 'What do you want?'

'Information.'

'Show me the footage.'

Freeman led him across the road to the Impala. Maja was sitting in the passenger seat with the laptop on her knees.

'Get in the back,' he told Crusty and climbed in the driver's seat. The back of the car visibly sagged as Crusty squeezed himself into the rear. He leaned forward between the front seats with his glued hair sliding across the ceiling.

'What you got for me, honey?'

'You asshole,' Maja snarled. She glanced at Freeman. 'Are you sure you want to do this?'

Freeman nodded. 'Show him file 20.'

Maja opened her laptop, and when the screen lit up clicked on the file.

For the next couple of minutes, Crusty wrinkled his nose as if he could smell something unpleasant. When it was over, he eased slowly back in the seat with his hands on his thighs.

'Who else have you got?'

'You know I can't tell you that,' Freeman replied.

'Shee . . . !'

'It's not good, Crusty.'

'Have the Feds seen this?' he asked.

'Not yet. They will in the morning.'

'Damn!'

'What was her name?'

Crusty closed his eyes and opened them again. He said, 'She said her name was Katja.'

'How did you meet her?'

'Let's go get a drink someplace,' Crusty suggested.

'I'll wait here,' Maja said, tight-lipped.

The two of them walked a block east to the Camelot Club. They sat at high-backed stools at the bar, with their backs to the pole-dancer on the stage, and ordered overpriced bourbon. Crusty was hunched over the bar, shaking his head and not even the topless bartender elicited his customary folksy charm.

'You know Cindy will have my balls for this.' Crusty's wife Cindy Buchanan was the only daughter of a Texas oilman and former state senator called Bobby Wentworth. It was Wentworth who had bankrolled Crusty's election campaign through the primaries and the general election. 'She'll turn a blind eye to most things but not a homicide. And the party's gonna be pissed. And the Democrats will have a field day. I got to find some way out of this. I need some help here.'

'What kind of help?'

'Come on, Michael. It's me. It's Crusty.'

'Spit it out, Crusty.'

'You could delete the file.'

'It's a felony to destroy evidence of a crime.'

'Don't preach to me, Michael. What are you going to do for me?'

'That depends,' Freeman said, after a pause.

'On what?'

'On what you do for me.'

'Shee . . .'

'Tell me how you met her.'

Crusty finished his drink and ordered another. 'Hell. It was one night a few months back. We'd had a late vote in the House. I wasn't ready for sleep. A few of us went out for a drink. The long and short of it is I ended up in a hot tub in Marty Fineman's yard in his place out on the River Road, shooting the breeze . . .'

'Marty Fineman?'

'Longtime defence lobbyist.'

'Go on.'

'It was late. Marty had passed out and there was just one other guy there, a skinny guy with a funny accent. He said he was French-Canadian though it didn't sound to me like that's where he was from. He told me his name was Olivier Davide. I got the feeling that wasn't his real name. We were alone. OK, there were some girls there but for whatever reason they went inside. I was talking about exotic pussy. Out of nowhere the guy in the tub tells me this story about these girls from Russia who were trained by the KGB. They're like modern-day geishas, expert in seduction and enticement. They're so good at what they do, this guy says, it's the fanciest fuck you'll ever have.'

'You believed him?'

'Hey, I was baked. The guy was convincing. He described it as a clandestine behavioural modification programme set up by the KGB during the later stages of the Cold War. He said that their aim was to teach these girls all the ways to exploit the sexual vulnerabilities of a man, so they could let them loose on us and gather secret information. He said the KGB had always believed that a whole lot could be achieved with sex because it opened up channels of communication more quickly than other approaches. He told me that the East Germans were the real pioneers of this stuff; they had their own special department in the Stasi. Their so-called "Romeo Spies" infiltrated all levels of West German government and industry. They had women inside NATO HQ and the German Chancellor's office. Did you know that? I didn't, but it's true. I checked. So he said the KGB wanted to go one further than the Stasi. They set up a school with a specially selected group of young girls, orphans in fact. They taught them politics and psychology and English and Japanese and stuff. But most of all they taught them how to fuck. I mean really fuck! The plan was that when these girls were sent over the wall the KGB was going to clean up. Only the evil empire came to an end too soon. The programme sputtered along after the fall of communism like much of this stuff, but eventually it fell apart for lack of funding. The girls were dispersed. Some were picked up by the Russian mafia. He told me there used to be a notorious brothel called the

Monkey House in Tiraspol in Transnistria with several of these girls in. But a few of them escaped. He said at least one of those who escaped was here in DC. She's now in her mid-twenties, a thoroughbred at the peak of her professional life. He said she was available to a very few select individuals – I mean very fucking few. I told him to give me a business card.'

'So you just had to have her, Crusty?'

'Hell, I was suspicious at first. I figured this guy Davide was all hat and no cattle. But I checked with Marty and he chewed me out for even asking him. He said Olivier Davide should never have told me. After that I knew it was true. Yeah, I had to have her. You know me, Michael. The fanciest fuck I'm ever gonna get? You think I was gonna pass that up? Nothing was gonna stop me. I called up Olivier Davide, and I told him straight out I wanted to have this girl. I didn't care what it cost. He was reluctant at first. He said it wasn't up to him. I had to work real hard to persuade him. But I did.'

'I bet you did. Where did you meet her?'

'At the Renaissance. I got a hotel swipe card in the mail. With it a sheet of plain white paper with the room number and date and time printed on it. I went early. I sat on the bed. When the time came there was a knock. I opened the door. The girl was standing there in a long coat and just looking at her I'm enslaved. I'm not kidding you. My jaw hit the floor and I got all bowed up. She wasn't alone, of course. Davide was there and there's this big buck nigger, no offence intended, standing beside her and holding a bag with her stuff in. She tells me in a very businesslike manner, "My name is Katja, this is Byron, he's going to make preparations with me while you wait outside." I can hardly speak but I manage to say, "Sure, whatever; in you go." Byron carries the bag into the room and I step outside with Davide. We don't say a word to each other. After maybe five minutes, Byron steps out and tells me she's ready. As he pulls the door behind him I get a glimpse of her. She's tied down but she's straining against it like some kind of wild animal. He tells me whatever I do not to untie her. At this point I'll agree to anything. Davide slaps me on the back and says, "You're a lucky man." So in I go. The best goddamn fuck of my life.'

'And what did they want in return?'

'Nothing.' He grimaced. 'Nothing the first time anyway.'

'Jesus, Crusty.'

'I had to have her again.'

'What were you thinking?'

Crusty sighed and gripped his head in his hands. 'It's fucked up,' he said. 'But I'll tell you she was everything that was promised and more, much more.'

'What did you have to do?'

'Nothing really. I mean it, hardly anything. Prevent a bill coming to the floor. That's all. I mean the Democrats were the ones supposed to deep-six it. I just had to make sure there was no motion to recommit and if that didn't work I was supposed to pack it with "gotcha" amendments to kill it. I was told any kind of stink bomb would do. You know, a porn measure maybe, something requiring contractors to fire any employee who ever downloaded pornography. You follow it with thirty-second attack ads accusing the Democrats of supporting child porn and you can be sure they'd drop it.'

'What bill?'

'Shee . . .'

'Come on!'

'All right, all right! It was the Stem Cell Research Advancement Act. And don't ask me what was in it, Michael, 'cause I didn't read it.'

'Then what happened?'

'I tried calling this guy Olivier Davide but the number was out of use. I spoke to Marty and he told me that if I knew what was good for me I'd drop it. I never saw him again. That's it.'

'They played you, Crusty.'

'What are you gonna do?'

'I'm not sure.'

'If you turn that file over to the Feds I'm finished.'

'Crusty, you're an out-and-out bigot. You pal around with

assholes! Answer me this: why the fuck should I give a moment's thought to your career?'

'Because I'm your battle buddy, pal. I was there beside you, remember – when the Jetsons beat the Flintstones.'

In Fifth Special Forces Group, at the end of 2001, when they were calling down airstrikes on Taliban positions they'd called it the Jetsons beat the Flintstones.

'That was a long time ago,' Freeman said, rising from the bar. He threw down a twenty.

'You never were a team player, Michael. That's your problem. You do this you'll regret it.'

'I'm sure I will, Crusty. I'm sure I will.'

Freeman walked out of the bar.

Maja was sitting waiting in the darkness with her crocheted hat pulled low over her ears. 'Well?' she asked as he climbed into the driver's seat.

'He killed a bill.'

'What bill?'

'Stem Cell Research Advancement Act.'

'What was in it?'

'He doesn't know. He didn't read it.'

'Jesus!'

He glanced across at her. 'Give me the hard drive.'

'What are you going to do with it?' she demanded.

'Give it to me, please.'

Grim-faced, she disconnected it from the laptop and handed it to him.

'Just because he's your friend doesn't mean he should get away with this,' she said. 'And just because Cannon was in the same unit as you doesn't mean he should walk away scot-free.'

'He's not my friend, and neither is Cannon,' Freeman protested angrily. 'What do you take me for?'

She didn't reply. He leaned back against the headrest and closed his eyes. He was utterly exhausted.

'You should go home to bed,' Maja told him.

'I will,' he said. 'In a couple of minutes.'

'I'm leaving,' she said.

Within seconds he was softly snoring.

Freeman woke with a gasp.

The door had been yanked open and a blast of cold air had rushed into the overheated cabin. Before he could react, he was dry-tasered – the Taser pressed to his neck – and then dragged by the collar, convulsing, out onto the slurry of ice and grit on the road. A man in a black ski mask, who was squatting above Freeman's head, forced a pistol into his mouth until he gagged. Another man, also in a ski mask, stood astride him and patted him down. He drew Freeman's gun from its holster and stuck it in his waistband. He threw Freeman's wallet, the cells and car keys under the car, and he pocketed the hard drive.

The gun was pulled out of Freeman's mouth. The two men ran off.

Freeman groaned and rolled over. He reached under the car for his things. Then he edged himself up the side of his car until he was standing straight. He looked around. There were no bystanders, no witnesses.

He called Maja's cell. She sounded dazed and confused. 'I've just been tasered.'

'Me too,' he said.

'They took my laptop. They got everything. All my stuff.'

'They cleaned us out,' he told her.

He called Crusty's cell. It went straight to voicemail.

'You asshole,' he said.

A snowplough drove by and sprayed him with grit.

TWENTY-FIVE

He found Maja standing in the street beside a bank of dirty snow. She had never looked more forlorn.

Freeman pulled up alongside her, reached across and opened the passenger side door.

'Get in. You look frozen.'

She climbed in and leaned her head against his shoulder; her cold nose pressed against his neck, her ungainly glasses jammed against his chin. 'Those bastards.'

'I know,' he said, his arm sliding down her back. He found himself wishing that he could reach out and lay a hand on her soft, blonde head, pull her tightly to him and kiss the crown of her head, tell her that it was all going to be OK, and that by protecting her hard enough he could see off any trouble.

She straightened up and blew her nose. 'Sorry. I'm just pissed at losing my Mac.'

'Let's go get a coffee,' he said.

'We're lucky they didn't kill us,' Maja said.

They were parked outside a Seven-Eleven in North-East. At midnight, the Seven-Eleven resembled a Rift Valley water hole, somewhere to go if you wanted to see the densest concentration of nightlife, from bottom-feeders to top-of-the-chain predators, hyenas to elephants: cops, dealers, civilians, district workers, lobbyists, a senator and his entourage; and outside, on the side-walk, ranging between the store and the mêlée of vehicles in the street, the trembling, muttering panhandlers.

'You have both the chairman and the ranking member of the House Rules Committee in your pocket and you have the power to prevent legislation ever reaching the floor. There's no way whoever is responsible would let the contents of that drive get out. Shit, I wouldn't want to be Byron Bastian right now. He was correct when he told you we can't protect him.'

Freeman was feeling bruised and hollowed out. 'What about the other two? How do they fit in to your theory?'

'Political cover,' she replied. 'If you want to kill a bill for sure you want to come at it from both ends and it helps for the politicians to feel the pressure. On one side you've got a religious conservative who runs a mega-church, he comes out against the legislation probably because it doesn't go far enough, and on the other side a liberal pundit who's attacking it because it will delay vital research and the development of new therapies. It's a stitch-up. A *coup d'état* in all but name.'

Freeman wanted to tell her that she was overreacting, that there was nothing to worry about but what if she was right?

'We're way out of our depth here, Michael,' Maja said. 'You're going to have to tell the FBI. You need to speak to McCafferty.'

'And tell him what? We've got nothing to show him. They took the hard drive.'

'You think it was Cannon's people?'

'Maybe,' Freeman told her. 'Someone's been following us.'

'What?'

'We've been followed. They're using several different cars.'

She was incredulous and angry. 'How long has this been going on for?'

'Since this morning.'

'Jesus, Michael, when were you going to tell me?'

'I didn't want to worry you.'

'Fuck! You really are an asshole!' She got out of the car and slammed the door behind her.

'Maja,' he called after her.

Without looking back at him, she flagged a taxi and got in. It drove off.

'Damn,' he muttered.

★ ★ ★

At twelve thirty, Hector and Eli parked in front of him in their unmarked Crown Victoria. They went inside the Seven-Eleven and came out a few minutes later clutching six-packs of Red Bull.

Hector got in the front passenger seat and Eli got in the back of the car and shimmied along the bench.

'Eli got a lead on Byron Bastian,' Hector said. 'A name of interest – a fellow named Dezmine Felder.'

He nodded to Eli who took up the story.

'Dezmine used to work corners with Byron back in the day, slinging crack. They did some time together before Byron got clean. Dezmine's traded up since then; there's a list of priors on the system – armed robbery, assault with intent, rape and theft. He now controls a business running Percocets and oxycontin into the District from boosted pharmacies in Maryland.'

'You think Byron went to Dezmine and asked him for shelter?'

Eli nodded. 'If Byron was looking for someplace to lay low then it makes sense for him to have gone to Dezmine. If that's the case, then Dezmine's likely got him hidden in a stash house somewhere in Anacostia.'

'Word is out,' Hector said. 'Uniform, informants – everyone down in Seventh District is looking for them. Don't worry. We'll have Byron by morning.'

Twenty minutes later Freeman arrived back at his apartment, kicked off his shoes by the door, and dropped his coat on the floor. He went through to the bedroom where he stood for a moment, absorbing the silence. No sign of Shawna. He went through into the kitchen and looked again at his wife's schedule. For tonight the entry was blank. Maybe she had stayed over an extra night in Chicago. He took down a bottle of Buffalo Trace from the cabinet and poured himself a drink.

He sat on the couch and put his cell and Renee's clamshell on the table. He drank the bourbon and considered his situation. He'd lost a key piece of evidence that suggested a broad conspiracy to blackmail politicians and he'd had his service weapon taken off him. He still hadn't found the only witness to the murder. He'd fallen out with Maja, his only friend. And he was beyond exhaustion.

He wanted a cigarette. Lately he had been thinking of taking up smoking again. He'd smoked in Afghanistan, sitting on ridgelines watching the contrails of B-52 bombers overhead and the ripple of detonations as they pummelled the Taliban lines. It had filled the time. That is what he craved – something to do in those abject hours in the dead of night when he was so often awake.

He switched on the television. MSNBC were running an interview from earlier that evening in which Chief Thielen was asked whether she believed that the missing fugitive Byron Bastian was involved in the unknown woman's murder in Rock Creek Park as well as that of his sister Renee and a defence lobbyist named Olivier Davide.

'It's a possibility,' she replied. 'Nothing's ruled out. We haven't put all their movements together yet. I think Byron should come in and tell us what he knows. We would appreciate his help.'

TWENTY-SIX

Harry was jumping up and down on his ridiculous Cambodian general's bed as if it was a bouncy castle. It was 2 a.m. and she was singing:

A you're adorable
B you're so beautiful

Jack was stuffing things in a backpack: GPS, binoculars, digital voice recorder, chargers and batteries. He was laughing at her; it only made her even angrier. She was outraged by his departure. How could he leave her when he had told her over and over again that he would never leave her?

C you're a cunt
D you're a cunt

'You should never sing,' he said. 'You have no talent for it.'

He did not understand what it meant to leave someone. 'I'm coming back,' he protested, but she was having none of it. That's what her dad said. Look what happened to him. She pointed at him, an outstretched and accusatory finger:

E you're an effing cunt.
F you're a fucking cunt

'That's it!' He threw down the backpack and sprang up onto the bed, gathered her up and threw her down. The foreplay was done. Within seconds he was inside her and she had her legs wrapped around his waist, her nails clawing at his shoulders and her mouth wide open and shouting at the top of her lungs. There were times when fucking Jack was like a jolt to the brain, a spasm of light that overwhelmed her senses and made her scream.

If the Old Her could ever somehow overhear the New Her, the Old Her's face would scald with embarrassment.

She came quickly, with a shudder that left her gasping for breath and afterwards she lay naked on her back with ripples of pleasure, like aftershocks, running the length of her thighs and her torso. The tips of her nipples burned. With her eyes closed, she whispered:

G you're a great big cunt

Beside her, Jack grunted contentedly.

H you're a helluva cunt

'Go to sleep,' he said. 'I'll join you in a little while.' He rolled off the bed and resumed stuffing things into his backpack.

'I love you,' she whispered.

TWENTY-SEVEN

Three a.m. Twenty-three hours since Freeman had parked his Impala on the Park Road Bridge and skidded into a railing built to deter suicides.

When he woke Freeman's heart was racing and his forehead was covered in a film of sweat. He rubbed his face with his hands and lay back again. His breath was short and his heartbeat thundered in his chest. His dream was still vivid: his father's face in agony as he neared the end; the tortuous rasping of his breath; and his look of unspeakable terror.

When his father became sick and quickly died, Freeman was fifteen. His mother had been gone for two years and in her absence her sisters had taken it upon themselves to look after him. When his aunts visited his father would often yell and make threats of violence but they were fearless and determined women and they had faced him down as if he were a barking dog. They brought their nephew comics and candies; they took him for haircuts and bought him clothes. After his father died they had supervised Freeman's upbringing in a routine fashion until he was old enough to join the army.

In the last months of his father's life they had maintained a vigil by the dying man's bedside, taking it in turns to sleep on the floor of the cramped one-bedroom apartment. Freeman remembered his father's head on the pillow, his face reduced to a skull by disease, his eyes gradually losing their shine as the fight went out of them. The aunts had prayed over him. By contrast the teenage Freeman had held back, advancing no further than the bedroom doorway. He had long ago given up on his father. Besides, he had his own battles to fight at school and in the ruins of the decaying neighbourhood. Life moved on: from Detroit to Iraq and Afghanistan and back to Detroit again. He had thought that he was invulnerable, that he had created a carapace to protect against further pain. But then Shawna came along and he had felt his heart leap in his throat and he had allowed himself to believe that there was hope for two people in this world.

He walked through the dark to the bathroom and groped for the switch. The light above the mirror was cruel. The nylon stitches on his bruised temple resembled dismembered insect parts strewn across a mottled background of purple and yellow. His cheeks looked grey and there were dark pouches under his eyes. His mouth tasted foul.

Twenty-four hours: a remarkable transformation.

He went out to the kitchen in search of something cold and sweet. He drank juice straight from a carton and stood in front of the refrigerator for a time, holding the carton and swaying slightly in the fluorescent white light.

TWENTY-EIGHT

Four a.m. Renee Bastian's clamshell phone was ringing.

Freeman had grabbed it up off the table, flipped it open and pressed it against his ear before he was fully awake. Byron was stoned and bitter and his voice meandered between anger and self-pity. Freeman struggled to comprehend what was being said to him.

'I once heard a girl say to her friend right in front of me, like I was invisible, "I'm so disgusted, my driver tried to talk to me." You know what the toughest part of my job is? I tell you. It's putting up with people with a sense of entitlement, who just see you as a labourer, somehow beneath them. The ones think it's disgusting that a driver, particularly a black man, should presume to speak to a customer. I need the pay cheque so I bite my tongue but I'll tell you, it's real hard sometimes. It takes strength. That shit stay with you. Beat you down. Are you a strong man, policeman?'

Freeman was shaking his head back and forth, trying to focus his attention. 'What are you talking about, Byron?'

'I never been in awe of anyone who got in my car because I don't put nobody on different levels, but I learned about the hold power has and what it can make a man do. Crack, meth – whatever – it ain't shit next to power. People rate themselves on how close to power they is in this town, but some of the people I've met are off the chart in terms of power. They can do anything they want, no matter how bad. You're never gonna get close to them. They're protected. Believe.'

Freeman was fully awake now, leaning forward on the couch, with the cell pressed to his ear. 'That's bullshit, Byron. Nobody gets away with murder.'

Byron laughed contemptuously. 'You think you're gonna solve this case?'

'Where were you last night, Byron? Were you at the senator's house?'

'People find a safe receptacle in me. They confide in me. You'd be surprised. That's because I'm not in their circle. They don't want my advice or opinion. They don't give a shit about that. They just want to vent. I don't think they remember what they've said more than five minutes after they've said it. I remember though. I know stuff I ain't supposed to know about. I got stories I could tell you.'

'Tell me.'

'You're a man of colour. Isn't that right?'

'I am.'

'Are you going to allow them to frame me for murder?'

'You have to tell me what happened, Byron, then maybe I can do something for you.'

'Some people brighten your life with a kind word. It doesn't matter what colour or class they are. Katja was like that. She was . . . like – I mean ain't never seen a female that fine. She had all the moves. She'd come sit up front with me. We'd joke about driving away together, somewhere out west. California, maybe, I always wanted to visit California. I didn't reckon I was special, though. Katja had a kind word for everybody. And everybody wanted a piece of her. You could see that from the way they looked at her, the politicians and lawyers and speechmakers and pastors; she once told me that there wasn't a man on the planet didn't want to fuck her inside of three minutes of meeting her. I believed her. Shit! That girl was a gift to mankind.'

'Did you know she was Russian?'

'Sure. Katja told me. She told me all about her life in the whore-house back in Russia. I knew the shit she'd been through. I knew everything.'

'Did you have sex with her that night, Byron? Tell me the truth now. We'll know soon anyway, we've got your DNA on file.'

After a pause, Byron said quietly, 'I didn't force her. I didn't have to.' And then, 'I didn't kill her.'

'Who did?'

'When I saw what that bastard had done to her I cried. Everybody was in shock. Nobody could believe it, it was so wrong. He was just standing there, with everyone looking at him with their mouths wide open. He had blood on his arms, and I'll never forget the look on his face.'

'Who, Byron, who was it?'

'He was laughing. His mouth wide open and his eyes shinin'. Scariest motherfuckin' thing I ever saw. He thought we was just gonna clear it up. I mean I could have done. Maybe I should have done. If I had I wouldn't be here all fucked up with a gun in my hand. But I couldn't face it. I ran right out of that house . . .'

Byron cut the connection.

Freeman boiled. In his frustration he wanted to throw the cell against a wall. Instead he took several deep breaths and told himself to calm down.

A minute later his cell rang. It was Hector. He sounded cheerful. 'We got 'im.'

'Where?'

'East of the river. The low-rises in Washington Highlands. I've requested an emergency response team from Special Tactics Branch on a code two – *silencio radio*.'

Freeman went through into the bedroom and felt under the bed for the unregistered Glock 17 that was taped there. He tore it away from the wooden slats.

'I'm comin'.'

TWENTY-NINE

'We like to call it inter-agency cooperation in the post-9/11 security environment,' the tactical commander explained. He'd brought his SWAT team over the river from the Pentagon.

Maja shook her head in disbelief, Hector rolled his eyes and Eli Wrath hawked and spat in the slush on the sidewalk. It was 4.20 a.m. and Freeman had just finished talking on his cell to the shift commander at the Joint Operations Command Centre. The shift commander had confirmed that the regular MPD SWAT team was otherwise committed and a SWAT team from the Special Operations Division of the Pentagon Police had been sent in their place. The District was awash with special weapons and tactics teams and Freeman had worked with most of them; the MPD, Capitol Police, Metro Transit, Treasury – they all had their own SWAT, but this was the first time he'd heard of the Department of Defense sending out one of their civilian police teams on a call like this. Their usual remit was providing an emergency response team for capital area military reservations, including the Pentagon. Here in Washington Highlands they were way off reservation.

Axley, the tactical commander, was standing at the back of a Lenco armoured wagon with its rear doors open. Beside him, a man in military fatigues who had been introduced to them as a pilot was sitting on the steps of the wagon with a control unit in a toughened aluminium case on his lap. With his hands he moved toggles that controlled a one-pound WASP micro-drone that was flying somewhere above them.

'What about the Fourth Amendment?' Maja demanded. 'Is this even legal?'

She still wouldn't meet Freeman's eye. She'd ignored him since she arrived.

Beside Freeman, Axley shrugged. 'It's a public airway . . .'

'There's somebody in there,' the pilot said. 'I got him on the infrared.'

Freeman looked across the road, through the chain-wire hurricane fence and the swirling snow, at the red-brick low-rises with their graffiti-covered walls and boarded-up windows. Byron was in there somewhere, hunkered down with a crack pipe and a gun.

'Can you believe this shit?' Hector muttered.

The two hundred or so abandoned units of the Highland Dwelling public housing complex sat on a hilltop overlooking the distant monuments, but for all their proximity to the capital landmarks, they might as well have been located on the moon. Contractors had put up a chain-link fence to deter thieves intent on stripping out the wiring but the fence was broken down in several places and a couple of the units had been gutted by fire. Until recently about a third of the city's murders had been generated by this small enclave, bounded on three sides by Oxon Run Park and on the fourth by Southern Avenue and the District line. No one in the department had been sorry when the complex was closed down. With its open spaces and bunker-like red-brick boxes, it was a perfect hiding place and a formidable defensive position for a man armed with a gun.

Axley broke radio silence: 'All units, you have compromise authority and permission to move to yellow.'

Yellow was the last position of concealment and cover.

They sprinted forward at a crouch, dodging and weaving like a Chinese dragon in a storm of freezing white confetti, looking for threats from all directions. The point man was holding a metal shield and those behind him were carrying an assortment of Beretta shotguns for *knock-knock* breaching and short-barrelled UMP-40 sub-machine guns for close-quarter combat. Their chest-rigs bristled with plasticuffs and flash-bang grenades. They crossed Yuma Street, clambered up a steep bank, eased themselves through a hole in the fence and dashed across the courtyard to the nearest bunker-like block. They crouched against the red-brick wall with clouds of steam rising from their Kevlar body armour and helmets.

Compromise authority was permission to fire.

Roach, the Delta team commander, risked a quick peek around the corner at the building that was believed to house the fugitive Byron Bastian.

The crisis site, the site of the breach: a red-brick two-storey building with boarded-up windows and a black door.

A voice broadcast from Atlantic Street, on the far side of the low-rises confirmed that Echo team, Delta's seven-man counterpart, was in place. Next, snipers from Hotel team called in. There was no movement inside the cordon.

Somewhere a dog barked.

Roach came back down the line to where Freeman and Hector were squatting in the snow, blowing on their fingers. Roach looked to Freeman, his eyes shining brightly out of the holes in his ski mask. 'You ready?'

Freeman hesitated. He glanced at Hector, who shrugged. 'That *cabrón* must have known we're gonna trace the call. So either he's expecting us or he's so fucked up he don't know what he's doing.'

'He's wasted,' Freeman said, 'and frightened and suspicious.' He put his hand on the ceramic plate on Roach's chest. 'He's a key witness. I need him alive.'

'I hear you.'

'I'm serious.'

'I hear you,' Roach repeated and spoke into his microphone. 'Delta is at yellow, permission to move to green?'

Green was the crisis site, the front door. Axley granted permission.

'All right, people,' Roach said, 'speed, surprise and shock action.'

'Let's do it,' Freeman said.

Then they were sprinting across the snow towards the door with their knees bent to absorb the recoil in case they had to fire. The breacher was front and centre. He attached a slap charge that resembled a strip of tyre rubber to the door. He removed the mechanical safeties on the control box and checked the detonating cord attached to the charge. He nodded to Roach.

'Delta at green,' Roach said.

'All units,' said Axley, 'stand by, I have control.'

Freeman took a deep breath. The assaulter beside him was holding his sub-gun in one hand and a flash-bang loosely in the other.

Axley began the countdown: 'Five, four, three, two . . .'

The breach charge blew.

They were in. They moved from room to room, throwing flash-bangs and shouting: 'Clear One, Clear Two, Clear Three . . . !'

They found Byron on the first floor. He was sitting on an old couch with the stuffing coming out in tufts and on the upturned cardboard box in front of him was a litter of soda cans, liquor bottles and cigarettes. He was holding a crack pipe and a lighter and he appeared frozen in an expression of mute surprise. He was thrown to the ground and cuffed. Hector read him his rights.

'I guess you don't remember calling me?' Freeman said, kneeling beside him.

Byron's bloodshot eyes rolled upwards in his head.

'Tell me you drove that girl to the senator's house!' He shook him by the shoulders. 'Who killed her, Byron?'

'He can't hear you, Michael,' Maja said. 'His eardrums are bust.'

Reluctantly, Freeman got up and watched as they hauled Byron to his feet. He stood for a moment, swaying back and forth with Hector and Eli supporting him.

'No way I killed that girl,' he shouted. 'No way on this earth.'

Axley had sent up the Lenco wagon. Within minutes they'd have Byron bundled safely inside and on his way downtown. Freeman was confident that within a few hours he'd have sufficient cause to search the senator's house. He felt a momentary surge of elation.

'Let's go,' Roach yelled.

They propelled Byron down the stairs, and thrust him out of

the door – out of cover – into the falling snow and they were halfway across the court, when suddenly Axley was shouting in their ears: a snatched warning, then his voice was cut dead by roaring static.

Interference.

They were sprinting and stumbling with Roach yelling, the assaulters' weapons raised and looking for targets.

Into the wash of revolving red and blue light.

And gunfire.

THIRTY

The sound of the front door slamming and Jack's boots on the porch steps woke her.

Harry listened to him speaking to the taxi driver without being able to distinguish the words. He was catching a dawn flight to Miami and from there, a flight to the Caribbean. She had no idea when she would see him again.

She wished that she had told him about the slip of paper and the job she had accepted. She reflected on the absurdity of her ridiculous need to please and how easily she had slipped back into a world that she was supposed to have put behind her. Should she rush after him shouting, *Jack, I need you, come back* ...

She lay in the darkness with her head pounding and her mouth as dry as ash and she thought of her father as she often did at such times. She never knew where he was during her childhood; he came and went without fanfare. Her mother later told Harry that for most of the time she had no idea whether he was alive or dead. Harry remembered complex childhood fantasies, imagining him in the wilderness, in the desert or the mountains, blowing up secret installations and rescuing hostages. Most of all she remembered the giddy excitement of him coming home from overseas, with only ever a few hours' notice; his backpack standing upright in the hallway, far too heavy for her to lift, with its taped-up straps, rolled rope and karabiners. His boots on the doormat with sand or mud baked in the seams. She remembered watching through the banisters, surreptitious as a mouse, as her parents embraced. But he always spotted her, his eyes drawn towards her with a faint look of surprise on his face, then the headlong rush down the stairs towards him; his arms effortlessly lifting her, the rough stubble on his cheeks.

He was a solitary man. Not a typical soldier. She remembered when he came back from the Falklands and she walked beside him, holding his calloused hand, as he hobbled to the corner shop each morning struggling against the pain of the frostbite in his toes.

In the end it was the IRA who killed him.

Snowflakes gusted past the windows. It seemed like the winter would never end. She had endured two boiling hot DC summers, when the humidity was such that you couldn't step outside the house for more than a few seconds before becoming sodden with sweat, and this was her second bitterly cold winter when on certain days it felt like the cold would flay the skin off your face. It really was a place of savage extremes. It was often described as a swamp, though strictly speaking it wasn't. Jack's line was that the founding fathers had deliberately chosen it as the location of their capital as a means of discouraging the formation of a political class and their hangers-on. If that was the intention then they had spectacularly failed – three and a half billion dollars had been spent lobbying Congress in the last year.

'Air conditioning,' Jack liked to say, 'the lobbyist's boon, it foiled the best efforts of Washington, Adams, Jefferson et al.'

THIRTY-ONE

'Cordon breach! All units! Intruder in the cordon. All units . . .'

Freeman was midway across the court, only a couple of steps behind Hector and Eli, who were supporting Byron between them, when Axley began shouting on the net and then, just as suddenly, his voice was drowned out by a barrage of noise.

Roach's mouth was opening and closing. He was yelling but Freeman couldn't hear the words. Freeman was trying to run faster, slipping and stumbling in the snow. He was buffeted by a gust of wind, a storm of snowflakes. He'd lost all sense of direction.

When the shooting began the sound of each shot was muffled and indistinct, the air bending around him.

Byron's head jerked backwards, a bloody piece of him torn away.

Roach went down like a toy soldier knocked off a shelf.

Hector pirouetting. As he turned, his mouth open in a mute expression of surprise, he sprayed arterial blood across Freeman's chest and face.

thump thump thump.

Then Freeman being pulled face down, the snow rushing up to meet him, and he was rolling over and over. With Maja holding him. It was impossible to tell which way was up or down. They came to a stop in a drift beneath a wall. The lever of a smoke grenade struck the brick above their heads and within a couple of seconds they were enveloped in a billowing red cloud.

'What the hell happened out there?'

It was 5 a.m. and Freeman was sitting in his Impala with the rattling heater ramped up to maximum, attempting to explain to

Chief Streeks what had happened; Maja was sitting beside him with a bottle of water and a rag. She'd been trying without much success to wipe the blood off his face and the collar of his shirt. It seemed that she wasn't angry with him any more.

Washington Highlands was lit up with spinning red and blue light. It seemed like every law enforcement agency in the city had descended on the place since the shooting.

'The weather conditions were extremely difficult,' Freeman explained, 'visibility was low and the security of the outer cordon was compromised. An unknown assailant overpowered one of the team snipers located on a rooftop on the cordon. He climbed the ladder put there by the team. He moved incredibly fast. The drone recorded it all. He used the sniper's rifle to kill Menendez, Roach and the fugitive Byron Bastian as we were bringing him out of the building. The killer then escaped, taking with him a frequency disruptor and a 7.62 semi-automatic sniper rifle, an M110. It's a kind of M16 on steroids. It comes with a sound suppressor, which is why we couldn't identify the direction of fire. It also has a times ten optic and a night vision scope.'

'Motherfucker! When did they start handing them out to SWAT teams?'

'Department of Defense started moving over to them in 2008; they must be supplying them to their civilian agencies.'

'Shit!'

'I think our killer is moving up in the world. He's progressed from his teeth, to a kitchen knife to a high-powered sniper rifle.'

'Chief Thielen is visiting with the Secretary of Defense in about thirty minutes.'

'She should ask why it is that we got sent a Pentagon SWAT team.'

'Hell, Michael, you think that they volunteered to go down there and get shot up?'

THIRTY-TWO

An hour before dawn. The cruellest hour.

When human beings were at their most vulnerable, when armies launch their attacks and when the police show up at your door with the worst kind of news. They arrived just after six. It was still snowing and the sky was dull white. There was one house with lights on and with figures moving behind the windows.

Freeman walked up the pathway with Maja at his side. They stopped in front of the door and she squeezed his arm and he felt pathetically grateful. He rang the bell. Four people opened the door, filling the doorway. Four girls from small to medium sized. They were dressed for an arctic expedition, with mittens and backpacks. They had shiny black hair beneath woollen hats with earflaps and they gave off an air of hyperactive excitement.

Behind them was Hector's wife. When she saw the expression on their faces she gasped and gathered the children in a desperate huddle around her.

'No . . .'

THIRTY-THREE

STRONG QUAKE ROCKS CAPITAL . . . LARGEST EVER RECORDED TREMOR
. . . PEOPLE ARE OUT IN STREETS CRYING, SCREAMING, SHOUTING.

Events in Washington had been consigned by the earthquake to an inside page of the *Washington Post*'s Metro section. What there was of a story was out of date, ancient history; there was a prison photo of Byron Bastian, heavy-lidded and scowling, looking for all the world like Willie Horton: *Fugitive sought in triple murder spree*. The *Washington Times* had the same photo and *Search intensifies for killer*. Freeman skimmed through the articles as he stood in the elevator at the Watergate: *Police will not confirm that limousine driver and ex-offender Byron Bastian is a suspect in the killing of three people including his sister Renee . . . yet the mystery that shrouds their deaths continues to raise more than a few eyebrows . . . Senator James Cannon's 'loquacious attorney' Abe Proust denies that the Jane Doe found naked in the park was killed on the senator's property . . . police will not confirm that she was a Russian prostitute nor will they confirm they are investigating a link between the third victim, a defense lobbyist named Olivier Davide, also known as Oleg Davidov, and the Russian mafia.*

It was all bullshit and misdirection. Cannon's work.

Freeman emerged angrily from the elevator and entered the office suite.

Winnie had been hard at work.

Jane Doe in the mosaic: lines of evidence radiating from her like spokes; photos and frame-grabs, X-rays, phone tracking records, maps and diagrams, witness statements and incident, autopsy and serology reports.

Freeman stood for a while in front of the array of felt room dividers and studied the photos of the three dead bodies on the autopsy table as well as photos of them at primary or secondary crime scenes: Oleg Davidov on his bed, Renee Bastian on the floor and Jane Doe in the snow. Arranged around the victim shots were driver's licence photos of Byron Bastian and Oleg Davidov/Olivier Davide and an employee photo of a blithely smiling Renee Bastian from Perfect Nails. There was a marked map of the District and surrounding counties with red pins for the homicides – two of them within a couple of miles of each other in the north-west quadrant and the other one in the south-east quadrant on the far side of the Anacostia River. There were blue pins with cotton thread linking them to frame-grabs of the Black Lincoln Town Car driven by Byron Bastian from the security camera on Shepherd and the traffic cameras on 16th Street and New York Avenue. There was also a blue pin in the corner of Connecticut and Porter, with a frame-grab of Davidov, minus a shoe, limping across the forecourt of the gas station. Head down and talking into his cell. There were black pins for Davidov's apartment, Harry Armstrong's house, Cardinal Limousine Services, Germline BioSciences Laboratories and Senator Cannon's mansion in Crestwood. There were photographs of the killer's bloody, splayed handprints from the row house in Congress Heights and the apartment in the Kennedy-Warren and beside them matching prints from the handgun that was thrown at Freeman.

Bite marks.

Freeman took three red pins from the edge of the display and stuck them in the map at Washington Highlands: Byron Bastian, Hector Menendez and the assaulter named Roach . . .

Six dead in total.

A killer with a sniper rifle on the loose.

What did he have to show for it?

He took a Sharpie off Winnie's desk and wrote *Katja* on a Post-it note. He stuck it on the mosaic, beneath a close-up of the barcode tattoo. He might have lost the drive with the flash files that identified her but for the purposes of the investigation, she now had a name.

Freeman strayed across to Special Agent McCafferty's desk and flicked through the piles of paper there, the printouts and photocopies, including a stack of lists: the top twenty contributors to Cannon's campaign committee; the bills that he had sponsored or co-sponsored; his staff salary expenditure by fiscal year for the last five years; and his voting record in the Senate on defence issues.

Freeman found two sets of divorce papers and beneath them the citation for Senator Cannon's Distinguished Service Cross. He paused to read it:

> The President of the United States takes pleasure in presenting the Distinguished Service Cross to James D. Cannon, Captain, US Army, for extraordinary heroism in action on 30 March 1969, during combat operations against the NVA while supporting 1st Infantry Division, ARVN operations in Quang Tin Province. Captain Cannon demonstrated the highest degree of courage and excellent leadership through his distinguished performance as Team Leader, Detachment B-52 while engaged in Jungle Combat Operations. His heroic actions throughout one of the most intensive firefights of Operation Masher were directly responsible for preventing enemy insurgent forces from overrunning the ARVN Force. Captain Cannon personally eliminated multiple enemy-controlled weapon positions, essential in turning the tide of the enemy's ground-force assault upon an ARVN company. His actions under fire as a leader were performed with marked distinction and bravery. Captain James Cannon's distinctive accomplishments are in keeping with the finest traditions of military service and reflect great credit upon himself, this Command, and the United States Army.
> *Department of the Army, Permanent Orders No. 111-08 (12 April 1970)*
> Home town: Jackson, Tennessee

As a former member of Fifth Special Forces Group, Freeman knew enough of his unit's history to know that although they had earned a lot of medals there, Vietnam had not been a particularly happy time for the unit. They were marginalised, pushed into a kind of twilight, living and fighting in the remotest jungle areas sometimes behind enemy lines and often in support of unreliable Vietnamese counterparts. They quickly slipped beyond anyone's official control. Things had come to a head in June 1969 when eight members of the unit involved in a clandestine intelligence-gathering operation called Project Gamma were arrested over the torture and execution of a suspected Vietnamese double agent.

Cannon had earned his medal just a few months before the Project Gamma incident, supporting South Vietnamese Hoc Bao Special Forces against an attack by the North Vietnamese Army in a remote mountainous province on the border with Laos. They may even have been in Laos. McCafferty had found two references to the attack on the Internet: the first from the memoirs of a Special Forces soldier wounded in the attack and the second from an army medic who arrived on the scene shortly after the battle had ended. They were stapled to the citation. Freeman read the first account:

> We were attacked at 0400 hours on the 30th by an unknown size enemy force. Two platoons of the ARVN strike force were on over-night leave, and many of the remaining strikers simply refused to fight or were secretly VC themselves. After four hours of fighting and despite several airstrikes, the NVA penetrated the inner perimeter and, low on ammunition, we were forced to abandon the position. The resulting casualties were two Americans killed and two Americans wounded, including myself. As I was being exfiltrated, Captain 'Jungle Jim' Cannon led several Nung camp guards back onto the knoll and recaptured it. Total enemy casualties were twenty-one killed and no wounded.

The word Nung was highlighted with a note in the margin in McCafferty's handwriting: *Vietnamese minority group, ethnic Chinese, fought with Special Forces.*

The second account by the medic who arrived after the fighting and tended to the American and ARVN wounded had a passage highlighted with yellow fluorescent marker:

> When I arrived on the hilltop there was an argument going on outside one of the bunkers. The leader of the Nung forces was shouting at the Special Forces captain. It might have turned violent if several of the Nung fighters hadn't stepped in and restrained their commander. The Special Forces captain then insisted that the bunker be destroyed. It was duly blown up. I later heard the captain got a medal.

Across the room, a landline rang. He hurried over to it and grabbed the receiver.

'Lieutenant Freeman?' asked a dispatcher from the Joint Operations Command Centre. 'There's a call for you from Georgia.'

'Put it through.'

The call was from a detective named David Vashadze of the Criminal Police of the Ministry of Internal Affairs in the Republic of Georgia.

'That Georgia,' said Freeman, looking around for the world map. A small, mountainous nation on the periphery of Europe, bordered by its bullying rival Russia to the north, thrusting Turkey to the south-west, and its fellow former Soviet Republics Armenia and Azerbaijan to the south and south-east.

'What time is it there?' Vashadze asked.

Calls between foreign police forces, in Freeman's limited experience, always began with the ritual establishment of the time difference.

'Early: 7.15 a.m.'

'I'm on the afternoon shift,' Vashadze said cheerfully. 'I saw your Interpol notice. I have some information for you.'

'Go on.'

'The fingerprints from your murders. We have the same ones.'

The fingerprints found at the murder sites of Renee Bastian and Oleg Davidov, Vashadze explained, were also found on the murder weapon used in the brutal slaying of a Georgian politician named Zurab Yakobashvili in 2008.

'The perpetrator is believed to be a member of a Russian criminal gang known as the Ras Serditye, which translates from Russian as the Furies,' Vashadze said. 'They operate out of a remote mountainous area called Svanetia. They've been hiding out up there since the mid-nineties. I'll email you the investigation report.'

Freeman shook his head. Under any other circumstances he might have assumed it was a mistake, a routine mis-identification, but nothing about this case was simple. He had a Russian victim, why not a Russian murderer?

'How did the perpetrator get here to the USA?' Freeman asked.

'You flew him there.'

'I'm sorry?'

'Your government flew him there.'

'How do you know that?'

'Everybody knows.'

'Define everybody.'

'Everybody here and some in your government there – speak to your CIA, your Pentagon. They know. You can tell them the Russians are mad as hell. Let me know if you catch the killer, OK?'

'I will.'

'I'll email that report.' Vashadze cut the connection.

Freeman shook his head in bewilderment and looked up to find Maja standing by the elevator.

'What's going on?'

'I feel like Alice in Wonderland. It's all getting curiouser and curiouser.'

'Are you OK?'

He shook his head. 'Not really.'

Maja headed in the direction of the coffee machine. 'You want one?'

'Please.'

He went through into his office and found Winnie curled up on the couch, with a blanket over her head. He sat at the desk without waking her and contemplated the piles of paper haphazardly arranged there while the desktop booted up.

He was convinced that Katja was killed on the senator's property;

it seemed equally likely that the Pentagon was intent on preventing the truth coming out. He supposed that a sex scandal involving a senior member of the Armed Services Committee and a Russian spy ring could have serious repercussions for the Defense budget negotiations. Maybe there was more to come out – the possibility of further, more damaging revelations. Of course they'd want to cover it up. But events in the Washington Highlands had left a question in his mind: Streeks was right when he said the Pentagon SWAT team wouldn't have deliberately walked into an ambush. There was some kind of wild card at play; somebody not playing by the rules.

He clicked on his inbox and found an email from Detective Vashadze with an original homicide report of the death of Zurab Yakobashvili, a member of the Georgian parliament; an English translation of the same report; fingerprints and crime scene and morgue photos – all glare and shadow in the brutal light of the camera's flash – close-ups of skin, of knife cuts and bite marks, each wound neatly circled in red.

A scattering of amputated fingers.

The Fury.

THIRTY-FOUR

McCafferty called from Quantico while Freeman was parked on Wisconsin Avenue, to tell him that the lab results had come through.

'She had sex with three different men before she was killed,' McCafferty told him. 'Do you have any idea how many people I had to have sex with to find that out? They've got a month-long backlog down here.'

It was 8 a.m. on Wednesday, day two of the investigation – twenty-nine hours since Harry Armstrong called 911. Freeman was sitting in the Impala watching the underground entrance to Sidwell Friends School, waiting for Sonia Rojas. He had his cell in one hand, a sausage and egg muffin in the other, and there was a sixteen-ounce cup of coffee squeezed between his thighs. It was his first food since a yogurt eaten at his apartment twenty-four hours before.

'Well?'

'We know the identity of two of them as a result of previous convictions,' McCafferty said, 'the limousine driver Byron Bastian and the Russian Oleg Davidov aka Olivier Davide; both now dead. Nothing yet on the third.'

'Thanks.'

She had sex with her pimp and her driver and one other. Then someone killed her. After that a prairie fire: Oleg, Renee, Hector, Byron and Roach . . .

'I heard you got a bite on your Interpol notice,' McCafferty said. 'You think it's the same killer?'

'Could be,' Freeman replied.

'We've got a legal attaché at the embassy in Georgia with a

couple of special agents attached. I'll give them a call and see what more I can find out.'

'Thanks.'

'There is something else,' McCafferty said in a more serious tone. 'The laptop found in Oleg Davidov's apartment is missing its hard drive.'

'Perhaps the killer took it?' Freeman suggested after a pause.

There was silence at the end of the line.

'Have you got it?' McCafferty asked eventually.

'I don't have it,' Freeman told him, which was true enough.

Just then, Sonia Rojas emerged from the school's access ramp, driving a silver Mercedes Coupé. She turned left on Wisconsin, heading downtown.

'I gotta go,' Freeman said, throwing the cell on the passenger seat.

He followed her for a while and then flipped on the red and blue dashboard lights as they approached Glover Park. She pulled over to the sidewalk. Freeman got out of his car and walked around to the passenger side door of hers. He paused and looked around. If he was being followed this morning, then they were hanging well back. He climbed in the car.

'Good morning,' he said.

'Good morning,' she replied, bland as warm milk. She was wearing make-up this time. Too much, he thought, though perhaps she had prepared herself for the television cameras. There was the same opulent smell of perfume.

'Nice car.'

'It serves its purpose,' she replied. If she was surprised by his bruised and battered appearance she gave no indication of it.

'It's an expensive school, Sidwell. Your ex-husband is an attorney, that's right?'

Freeman had done his homework. He knew that she was divorced from a lawyer, that she had a daughter and that she had handled public relations for a television network before going to work as Communications Director for the senator.

'That is correct.'

'Attorneys clean up in this town,' Freeman mused. 'My wife

wants me to switch, re-train at law school. Sometimes I'm tempted. I mean it gets to you: the bodies on slabs, the things that people do to each other. That girl for instance, the one who was dumped in the woods; we think her name was Katja and somebody beat her to death with a hammer. He took his time about it. He tied her down. He may have been one of the three people who had sex with her. Then he smashed her face with such force we found several teeth in her lungs. And nobody has come forward to claim her. She's not a missing person. Nobody seems to care. It's depressing. Who would have a daughter in such a world? Do you think I'd make a good lawyer?'

'I think this town has enough lawyers, Lieutenant.'

'That doesn't really answer my question. Is your daughter in the same class as either of the Obama girls?'

'No.'

'Pity,' he said and stared at the passing traffic. She was silent, waiting for him to speak. He realised that he had rattled her somehow. Something he had said. That he had given the victim a name or perhaps the manner of her death? He made a mental note of it, something to explore further later. 'I wanted to thank you for the senator's press conference yesterday. It was very helpful of him to call on witnesses to come forward like that. Perhaps someone will have a crisis of conscience. You must have got his wife and daughter on a plane to DC in a hurry.'

'Is there something that I can help you with, Lieutenant?'

'Sure. You can tell me who's killing my witnesses.'

'I have no idea what you are talking about.'

'I lost a colleague last night. He left behind a wife and four daughters.'

'I'm very sorry to hear that. But I can't help you.'

'What's the senator doing today?'

She pushed her hair back behind her ears and looked at him. 'He's delivering the keynote address at a Defense conference at the Cosmos Club in about half an hour. I'm on my way there to meet him. Then he's in on the Hill preparing for the committee hearings tomorrow.'

'I've never heard him speak,' Freeman said. 'I heard he's quite the orator. Maybe I'll follow you to the Cosmos Club. How's that?'

She made a show of thinking about it, weighing the pros and cons. 'Of course,' she said eventually.

'You want me to put the siren on?'

She was momentarily vexed.

'I'm just kidding,' he said.

Freeman followed Sonia Rojas up the broad staircase to the first floor of the Cosmos Club, once again trailing in her scent. She really did have great legs, her thighs swishing in nylons as she climbed. She stood beside him while the administrative staff issued Freeman with a handwritten name badge and waived the six-hundred-dollar registration fee. He handed over his cell in exchange for a numbered plastic token and was given a folder bearing the title *Warring Futures: the outlook for policy and defense business in the Singularity.*

'The singularity?'

'The future, Lieutenant, that's what it means. If you'll excuse me.'

'Of course.'

'I'll see you afterwards.'

She went back down the staircase and out onto the street, presumably to wait for the senator's arrival.

'This way,' said a young woman, showing him into an anteroom that smelled of bacon. Catering staff wearing black and white uniforms were standing behind a breakfast buffet, while men and women wearing name badges stood around holding plates. Most were wearing suits, but some of them were in military uniform. The only other black man was a Marine Corps general whom Freeman vaguely recognised. He helped himself to coffee. Adjacent to the anteroom was a large ballroom with painted wood panelling on the walls and gold filigree scrollwork decorating the high ceiling. The room was filled with round tables and with a podium at one end on which were set a lectern and a table with four empty seats.

At the lectern an air force colonel was speaking to an audience of just a few people dotted around the room, 'The wars in Iraq and Afghanistan have driven the rapid development and utilisation of unmanned surveillance and attack aircraft. Last year the United States Air Force trained more pilots of unmanned aerial vehicles than actual pilots of combat aircraft.'

Freeman noticed that there were several television sets mounted on brackets on the wall and they were broadcasting views of the people in the anteroom. Freeman realised that the footage was being broadcast from a tracked vehicle that was moving among the conference-goers; it was being controlled by a young man with a crew cut who was standing beside a pillar. He was wearing a dark business suit and had a desert camouflage backpack on his back and what looked like a PlayStation module in his hands. With a start, Freeman recognised him as the man who had controlled the drone over Washington Highlands during the ambush the night before.

'Not only dull, dirty and detailed jobs but dangerous ones too. Fifty-two per cent of casualties happen on first contact with the enemy. That's why the point man position is so unpopular. I say that's a great job for a robot.'

The colonel finished speaking and a man who identified himself as the moderator stepped up to the microphone.

'Ladies and gentlemen, please take your seats for our keynote address.'

Freeman joined the general movement of people into the ballroom. He chose a seat at a table at the back, right beside the exit. He flicked through the folder, glancing at the letter of introduction and list of participants. The conference programme listed three chairmen: a former Under-Secretary for Defense Acquisition, a former Principal Deputy Assistant Secretary of Defense for International Security Policy and a former Director of the Defense Science Office. He assumed that they were the three people who had just entered and were now sitting either side of the senator at the podium.

The senator was listed under opening keynote address as a ranking member of the Subcommittee on Emerging Threats and

Capabilities. He was introduced by the former Director of the Defense Science Office who referred in glowing terms to the senator's wartime service in Vietnam, his voting record on the Armed Services Committee and his unwavering commitment to maintaining the technological superiority of the US military.

When the clapping was done, the senator stood for a while with his large hands gripping the lectern and his gaze ranging across the room. The crowd grew still: a sudden gravity and portentousness filled the room. Standing there, the senator was a consummate public man, a presence. He broadcast his power like a beacon.

'Ladies and gentlemen, I don't need to tell you that we stand on the cusp of a technological explosion, the so-called *singularity*,' the senator said. He spoke without notes. 'Rapid advances in molecular nanotechnology, genetic engineering and robotics mean that within the next twenty years, the exponential trend of accelerating change will continue past the limits of human ability. Shortly thereafter, the human era as we understand it will be over.

'What do I mean by that in practical terms? Let me give you some examples. I'm talking about autonomous machines with the ability to locate their own power sources and choose targets to attack with precision weapons; computer viruses that can evade elimination and have achieved cockroach intelligence; metabolically dominant soldiers that can run Olympic-quality sprints for fifteen minutes on one breath of air, that can do without food and sleep for days on end; plants, microbes and small animals that can act as remote sentinels for reporting the presence of chemical or biological particles; I'm talking about brain–machine interfaces, real-time connections between individual living neurons inside the skulls of humans and wires that lead to computers; I'm talking about armoured exoskeletons that respond not to your muscle movements but to your brain's commands. I'm talking about a radical transformation in the conduct of future wars.

'We know that whenever technology approaches a barrier, new technologies will cross it. We also know that technology is a double-edged sword. It will provide us with the means to overcome age-old problems like poverty and illness, but it will also empower the destructive ideologies of those who are ranged against us. Biological viruses, software viruses and missiles already cross international boundaries with impunity. The new technologies will be no different. A self-replicating pathogen, designed and built in a laboratory in a distant land, whether biological or nanotechnology-based, could destroy our civilisation in a matter of weeks.

'The challenge for us is to secure the profound benefits of the singularity while diminishing its risks. We must urgently increase our investment in defensive technologies to address this new and under-recognised existential threat to humanity. We must stream-line the regulatory process for genetic and medical technologies to ensure that the first super-enhanced humans are our super-enhanced humans and not our enemies'. We must establish a programme for monitoring and if necessary replicating unknown or evolving pathogens. We must build the nanotech assemblers, the reconnaissance robots, the autonomous weapons platforms. Because if we do not our enemies surely will.

'We cannot let fear of the future inhibit us from exploring the future. We must fully understand the nature of emerging threats and the capabilities required to neutralise them. We must radically innovate. Only then can we build a future for ourselves that ensures the continuation of our current way of life. Only then can we retain our dominant position. Thank you. God bless America.'

The senator finished. The impressive register of his perfor-mance brought the audience to their feet. They were clapping enthusiastically. Freeman felt obliged to stand. There was a palpable stir in the room as the senator strode towards the exit with his entourage. Then he spotted Freeman and paused mid-stride, as if he might turn back, but the press of people around him left him no alternative but to continue. They were thrown together. Freeman walked alongside him.

'What did you think, Lieutenant? the senator asked.

'I'd say it rates fairly high on my weird-shit-o-meter.'

'Really? I'd have credited you with more imagination,' he said coldly, his whole body projecting a sense of power under restraint.

'Can you tell me what your connection is with Germline BioSciences?'

There was a brief flicker of interest in the senator's eyes. 'Why do you ask?'

'One of the bodies we found yesterday was of a man named Oleg Davidov, also known as Olivier Davide. He worked as a lobbyist for Germline BioSciences. Did you ever meet with him?'

'No, I don't believe that I did. Now if you'll excuse me.'

He pushed forward. Freeman found himself walking through the lobby beside Larry Lumpe, the senator's chief of staff, the man who had been with him at the house on the night Katja was killed.

'Did you know Oleg Davidov?' Freeman asked.

'No.' Lumpe shook his head emphatically, refusing to meet Freeman's eye.

'Lieutenant Freeman?' They were joined by a small, chubby man holding a briefcase. 'I'm Abraham Proust, the senator's counsel. How is the investigation going? Have you caught Byron Bastian yet?'

'Byron is dead,' Freeman told him. 'He was shot in the early hours of this morning.'

Proust didn't seem surprised. 'Your chief suspect is dead. Does that mean the investigation is over?'

'No.'

Proust shook his head. 'Lieutenant, I don't know where you are going with this but I can tell you I'll be speaking to your superiors and I promise you that if you continue this unwarranted harassment of the senator and his staff you will regret it.'

'Are you threatening me, Mr Proust?'

'Heaven forbid, Lieutenant. If you'll excuse me also.'

Freeman watched from the top of the steps as they climbed into a black Chevy Suburban. After they had pulled away, he looked across to find Sonia Rojas standing by his side.

She handed him his cell phone.

'What happened that night?' Freeman asked her.

'I don't know,' she replied coldly. 'I wasn't there.'

THIRTY-FIVE

'Excuse me for asking, miss, but how long have you known Dr Markoff?'

The questioner was tall and muscular with a soul patch on his chin and when he opened his mouth to speak she saw that he had a gold incisor. He was wearing a black beanie hat and a black windbreaker with RAEBURN stencilled on the back in white lettering and BUCK GROLIG written in red on his left breast.

'Since yesterday afternoon,' Harry replied.

She had arrived at the gate at eight forty-five, fifteen minutes early for work. The same two men had searched the car and patted her down as thoroughly as they did the day before. They had given no indication that they recognised her but when she pulled up beside the house, Grolig was waiting on the steps. He'd told her that he was head of security, working on contract for the Daedalus Foundation who owned the house and had loaned it to Dr Markoff and his family.

'So Dr Markoff just hired you out of the blue?' Grolig asked.

'That's right.'

He was smiling but his eyes were cold. 'See, I'm having trouble figuring that out.'

'Perhaps he thought you needed the help?'

He didn't like that much. 'What's your interest in Dr Markoff?'

'He offered me a job and I accepted the offer.'

'Who do you work for?'

'I'm self-employed.'

'We're gonna do some checking up on you, miss.'

'Be my guest,' she said. She consulted her watch. 'I'd like to stay and chat but I don't want to be late for my first day. Excuse me.'

She was conscious of his gaze on her back as she climbed the steps.

'Good morning,' Harry said.

Without replying, Yuri stood aside from the double doors and gestured for her to enter.

She stepped into a large room bathed in morning light. Like Dr Markoff's study, one wall was entirely made of glass. The only man-made thing in sight was the spire of the National Cathedral, otherwise it was just trees, stretching away as far as the eye could see.

The polished wooden floor was covered with vinyl tumbling mats and at the centre of the room was a set of freestanding six-foot-high parallel bars.

Eva was poised at the upmost point of a swing, a vertical dart with her toes pointing at the ceiling. She was wearing a black leotard cut high on her hips and bandages on her upper arms, and her hair was in a ponytail that hung down between her locked arms. She held the handstand for a couple of seconds more and then about-faced in a Diomidov, supporting herself momentarily on one arm. She grunted and her legs swung down and as she rose above the bars again, they spread like the points of a compass. She released her grip on the rails, and for an instant she was flying.

Harry gasped.

Eva grabbed the rails again and her legs came together. She rocked back and forth in a basket swing, raised herself into a hand-stand again, switched hands on the rails and swung forward into a double back flip, ending with her toes pointing forward. Again a handstand. More back flips. Harry marvelled at the young woman's strength and balance, watching as she effortlessly swung herself back and forth in a series of rolls, full turns, peels and twists.

She knew enough about gymnastics to know that the parallel bars were usually reserved for men.

Eva dismounted from a handstand without bending her knees, swinging into a triple back flip and landing on the mat with a punch, an exclamation, her arms outstretched, grinning.

Across the room a woman in a black leotard was clapping. She was petite with long blonde hair in a ponytail that reached down to the small of her back.

'Bravo,' she said.

Eva picked up a folded towel off the back of a chair and walked over to her, rubbing the back of her neck and under her armpits. A large purple bruise on the back of Eva's thigh caught Harry's attention. It looked like a horse had kicked her.

Eva and the woman were signing. After a few seconds, the woman looked at Harry. 'She says do you want a go?'

Harry laughed. 'I don't think so.'

'Have you used the bars?' the woman asked.

'The uneven bars,' Harry replied, 'but not since I was at school. Anyway, ballet was more my thing.'

Eva was watching them talk.

'Dr Markoff would be very pleased if his niece was a ballerina,' the woman said with a smile. 'But she doesn't have the patience for it. I'm Anna.'

She held out her hand and Harry shook it.

'I'm Eva's gymnastics teacher. I'm from Estonia.'

'I'm Harry,' she replied, 'from Scotland.'

'So we are both used to having loud and aggressive neighbours, I think?'

'Something like that,' Harry replied.

'The lesson is over,' Anna said. 'Excuse me.'

She kissed Eva on the cheek, nothing unusual in that, but then in a moment of intimacy, she pressed a finger against Eva's lips and held it there for a few beats, before turning away and walking straight out of the room without looking back.

As soon as she had left, Eva walked over to Harry and stood for a while studying her. Harry found herself feeling coy, almost embarrassed to be the focus of Eva's attention. The girl provoked such strange emotions. There was a strong smell rising off her skin, but it was sweet and musky, not at all unpleasant. Eva reached out and took Harry's hand in hers. She smiled reassuringly. Then she led her out past Yuri and along the corridor to another set of stairs. They went down the stairs to a narrow corridor on the ground floor. Eva's bedroom was at the back of the house, with sliding French windows that looked out on a broad wooden deck and beyond it on the grass, a mature magnolia tree. Behind the tree was a twelve-foot brick wall that marked the perimeter of the property and the boundary of Rock Creek Park.

Eva threw the towel down on a bench at the foot of her bed and stripped naked, kicking her leotard into a laundry basket on the far side of the room. She removed her scrunchy and shook out her hair. As she pulled off her wristbands Harry noticed the bruises and scraped skin on her knuckles and the backs of her hands. Eva's hands looked a size too big for her body, like a puppy's paws.

Harry glanced back at the open door, making brief eye contact with Yuri who was standing in the shadows. She stepped up to the door and pushed it closed with her toes. Spotting Eva's Curve on the bed she picked it up and typed a message in MemoPad.

Does Yuri go everywhere with you?

yes

Is he deaf too?

nope YURI has a problem with his vocal chords our family has many problems

He's family?

She laughed, an unnerving mewling and hacking sound.

kind of!

She padded through into the adjoining bathroom and switched on the shower. Harry looked around. It struck her that there was nothing personal in the room: no photos of loved ones, nothing that placed Eva or suggested where she had come from. The bed was large, dark cherry wood, in a sleigh design with an ivory-coloured, hand-stitched silk quilt with matching cushions. Beside the bed there was a tall nightstand in the same dark cherry wood. She saw that on top of the nightstand beside a half-empty water glass and a face-down Russian paperback cracked open on its spine, there was a white cardboard box from a pharmacy with *Progesterone Injection USP* written on it.

Abruptly, Harry's attention was caught by the sight of Eva's uncle striding across the deck outside. He was shouting into a phone. She crossed to the window. The soundproofing of the house was so effective that it was impossible to hear what he was saying.

Harry looked back. Eva had emerged from the shower and was towelling herself. When she was done she threw the towel on the floor and picked up her Curve.

> Uncle SASHA is upset he does not think it is safe 4 us 2 stay
> Who is he talking to?

Eva shrugged.

> pentagon mayb

She crossed to the dresser and opened several drawers, removing socks, underwear, jeans and a folded check shirt. Harry found herself staring admiringly at Eva's lithe and muscular body, her narrow waist, rounded breasts and taut stomach. The only marks on her were the bruise on her thigh and the broken skin on her knuckles and the backs of her hands. She watched as Eva sat on the edge of the bed and from a bedside drawer removed a syringe and a sterile swab and from the box a small bottle of progesterone. She drew off 10cc, swabbed a patch on her stomach and injected the hormone.

'What are you doing?' Harry asked, making a gesture that was somewhere between a frown and a shrug, and pointing with her palm.

Eva evidently found this hilarious. She held out her Curve for Harry to see:

> ur a gr8 communicator :)

Undeterred, Harry repeated the gesture. Eva typed another message:

> i am making eggs

THIRTY-SIX

Cloak and dagger shit, Freeman thought.

His cell had begun to vibrate as he was walking out of the front door of the Cosmos Club.

Number withheld.

'Hi, Michael,' said a voice that he had last heard almost a decade before in the ruins of the Qala-i-Janghi fort in Afghanistan. 'It's Baba John . . .'

Back then 'Baba John' Bohlayer had been one of the CIA paramilitary officers assigned as an adviser to General Dostum's Northern Alliance.

'What can I do for you, John?' Freeman asked.

'In front of you, can you see a woman on a motorbike?'

You couldn't miss her. At the bottom of the steps there was a figure in matt black armour, from full-face helmet to gauntlets to injection-moulded boots, standing astride a 1000cc Yamaha bike.

'Yes.'

'Give her your cell and get on the back.'

The woman flipped up her visor and removed her gauntlets as he walked towards her. Her eyes were grey and almost colourless. She handed him a helmet and he gave her his cell. She removed the cell phone's battery and zipped it into a pocket while he put on the helmet and fastened the chinstrap.

'Get on,' she said, handing him back the cell.

He threw his leg over the seat behind her. He put his arms around her, conscious of the woman beneath the mesh fabric and armour panels.

She walked the bike a few steps down and then put it into gear. The bike roared. She performed a complicated circuit of local streets and back alleys in Dupont Circle, Freeman assumed, to shake off any possible followers and then down New Hampshire and a surge along Ohio Drive, roaring past the Lincoln Memorial.

She stopped beside the Potomac and flipped up her visor again. He dismounted and undid the fastening under his chin. He handed her the helmet.

'Where do you want me to go?' he asked.

'The Jefferson Memorial.'

She roared off.

With my cell battery, Freeman thought.

He walked along Ohio Drive between steep banks of snow, heading towards the memorial while Black Hawk helicopters crossed the river from the Pentagon and thudded overhead. The tidal basin was almost completely frozen over and the jumbled plates of ice had a light covering of snow; only a small circle of choppy water at the centre of the lake was moving.

He climbed the memorial steps to the President's statue. John Bohlayer – Baba John – was standing beneath the dome beside the south-east wall, in front of the inscription that was redacted from a letter written by Jefferson in 1816:

We might as well require a man to wear still the coat which fitted him when a boy as civilized society to remain ever under the regimen of their barbarous ancestors.

His wife Shawna called it Jefferson's 'saving grace': she liked to think of it as a statement of opposition to slavery by a reluctant slave owner.

Bohlayer was short and whip-thin like a jockey and when he smiled all his teeth showed. Freeman had first met him at the landing zone in the Darya Suf Valley on the night in October 2001 that he had first arrived in Afghanistan. Bohlayer had been attached to the Uzbek warlord General Dostum who was fighting with the Northern Alliance against the Taliban. The Afghans knew him as Baba John, or Brother John. They liked him. He spoke Dari and Pashtu. He was polite and respectful and, unlike most of the foreigners they encountered, he didn't lecture them and he rarely spoke his mind.

191

'It's been a long time,' Freeman said.

'I just got pulled out of Islamabad,' Bohlayer told him.

'You found Bin Laden yet?'

'You know better than to ask me that.'

'What can I do for you, John?'

'This homicide case you're investigating.'

'Yes?'

'Let me put it this way. You've been red-flagged. Any call you make, any email you send, any search engine you access – alarm bells ring across several agencies.'

It wasn't exactly a surprise. 'And I'm being followed,' Freeman told him.

Bohlayer nodded. 'They're queuing up behind you.'

'Who is?'

'Cannon has people on you.'

'I suspected as much.'

'And we think the Russians do too.'

'The Russians?'

'We're not sure if it's state-sponsored, i.e. the SVR, the successor to the KGB, or if it's the Russian mob, the Bratva. It may be a mixture of both.'

'Great.'

'Thing is, Michael, we need your help.'

'We?'

'The Agency.' He gave a pained look. 'I'll be frank with you, we're scrambling to catch up here.'

'You are?'

'I need you to tell me everything you know.'

'They pulled you out of Islamabad to ask me that?'

'That's about it,' Bohlayer confirmed.

Freeman shrugged. 'I've been red-flagged. You know what I know.'

'Come on, buddy.'

Freeman stared out across the fractured ice in the tidal basin. The thing was, he wanted to trust Bohlayer and there weren't many people he felt that about.

'Believe me, I'm on your side, Michael. Tit for tat. If you tell me what you know, I'll tell you what I know . . .'

'OK,' Freeman said, thinking that sometimes you had to go with your gut. He told him about the hard drive that he had recovered from Oleg Davidov's laptop that had been subsequently stolen and his belief that he had uncovered a spy ring that had been trading sex for influence in a broad conspiracy to subvert the legislature. He described a clandestine behavioural modification programme called Progress that was run by the Soviet KGB. He said that the dead girl was part of that programme. She was trained to exploit the sexual vulnerabilities of men. He told Bohlayer that someone was savagely killing witnesses and anyone even tangentially connected to the case. He said that there might be a connection to a criminal gang operating in Georgia, the Ras Serditye – the Furies.

Bohlayer listened attentively throughout and when Freeman had finished he nodded thoughtfully.

'Your turn,' Freeman told him.

'You don't get to share this information,' Bohlayer insisted.

Freeman nodded to show that he understood.

'Back in August 2008. Just after the Russia-Georgia war kicked off, the CIA station chief in Georgia received a request from the Pentagon to lift a party of four Russian nationals all from the same family out of Tbilisi and deliver them to an airfield in North Carolina, no questions asked.'

'And?'

'That's it. We did it. We re-routed the return leg of a rendition flight. We didn't ask any questions.'

'Jesus,' Freeman said. Detective Vashadze had been right.

'It doesn't look so smart now,' Bohlayer conceded. 'The Monday morning quarterbacks at Langley are having a field day.'

'What does the Pentagon have to say about it?' Freeman asked.

'They're in lock-down, full-fledged denial. Ever since we asked them what the hell was going on they've been treating us like a hostile nation. Whatever they think they were doing organising for this family to come into the US they miscalculated in a big way. Our guess is, they're in all kinds of shit.'

'What about Senator Cannon?'

'He's implicated, that's for sure. Why else would he have people following you?'

'So what are you going to do?' Freeman asked.

'I'm going to report back on what you told me. I'm going to wait on further instructions. What I can tell you is the Agency is very unhappy about being dragged into this.'

'What about a name for the family you transported?'

'Markoff. That's what they submitted on the passenger list. That's all I've got, buddy.'

'Great.'

'Be careful out there,' Bohlayer said. He took a cell phone battery out of his pocket and handed it to Freeman. 'I'll be in touch.'

THIRTY-SEVEN

Seven missed calls.

Freeman inserted the battery and switched on his cell as he trudged back along Ohio Drive and seconds later it began pulsing in his hand. Two from the Chief of Police's office, one from Assistant Chief of Police Streeks, one from the Medical Examiner Kaplan, one from Maja, one from Winnie Love Diggs and one from his wife. He dialled the Chief of Police's office first and was put straight through to Thielen.

'I got a call from the senator's office,' she said. 'Do you have any hard evidence that places the car, the lobbyist, the driver or the Jane Doe at the senator's house on the night of her murder?'

'We're calling her Katja. The Jane Doe, I mean.'

'What are you up to?'

'I'm just ruling out all eventualities,' he said evenly, reminding himself that the Chief had every reason to worry. If it turned out that Katja was killed on the senator's property then her decision to join the mayor at the senator's house so soon after the murder was going to look incredibly naive.

'Don't pretend you're that stupid, Michael,' she said. 'You move in political circles. You know the trouble you're causing.'

'I'm doing my job, Chief.'

'It's a high stakes game you're playing, Michael. You put a foot wrong it won't just be your job you lose. Do you understand me?'

'I understand.'

She cut the connection.

He spotted a cab and started waving his arms. On his way back to the Cosmos Club to collect his car, he called Assistant Chief Streeks's office and was told by a receptionist to report to him immediately.

'I'm on my way,' he lied.

He called Kaplan but the Medical Examiner's phone was switched off. He called Maja who told him that she'd found a former spy up on U Street who could visually read a barcode.

'I'll meet you there in fifteen,' he told her.

Next, he called Winnie who told him that she had been reviewing footage from the cameras in the lobby of the Kennedy-Warren on the night of the murder. She had Oleg Davidov getting into Byron Bastian's Town Car at 9.22 p.m. on the night of the murder.

No sign of Katja.

'They must have collected her from somewhere else,' Freeman said.

Freeman contemplated returning his wife's call but decided to put it off until later.

He spotted Maja standing on the sidewalk, beside the empty lot that hosted the flea market at the weekends. Beside her a tall, sharp-featured black man with a receding hairline was staring gravely into the trunk of an ancient Pontiac Bonneville complete with fins. Freeman guessed he was in his sixties. He was wearing a Barbour jacket, its waxed cotton gone the shade of cow dung. As he joined them, Freeman glanced in the trunk at the rows of container store boxes packed with electronics.

'Is this the fellow?' the man asked in an imperious tone.

'It's him,' Maja confirmed.

The man gave Freeman his business card. It said: *Hagos Afwerki. Code breaker. Former Counter Revolutionary Investigation Department.* A DC cell number.

'Counter Revolutionary Investigation Department?'

'Ethiopian intelligence services,' Afwerki explained.

More cloak and dagger shit, Freeman thought.

'Show me the barcode,' Afwerki said.

Freeman produced a blow-up of the tattoo from his jacket and handed it to Afwerki who retrieved a jeweller's loupe from his voluminous pockets and proceeded to examine the photo in detail.

'How old is the tattoo?' Afwerki asked, without looking up.

'At least ten years,' Freeman replied.

'It's a 128 barcode,' Afwerki told them, 'commonly used in shipping and distribution, a superset of the Universal Product Code system. The tattooist has inked black bars on a white rectangle, thereby including the spaces and quiet zones. It's skilfully done. The symbol is made up of a leading quiet zone, a dialect code, the data itself, a check character, a stop character and a trailing quiet zone. All 128 barcodes have the same stop bar pattern on the right side of the barcode symbol, so provided that the skin has stretched evenly in the intervening time it should be possible to calculate the weights and values of the coded bars and spaces using the stop bar pattern as a key. Let me see.'

They waited patiently while Afwerki minutely inspected the photo.

'There are three dialects of 128 – A, B and C. This is C, which is numeric only. It is followed by what looks like a country of origin number, a factory number, batch/lot number, a production date and an individual serial number.'

'What's the country of origin?' Freeman asked.

Afwerki looked at him. 'It's no longer in use.'

'What is it?'

'The Soviet Union.'

'You're sure.'

He shrugged. 'I trained there.'

'And the factory?'

Afwerki ran a hand over the dome of his forehead. 'It's triple zero. I thought it was a myth, a story you told recruits to scare them. It's the Scientific and Experimental Production Base in Stepnogorsk.'

'So?'

'They made weapons there, Lieutenant, biological weapons, smallpox, anthrax, stuff like that.'

Freeman and Maja exchanged nervous glances.

'I'll call the Medical Examiner's office,' Maja said. She took out her cell and walked to the corner.

Afwerki and Freeman were left staring at each other.

'Do you have paper and a pen?' Afwerki said. 'I'll write down the numbers for you.'

Freeman passed him his notebook and pen. He glanced towards Maja. She was standing at the kerb with an index finger raised, listening and nodding gravely.

'She's a special lady,' Afwerki said and handed him back his notebook.

'She is,' Freeman agreed.

'Do me a favour. Look after her, will you?'

'Of course.'

Afwerki gave him a sceptical look.

Maja summoned Freeman over. 'A Homeland Security Hazmat response team arrived at the morgue with a team of US marshalls and a warrant about an hour ago. They took the bodies.'

THIRTY-EIGHT

The Medical Examiner's building was cordoned off with yellow incident tape.

Freeman and Maja arrived at 1 p.m. The bodies were long gone but there were still several Homeland Security and US Marshall Service vehicles parked in front of the entrance and officers in Hazmat suits and respirators going in and out carrying bottles of disinfectant. In response to his demand to see the warrant Freeman was shown one signed by the Office of the Inspector General of the Federal Emergency Management Agency FEMA.

'Where have you taken them?'

'Bethesda Naval Hospital,' a marshall told him. 'They are now under military jurisdiction.'

'Department of Defense is behind this?'

The marshall shrugged. 'Couldn't say.'

Freeman turned to Maja who was approaching from the parking lot; behind her the morgue's staff were standing shivering in the snow.

'Where's Kaplan?'

Maya shook her head. 'Nobody knows. He went missing shortly after these goons showed up acting all *X-Files*.'

Freeman called Kaplan's cell but got put through to voicemail. 'Call me,' he said, after the tone.

'What's going on?' Maja asked. He'd never seen her look so unsure of herself.

'Pentagon is clearing up,' he told her. 'Without the bodies we've got no case.'

'What are you going to do?'

'Go talk to Streeks.'

★ ★ ★

Half an hour later at Police Headquarters, Assistant Chief of Police Streeks looked up from the report on his desk and stared stony-faced at Freeman.

'What do you expect me to do with this?'

'I thought it was important that you were in full possession of the facts.'

'What facts? I see no facts.'

Streeks was a man who dealt in certainties. The first time he'd been called to the Assistant Chief's office, soon after his transfer from Detroit, Streeks had pointed a finger at Freeman and said, 'Don't ever take a step in my office without being prepared to back up whatever it is you have to say.'

'I'm making progress,' Freeman insisted.

'Are you?'

'Yes.'

There was a pause. Streeks made no effort to hide his disappointment. 'That's it? Just yes? I could suspend you now for gross negligence and wanton conduct. By your own admission you have caused the loss of a computer hard drive containing evidence that might have been vital in solving this case. And I don't need to tell you how bad it looks that you have lost your service weapon.' He paused and looked again at the report on his desk. 'I should remove you from this investigation.'

'That would be a mistake.'

Streeks shook his head. 'You insist on calling the victim Katja. You claim that she was a Russian spy, you claim that she was part of an elaborate plot to blackmail senior politicians, you suggest that she was killed at the senator's house, you suggest a cover-up involving a mysterious assassin who belongs to a criminal gang called . . . let me get this straight – the Furies. On top of that you accuse the Department of Defense of tampering and obstruction, but you have produced not a shred of credible evidence to back up any of your allegations.'

'I want her body back. I want all the bodies.'

'I've been told that's impossible. The Department of Defense will retain the bodies for further testing. There is a risk of infection. They may have to be destroyed.'

'It's bullshit. This is a blatant attempt to close down this case.'

'It may be.'

'Of course it is. I'm getting too close to the truth here.'

'What you're doing is making it very difficult for this department to defend you or your conduct of this investigation.'

'I'll solve this case,' Freeman said, and then for effect, 'if it's the last thing I do.'

Streeks was unimpressed. 'The way you're going it may be the last thing you do.'

THIRTY-NINE

Across town at the Watergate, Freeman hurriedly gathered his team in the basement garage, away from the microphones. It was 2.30 p.m.

He could tell from the expressions on their faces that the death of Hector had hit them hard. They had lost Byron, the only known witness to Katja's murder and they now believed, as he did, that the Pentagon was deliberately impeding the investigation. It was no surprise that they were beginning to lose their confidence in his leadership. He had failed in his duty of care and one of their number had paid the price. But he would not give up and he would not let them give up either.

He needed to re-focus them on doing their jobs, to coax them into his way of thinking.

'Let's track this thing through,' he said, 'from the beginning. Step by step. Winnie, you start. Last movements.'

She tucked her thumbs into the waist of her voluminous pants and stared at the floor for a time before responding. 'Byron Bastian attended his regular NA meeting. He did not share. We know he rarely shared and he never talked about his work. He then took a bus over the Anacostia and reported promptly for work as usual at the Cardinal Limousine Services yard at 8.45 p.m. He picked up a freshly valeted Lincoln Town Car and drove it out the gate at 9.00 p.m. exactly. The client was a defence lobbying company called Potomac Global Security. It was a regular job, two or three times a month. Always the same driver, Byron Bastian, and always the same first stop. At 9.20 p.m. he pulled up at the lobby of the Kennedy-Warren and Oleg Davidov, also known as Olivier Davide, sole director of Potomac Global Securities, got in. He was wearing a suit and a pair of shoes both purchased at the Bloomingdales in Friendship Heights in October last year. We have witness testimony from the doorman and camera footage from two vantage points. The vehicle was filmed entering Crestwood shortly after ten p.m. At 1.15 a.m. the same Town Car was captured on camera leaving Crestwood in a hurry and subsequently runs lights at 16th Street and New York Avenue.'

'So we have just under three hours to account for,' Freeman said. 'What happened?'

'Katja was tied down and had sex with three men,' Maja said, 'including Byron Bastian and Oleg Davidov.'

'How do we know she's called Katja?' Eli asked.

'We just do,' Freeman told him.

An uncomfortable silence followed.

'A gang-bang?' Kari Marschalk asked eventually. 'Is that what this was?'

'If she was tied down she may not have been able to defend herself,' Maja said.

'Let's play at conjecture here,' Freeman told them, because without the hard drive that was all that he had to offer them. 'We'll throw some ideas around. Let's just say, for a moment, Oleg Davidov's lobbying activities extend to pimping out the victim, who is also Russian, in order to obtain political favour on behalf of a client.'

'If she's some kind of high-end Russian escort what is she doing having sex with the driver?' Marschalk asked.

'Maybe he's part of the service,' Maja said. 'A big black stallion. Available to perform if required.'

'Go on,' Freeman said.

Maja took it up. 'She was tied down on a flat surface, possibly a table, using nylon straps. She had sex with three men and then she was murdered. She was beaten to death with a hammer. Twenty or thirty blows. The killer took his time. He was careful to entirely erase her face. It's a distinctive method of operation.'

'Where are we on forensics?' Freeman said.

'Nothing,' Maja replied. 'No prints, hair or fibres.'

'Anyone know where we are on cold cases?'

'McCafferty's not saying,' Winnie told him.

'OK, we'll come back to McCafferty,' he said. 'So what happened next?'

'Byron panicked,' Eli told them, hunching forward in his chair, pulling on his beard. 'This was not the outcome he expected. He'd put all that stuff behind him. And he'd got a thing for Katja. Faced with a murder, he freaked out and drove away, leaving Davidov holding the body, literally.'

'That's consistent with what Byron told me last night. He said the killer was laughing at them.'

'Of course he was,' Maja said, 'he'd implicated them in the murder. Maybe he even knew their DNA was on file. He invited them to have sex with the girl and then he murdered her. Davidov, who had brought the body, wasn't left with any choice but to dispose of it.'

'So what happened next?'

'The witness, Harriet Armstrong, saw Oleg Davidov in the park trying to carry the body away from the scene of the crime wrapped in a tarpaulin,' Maja answered. 'But he wasn't strong enough. It was snowing, he was freezing cold, he wasn't dressed for it and he lost a shoe. So he dumped the body and fled. He ran south on Beach Drive and west on Porter to Connecticut. Back at his apartment in the Kennedy-Warren he strips off his clothes and sticks them in a bag under the sink. He takes a shower. We don't have his cell phone, but we have video footage of him using it as he was walking back, and not long after he arrived someone turned up at his door. Oleg knew his killer, or had reason to trust him, because he opened the door to him. Either way it was a big mistake. He was savagely attacked and then killed.'

They were on a roll. 'Come on,' Freeman demanded, 'what happened next?'

'Davidov's killer went straight to the site where Katja's body was dumped,' Maja said. 'My guess is he was expecting to find the body there and recover it. He didn't know that Davidov was spotted dropping the body. He wasn't expecting the police. When he was disturbed at the scene, he hospitalised a uniform from the Park Police and gave you a nasty gash, Michael.'

'Next?'

'The break-in at Cardinal Limousine Services,' Eli responded. 'The killer went in over the fence and pulled Byron Bastian's address from his personnel file and headed down to Anacostia. Byron wasn't in but his sister Renee was. The killer broke down the door and attacked and killed her.'

'Why kill Renee Bastian?' Marschalk asked.

'The killer does not value human life,' Maja said. 'He lacks empathy.'

'Somebody is eliminating potential witnesses or enacting revenge on those who stood by and watched the murder,' Freeman said. 'And he doesn't hesitate to kill anybody like Renee who gets in his way. Let's go back to Byron.'

'He dumped the car in the river,' Eli said, 'and headed out to find his old friend Dezmine Felder and ask him for shelter. Dezmine stuck him in a stash house in the abandoned low-rises in Washington Highlands. Byron, who was more than aware of how much shit he was in and who had been clean since he went down for manslaughter, decided for no good reason it was time to get high.'

'Then what?'

'Byron called you,' Eli said. 'We traced the call to Washington Highlands and tasked an emergency response team. Instead of the usual we got a SWAT team from Pentagon Police. They broke down the door. We arrested Byron. 'Bout the same time, our killer overpowered one of the snipers on a nearby rooftop. Smashed his head up and down on the balustrade until he was unconscious.'

'How do we know it's our killer?'

'Prints on the sniper's helmet match those recovered from Renee and Oleg's murder scenes.'

'Have we got a description from the sniper?'

'Naw,' Eli said, 'it was all over too fast.'

'Go on.'

'As we were bringing Byron out the killer shot us up with a mil spec rifle. Hector went down, then Byron, then one of the Pentagon assaulters named Roach.'

'When we lost Byron, we lost the only person who could ID the killer,' Marschalk said.

'Maybe not the only person,' Freeman said. 'We need to know who the third man that Katja had sex with is. If it's not the killer then it's someone who likely witnessed the murder and can identify the killer.'

'We should ask the senator and his chief of staff for voluntary DNA samples,' Maja suggested.

'Unless we can prove that Katja was killed on the senator's property,' Freeman said, 'there's no reason for them to agree to it.'

'Public pressure might do it.'

'What do you mean?'

'What if an anonymous source tips off the press that Metro PD are considering a request to the senator and his aides to give DNA samples to rule them out of the investigation. The cable networks will go wild for it. If the senator looks like he might refuse he appears guilty in the public eye.'

'Do it,' Freeman said. Next, he looked at Eli Wrath and Kari Marschalk. 'I need you two to review the case notes the detective from Georgia sent over. I want to know for sure it's the same killer.'

'Sure,' they said in unison.

He glanced at Winnie. 'Davidov was registered as a defence lobbyist working for Germline BioSciences. Senator Cannon's subcommittee approves research grants for defence projects through DARPA, the Defense Advanced Research Projects Agency. Take a look at their budget estimates. See if you can find a grant to Germline BioSciences. Then maybe we have a link.'

'OK, boss.'

'Yes, and find out what the hell has happened to Kaplan. Speak to his wife.'

'What are you going to do?' Maja asked.

'I'm going out to Maryland to Germline BioSciences.'

FORTY

They had been walking in the grounds, following the perimeter wall.

By mid-afternoon, Harry could feel the effects of last night's drinking in the dull ache between her eyes. What had she been thinking, getting wasted the night before her first day at work? Note to self: *get a grip!* She was wearing a pair of Eva's wellington boots that were several sizes too large for her and she gracelessly clomped through the snow. Eva had surprisingly large feet. And large hands. Everything about her was surprising, unnerving even, from her acrobatic skills to her flirtatious smile. Harry couldn't get enough of that smile. It cut right through her hangover and left her wanting more. She felt giddy and impetuous.

She tried to concentrate on the job in hand, protecting Eva. The more she thought about it, the more she wondered what she had let herself in for. The place was an armed camp in a state of obvious readiness. As far as she could tell there was only one way in or out of the property and that was through the front gate. Cameras and motion sensors were sited on the perimeter and throughout the grounds. There was a two-man twenty-four-hour guard in a booth at the gate with an intercom linked to the house and another guard monitoring the video screens from a small room adjacent to the front door of the house. There was a direct line to the Uniformed Division of the Secret Service and a panic button in every room. The windows were bulletproof. The house even had a stronghold, a fortified panic room with its own air supply on the first floor. She could tell from the outline of his suit that Yuri was armed. They appeared about as ready as they could be, Harry thought, but ready for what – a full-frontal assault? So much for the babysitting job she was promised.

Eva passed her the Curve.

do u like USA?

Harry stopped and typed:

The people are very friendly and generous

i like AMERICA also u can b whatever u want 2 b where i come from its impossible!

Tell me about yourself?

What do u want 2 no?

Start at the beginning

Eva smiled as if they had agreed to play an amusing game.

ok i was born in KAZAKHSTAN u know it?

Two I mean 2! up from Afghanistan?

yupp!!!

Harry smiled back. She watched Eva crinkle her nose as she concentrated on composing a longer message:

KAZAKHSTAN was still a part of USSR though not for long we lived 20 miles outside STEPNOGORSK on the steppe like nomads my uncle SASHA was running primate breeding programme PROGRESS & collapse of USSR meant it was very difficult :-(there was no money no food 4 years & years & we had problems – the lab burned down & gangsters came & we had 2 run away & we went to hide in SVANETIA u know where it is???Harry shook her head.

a cold place!!!hi up in CAUCASUS mountains

What happened to your parents?

Eva looked at her feet.

they r dead

I'm sorry to hear that

She looked up.

what about u?

Harry shrugged and typed.

My mother is an academic. She teaches a dead language. She doesn't approve of what I do. My stepfather is also an academic. He has a very high opinion of himself

ur real father?

She shook her head.

My real father died when I was 13

u understand

They began walking again. After several steps Eva reached out for Harry's hand. Harry remembered it well, the time before her father's death. They were living in Edinburgh, in army quarters close to Redford Barracks. Her father came and went, disappearing for days at a time and then reappearing out of the blue. Suddenly, he'd be there waiting for her at the school gates.

'How's school?' he'd ask, the same way he did every time.

'Fine.'

'What did you learn?'

'Stuff.'

'What kind of stuff?'

'All sorts of stuff.'

Silence would fill the car and in case he tried again she'd respond in kind: 'How's work?'

'Fine.'

'What did you do?'

'Stuff.'

There were no lies and no truths in their relationship. Only ambiguities. He was usually gone again the next morning. Then one time he didn't come back. Over time, Harry had come to realise that with each year that passed a child took a step away from its parents, but when you had lost a parent, you were walking backwards, still moving away but looking to the past for clues and hints about your loss.

On 13 June 1988 Harry's father's car was blown up outside a pub in Crossmaglen, Northern Ireland. He was a thirty-five-year-old soldier on an undisclosed assignment. The army told the family only that he had died at the scene. The regiment treated the family well. The body was shipped back to England, and they covered all funeral expenses, and organised for her father's name to be added to the list of those fallen on the clock tower at Hereford.

But no one ever explained what happened or why. And because it was so sudden Harry never really believed that he died. Her parents had been fighting a lot before he died and she thought that her father wanted to leave. Maybe he had received prior warning about the bomb placed beneath the wheel arch of his car. He had slipped away. He'd run across the fields and disappeared into the woods. He was living a parallel life in Brazil, with a beautiful Brazilian wife and better looking children.

That's why they never saw the body. Her brother had speculated that it was because he was 'burned beyond recognition'. Harry knew better. But she had the sense not to talk about it. She kept the truth to herself.

It made you wary, losing a parent.

They had stopped again. Eva was standing typing. Behind them, Yuri had also stopped, as if playing grandmother's footsteps. Harry had decided that there was something definitely creepy about him. Eva nudged her with the BlackBerry:

we hav 2 go 2 the lab :-)

why?

4 a sonogram & 2 see the PEACEFUL

Peaceful?

BONOBOS – a kind ov ape

What will your uncle say?

Eva smiled. It lit up her face.

its fine we can take the TANK

With that, she kicked away her wellington boots and took off across the grounds in a string of spectacular cartwheels and flips. When Harry caught up with her she was dusting the snow off her hands.

Harry passed her the boots and her Curve.

Eva linked her arm through Harry's again and they walked back to the house.

It turned out the tank was a two-and-a-half-ton armoured Chevy Tahoe with half-inch-thick windows, run-flat tyres and a Cambodian driver known only as Suthy. Yuri rode in the front with him and Harry and Eva sat on the cream leather seats in the back. The outside world seemed muffled and indistinct.

They glided north along Connecticut.

FORTY-ONE

The facade of Germline BioSciences Laboratories was an undulating wall of mirrored glass, a two-hundred-foot-long oscillation wave. It was set back from the road on a snow-covered lawn dotted with several mature trees, oaks and magnolias. There was a small demonstration outside. Five people, men and women dressed in hats and parkas, with colourful scarves and wellington boots, were waving handwritten placards, with quotes from the Old Testament: *And if a man lie with a beast, he shall surely be put to death: and ye shall slay the beast.*

More crazies making death threats, Freeman thought. They crowded around the car as he approached the gates. One of them slapped a hand on the window of his car and Freeman hit the siren and lights simultaneously and they scattered. Two uniformed guards emerged from a booth and stood by as the gates opened. Freeman drove past them and up the sweeping driveway to the building. He parked in a space reserved for visitors and approached his reflection in the mirrored wall.

'Lieutenant Freeman,' he said to the freestanding brushed-steel intercom. 'DC Homicide.'

'Homicide,' a voice repeated, politely but neutrally, as if the word was unfamiliar.

'That's right. I'm police.'

'Yes,' said the voice. 'We don't have any record of an appointment.'

'I can be back here with a warrant and a SWAT team in an hour or so and we'll break some glass. You want to go down that road?'

'One moment please.'

Freeman looked away. Traffic swished by on the Rockville Pike.

He saw that the protesters had given up waving their placards and were now huddling around a fire in an oil drum. On the lawn an old Hispanic man was shovelling snow into a mound against the perimeter fence. It was a beautiful winter's day. The light seemed preternaturally clear and bright.

A door opened in the glass behind him and he turned to see a glowing white room and a small man in a dark blue blazer with an apologetic smile. The word RAEBURN was written in white lettering on his left breast.

'I'm sorry about the delay,' he said. 'Please come in. Our Chief Scientist will be with you presently.'

The man crossed behind the reception desk and sat down in front of a monitor with a camera mounted on it. On the wall behind the desk there was a six-foot-long multicoloured horizontal band, like a candy cane, made up of what looked like several hundred vertical strips of bright blue, red, green and black. Below it, at the right end of the band, GERMLINE BIOSCIENCES was written in black lettering.

'Your badge?'

Freeman handed it over to him.

'Place your thumb on the pad on the desk. And look into the camera. Thank you.'

'That's an interesting logo.'

'It's a barcode.'

The man handed Freeman back his badge and then a minute or so later a pass on a lanyard, with his photo and fingerprint on it and VISITOR written in large red diagonal lettering. As he was hanging it around his neck, a set of double doors on the far side of the room hissed and thumped on hydraulic-cushioned hinges, and a tall, slightly stooped man entered the room. He had very pale skin, watery blue eyes and swept-back grey hair that fell either side of his forehead. He strode towards Freeman with a plastic and placatory smile on his face.

'I'm Dr Alexander Ilyanovich Markoff,' he said, holding out his hand for Freeman to shake. 'Very pleased to meet you.'

Markoff was the name on the passenger list of the family flown out of the Republic of Georgia by the CIA, that's what Baba John Bohlayer had told Freeman that morning. Was the dead girl in Rock Creek Park related to this man? Had she come to America with him on the rendition flight?

'I was asking about your logo,' Freeman said, to give himself time to think.

'Of course.' Dr Markoff's smile widened. His hands were soft and his nails were manicured. 'People are often interested.'

Freeman got the feeling that they weren't.

'What is it?'

'It is what we call DNA barcode. It uses a short DNA sequence from a section in the genome as a diagnostic for species identification.'

'What does that mean?'

Dr Markoff raised his eyebrows. 'Very well, it's a colour-coded chart of a sequence of four nucleotides in the Folmer region of the genome. The four nucleotides are cytosine, adenine, thymine and guanine. In this particular case blue, green, red and black. The arrangement of patterns determines whether your eyes are blue or brown, Lieutenant, or whether an organism is a zebra or perhaps a zebra fish. By recording the precise order of the nucleotides we produce a de facto barcode that defines each unique species. And it resembles a supermarket barcode, yes?'

'What is it?' Freeman asked.

'I'm sorry?'

'The barcode on the wall, what species is it?'

The smile became a painful grimace. 'It's a confection,' Dr Markoff explained, 'a mixture of species. Not a real thing. For fun, really.'

'I see.'

There was a pause.

'What am I able to do for you, Lieutenant?'

'I'm investigating a homicide. Several in fact.'

Dr Markoff frowned. 'I'm very sorry to hear it.'

'One of the victims appears to have had a link to this company. Oleg Davidov, also known as Olivier Davide.'

'I'm sorry, I don't recognise these names. He's not an employee of Germline BioSciences, I think.'

'He was a registered lobbyist and according to Congress you were his client.'

Dr Markoff lifted his eyebrows again. 'How strange. I don't believe we undertake any manner of lobbying activities.'

'I'd like to know more about what you do here,' Freeman said, after a pause.

'How about I give you a tour?'

'OK.'

'Please, follow me.'

Dr Markoff led him to the double doors. 'Put your thumb on the pad.'

The doors hissed open. They were in a long corridor with the same glowing backlit white walls as the reception area. Air ventilators throbbed loudly. On one wall there was a row of high windows looking onto a large courtyard with a glass floor suggesting a cavernous underground atrium. Dr Markoff led him towards a waiting elevator with mirrored glass walls.

'Are you Russian, Dr Markoff?' Freeman asked.

'That's right, although I was born in Kazakhstan which at that time was part of the Soviet Union. My parents and grandparents were Russian.'

'How long have you been here?'

'Since 2008.'

'You came here from Russia?'

'We came out through Georgia, as a matter of fact.'

'We?'

Dr Markoff hesitated. 'My family.'

'I see.'

'Please.'

There were three buttons on the elevator, the numbers running backwards, like in an underground garage:

Level One   Subject containment area
Level Two   Subject containment area

Level Three Main Lab

'We're going to visit with the bonobos,' Dr Markoff said, pressing the button for Level One.

'Bonobos?'

'Bonobo means ancestor in the Bantu language. Our closest relations, *Pan paniscus*, previously known as the pygmy chimpanzee; they are an endangered species of ape found in the wild only in Democratic Republic of Congo.'

With barely a whisper, the elevator took them down one floor. The doors slid open. Beyond them was a space covering several acres, a covered concrete walkway skirting a large courtyard with a glass ceiling that was flooded with light from the atrium above. A wire mesh enclosure filled the courtyard. Inside the enclosure there were a few trees and hardy shrubs, rope swings and children's playground equipment. There was a penetrating odour in the air, the muskiness of a zoo.

'There's a tunnel at the back of the enclosure that leads to a two-acre park behind the building with a high fence. The bonobos come and go as they please.'

Dr Markoff approached the mesh and Freeman followed. Just the other side an ape was sitting on a tyre chewing on a piece of sugar cane.

'This is Frank.'

The bonobo was slender with a flat face and a thick black thatch of hair on his head. His body hair was sparse though, revealing tautly muscled arms and a broad chest. He stared through the mesh at Freeman with bright black eyes and his pink lips made soft smacking noises as they chewed on the sugar cane.

'Say hello,' Dr Markoff urged Freeman, nodding his head in encouragement.

'Hello, Frank,' Freeman said, feeling self-conscious.

Frank stopped chewing for a moment and then his face stretched, and he peeled back his pink lower lips to reveal gums and sharp-looking teeth.

'Don't worry, he's smiling at you,' Dr Markoff said with what seemed like genuine enthusiasm. 'Bonobos smile and laugh just like regular human beings. They are also capable of altruism and compassion. As a matter of fact, bonobos are barely different from humans. Their blood type is indistinguishable from the human A negative blood type. And reproductively they are almost identical. The menstrual cycle is one week longer, but the physiology of the reproductive tract and the timing and amount of hormones secreted by ovaries are almost exactly the same.'

Beyond Frank, something caught Freeman's attention. Two bonobos were hanging from the same tree branch facing each other. One had its arms wrapped around the other's waist. They had swollen, pale pink genitals, which they rubbed together in a rhythmic sideways motion, making the branch vibrate.

'What are they doing?' Freeman asked.

'It's called genital-to-genital rubbing,' Dr Markoff explained with a rueful smile. 'Also tribbing.'

'Am I right in saying that they are both females?'

'That's correct. They are rubbing their vulvas together. Sexual bonding helps females form close relationships. It is an expression of friendship and for the relief of tension. Casual sexual contact, including significant homosexual activity, is common among bonobos. It is how they resolve differences. They have sex a lot. Here in captivity they initiate sexual contact on average every fifteen minutes.'

'That is a lot,' Freeman agreed.

'There are sound evolutionary excuses. Other apes, chimps and gorillas for example, have a limited oestrus cycle, so when they come into heat there is much competition and aggression, but bonobo females are sexually available all the time. There is no reason to fight over sex and so they live more peacefully than other apes. As a matter of fact, there are no confirmed observations of lethal aggression among bonobos, either in the wild or captivity. They do not do murder. The result is an increase in the survival rate of young. They make love not war.'

'It sounds like we could learn a thing or two.'

'We are learning all the time, Lieutenant,' Dr Markoff replied.

'The question we are currently trying to answer is why they don't overpopulate. Given how promiscuous they are, what keeps them from getting pregnant every time they ovulate?'

'And do you have an answer?'

'We believe that bonobos produce a pheromone, a kind of chemical signal, that acts as a contraceptive. By studying these pheromones scientists at Germline BioSciences hope to come up with a human contraceptive that is reliable, safe and easy to use. Our primary aim is to relieve women of the burden of prescriptions, injections, implants and surgery, to free women from weight gain and depression, and offer women real choice and control over their bodies. We have identified the human gene that is linked to pheromones. This gene makes a protein that allows humans to detect them. The protein is found in the mucus membrane lining the human nose.' He squeezed his nose for effect. 'Imagine, if you can, a jar of scent that a woman has only to sniff once a week. A jar that could last for her whole reproductive life. Can you imagine what the consequences for society would be?'

'Free love?'

'When overpopulation stops, competition for resources ends and so does violence.' He winked. 'We'd put you out of a job, Lieutenant.'

FORTY-TWO

Dr Alexander Markoff glanced at his watch, a stainless-steel Cartier Roadster. 'I'm afraid I have an urgent meeting at four, Lieutenant. So I'm sorry that's it for our tour.'

'You've been generous with your time but before I go could you tell me what happens on the other levels?'

'On Level Two we have another ape colony and on Level Three we have the Main Lab. That's where we undertake our research and development.'

'And if I wanted to see the other levels?'

Dr Markoff smiled apologetically. 'I'm sorry it will not be possible to visit them at this time.'

'Why not?'

The smile widened into a grimace again. 'Your pass won't allow access to those levels.'

'So give me a new pass.'

'I'm not authorised to escort you there.'

'I thought you were in charge here?'

Dr Markoff shifted from foot to foot. 'The terms under which we are funded are quite specific.'

'I'd like to see the other levels,' Freeman insisted.

'Technically speaking, the lower levels of the building are a Department of Defense restricted area under military jurisdiction. You would require special clearance from the Pentagon to access these areas.'

'You're funded by the Pentagon?'

He grimaced. 'I'm not permitted to discuss it.'

There was a pause.

'Have you heard the name of a KGB programme called Progress?' Freeman asked.

Dr Markoff smiled uneasily. 'I'm a scientist, Lieutenant, not a spy!'

'What about a place called Stepnogorsk?'

'No, I'm sorry.'

'It's in Kazakhstan. You told me you were born in Kazakhstan.'

'I have never heard of this place.'

'What about a gang called the Furies?'

'No.'

'A young woman called Katja?'

'No.'

'She's dead. Somebody beat her to death with a hammer.'

'I'm sorry. This is ridiculous.'

Dr Markoff pressed his thumb to the pad to summon the elevator.

'Why did you come here, Dr Markoff?' Freeman asked.

'To America? There is funding for my work here.'

'How long have the protesters been outside the building?'

'Since last year.'

'What are they protesting about?'

'Frankly speaking, nobody is really sure. They are not very articulate. Because my work with primates has human benefits they say that I am meddling with what it means to be human.'

'Are you?'

'We are trying to find a way to stop human beings from over-running the planet. I don't call that meddling, I call it progress.'

'Progress . . . ?'

Dr Markoff stared at him for a moment. 'I think you are reading too much into my choice of words.'

The elevator doors opened. Two women and a large bald man, as broad as he was tall, stepped out. Freeman recognised Harry Armstrong instantly. He saw the shock of recognition in her face, a tremor like the extra beat of a heart. Beside her there was a beautiful young woman with startling blue eyes.

The bald man stepped in front of the young woman to shield her, reaching across his body for the pistol in his shoulder holster.

'Don't even think about it,' Freeman said, reaching behind him for his weapon. Beside him Dr Markoff flinched.

The young woman smothered the big man's arm, preventing the gun from clearing the holster. She was wearing an amused, almost mocking expression on her face.

'It's all right, he's a policeman,' Harry added quickly, her hands out in a restraining motion.

Dr Markoff turned sorrowfully to Freeman. 'Are we really going to kill each other here?'

The stand-off ended as abruptly as it began. The bodyguard relaxed and stepped away. Freeman released his grip on the Glock in his holster and breathed out loudly.

'What the hell are you doing here?' he demanded of Harry, unnerved by the composure of the beautiful young woman beside her.

'I'm working for Dr Markoff,' Harry told him. 'I started this morning. This is Eva Markoff, the doctor's niece. I've joined her security detail.'

Freeman looked from Eva to Dr Markoff. 'You're her uncle?'

Uncle.

A mental flash of Katja on a bed, rolling a stocking up her leg: *All I know is, Uncle brought me here to America.*

'Katja,' Freeman said, watching Eva Markoff's face for a reaction. 'Did you know Katja?'

The girl stared evenly back.

'She's deaf,' Harry said. 'She can't answer your questions.'

'If you want to interview my niece,' Dr Markoff said, 'I want a lawyer present.'

Freeman glared at Harry, who still seemed shocked. Was it an act? Was it all an act? She claimed that she had been out running when she found the body and now it turned out that she was working for Dr Markoff who he was convinced had brought the dead girl with him from Georgia. Freeman didn't believe in coincidences. Harry must have lied to him, just as Dr Markoff was lying to him now.

'Please,' Dr Markoff said to Freeman, calmer now, gesturing towards the elevator.

'Come on Eva,' Harry said, steering the young woman towards the mesh enclosure.

Freeman stepped into the elevator with Dr Markoff at his side. As the doors closed, he told Harry, 'I'm going to want to talk to you again.'

There was a US marshall sitting waiting in the reception area. As they emerged through the doors, she slipped a plain envelope from her briefcase and stood up.

'Alexander Markoff?'

Dr Markoff stopped and stared uncertainly at her.

'Yes?'

She handed him the envelope. 'I am serving you with a subpoena pursuant to an authorised investigation by the Senate Armed Forces Committee. You are hereby required to attend, give testimony and produce any books, records, correspondence, memoranda, papers or documents relating to federal funding of your research work at a hearing of the Subcommittee on Emerging Threats and Technologies tomorrow at 2 p.m.'

With that she turned and exited through the door.

FORTY-THREE

As he drove out of the gate after the marshall's vehicle, Freeman's cell began to vibrate. *One missed call.* Winnie. He rolled to a halt at the kerb and called her right back.

While the phone was ringing he spotted a patrol car from Montgomery County Police Department parked alongside the protesters' makeshift encampment and a black patrolman speaking to the huddle of protesters.

'What have you got?' Freeman asked when Winnie answered.

'Zip.'

'What do you mean zip?'

'I've been back through five years of budget estimates and there is no record of defence funding for Germline BioSciences.'

'That doesn't make any sense. They've got two whole levels off-limits here and under military jurisdiction. The Chief Scientist here just got hit with a subpoena from the Armed Forces Committee and he didn't look very happy about it.'

'I'm telling you there's nothing.'

'Keep looking.'

'I will. Oh, yes, I spoke to the Medical Examiner's wife. Mrs Kaplan. She told me her husband took a flight to Boston. He was heading for Cambridge, Massachusetts, talking about some machine they've got up there at MIT.'

'Thanks, Winnie.'

Freeman ended the call. He got out of the car and walked over to the protesters.

'What's going on?' he asked, showing his badge.

'We've received a complaint,' the patrolman explained, pointing to a small serious-looking man with black spectacles. Freeman

222

recognised him as the man who slapped his hand on Freeman's window as he went through the gate. 'These people have been harassing vehicles entering the facility.'

'I've told you,' the man said in an aggrieved tone. 'All we're doing is recording the plate numbers.'

'Are you tracking vehicles going in and out of the building?' Freeman asked.

'That's right. We note it all down, even the mail vans and the laundry.'

'You have the plate numbers of every vehicle that's come in and out?'

'That's right.'

The patrolman looked at Freeman and together they walked some way off from the protesters. 'What's your name?' Freeman asked.

'Burgess.'

'Well, Burgess?'

'Look, these aren't bad people, Lieutenant. I've never had any trouble with them. One of them is in the same congregation as I am. They just have a problem with what goes on in that building and if half of what they say is true then so do I.'

'I understand,' Freeman said. 'Can you leave this with me?'

'Sure.'

Burgess got into his patrol car and drove off.

Freeman walked back to the protesters.

'I told them you were a cop,' the man with black spectacles said. 'I told them no G man would be driving that heap of junk.'

'I'm with DC Homicide. Lieutenant Michael Freeman.'

'I'm Eric Schwenk. I'm sorry that we crowded your car before.'

'That's OK. Can I ask you a question, Eric?'

'Sure, fire away.'

'Did you see a vehicle come in after I did, possibly with three passengers, two women and a man?'

'It was a Chevy Tahoe.' He produced a notebook from his pocket and opened it. 'I've got the tag number.'

'Let me see that,' Freeman said.

Schwenk handed him the notebook. Inside were handwritten lists of vehicles with plate number, make and model, colour, number of passengers and times of entry and exit meticulously recorded; there was a black Chevy Tahoe down as entering at 3.25 p.m., about twenty minutes after Freeman. He called Winnie back.

'I need you to check a plate number for me.'

He read it out to her. While he waited for the response, he flicked absentmindedly back through the pages.

'We have records going back to when Dr Markoff started working at the lab,' Schwenk told him.

Winnie came back on the line. 'The Tahoe is registered to Raeburn Correctional Services, a private company registered in Tennessee that runs sixty-three adult and juvenile correctional facilities in twenty-one states.' Raeburn had been the name on the jacket of the security guard at reception. 'I got a list of the board of directors. Guess who's on it?'

'Tell me.'

'James D. Cannon.'

'That figures.'

A private prison company associated with Cannon was providing security for the research laboratory and armoured transport to its Chief Scientist's niece, not to mention his witness, Harry Armstrong. While he was pondering this, Freeman flicked back through the pages again, scanning the comings and goings over the last couple of days.

He stopped, staring at the page in front of him.

On the night of the murder a Black Lincoln Town Car arrived at 9.37 p.m. and departed at 9.48 p.m. Tinted windows – *number of occupants unknown.*

'Hang on, Winnie. I've got another request. Give me the plate number of Byron's Town Car.'

Winnie read it back to him.

'Shit,' Freeman breathed. It was a match. Byron Bastian had spent eleven minutes at Germline BioSciences on the night of the murder. He must have come straight here from the Kennedy-Warren after picking up Oleg Davidov at 9.20 p.m. Freeman realised that this must be where they'd collected Katja. From here they'd driven her to Crestwood on her final journey.

'Winnie, I'm going to send someone to you in a taxi. He has a notebook which I want you to log as evidence.'

He glanced at the man in the black spectacles who was watching him expectantly. 'Mr Schwenk, I need you to go downtown and give a statement.'

'I'd be happy to.'

'Can I ask you a question?'

'Sure. Anything.'

'What is it you think they're doing in there?'

Schwenk took off his glasses and wiped them with a handkerchief. 'Don't you know?'

'Illuminate me.'

'They're building monsters, Lieutenant. Real-life monsters.'

FORTY-FOUR

There was no time for hesitation. No time for second thoughts. No time to wonder what the hell a battered-looking Michael Freeman of the DC Police was doing here at the lab.

Eva took her firmly by the hand and propelled Harry to a small door set in the cage containing the bonobos. She placed her outstretched palm against an electronic pad and the door clicked open in front of them. They were in. The cage door clicked shut behind them. They were trapped. The apes were swinging down from the trees and Eva was gesticulating with her fingers, repeatedly interlocking her index fingers.

'What are you doing?' Harry asked, frozen on the spot.

Eva squatted and pulled Harry down beside her. She squeezed Harry's arm and then stood up again and backed towards the door. Suddenly they were too far apart to pass the BlackBerry back and forth. When Harry gave her a panicked look, Eva motioned for her to stay put.

'aaai tol 'em 'ur fr'en'ly . . .'

The apes formed a watchful semicircle around Harry. Five adults, including a couple of mothers cradling infants. They gave off an incredibly strong and musky odour.

'Fuck,' Harry muttered.

The apes were shooting nervous glances in Eva's direction.

'iii's o'ay,' Eva said, signing to the chimps.

The nearest bonobo reached out for Harry's hand. It was a large male.

'aaats 'Ank.'

'Ank (Hank, Frank, whatever . . .) lifted Harry's hand to his mouth and kissed it. She felt the warm wetness of his tongue on her fingers. He looked into her eyes and pulled her to him, stroking her back and neck with his leathery palms.

''eee's fr'en'ly.'

'Friendly?'

''es!'

What the hell, Harry thought and started stroking him back. Her nose was filled with the smell of 'Ank's fruity breath and the musky odour of his skin and fur. The long hair on his back was like rough raw silk in her hands. His muscular chest was pressed against her breasts. It wasn't an unpleasant experience; in fact, it was a bit like cuddling a large and rather smelly teddy bear.

'Ank began to vocalise, a high-toned moaning with short vowel sounds and pants, and then suddenly Harry became aware of his penis, long and erect, brushing her thighs. Embarrassed, she pulled away and the ape immediately released her. He turned and climbed up a nearby pole to a platform where he busied himself with an old running shoe, ripping and closing the Velcro fastening. The rest of the bonobos retreated.

Eva was standing by her side again, offering the Curve.

    ur blushing!!!

Harry typed a response:

    A monkey never made a pass at me before.

    APE not MONKEY! its time 2 go wave w/ right hand

Harry looked up at the ape on the platform and waved. 'Ank waved back.

They were in the elevator. Eva had paused with her finger about to press the button for Level Three. Harry was showing her the Curve.

    What's on Level 2?

Eva was wearing the same expression as when Harry first met her beside the monstrous snowman in the grounds of the Chevy Chase house: half mocking, half mischievous.

    more APES

    Can I see them?

    r u sure u want 2?

Harry smiled.

Yes. I'm obviously a big hit with the apes on Level 1, why not Level 2?

difrent kind ov APE

So show me!

Eva pressed the button for Level Two.

FORTY-FIVE

They emerged from the elevator into a dimly lit and humid space. The smell was eye-watering: a pungent mix of sweat, faeces and ammonia.

UNCLE calls it the DIRTY PROTEST

Unlike the bonobo habitat, the enclosure on Level Two was behind a floor-to-ceiling wall of reinforced glass; at first glance it seemed to be almost opaque but as she drew closer Harry realised it was smeared with shit. Eva tugged on her arm. It was the first time that Harry had seen her display any sign of nervousness. She tugged again.

dont touch the glass!!!

What are they?

HAMADRYAS BABOONS

Harry was just a foot or so from the glass, when a shadow fell across her face. A fleeting glimpse of a jutting mouth, its crooked teeth bared in a snarl and then a fully spread and very human-looking hand slapped against the glass so that it vibrated like a gunshot.

Harry stumbled backwards, startled.

Eva grabbed her and pulled her towards the elevator.

Shapes moved at frightening speed in the darkness and there was a frenzied howling. Fists pounded on the filthy glass.

Inside the elevator Eva punched the button for Level Three.

FORTY-SIX

They exited the elevator on Level Three. Harry stumbled out into a white foyer with two bulkhead doors and a sign that read: AUTHORISED PERSONNEL ONLY BIOLOGICAL HAZARDS PRESENT, NO EATING, DRINKING OR SMOKING.

She stood half-bent, catching her breath with her hands on her thighs.

Standing in front of her, Eva was holding up her Curve with her familiar mocking expression restored:

i guess they didnt like u on L2 :-(

Harry snatched the Curve off her:

What happened to them?

UNCLE gave them bigger brains & better working thumbs

'What the hell?'

its PROGRESS! come on

Eva opened one of the bulkhead doors into an all-white, windowless corridor that curved away to the left and right and appeared to have no end.

its called THE BELTWAY come on

As they proceeded, a shaggy and reddish-brown shape appeared out of the dissolving whiteness.

Harry stopped in her tracks.

Eva looked from Harry to the shape shambling towards them and back again.

Its OK we r on L3

'Is that supposed to be reassuring?'

It was an orang-utan.

He was about four foot high and grossly obese, Harry guessed more than three hundred pounds. His long arms and broad

230

shoulders were covered in a cloak of matted auburn hair that was shot through with streaks of grey.

Eva squatted down beside him. Initially he shrank back, but then she put her arms around him and he pursed his lips and kissed her. He had a broad flat face framed by cheek flaps, a huge upper lip and tiny nostrils. A red-tufted beard. Pendulous man-breasts. Eva released him and showed Harry the Curve:

JOSEF

'Right,' Harry said. 'As long as he doesn't bite.'

he has 100 RUSSIAN signs! u can say hello

'Hello,' Harry said.

The orang-utan reached over Eva's shoulder with an incredibly long arm and shook Harry's hand. His palm was dry and leathery. His eyes were hooded and watchful. When he let go, Eva signed at him and after a pause he signed back, his hands moving slowly and deliberately. Then he grunted and continued on his way, leaving Harry staring after him. Eva nudged her with the Curve:

he says ur very pretty he likes blondes ;-)

Eva took her by the hand.

After a hundred yards or so they came to a door with a sign: MAIN LAB.

They heard Dr Markoff before they saw him. He was in a rage. A technician in a white coverall and face-mask scurried past them in the corridor, fleeing the scene.

'A fucking subpoena!' Dr Markoff hissed. 'Signed by a majority of subcommittee members, personally brokered by the chairman, that bitch Oberstar. I'm telling you she wants to destroy me!' He was standing with a crumpled piece of paper in one hand and a landline on a short cord attached to the wall in the other. Opposite him was a large pane of glass and on the far side of the glass, a startled technician in a respirator and biohazard suit had stopped work at her bench and was staring at him, pipette in hand. 'What do you mean I have to show up?' he demanded. 'No choice? I pay you to give me choices. No, I don't want to be locked up. No, I don't want to go back to

Russia. What? What? What?' His face was bright red. 'Listen to me, Cannon told us we would never testify. He gave assurances!'

Spinning around, Dr Markoff saw them standing, watching him. He put a hand over the phone.

'If I don't give testimony they're going to lock me up. Maybe deport me. I'm not going back to Russia! You've got to get us out of here, Harry.'

'Right,' Harry said, not sure how to respond.

Dr Markoff returned to his conversation. 'What will I say? I'll tell them straight. I've done everything asked of me and more. And if they don't like my methods then maybe I'll go work for the Chinese . . .'

He put his hand over the phone again.

'It's time for her sonogram,' he said.

Harry was sitting on a wooden bench in a locker room, wondering if she shouldn't have paid more attention to Neil Trefoil at the ambassador's residence last night when he urged caution. She really had jumped in the deep end. And now she was struggling. Dr Markoff and his niece clearly thought she was a spy and the DC cop Freeman had obviously concluded that she was implicated in the murder of the girl in the park. The weirdness of her surroundings – the space station corridors, the silent elevators and hissing doors, the priapic bonobos, the sinister and aggressive baboons and the signing orang-utan – none of it helped.

She wished she could talk to Jack. There was no one to turn to. No advice forthcoming.

Across from her, Eva had stripped naked and was tying on a backless gown. Harry couldn't make up her mind about Eva. There was something mercurial about her, she seemed to struggle with the distinction between appropriate and inappropriate behaviour and she made even the most basic human interactions seem strange, somehow off-kilter.

Resisting the urge to pick up and fold Eva's haphazardly discarded clothes, Harry instead picked up the Curve and typed a message. She held it up for Eva to see.

Why was the police lieutenant here?

Eva shrugged. Harry typed again.

Did you know the dead girl?

She was a whore

Harry was taken aback.

She was a person. She was somebody's daughter

Eva shrugged petulantly. She looked away. Something had made her angry. She wrote another message and thrust the Curve in Harry's face.

do u think MONKEYS hav souls???

I'm not sure human beings have souls

Eva took the Curve from her and refused to hand it back.

Weirder still.

Ten minutes later, Eva was lying on an examination table with her feet in stirrups and her legs wide open. Harry was holding her hand. A female technician in green scrubs had drawn two test tubes of blood through a catheter in Eva's arm and Dr Markoff, who had calmed down considerably, was sitting between Eva's parted legs holding a long white probe with a condom on the end. He inserted the probe, moved it back and forth, and studied the grainy black and white images of ovarian follicles on the screen. To Harry's untrained eye the black fluid-filled sacks looked like the chambers in a revolver.

'Six follicles,' Dr Markoff said, apparently content. He removed the probe. 'As long as the blood work tells me it's all OK we'll be ready in two days.'

'Then what?' Harry asked.

'We harvest the eggs,' Dr Markoff replied in a matter-of-fact way, stripping off a pair of blue latex gloves.

'What do you do with them?'

'We fertilise them, of course. After that we freeze the embryos or implant them in a host.'

When Dr Markoff had gone, Eva hopped down off the table and Harry followed her back into the changing room and watched her get dressed again. She was not sure whether to feel appalled or outraged. She snatched the Curve and typed a message.

What did he mean implant them in a host?

Eva seemed annoyed.

a surrogate mother

I don't understand. What is going on here?

Eva snatched back the Curve and walked out of the dressing room, Harry trailing in her wake.

As they emerged from the underground car park in the armoured Tahoe, Harry's cell phone found a signal. She had a new voicemail. It was Neil Trefoil from the embassy and he didn't sound happy. She could imagine what it must have cost him in swallowed pride. It seemed the British intelligence community was interested after all.

'Hi, Harry, Neil here. I hope your first day in the new job is going well. Listen, I know it's short notice but I'm hoping that you can be at the Restaurant Eve in Alexandria at 7 p.m. or shortly thereafter. There's somebody over from London who wants to meet you. I'd be grateful if you could let me know whether you can attend. Just a text will do. Thanks very much. Bye.'

Harry consulted her watch. It wasn't long after 5 p.m. If she headed over to Alexandria as soon as she was due to finish for the day she could probably make it on time. She held out her hand for the Curve. Eva took it out of her pocket and handed it over.

It's the embassy. They want to talk to me.

Eva shrugged. Harry typed another message:

Do you want me to talk to them?

When she didn't receive a response, Harry texted back to confirm that she would attend and two minutes later received a reply from Trefoil.

Excellent. Thanks very much.

Eva prodded her with the Curve.

uncle SASHA sez ur our best hope!?!

What do you think?

wot does it matter! im a fukin factory hen!!!

Eva sank further into her seat and started playing a game on the Curve in which she used her thumb on the trackpad to move a cube through a puzzle towards a hole.

FORTY-SEVEN

Freeman followed the armoured Tahoe from Germline BioSciences to a compound in Chevy Chase.

It was twilight. Not long after 5 p.m. As he drove by the compound, he caught a glimpse through the gate of the Tahoe driving through lengthening shadows towards a low dark building resembling a bunker. He pulled over and parked out of sight of the two men in the guard hut by the gate. Then he called the Watergate and asked Winnie to check the county records.

Winnie called back half an hour later with the news that the house was owned by the Daedalus Foundation, a 501(c)3 not-for-profit organisation established in the 1920s with railroad money. Their most recent 990-PF tax form put them at number eighty-nine in the table of top US foundations by total giving, dispensing about seventy million dollars annually, the bulk of which went to programmes on the cutting edge of sciences – genetics, robotics, nanotechnology. The flagship programme was the Daedalus Prize that was awarded without fanfare each year to a scientist who was breaking boundaries at the forefront of science. Last year's laureate was listed as the Russian geneticist Dr Alexander Ilyanovich Markoff.

'Bingo,' Freeman said.

'I've got the foundation website up in front of me,' Winnie told him. 'It says the foundation was named after Daedalus, the mythological artisan and sculptor. There's a mission statement. The mission of the Daedalus Foundation is to ensure the perpetuation of American global technological dominance. There's also a founder's statement: "To get a bargain price you've got to look to where the public is most frightened and pessimistic."'

'Nice. Anything else?' Freeman asked, watching the two men in the guard hut by the gate, their faces lit up by video monitors.

'There's an address in Tennessee,' Winnie told him. 'A telephone number. There's a posting saying that they are not currently accepting grant applications. Hang on. Here we go. I got a list of seven trustees. Senator John T. Cannon is listed as chairman of the board.'

The Markoff family lived in a house owned by a foundation controlled by Cannon, and a private company, also controlled by Cannon, provided their personal and workplace protection.

'What about Germline BioSciences?'

'That's going to be more difficult. So far all I've got is an attorney's address in the Cayman Islands.'

'Keep digging. And tell Eli and Kari to get over here and watch the house.'

'Sure thing.'

Maja called to tell him that Cannon's attorney had issued a statement repeating the denial that the girl was on the senator's property the night she was killed. He was accusing the DC police of not fully investigating the link between the murders and the dead fugitive Byron Bastian. He was calling on the FBI to take control of the case. Cannon's wife had also issued a statement in support of her husband expressing concern about what she called a politically and racially motivated vendetta against the senator by elements within the DC police force.

'Do you think she means you or Chief Streeks?'

Forty minutes later, Eli Wrath tapped on the Impala's window and slipped into the passenger seat. He passed Freeman a gatefold brochure. 'I picked it up in the foyer of the American Enterprise Institute.'

'Thanks.'

According to the six-page brochure, which Freeman spread out on the steering wheel before him, and read by torchlight, Daedalus built the Labyrinth for King Minos to safely contain the mythical beast, the Minotaur, which was part man and part bull. With its

236

metallic ink cover, gloss laminate and silver foil embossing, the brochure looked like it ought to be selling luxury yachts rather than promoting the latest in biological research. It claimed that the Daedalus Foundation's programmes were devoted to scientific breakthrough and a vigorous defence, at home and abroad, of the vitality of American innovations and institutions. It stressed collaborative work with the National Institute of Health, MIT and the Defense Advanced Research Projects Agency (DARPA). It committed itself to placing America at the forefront of somatic and germ-line engineering.

On the back cover there was a quote from the eugenicist Francis Galton: 'What Nature does blindly, slowly and ruthlessly, man may do providently, quickly and kindly.'

Freeman switched off the torch.

'There's nothing kind about it,' Eli said after a pause. It was unusual for Eli to venture an opinion in this way.

'You got something to say?'

'Maybe,' Eli conceded.

'Well, spit it out.'

Eli tugged on his beard and then began talking. 'When I was sixteen my grandpa drove me down to the Western State Hospital in Staunton and told me the story of what had happened to two of his uncles, back in the thirties. They were Brush Mountain folk. Hill people. They got lifted in a round-up by the Montgomery County Sheriff's department and trucked down to Staunton where they were judged feeble-minded and unfit to reproduce by Virginia state law. They were sterilised. Grandpa said there was no use fighting it. They gave them some pills that made them drowsy and then they wheeled them up to the operating room.'

'Where are you going with this?'

'They got a plaque on the wall at the Western State says it was built with a grant from the Daedalus Foundation.'

Freeman swore under his breath.

A moment later, Eli said, 'It wasn't just the Western State and it wasn't just hill people.'

'If he's complicit in the girl's death then Cannon will go down,' Freeman told him.

'We're with you on this,' Eli told him. 'All the way. Winnie, Kari, Maja and me. We'll see this thing through.'

'Thank you,' Freeman said.

'You got any specific instructions?' Eli asked.

'Yeah. Watch the house. If anyone leaves follow them.'

'Will do.'

'How did you get on with the case file sent over by the Georgian detective?'

'It's the same killer all right,' Eli said, lifting his cap and scratching at his head. 'The bite marks match. They got as many murders over there as we do here. Victims were local politicians and community leaders mostly. This gang the Furies, it looks like they got a remote corner of that country locked down.'

'Good. Thanks.'

Eli went and climbed in the back of the surveillance van.

Freeman started the car. He had an event to attend.

He was on Rhode Island Avenue, heading out of the District when he realised that his followers had given up any pretence of concealment.

The nearest car was a red Toyota Corolla with two men inside. They were several cars back but as he crossed Florida they moved in close. He drove under the raised metro tracks by Home Depot and braked for a red light. The Corolla was directly behind him. He put the car in park, pulled the handbrake and in a single fluid motion exited the car and drew his gun from its holster in the small of his back. He advanced on the car behind.

'Driver, shut the engine! Passenger, put your hands out the window. Both hands!'

Freeman crossed to the driver's side and told him to drop the keys out of the car. The driver had a Frank Zappa moustache that gave him a piratical look and his colleague in the passenger seat had short ginger hair and freckles on his face and hands. Panicked drivers were reversing or swerving around them.

'Is that a service weapon?' asked the driver.

'I'll fuck you up.' Freeman darted in and chopped him across the bridge of his nose with the barrel of the gun. 'Now step out of the car. Both of you! Keep your hands where I can see them.'

Clutching his bloody nose, which was running grossly and copiously, the driver climbed out. The passenger did the same. As he was watching them, Freeman was aware of a blue Camry several cars back doing a U-turn and speeding away south on Rhode Island.

'You're on your own, boys, your back-up's fled. Now get down in front of the car where I can see you. Right now! Put your hands behind your back and cross your legs.'

He cuffed them and emptied their wallets out on the tarmac; both of them were carrying Tennessee driving licences and IDs for Raeburn Correctional Services.

'You planning on taking me to prison?'

'For sure, that can be arranged,' said the ginger-haired man.

Freeman stamped on his head. 'Shut the fuck up.'

He crossed back to the car and quickly searched the footwells and under the seats. He could hear the manic Doppler effect of approaching sirens. He opened the glove compartment. Inside he found two ski masks, a loaded SIG 9mm pistol and a police-issue double-shot X26 Taser. He threw the gun on the tarmac and walked back to the men lying on the road with the Taser in his hand.

'You're the motherfuckers that zapped me.'

'You don't know who you're messing with,' the driver said.

'Sure I do. Senator Jim fucking Cannon.'

Freeman knelt down beside him, put the Taser to his neck and pressed the button. The driver started spasming.

Watching his colleague with something like embarrassment, the ginger-haired man said, 'I don't blame you for doing this.'

'I'm glad you understand,' Freeman said and tasered him next. 'Now I have to go find my wife.'

He stood up and held his badge in the air as the patrol cars converged.

FORTY-EIGHT

'Puck,' she announced, bustling to her feet as Harry approached, 'as in hockey. Allegra Puck.'

Allegra Puck had a firm handshake and a forthright gaze. There were several chunky rings on her fingers with brightly coloured stones and her frizzy shoulder-length hair was streaked with grey. She was dressed in a spectacularly creased blue linen trouser suit that suggested that she had come straight off a transatlantic flight.

'Harry,' she said, with a warm smile. 'Everybody seems to call you Harry so I will too. I'm just Allegra. My husband calls me Legs but frankly speaking I think I've passed the day when I could carry that off in public.'

Harry had walked into the bar at Restaurant Eve and found Allegra Puck rummaging in a voluminous handbag. Much of the contents of the bag, including pens, hairgrips, receipts and several cell phones, were spread out on the sofa around her like flotsam.

'Sit down,' Allegra said, after shaking Harry's hand. 'I won't be a minute.'

Harry perched on the only available space on the edge of the sofa and watched as Allegra continued to remove items from the bag.

'This one,' she said triumphantly and pulled out a black clam-shell phone. 'I can never find the right one. Hang on.'

She fiddled with the phone for a while and then held it to her ear.

'Yes,' she said, 'I came straight here. Yes, she's here.' She winked at Harry. 'Yes, I'll call you later.' She ended the call. 'That's it.' She held the open bag at the edge of the sofa and swept all the things back into it. 'Do you want a drink first? Or shall we just eat? Are you hungry? I know I am. I can't bear to eat on planes. Now I could eat a horse. Let's eat.' She sprang to her feet again and guided Harry towards the hostess. 'You've had a busy few days. I thought you deserved a decent meal on expenses. Besides, I've always wanted to try this place and I don't get over here as much as I used to. In fact I don't get out much at all.'

They were escorted to a corner table in the chef's tasting room reserved in the name of Moncure. Once they were seated, a waiter handed them their menus, parchment scrolls wrapped in green ribbon.

'I've just become a mother again at forty-six,' Allegra told Harry, in a conversational tone. 'An accident? More like a bloody miracle. My husband is holding the fort until I'm back. I had to spend half a day attached to a breast pump before I could leave for the airport. I don't mind telling you it's a bloody relief to be away from all that. Look, if we bump into someone you know, Harry, which is sod's law in this game, don't bother explaining who I am. If you're forced to it I'm your old career development adviser from Hendon. Got that?'

'Yes.'

'Still doing ballet?' Allegra Puck asked casually. She undid the piece of green ribbon and unrolled the menu, holding it at arm's length before rummaging in her bag for a pair of reading glasses.

Harry shrugged. 'Now and then.'

'Where?'

'The school of ballet on Wisconsin. They run open adult classes.'

Harry unrolled her own menu. There were five named courses: *Creation, Ocean, Earth and Sky, Age* and finally *Eden.*

'And shooting? Pistol, wasn't it? Still shoot, do you?'

'Yes.'

'Where?'

'A small arms range near Andrews Air Force Base.'

'What's your shooting like?'

'Middling.'

'I'm serious.'

'Well, good, I suppose.'

Allegra studied her over the rims of her glasses. 'I heard you were cheated of a bronze in Finland.'

Harry blushed. It was true that she had competed in the International Shooting Sport Federation world championships in Lahti, Finland, in 2002. She'd reached the final six contestants, but been beaten into fourth place by a Bulgarian and two Chinese shooters.

'I was happy with the result,' she said. It was laughable really, Harry thought, the contrast between the ebullient young girl who wanted to be a ballerina and the woman who became a protection officer and shunned the limelight.

'And sailing?'

'Weekends mostly.'

'On your friend Gary's boat.'

'That's right.'

'You must rather feel he's dropped you in it?'

'That about sums it up.'

'Let's order food,' Allegra said. She glanced around expectantly and within seconds their waiter was standing attentively beside them. 'I'll have the parmesan crème brûlée, the black bass, the sweetbreads, the cashel blue and the ginger snap ice cream. How's that?'

The waiter turned to Harry who grimaced.

'I'll have the same,' she said quickly.

Allegra lifted her eyebrows. 'You can have whatever you like.'

'Same as you is fine with me.'

'Douglas says you're no trouble.'

'You know my father-in-law?'

'I used to brief him when he was a junior minister at the Foreign Office. We've kept in touch. You should know he speaks very highly of you. He says that you'll rise to any occasion.'

'He's my father-in-law. He has a rosy view.'

'He's not the only one. At Protection Command they'd take you back like a shot. In fact, I was hard pressed to find anyone with a harsh word to say about you. You were one of only fifty police officers nationwide selected for the High Potential Development

Scheme. I've seen your attachment reports from robbery, burglary and the Community Safety Unit. You were being groomed for the top. You did retire early, when you think about it. It's not everyone who gives up a promising police career in favour of becoming what exactly?'

'I'm enjoying being married.'

'Of course you are. And such a catch. He's as handsome as his father. Not without a downside though. You must hang around a good deal waiting for him to come back from wherever?'

'He travels a lot,' she acknowledged.

'I suppose that's what all the running after dark is about. Take your mind off it. Where is he now – the earthquake?'

'Yes.'

'Have you heard from him?'

'He'll call when he gets the chance.'

Allegra Puck smiled sympathetically. 'I'm sure he will.'

'What about Pakistan?' Allegra asked, between the first and second courses. 'What happened there?'

'What do you mean?' replied Harry stiffly.

'I mean you didn't leave the police because of Jack, did you?'

'I'm sure that you've seen the investigation report.'

'I read it on the plane. But it's not the same as hearing it from the horse's mouth, is it?'

'You want me to tell you what happened?'

'Yes.'

How to explain the difference between New Her and Old Her? *Start at the beginning*, that's what Jack would have said.

There were inevitably times as a police protection officer when you felt like an inconvenient piece of baggage, hauled along from place to place. Your advice ignored. Your job made near impossible. But there was a limit, and without giving it much thought, Harry had believed that no one would put themselves and those around them deliberately at risk in search of a passing headline in a tabloid newspaper. She had been wrong, of course.

In 2006 Harry was asked to 'guest' on an overseas protection job, providing supplemental security. She was informed that she had been selected along with four Special Branch colleagues to accompany the Secretary of State for International Development on a fact-finding trip to Pakistan.

The Secretary of State (SoS) had a reputation for falling out with her security detail. She routinely disregarded advice and was often extremely antagonistic, particularly towards middle-aged men. From the outset Harry had understood that she had been included on the team because she was a woman and that someone at Protection Command had the bright idea that if there was a woman on the team the Secretary of State might be more inclined to listen. The trouble was it didn't work. If anything Harry made her more aggressive. She seemed to perceive Harry as a provocation. She only spoke to her once on the entire trip and that was just before the incident kicked off.

Harry had been over her testimony a thousand times. She could put herself back in front of the five-member panel and she could hear her own voice, the competing claims of her need to be accurate and her self-righteous anger, the struggle to maintain her composure. She could recite it almost word for word.

She did so again. This time for Allegra Puck with the same flat, declamatory tone of voice.

'We flew with the SoS and her private secretary from Gatwick to Islamabad where we met with the British High Commissioner and a Pakistani security team. It was a nightmare from the very beginning. No one knew how secure the Pakistani police or intelligence services were or how trustworthy. The drive from the airport to the High Commissioner's Residence was extremely chaotic. There were cars swerving all over the road and cars coming out of side roads, and people in them pointing AK-47s out of the opened windows. We didn't know who were police and who weren't. And that was the way it was for the rest of the trip. It was particularly bad when we made a courtesy call on the Pakistan President, Pervez Musharraf. Everywhere we went there were crowds of people, unidentified gunmen and a media scrum. The SoS was getting denounced in the local press for being an

American lackey and it didn't help that we were travelling in a GMC Sedan with American diplomatic plates that had been provided by the US Embassy because our own High Commission didn't have a sufficiently armoured vehicle available.

'At the end of the first day, the SoS decided that she wanted to visit one of the refugee camps that was receiving British aid. The High Commissioner and her private secretary were against it but the more problems that were pointed out to the SoS the stroppier she got. Eventually, as a compromise, it was decided that she could visit a World Food Programme depot in Peshawar. The Pakistani military agreed to fly her up there and in the morning I went ahead by road with Ned, the team leader, to recce the site. It was like the Wild West up there. There was a level of hostility towards us in the villages we drove through that was unnerving and when we stopped for fuel we were forced to draw our weapons because we observed several armed men enter a house that overlooked our position. We got out of there as quickly as we could.

'When we got to Peshawar Ned called the High Commission on the sat-phone and told them that the visit was too risky. The answer came back that the SoS was going no matter what. She was not going to be intimidated.

'So we headed out to the air force base where she would arrive. She came in on an old Sea King helicopter that looked like it had seen better days. Ned said that the Pakistani military must have decided that if they were going to lose a helicopter it might as well be an old one. Once the chopper had landed I went ahead with one of my colleagues to the food depot. The depot consisted of a large warehouse full of food sacks surrounded by a fence and about thirty brightly painted trucks and several dozen drivers. The immediate problem was that the depot was adjacent to a large refugee camp and the level of local security was insufficient in our opinion. It was exactly the sort of situation we had been trying to avoid. We hadn't been there long when the media arrived. They had obviously been tipped off. Their arrival prompted a lot of interest from the camp next door and by the time the Secretary of State's convoy arrived there was a substantial crowd of onlookers at the gate. She got out of her car and was immediately surrounded by the truck drivers. Then the guards on the gate relented and allowed the TV crews to enter. Seconds later they had completely lost control of the situation. There were people everywhere, rushing into the depot from the camp. The SoS seemed oblivious to the situation. She was intent on speaking to the crowd. I tried to prevent her from being crushed and started pushing people away to create a safety gap. She became extremely angry with me. At that point there were only two of us from Protection Command in close proximity to her. The other two were carrying Heckler & Koch carbines and needed a wider arc of fire, so they were forced to stay clear of the crowd. Then one of the Pakistani security team told us that there were suicide bombers in the crowd.'

She remembered the chair of the panel leaning forward over the table, a kindly expression on his face. 'Then what happened?'

'Ignoring her protests, I grabbed the SoS by the arm and pulled her towards the armoured car. Then the first bomb went off. It was by the gate. People were running in every direction. There was a lot of confusion. I drew my weapon. We had almost reached the car when a man came running out of the smoke. He was wearing a bulky vest with full pockets and wires connecting it up. I shot him. Double-tap. Head and chest. I killed him. That's it.'

'I didn't have any choice,' Harry said in a low voice.

'You were fully justified,' Allegra told her. 'It's there in the report, in black and white. I'm surprised they didn't give you a medal.'

'We shouldn't have been there in that place.'

'Of course not, but that's not really your fault, is it?'

'No, it's not.'

'And the Pakistani government subsequently claimed that the man you shot was a border policeman?'

'I know what I saw.'

'So why did you resign?'

'I didn't resign because I killed someone, if that's what you think.'

'So why did you?'

'I always knew that I might have to kill someone. I was at peace with that. You don't go through all that training and then back out. You do your job. But I didn't expect to have to do it because of the stupidity and vanity of a politician.'

'So you resigned.'

'Yes.'

'You made your little protest.'

'Yes.'

'And now you get by on odd jobs and think about having a family?'

Harry was finished speaking. She stared at her plate.

'I guess what I want to know, Harry,' Allegra resumed after a pause, 'is whether you'd like to have another go. Not at protecting some vainglorious politician, but at serving your country.'

She beckoned for the check.

'You're leaking,' Harry said.

'I'm sorry?'

'You're leaking milk.'

Allegra looked down at the spreading stains on her blouse. 'Oh bollocks!'

FORTY-NINE

'Why you? It's a good question, Harry. Fate, I suppose. You were in the wrong place at the wrong time. If you hadn't been in the woods that night you wouldn't be here now talking to me. Look on it as an opportunity.'

They were in the restroom and Allegra was standing in her bra, holding her blouse over the sink and dabbing at it with a damp napkin.

'But why did Markoff hire me?'

'Because he's devious. Because he thinks you're working for us. Because the Pentagon have abandoned him. My guess is that if you checked with your friend with the yacht you'd find that Markoff asked for you by name, which means he found out who you were pretty damn quick. He's got himself in a mess and he's flailing around, looking for a way out. He's added two and two and come up with five. Who can blame him?'

'What does that mean exactly?'

'Dr Markoff's unique set of skills are of interest to a number of intelligence agencies, Harry, both friendly and unfriendly. He's being watched and he knows it. His fate is being determined. When you discovered the body of the young woman in the park he assumed that you were working for us and given your background that's not entirely surprising. Furthermore, by stepping out of the shadows as a witness he must have assumed you were making an overture.'

'And now you want me to make that overture real?'

'Let's just say we're open to exploratory talks. There's an opportunity here for us. The Pentagon and the CIA have fallen out with each other over this. And the CIA have asked us to help.'

'I still don't understand.'

'The Pentagon believed that they'd pulled off a coup in persuading Dr Markoff to defect, a shot in the arm for their research programmes. But they got more than they bargained for. Dr Markoff's style of operating owes more to the modern Russia than to the Cold War era, and now he's really landed them in it. The repercussions of the young woman's death in Rock Creek Park have yet to be fully felt. And needless to say our friends at Langley are furious. They feel that they are going to be landed with some of the blame for the Pentagon's stupidity and with good reason. After all, the CIA brought Dr Markoff and his family over here on the return leg of one of their rendition flights. They are especially eager to minimise the impact of this and they don't mind ruffling a few feathers to do it. That's where we come in. It may be that we can help and in the process earn ourselves some good will. God knows we need it. Langley haven't been too keen on sharing information with us since our courts started publishing details of some of their more secretive activities.'

'How are we going to help exactly?'

'We're giving serious consideration to an offer of asylum to Dr Markoff and his family. Not in the UK, but possibly in one of the Overseas Territories, provided, that is, we can persuade the local authorities there to go along with it.'

'What is the link between Dr Markoff and the dead woman in the park?' Harry asked.

'We understand that the woman whose body you found in the park came over to this country with Dr Markoff in the summer of 2008. We believe that she was what's called an "illegal", which means she was trained by Directorate S of the KGB.'

'She was a spy?'

'That's right. She belonged to a select group of "illegals" who were part of a Directorate S programme known only as Progress that was set up in the early 1980s and was closed down a decade later. On arrival here in the States Dr Markoff appears to have utilised her as a means of acquiring political influence, as an incentive or by means of blackmail. She was made available to selected politicians of influence, senators and congressmen, either because they controlled the funding for Dr Markoff's research work at Germline BioSciences or because they were connected with legislation that posed a threat to that research.'

'Made available?'

'She had sex with them,' Allegra explained in a matter-of-fact way, 'a common-or-garden honey trap. But now somebody's killed her. If the Berlin Wall was still up this would be a scandal of almost unimaginable proportions. You can imagine the headlines – "Russian Mata Hari infiltrates key congressional committees".'

'Who killed her?'

'We don't know. Frankly speaking, we don't want to know.' She put her blouse back on and buttoned it up. 'Come on, let's go.'

They were driving north on the Rock Creek Parkway, between banks of freshly ploughed snow.

'What's Dr Markoff's background?' Harry asked. 'What makes him tick?'

Allegra did not respond at first, she was staring out of the window at the forested ravine rising either side of them, the trees loaded with snow. Then she said, 'He comes from a family of scientists who have fallen in and out of favour with the Soviet and then after them the Russian authorities. His grandfather Ilya Ivanovich Ivanov was a biologist back in the twenties who specialised in artificial insemination and hybridisation of animals. He came to the attention of Stalin and he enjoyed a brief period of popularity but he failed to deliver results. In 1930 he was arrested in a political purge and exiled to Kazakhstan. He died there a couple of years later. We don't know much about his son who was also called Ilya. He may have worked at the Kazakh Veterinary-Zoologist Institute. We do know he was involved in his father's work and travelled with him to Africa on specimen-seeking trips in the twenties. The grandson, Alexander Markoff, known as Sasha, first rose to prominence in the mid- to late eighties when Gorbachev was in power. Our information suggests that he went to work for an organisation called Biopreparat, breeding primates for biological warfare testing. It is not a commonly known fact, Harry, but at the same time as the Soviets were reducing their nuclear stockpile they were ramping up their work on bio-weapons.

'Known as "the Concern", Biopreparat was the hub of Moscow's germ effort, a vast network of secret cities, production plants and centres that studied and perfected germs as weapons. For the Soviets it was their equivalent of the Manhattan Project – the American programme that produced the first atomic bomb. In the late eighties they had more than sixty thousand people working on bio-weapons, thirty thousand of them, including Dr Markoff, at the Scientific and Experimental Production Base in Stepnogorsk, in Kazakhstan. It was a huge complex but it wasn't listed on any map. Its address was a post office box.

'We in the western intelligence services didn't get a look inside Stepnogorsk until 1995, by which time the base was in a terrible state of disrepair, but the inspectors did see the first evidence of a KGB Directorate S behavioural modification programme called Progress that had been hidden within the Biopreparat programme. All very Russian – like a doll within a doll. It was written up as a footnote in a report, indicating a requirement for further investigation, but of much less significance than the need to secure Soviet bio-weapons stocks to prevent them falling into the hands of terrorists or rogue regimes.

'I'll be frank with you, Harry. Nobody gave Progress much thought then or subsequently. Let me put this in context: it was a period of turmoil in the former Soviet Union and the Russian Secret Services were largely left behind in the mad rush to market reforms and democracy. Although Directorate S of the KGB survived as part of the newly constituted Russian Foreign Intelligence Service, or SVR as it's known, many clandestine programmes like Progress collapsed during the transition.

'And then, out of the blue, Dr Markoff approached the Americans. He passed a dossier to the US defence attaché from Tbilisi, who was on an assessment mission in the breakaway region of Abkhazia. We haven't seen the dossier and neither have our friends at Langley but we understand from the Pentagon that it contains information that suggests he got a lot further along with some of his research than we realised.'

FIFTY

Rather than cancel the event, the organisers had re-billed the thousand-dollar-a-plate fundraiser as a benefit for the earthquake. It was being held in a red-brick McMansion with a jumble of chimneys, dormers, pilasters, quoins, columns and roof peaks. It was one of several dozen luxury homes set in clear-cut lots in an all-black exurb in Prince George's County; since 1960 more than nine million African-Americans had fled the inner cities of America for suburbs and outer edge cities, some of them, the more affluent, to gated communities like this.

Freeman parked his dented, government-issue Impala along-side the rows of immaculate BMWs and Mercedes parked in the tree-lined avenues.

He got out of the car and looked himself up and down. There was blood on his cuffs, and mud and slush on his shoes. His fore-head was a mess.

He was late.

Shawna would understand.

He walked up the drive and entered the house. Inside Hispanic waiters carried trays of canapés among the mix of doctors, admin-istrators, business owners and professional athletes. Freeman spotted his wife Shawna, a head taller than those immediately around her. She was talking to the candidate, a Democratic incum-bent with a seat considered safe in all predictions for the 2010 mid-terms. Among those listening to them, Freeman recognised a local news anchor and the influential pastor of a local Baptist mega-church.

Spotting him, Shawna was briefly startled. She excused herself and began working her way through the crowd towards him, stopping now and then to acknowledge a greeting, her hands reaching out to make connections, a forearm gripped here, an upper arm stroked there, her flawless smile bestowing a moment's intimacy on whoever it was directed at. It was an impressive performance, Freeman thought, not for the first time. He was so incredibly proud of her.

'What are you doing here?' she demanded.

'It looks worse than it feels,' he said ruefully. 'My head, I mean.'

'Why did you come?'

'I wanted to see you.'

He reached forward to kiss her on the lips and she turned away, offering him her cheek instead.

'You haven't been home, have you?'

'Not since before dawn,' he explained. 'If I'd had the time I would have changed. I'm sorry. I've been flat out on a case. It feels like we've been fighting a prairie fire.'

She shook her head in disbelief.

'What?' he asked.

'Tens maybe hundreds of thousands of people have died in the earthquake and you're obsessing about a murdered Russian prostitute.'

'How do you know she was a prostitute?'

'She wasn't?'

'At last count I had six dead,' Freeman told her, 'two women and four men. Two cops. Two African-Americans in the mix. They deserve justice as much as anyone else.'

'Then don't let me stop you working the case.'

'I need to ask you a question,' he told her.

She shook her head. 'What?'

'The time that we went to Senator Cannon's house for a party, why was it you asked me not to leave you alone in a room with him?'

'Don't even go there,' she snapped. 'We need Cannon to abstain on healthcare.'

He stared at her.

'Stop it, Michael,' she said.

'What?'

'You're doing that thing.'

'What thing?'

She looked away. She seemed profoundly sad. 'That thing that you do.'

A hand gripped Freeman by the shoulder and a familiar voice, accented with money and education, greeted him in a confident tone: 'The diligent investigator . . .'

Freeman turned to face the man. Gideon Wu's features were angular and his skin had an exfoliated sheen. His suit was navy blue and expensively tailored with a flag-pin on the lapel. If he was uncomfortable with being the only non-black at the event he wasn't showing it. Under Freeman's gaze he turned his cheeks, one way and then the other like a man shaving. 'What are you doing here?'

'Michael came straight from work,' Shawna replied for him.

'I see,' Gideon said, as if there was some significance in the remark. He looked away. 'Good turnout, isn't it?'

'It is,' Shawna said, a little too quickly, to fill the silence.

'I hate to break this up, Lieutenant, but we have to circulate,' Gideon told him with an easy smile full of even white teeth. 'There are people here with deep pockets who need to be mobilised. Excuse me.'

Gideon Wu took Freeman's wife by the elbow and steered her away through the crowd, leaning in now and then to whisper in her ear, leaving Freeman wondering when she had stopped wearing her wedding ring.

He stood for a while, alone in the midst of the babble of the crowd, with the uncomfortable realisation that he wasn't welcome at the event. There was a time when his military record, his silver star, and his career in the police had been a boon to his wife's ambitions. Something had evidently changed. He took a glass from a passing waiter and eased himself towards the back of the room. He was most of the way there when he spotted Assistant Chief of Police Streeks, standing by himself at the bottom of a staircase, looking ill at ease.

'I wondered if you'd be here,' Streeks said, when Freeman reached him. He didn't look particularly happy to see him.

They stood side by side and surveyed the crowd. The mayor was standing near the centre of the room, where the sound of people was most intense. Two men were talking to him, falling over themselves to communicate with him. Another was removing a business card from his wallet.

'If it's proven that Katja was killed on the senator's property then Chief Thielen's presence at the house in the aftermath of the murder and her reluctance to involve the FBI suggests the makings of a cover-up. If it comes to that her position will become untenable,' Freeman observed. 'The mayor will be looking for a new Chief of Police.'

Streeks glanced at him. 'You suggesting I go kiss some ass?'

'Something like that,' he acknowledged.

'Don't be impertinent, Michael.'

There was a pause between them.

A waiter had appeared at Freeman's side. 'There's a man waiting for you outside,' he said and inclined his head towards the kitchen at the back of the house.

Freeman nodded in acknowledgement. 'Excuse me,' he said to Streeks.

He followed the waiter to the kitchen.

FIFTY-ONE

Jay Albo, the mayor's driver, business partner and co-chair of his re-election campaign, was standing in the shadows by the trash cans, just beyond the pool of light cast by the kitchen window. Freeman might not have seen him but for the burning tip of his cigarette. As he closed the door behind him, and descended the steps, Albo crushed the cigarette beneath his shoe.

'Come on,' he said.

Freeman followed him across a darkened lawn and alongside a row of parked cars to an intersection where a black Suburban with North Carolina plates was standing, idling. As he approached the vehicle, one of the darkened rear windows descended and he saw a woman's face looking out at him. Her eyes appraised him openly, as if he might present a threat or an opportunity.

'Do you know who I am, Lieutenant?'

'Yes, Senator.'

He had recognised her immediately. She was Elizabeth Oberstar, the senior senator for the state of North Carolina and chairman of the Emerging Threats and Capabilities Subcommittee of the Armed Services Committee. Cannon's main political rival.

'Will you speak with me?'

'I'd be happy to.'

'Get in, please.'

Freeman glanced over his shoulder at Jay Albo who was already walking away. It seemed the mayor's friendship with his Crestwood neighbour Senator Cannon was not as tight as it had been. Ties of allegiance were shifting.

He opened the rear door of the Suburban and climbed in. Senator Oberstar had shifted along the cream leather seat and was sitting with her legs crossed with a folder in her hands. Special Agent McCafferty was sitting facing her in a jump seat with his back to the tinted glass screen that separated them from the driver. He nodded to Freeman but didn't speak.

The senator was wearing a navy blue raw silk dress, sheer hose and a string of fat pearls, diamonds at her ears and a large rock of several carats on her finger. A smooth, Botoxed forehead and brunette hair that fell in luxurious waves to her shoulders. The unmistakable scent of Chanel No 5.

A senator's immaculate gloss.

'How are you, Lieutenant? I gather from Special Agent McCafferty you've had a difficult couple of days?'

'I'm well, Senator, thank you.'

If she found Freeman's somewhat dishevelled appearance distasteful, she was too much of a professional to show it. It was impossible to judge her age; she looked like she was in her late forties but she might have been ten or fifteen years older than that.

Before beginning, she glanced at McCafferty, who gave her an encouraging nod.

'Very well,' she said. She looked Freeman straight in the eye. 'Lieutenant, when I took over as chair of the subcommittee I fully expected to learn secrets, often unpleasant ones. I did not expect to discover that the previous chairman, Senator James Cannon, had run the subcommittee as if it was a personal fiefdom. It has been my intention since I took over as chair to cast light on defence research and its funding. To provoke a public discussion about what kind of future it is that we seek for our nation. I had not counted on the resourcefulness of my adversaries. I have been blocked at every turn. I find myself forced to take matters into my own hands. I propose to show you something that may help you with your investigation. Then I'm going to ask you to do me a favour, which I hope that you will be happy to undertake. First, though, I have to ask you if you can keep a secret?'

'I'm investigating a series of murders, Senator . . .'

'I understand. I really do. I simply ask you not to reveal that I was the source of the information that I am willing to share with you.'

He nodded. 'OK.'

She smiled as if his answer had been in doubt. 'Good. Now, Lieutenant, I understand that you are searching for a link between Senator Cannon and a biotechnology company called Germline BioSciences. Is that correct?'

'That's correct,' Freeman said.

'Good,' she said. 'Very good. Now, do you understand what pork is, in a budgetary context?'

'You mean a congressional earmark?'

'Yes, a legislative provision by which a congressional member can secure funds for a specific project without subjecting it to congressional debate, or to the scrutiny and oversight of the public.'

'I understand.'

'I take it you are aware that the subcommittee of which I am a longstanding member is responsible for the allocation of several billion dollars annually to the Defense Advanced Research Projects Agency, the research and development agency for the Department of Defense.'

'I am.'

'Are you also aware that the subcommittee allocates more than a hundred million dollars to classified programmes?'

'I didn't know that.'

'Now you do. I'm going to show you something, Lieutenant. A secret earmark allocated by the chair of the subcommittee, Senator Cannon, to Germline BioSciences to the value of sixty-three million dollars.'

She opened the folder on her lap and extracted a single sheet of paper which she held up for him to see.

TOP SECRET

The Department of Defense, Defense Advanced Research Projects
Agency (DARPA), Fiscal Year (FY) 2009 Budget Estimates
Materials and Biological Technology:

The Metabolically Dominant Soldier Program
'War fighters experience a wide variety of operational stressors, both
mental and physical, that degrade critical cognitive functions such as

memory, learning and decision-making. These stressors also degrade the war fighter's ability to multitask, leading to decreased ability to respond quickly and effectively.'

FY2008 Plans

1. *Identify and characterize the genetic targets behind the adaptive vs. dysfunctional response in war fighters to stress, exploring a minimum of four stressors (cognitive, physical, sleep deprivation, illness, etc.).*

FY2009 Base Plans

1. *Design genetic interventions for prevention of stress-induced cognitive dysfunction in war fighters based on observations.*
2. *Identify targets for modification.*
3. *Establish an in vivo anatomical and molecular pathway in a human model.*

Senator Oberstar slipped the sheet of paper back into the folder and looked expectantly at Freeman who was still trying to discern its meaning.

'A human model?' Freeman said cautiously. 'All I saw were apes.'

'How much of the building did you visit?'

'Only the first basement level,' he conceded. 'There were two other levels below that.'

'It is my belief that they are tampering with human beings on the lower levels, Lieutenant.'

'Tampering?'

'That's right, Lieutenant.' Her eyes were shining, excited. 'That's it exactly. I couldn't tell you what form that tampering takes but I can tell you I mean to find out and if necessary put a stop to it.' Her manicured fingers impatiently drummed the cover of the folder. 'Now that I have shared with you what I know, I have that favour to ask.'

Freeman found himself nodding.

'I have subpoenaed Dr Alexander Markoff, the Chief Scientist at Germline BioSciences, to appear before the subcommittee tomorrow. I can't ask him about confidential programmes without closing the hearing and I don't want to do that. I want the public to know. What I can do is ask him under oath about his previous work in Russia. It is my belief that what he is doing over here is a re-creation of what he was doing over there. What I need you to do, Lieutenant, is to make sure that Dr Markoff makes it to the hearing. Can you do that?'

Freeman looked from the senator to McCafferty. McCafferty nodded.

'OK,' Freeman said. 'I'll get him there.'

FIFTY-TWO

Freeman was startled awake by someone tapping on the driver's side window. He looked groggily around him. He was in his Impala. More tapping. He opened the window.

A blast of freezing air.

'Move along now, sir,' said a uniformed security guard. He was standing holding a flashlight, surrounded by swirling snow.

Freeman rubbed his face and glanced at his watch. It was ten twenty. He remembered Senator Oberstar leaving with McCafferty and then walking over to his car and getting in. He remembered switching on the heater. He'd called Eli and Kari and checked that they were still outside Markoff's Chevy Chase compound in the van. He'd called Kaplan's number but got no answer. He dimly remembered thinking that if he could just have a moment's rest he would be able to go on. After that, nothing: he must have fallen asleep.

'I need you to move along,' the security guard repeated.

'I have to find my wife,' Freeman said, showing him his badge. The security guard stepped back to allow him out of the car and stood by, watching, as he walked back up the drive to the McMansion. All the vehicles had gone.

Inside, the fundraiser was over and the catering staff were clearing up. There were no remaining guests. A sympathetic woman, whom he assumed was the hostess, told him that his wife was long gone.

Something was wrong. He returned to the Impala. The security guard followed him in his patrol car all the way to the community gate.

Physically, Freeman felt almost normal; the pain in his temple had receded but mentally he was in overdrive, a by-product of exhaustion, the details of the case turning over in his mind as he rushed home.

He bounded up the stairs two at a time, unlocked the door and entered. Stopped in his tracks. Suddenly he understood why she'd asked him whether he'd been back to the apartment today.

The words of his old commanding officer came to him: he missed nothing given time. He'd missed this. How could he have been so blind?

Shawna had been thorough, as she was in all things. There were no chairs or tables, rugs or curtains, books or bookshelves, no china, glasses or cutlery. In the bedroom only the bed and the sheet on it remained. He remembered how difficult it had been to get the bed up the stairs and into the apartment. She had stripped it of blankets though. He walked from room to room, feeling bruised and empty as if he'd been robbed. The only other thing she had left was the half-empty bottle of Buffalo Trace in one of the cupboards. He pulled the cork from the bottle. A searing mouthful.

He called his wife on her cell. It took an agonising time for her to answer.

'Michael.'

'Where are you?' he demanded.

'There isn't an easy way to say this. I don't love you. I love Gideon.'

And then it was as if he were in deep and treacherous water and his fingers had reached out but failed to find purchase and he was sinking and suddenly unable to swim. 'How can you do this?'

She ended the call. In the living room he slid down the wall, his body racked by dry heaves.

'Fuck . . . fuck . . . fuck!'

He slurped greedily at the bottle. He'd like to get his hands on Gideon Wu's hand-tailored lapels. He'd shake him till the shit ran.

This wasn't supposed to happen to him.

His cell rang. Caller unknown.

It must be Shawna. His spirits soared. She would be

repentant, pleading; it had all been a terrible mistake. They were words, she'd say – just words – spoken in anger, easily retracted, easily forgiven . . .

'I haven't disturbed you, have I?' Senator James Cannon said.

Freeman sat up. With the clarity of someone shocked awake, he saw all the details around him: the scuffed floors, the picture hooks on the bare walls, the shadows cast by adjacent buildings, a discarded roll of packing tape.

'No,' he said.

'I find I'm at my most active late at night,' Cannon said. 'I'm sure it's the same for you in your profession, Lieutenant? As a species we prefer to kill at night.'

'We?'

'You, then.' He laughed softly. 'After all, the perpetrators of crime in this city resemble you more than they do me, isn't that right?'

Breathe, Freeman told himself. Breathe. 'I try not to distinguish between people on the basis of their colour or how much money they have.'

'Justice is blind, Michael?'

'What do you want, Senator?'

'I must congratulate you for that stunt you pulled on Rhode Island Avenue tonight.'

'I don't like being followed.'

'A couple of over-zealous rent-a-cops,' the senator said airily. 'I can assure you that they have been severely reprimanded. No hard feelings, I hope? You know that I hold you in the highest regard. After all, I was the one who told the mayor that you were the man for this case. That's right. I insisted on you. You know why? Because you're a patriot. Just like I'm a patriot. We're similar, you and me. Both Green Berets, of course. But more than that, and I've only just discovered this, we both grew up without a mother. In the absence of family, country came first. I do what I do, Michael, because I love my country, because I want to keep it safe against those who seek to weaken it and undermine it. I know you are stirred by the same emotions. You have a bright future,

Michael; if you make the right choices, the smart choices, there's no telling where you might end up. I can help you.'

'I don't think so.'

'I sincerely hope that we can work together to swiftly solve this case, Michael. We can get your career back on track. Who knows, maybe your wife will move back in?'

'Fuck you.'

Freeman threw the cell at the far wall and watched the casing break and the battery pop out. He grabbed his jacket and headed out of the door.

As he rushed to Georgetown, driving the Impala down empty streets with the heater on full blast, melodramas filled Freeman's head: Shawna was repentant and he was magnanimous; she was bitter and angry but he was tolerant and understanding; she didn't really love Gideon; he convinced her to come home; their hearts softened; she was going to find time for him and he was going to find a new career. All the variations in between and all of them ending up in bed. Except for the last few months, the sex had always been great. It could be again. The night would end with a tumultuous fuck.

And in the morning he would solve the case.

It didn't work out that way.

He screeched to a halt outside Gideon Wu's Georgetown home, jumped out of the Impala and in two bounding strides was at the door. He pressed the doorbell several times and then started banging on the door with his fist.

'I need to talk to you!' he yelled. He continued banging on the door. 'Shawna! I know you're in there!'

Eventually, Gideon opened the door. He stood in the hallway in his socks and said in a measured tone, 'I've called the police.'

'I am the police,' Freeman retorted.

'Then behave like it.'

'I'll tell you what, I'll give you a lesson in police brutality,' he said and punched him in the face.

Gideon staggered backwards and sat down heavily at the

bottom of the stairs, with his hands in front of his face and an impressive amount of blood dripping onto his open-necked shirt.

'You bwoke my dose,' he complained.

'Second one of the night,' Freeman told him triumphantly.

Shawna rushed down the stairs and put her arms around her lover. She glared accusingly at Freeman and snarled, 'Get out!'

He was stunned by the ferocity of her expression.

FIFTY-THREE

'The girl is the key to this,' Allegra said.

It was well after eleven. They were in Allegra's suite at the Hay Adams Hotel, drinking Scotch from the mini-bar. Allegra was sitting on the edge of the bed and Harry was ranging here and there.

Harry had described her first impressions of Dr Markoff's mysterious niece Eva and the unsettling bodyguard Yuri and then the interview itself. She had described the strange and exhilarating day that she had spent in the company of Eva: the friendly, intimate walk in the grounds of the Chevy Chase mansion; the drive out to Germline BioSciences in the 'tank'; the encounter with the DC police lieutenant Freeman; the tour of the primate facilities and labs; the promiscuous bonobos, the violent baboons and the signing orang-utan; Markoff's subpoena and the results of the sonogram.

'In what way is she the key to this?' Harry asked.

'Her eggs. That's what Dr Markoff's got to offer. The promise of a whole new generation.' She gave Harry a cell phone from her handbag. 'This one's for you. Use it to call me. My number is saved in the memory. It's the only one. I'll be waiting at the embassy for your call. Now you better go and get some sleep. You look like you need it.'

Harry was driving north on 16th and had just passed the sphinxes outside the Freemasons' House of the Temple, which Jack liked to call the Pharaoh's Bunker, when her cell phone beeped. She grabbed it off the passenger seat expecting a message from him – he was safe, he'd reached the border of the affected country, the earthquake zone – but when she looked at the screen she saw it was from Eva. With a sinking feeling she pulled over to the kerb.

wat r u doing?

I'm driving home. Where are you? Are you at home?'

how was ur meeting?

Fine

do THEY want us?

What do you mean?

are THEY making us an offer??

Honesty seemed like the best policy:

An island in the Caribbean.

is that the best u can do 4 us???

Harry was climbing the stairs and had almost reached the bedroom; Jack's preposterous bed had never looked more inviting, when her phone beeped again.

wat r u doing now?

She stopped and wrote a reply.

Going to bed. Where are you?

LOVE the club ;-) want 2 come?

'For fuck's sakes,' Harry muttered. What the hell was Eva doing out of the house at this hour? She wasn't allowed out after dark. Harry leaned against the wall, the prospect of bed receding like a retracted zoom lens. 'I don't believe this.'

please please come

She didn't have any choice.

OK I'm coming

ur names on the door :-)

FIFTY-FOUR

Harry arrived at Love as clubbers were spilling loudly out onto Okie Street and snowballs were flying. She parked in a makeshift parking lot ringed by dirty mounds of snow and gave a man in a ragged flight-suit five dollars not to vandalise it. As she approached the entrance, Harry saw a woman she thought was Rihanna tottering across the ice in heels. Bodyguards surrounded her and every now and then one of them reached out and steadied her. She climbed into the back of a black Navigator.

Harry joined the VIP line, gave her name and the bouncers stepped aside to allow her in. Inside, a wave of heat and noise assaulted her senses. It was a massive space, full of hundreds of gyrating bodies and spinning lights and pulsing shapes on plasma TVs. She removed her jacket, stripping down to her sleeveless vest and squeezed between the press of people, skirting the edge of the dance floor. The club rose several floors above her and at the edge of the dance floor there were private rooms and roped-off areas.

She texted Eva:

Where are you?

the top!!!

She climbed the stairs, weaving between groups of people. Sweat ran off her forehead and down between her breasts. Several times she brushed past men who reached for her or attempted to shout in her ear. A bald-headed man with a goatee and too much jewellery made a grab for her on the third floor and she stamped on his toes and left him hopping and cursing.

The fourth floor was pounding out vintage Detroit techno. If she felt about ten years too old for the crowd, she told herself she was the right age for the music. For a moment, she thought she glimpsed Eva through the crowd. She was in a clinch with a woman wearing a straw Stetson. Harry pushed forward, using her elbows to clear a path. Someone behind her protested. Someone jabbed her in the ribs. It was like one of her bad dreams of being hemmed in with no clear fields of fire. She turned side-on, still pushing forward. Then a hand reached out and took hers and drew her in and a moment later she found herself up against a bar and sandwiched between Eva on one side and Anna, Eva's gymnastics tutor, on the other. They were both wearing shorts and muddy wellington boots, and Anna had the crumpled Stetson pushed down over her ears. Anna was high as a kite – her pupils were compressed to pinpricks and she was grinning and clapping, pointing past Harry at the swirling patterns on a plasma screen. There were streaks of dirt across her face and a cut above one eyebrow.

Eva's hands roved up and down Harry's torso and hips. A small space opened up around them as if in deference to how wasted they were and they staggered back and forth without anchor, and for a split second they were on the verge of tumbling onto the floor but Harry grabbed the bar and they righted themselves.

Eva was laughing and Anna was laughing too.

Harry turned and ran her hands around Eva's waist and across her buttocks until she found the Curve tucked in the back pocket of her alligator-print shorts. She held it up above Eva's head and typed a message. Then she shook her and made her read it.

We're leaving

Eva squinted at the screen, wrinkled her nose and shook her head. She held up three fingers to a passing barman and soon there were three shots of tequila in front of them and Anna was pushing crumpled notes across the bar. Harry grabbed Eva by the wrist. There was crusted blood beneath her fingernails and more blood on her forearms. She raised a questioning hand but Eva just shrugged her off. She downed a shot and upended the glass on the bar. Anna did the same. Eva held up the remaining glass for Harry. She refused. She wrote another message.

Yuri and Suthy are outside

Eva looked outraged. She mouthed: *No!*

Yes

Eva took a step back with her arms out and mouthed: *Why?*

I take my job seriously

She seized Eva by the hand and led her away from the bar and across the crowded dance floor. To her surprise Eva did not struggle and Anna meekly followed. They went down the stairs and out onto the street where Suthy and Yuri were waiting by the armoured Tahoe. It was like stepping from an oven straight into a freezer – Eva and Anna howled and ran across the gravel parking lot with their hearts galloping. Eva staggered up to Yuri and kissed him on both cheeks. Harry was struck by the ferocity of the expression on Yuri's face. He looked like he wanted to hit her or worse. Harry hurriedly bundled Anna into a cab and returned to the Tahoe to find Eva sprawled on the back seat and Yuri standing by the open door watching her and looking like he was about to get in with her.

Harry knew she should go home and get some sleep but she didn't want to leave Eva on her own with Yuri. She glanced up the street in the direction of her car. It would be OK for a few hours, she thought. She could get a cab back here and pick it up in the morning.

Her mind made up, she pushed past Yuri and got in the back with Eva. Yuri turned away with an angry grunt and got in beside the driver. With the door closed it was almost as hot as the club and as they drove away, Eva kicked off her wellingtons and sat cross-legged on the seat with a reproachful look on her face. She couldn't maintain it though and within minutes had dissolved into a fit of giggles.

What have you taken?

nothing

What about Anna?

a pill

What was it?

i dont no

How did you get out of the house?

!i jumpd da fence!!

She held her bloodstained hands up high like a winning boxer.

What about the motion sensors?

!!!not touch ground!!! from tree 2 tree like TARZAN :0

Whose blood is that?

not mine!

She beat her chest. Harry shook her head and suppressed a grin; she found it difficult to be angry with Eva. She reached across and fastened Eva's seat belt. Then she took a bottle of water from the cool box and handed it to her; that done, she fastened her own seat belt. Eva drank from the bottle, pouring some into her cupped hand and running it through her hair. She typed on her Curve for a while, leaning into the bends as the Tahoe turned.

do u know 1000 NITES & 1 NITE?

The Arabian Nights?

yes :-) Do u know story of KINGS DAUGHTER & THE APE

Harry shook her head. Eva wrote a swift message and held up the Curve for Harry to see.

1ce ^on a time a PRINCESS fell in LOVE w/ an APE

Harry nodded uncertainly. Where was this going? Eva resumed typing with an expression of intense concentration. Eventually, she thrust the screen in Harry's face.

PRINCESS loves loves loves SEX! every 2 hours SHE wants 2 FUCK! no MAN can meet her need :-(SHE is going up the walls! then her HANDMAIDEN tells her nothing is as LUSTFUL as an APE! her mind whirrs! now 1 day a trader goes by HER window w/an APE & SHE immediately unveils her face & the APE stares in2 her eyes & sees the LUST there!!! HE breaks his bonds & climbs up 2 the PRINCESS & they FUCK :-) - AMAZING!!! - NUMBER ONE LUST! thereafter SHE hides him in her apartments & HE lives there night & day eating drinking & FUCKING . . .

Eva took another swig of the water bottle and wrote again.

to escape the WRATH of her father the KING the PRINCESS flees 2 CAIRO with her APE lover! every day she buys meat @ the market for the APE from a young MAN – a BUTCHER who falls 4 her gr8 beauty :-) but SHE comes each day 2 the market in a real state ;-) 1 day the BUTCHER decides 2 follow the PRINCESS home & is amazed to see her change into rich garments & wine & dine with a great big APE and then FUCK & FUCK with the APE until she passes out!

convinced that the PRINCESS must b under a malicious SPELL the young BUTCHER breaks in2 the house & confronts the APE !!! the APE is big and strong but the butcher plunges a KNIFE in2 the APE cutting him open!!! Startled awake by the noise, and coming upon her dying LOVER the PRINCESS shrieks & shrieks & shrieks . . .

the gallant butcher pledges 2 stand in for the APE but he is unable to cope with the PRINCESS's ravenous sexual appetite . . .

Eva took Harry's hand, held it for a while with her eyes shining and then slipped it under her vest. She held it against her chest so that Harry could feel her racing heart. Then she turned slightly so that one of her breasts was cupped in Harry's hand. When she made to pull away, Eva's grip tightened and Harry felt the nipple harden against her palm. Harry tried to push it away but Eva was incredibly strong. She was leaning into Harry who was pinned against the seat. Eva was kissing Harry's neck and her cheek and her free hand slid under the waistband of Harry's trousers.

The snowplough hit them side-on, knocking the Tahoe over on its side and pushing it across the road in a shower of sparks. It burst through a snow-bank and a row of parked cars, and up onto the sidewalk.

FIFTY-FIVE

Freeman ignored the buzzer and continued drinking.

Whoever it was would give up eventually and sure enough after five minutes or so the buzzing stopped. They could all go fuck themselves: Streeks, Oberstar, the FBI, the KGB, Cannon, Harry Armstrong, Dr Markoff, his niece Eva – every last one of them. Then someone started banging on the apartment door. He cursed the neighbour who had let them into the lobby. He yanked the door open. 'What?'

It was Maja.

'How come you're not answering your phone?' she demanded.

'What do you want?'

'I got a call from Second District,' she told him. 'Is it true you punched White House counsel?'

'I hit the man who's been screwing my wife on the President's time, if that's what you mean.'

He walked back into the living room with Maja following on his heels. She said, 'Do you have any idea how much trouble you could be in if he decides to press charges?'

'I wasn't giving much thought to the consequences.'

'Obviously.'

He picked up the bottle again and took a slug.

'Are you in the mood to share?' she asked.

'There aren't any glasses.'

She held out her hand for the bottle. 'We'll assume you don't have any communicable diseases.' She took a mouthful and looked around. 'She really cleared you out, huh?'

'She really did.'

They passed the bottle back and forth.

'You know something?'

'What?'

'I never liked Shawna much anyhow.'

They were kneeling on the bare, wooden floorboards. She was holding him while dry heaves racked his frame. He was sobbing. He couldn't control it; it had just welled up and out of him. 'What is happening to me?'

'Michael, you've got to stop punishing yourself,' Maja said.

'She used to love me. Now she hates me.'

'It's not your fault. You weren't right for each other. You know that. She was never going to make you happy. Now she's gone. You should be grateful.'

'How can I be?'

'Because you're free, because you can love whoever you want.'

Her hair against his face had a sweet, musky smell. She felt warm. He couldn't remember when someone had last held him like this.

'You can make someone genuinely happy.' She sighed and gripped him harder. 'Someone who gives a damn. Christ, Michael, you're so fucking slow sometimes . . .'

At that point she took off her clunky black-framed glasses. It was such a corny and comical act that he let out an involuntary burst of laughter.

'Are you laughing at me?' she demanded, poking him in the chest.

'Miss Hadžios, I didn't know you cared,' he said with tears streaming down his cheeks and poked her back.

'Bastard!'

A spark from eye to eye.

They were very still. Her hands were splayed on his chest and her eyes were shining ever so brightly. Time had come to a crashing standstill. The air around them shimmering like the air over a scorched road.

Then they were kissing.

Their lips pressed against each other, their tongues darting.

Their hands moving all over each other, touching everywhere, loosening and unbuttoning, swiftly stripping their clothes off and letting them fall away. He was kissing her mouth, her neck, her cheeks and her hair.

He picked her up and carried her to the bed. She spread her legs and raised them so that her knees almost touched her chin and he pushed aside the damp slip of cotton between her legs and within seconds he was deep inside her, plunging into her until she cried out, half sob and half laughter, and he was making a sound like a drowning man hauled back aboard, and something was leaping violently in his chest, and darkness was rushing towards him and he was lost in an extremity of emotion and abandon that he had never before experienced.

FIFTY-SIX

Silence. A sigh. A groan. The seat belt tightening across her chest.

When Harry came to, she found herself hanging in the back seat with the car door beneath her. Blinking, she looked around. Suthy was in front of her, with his face buried in an airbag and Eva was below her. Yuri was diagonally opposite, upside down with his head at a right angle to the rest of his body.

Harry pressed her fingers to Eva's neck and felt for a pulse. Satisfied that there was one, she reached around and undid her seat belt. She rolled across Eva and slid into the footwell below. She could see Yuri's purplish face squashed against the armoured glass. He was unconscious, possibly dead. She reached around the seat in front of her and, after several seconds of fumbling, slipped his gun out of his shoulder holster. It was a Glock 17. Nineteen-round magazine. She made ready just as she felt the thud of boots on the car's bodywork. Someone had jumped on top of the vehicle. Looking up, she caught a glimpse of a man in a black ski mask kneeling on the driver's door and slapping a charge down on it. Then he jumped free.

'Oh fuck!' She curled up in a ball with her hands over her ears.

The explosion was more muted than she expected. It sucked the air out of her lungs, leaving her gasping. When she opened her eyes, she had a clear view of the sky above, the dense clouds tinted orange by the city's sodium glow and the drifting snowflakes. Then a small, black, perforated cylinder flew in through the hole and rattled as it bounced off the dash and landed in her lap.

Flash-bang grenade.

She grabbed it and threw it back out through the hole.

It went off, emitting a blinding million-candlepower flash and a subsonic bang. Then Harry, who was taught to take best advantage of the space created by a bang, and had spent hour after hour practising such an event, was scrambling up and out of the car, rolling off the upturned side and landing on her feet. The man in the ski mask who placed the charge had dropped his weapon and was stumbling backwards towards the street with his head in his hands. He collided with a parking meter, fell and struggled to get up again. Harry advanced on him. The man rolled over on his back and pulled off his ski mask. Blood was running out of his ears. Harry put two rounds into his chest, stuck the Glock in her waistband and picked up his discarded weapon, an MP-5K submachine gun. She ejected a round and pumped a new round into the chamber to check the working parts.

To her left, a man jumped down from the cab of the snowplough. He was about sixty feet away, also armed with an MP-5. Harry knelt, fired a three-round burst in his direction and scuttled back around the side of the Tahoe.

'Eva!' Harry shouted and banged on the roof of the car. But of course Eva couldn't hear her and Harry couldn't hear either. It felt like she was underwater. She raised a hand to an ear and it came away sticky with blood.

At the rear end of the Tahoe, she risked a glimpse. The man who came out of the snowplough was dragging himself away across the ice and snow, a bright red stain on white.

There was a second vehicle, a white van. It had come out of the same side street as the snowplough.

Snow kicked up around her and a round nicked the car's bodywork above her head. She ducked into cover and behind her the plate-glass frontage of a CVS pharmacy turned opaque and collapsed. She ran to the front end of the Tahoe, took a breath, popped up out of cover and fired a three-round burst at the van. She dropped back out of sight as they returned fire. There were three of them. One was kneeling by the van's front wheel providing covering fire. The other two were running diagonally across the street in the direction of the nearest parked cars. They were trying to get around behind her. She ran back to the rear end of the Tahoe, thumbed the switch to automatic and sprayed the line of parked cars from end to end until she was out of ammunition. She threw the MP-5 away and drew the Glock. She had seventeen rounds left. As she scrambled to achieve a new fire position, a shadow passed over her, Eva leaping from the upturned vehicle and landing in a crouch beside her.

She fired three more shots and dropped down again. Time to think about an exit.

As if reading her mind, Eva was pointing at the CVS. Harry nodded and together they sprinted for its garishly lit interior. They hurdled the low brick wall, skidded across a linoleum apron sparkling with chips of fractured glass and ran down a carpeted aisle between rainbow stacks of candy. At the back of the store, by the pharmacy counter, Harry shot out the lock on a door marked STAFF ONLY. Then they were running past a row of cardboard boxes, and out through an emergency exit past a line of trash-cans dripping ice stalactites and across a staff parking lot that was as sheer as an ice rink.

Slipping and sliding, they ran between parked cars and diagonally across a road towards a dark mass of woodland. At the road end they jumped a crash barrier and tumbled down a snow-covered slope into a ravine.

FIFTY-SEVEN

Freeman ran a hand down her flank and across her thigh. He was lying on his back with Maja's head resting on his shoulder and her heavy breasts pinned against his chest. She pressed closer and he felt the strength of her.

'I know that in the cold light of day you're going to regret this,' Maja told him, lifting herself on one elbow and looking down at him, 'so don't worry, we can pretend it never happened. My mother always said I had shitty timing.'

He wanted to press a finger gently to her lips to stop her. 'Don't ruin the moment,' he whispered.

'It's OK, Michael.'

He smoothed back a stray lock of her hair. 'Thank you,' he said.

'For what?'

'For this.'

They kissed again.

Her cell began chirping like a cricket. She grimaced, rolled off the bed, scrambled among her clothing, hauled it out of a jacket pocket and held it to her ear.

'Yeah, what?' She listened and grimaced again. 'When? Just now?'

A male voice, tinny and indistinct, leaked from the phone. Maja looked at Freeman and raised an eyebrow. Freeman groped for his watch. It was 3.15 a.m.

'Yes, he's with me now,' she said. 'We'll be there in ten.'

She ended the call.

'That was Eli. Your friend Harry went out again a couple of hours ago. She met up with Eva. Somebody's just had a pop at them.'

★   ★   ★

They hurried past hissing red flares dropped in the road and through the cordon of patrol cars and FBI vehicles.

EliWrath and Kari Marschalk were standing beside the upturned Tahoe. Beside them was Special Agent Gunning, head of the FBI's local field office in DC. Kari was nodding helpfully and Eli was scowling and lighting a cigarette off the stub of another.

There were five dead bodies sprawled on plastic sheeting in the road: one by the white van, one by the snowplough, two by the line of cars at the kerb and the fifth in front of the Tahoe. FBI investigators were planting coloured flags to mark the locations of shell casings. Inside the Tahoe was a sixth body. It was Yuri, the massive bodyguard that Freeman had met at the lab that afternoon. His head was at an unnatural angle, his face purple, his neck broken.

'Gonna need a crane to get him out,' Eli said.

'What happened?' Freeman demanded.

'We were crossing the bridge,' Kari explained. 'It happened right in front of us. The snowplough came out of Macomb and rammed the Tahoe side-on. The second vehicle, the van there, also came out of Macomb. There were two explosions – tap, tap – one after the other. Then the shooting started.'

'They used a slap charge to blow the door open,' Gunning added. 'That's the first explosion. The second explosion was a flash-bang grenade. It's there on the ground.'

Freeman stared down at the perforated black cylinder on the tarmac.

'It's a throw-out,' Eli said. 'Harry came out after it and put two rounds in this guy here, two in the first body there by the line of cars and three more in the guy there by the snowplough.'

Harry didn't hesitate. She came under attack and she responded ruthlessly and efficiently. Difficult not to admire her decisiveness, Freeman thought.

'The other girl came after her,' Kari said.

'Eva Markoff,' Freeman said. 'Then what?'

'We flipped on the lights and the siren. Soon as we did that we came under fire. We got out of the car and returned fire, took the last two down. One by the van, one by the parked cars.'

'The two females ran out through the back of the CVS and into the park,' Gunning said. 'Uniform are in the woods and we've put out a BOLO on them.'

'The driver?'

'He's in an ambulance on his way down to the Correctional Treatment Facility. We should be able to talk to him in a couple of hours. The Tahoe is registered to a Tennessee company, Raeburn Correctional Services.'

'I know them,' Freeman said.

He returned his attention to the body of the dead attacker at his feet. He had pale translucent skin and lank blond hair.

'Who is he?'

'No wallets or ID. We're waiting on prints. Look at this.' Gunning knelt down and lifted a dead hand. The attacker was wearing leather gloves with the ends of the fingers cut off and his fingertips were stained with ink from where the techs had taken an impression. Gunning peeled off the glove revealing that the man's fingers were tattooed above the knuckles with prison markings – ill-formed blue symbols made from an ink of charred boot heel and urine: Cyrillic characters, a cross, a stack of skulls. 'We think they're Russians.'

'It was a professional hit,' Maja said.

'Guns and vehicles?' Freeman asked.

'Both the snowplough and the van were reported stolen earlier this evening,' Gunning explained, 'and the sub-machine guns were boosted from the Harvey police range in Chicago last year.'

'Shit!' Freeman said.

'What is it?' Maja demanded.

Freeman had remembered his promise to Senator Oberstar. He was already running for the car. 'Dr Markoff . . .'

FIFTY-EIGHT

They had come tumbling down through the trees in the darkness onto an old roadway with fractured plates of tarmac thrusting up through the snow.

At the bottom Harry pulled Eva down and they crouched against a bank, gasping for breath. Her hands were shaking. She jammed them together. She was cold and getting colder. She was going into shock, she thought, her peripheral blood system shutting down. *Not now*, she told herself. With an effort, she raised herself up to look and she saw the wash of red and blue police lights on the bridge and the flashes of gunfire but she still couldn't hear anything except a buzzing sound like a swarm of flies in her ears. Eva tugged at her sleeve and led her along the road and across a frozen stream into the woods on the far side. Soon they were among closely packed firs and pines, where the snow had hardly penetrated. Eva seemed to know where she was going. She pulled Harry down onto her knees and they crawled forward across a carpet of pine needles as dark and ragged shapes like monstrous antlers loomed above them, a massive deadfall. Eva led her into a narrow tunnel beneath interlocking branches, towards a hollow space at the centre of the deadfall.

It was warmer than the outside and there was a sharp, stale smell.

Harry remained still as Eva rummaged in the darkness for something, then a red-filtered torch flicked on, illuminating a narrow space with a sleeping bag, a waterproof duffel bag, a steel Thermos and some discarded takeout boxes. It was some kind of bolthole, a temporary resting place sheltered from the elements. Eva's evident familiarity with the place suggested that she'd used it before. This was where she came at night?

Eva had unzipped the sleeping bag and climbed in and was gesturing for Harry to join her. They huddled together. Eva smiled and smoothed the hair from Harry's face. She switched off the torch and pressed Harry's cold hands to her warm torso.

She could see glimpses of torchlight and as her hearing returned Harry could hear men calling to each other in the trees. She was sure that they would soon be discovered. She would be arrested and questioned, forced to explain what had happened. It had been mostly instinct, action unhindered by reflection. She now wished that she hadn't shot the first man, the one closest to her who was stumbling backwards, stunned and defenceless. But there were too many of them and he was too far inside her space. She couldn't afford to leave him so close. She was protecting Eva; she was doing her job. She told herself she didn't have any choice, everything in her training confirmed that, but a counter voice said there was always a choice. She had no idea who the attackers were; what if they were cops? What the hell was she going to say to Jack? She wished she could speak to him but what reassurance was there that he could offer?

She felt a plunging sense of despair. Eva wriggled against her and held up her Curve for Harry to see.

give me yr phones

Harry handed over the two cells, her personal one and the one given to her by Allegra Puck. Eva popped the cases with a nail and removed the batteries, stashing the disassembled pieces in the pocket of a down jacket that was leaking white feathers from several tears.

Harry took the Curve and typed a message:

What just happened? Who were those men that attacked us?
RUSSIANS mayb
Why?
they want 2 take me back 2 Russia
Why?
bcoz ov my eggs
What's so special about your eggs?

Eva just shook her head and popped the battery on the Curve.
'SSSleee . . .'

'Sleep! Are you crazy?' Harry said and then because it seemed
so ridiculous, given the dire situation they were in, she started
giggling. A strange, strangled kind of giggling that was really just
the adrenalin working its way out of her via the most inappropriate channel that it could find.

Eva gripped her tighter.

'SSSleee . . .'

Fuck it, why not? Harry thought. She couldn't be more tired.

She closed her eyes. She felt her heart pounding in her chest.
Concentrate on your breathing, she told herself; in through the
nose and out through the mouth. Let the breath fill your tummy
and your chest.

She felt her heart gradually slowing as she relaxed.

There was nothing to be done.

She gave herself up to sleep like someone falling.

Down. Down.

Into the realm of dreams – eddies in the unconscious – images
coming together and moving apart, bumping and swirling like ice
floes in a fast-running river.

FIFTY-NINE

The bodies were still warm.

The gate was wide open and the security guards were slumped over the monitors in the sentry box. The screens were blank, the video feeds disconnected.

'Call back-up,' Freeman said, drawing his Glock.

Together they ran up the gravel driveway to the house.

The front door was standing ajar. The third guard was slumped at the bottom of the steps; he'd crawled out of the house before dying, leaving a trail of blood on the steps behind him.

Eli and Kari took the ground floor, Freeman and Maja the first floor. They moved from room to room, shouting, '*Room clear!*'

The panic room door had withstood a slap charge.

They advanced through the swirling dust down a narrow corridor that still reeked of the tarry smell of burned explosives. The door was scarred and blackened, the CCTV camera above it was hanging off its mounting, but the intercom still worked.

Freeman pressed the button and spoke into the microphone. 'Dr Markoff?'

The response was immediate. 'Yes?'

'It's Lieutenant Freeman, with the Metropolitan Police Department. We met at the lab yesterday. It's safe for you to come out now, sir.'

'Stand back.'

With a dull thud the door opened. Dr Markoff was standing wild-eyed in his pyjamas.

SIXTY

Harry was jolted awake by the sound of someone scrambling down the tunnel towards her.

She grabbed the Glock and the torch. Whoever it was stopped suddenly.

'Who's there?' she called out, pointing the gun, remembering that she had fourteen rounds left. Where the hell was Eva?

No response.

She switched on the torch. Gasped.

Eva loomed out of the darkness on her hands and knees. Her eyes were black in the light from the torch and as glossy as marbles. She was wearing the black down jacket and on the crown of her head were a pair of bulky goggles. She was carrying a bundle of clothing and a couple of paper bags with grease marks that shone in the torchlight.

She eased herself in beside Harry and handed her one of the bags. Inside was a cold burger still in its greaseproof wrapping and a handful of loose fries. Dumpster food, Harry thought. She handed it back.

Eva shrugged and swiftly consumed the contents of both bags.

As dawn broke, they were trudging north on a ridge-top trail through jumbled snow-covered rocks and beech trees with the frozen ribbon of Rock Creek below them.

Eva led the way and Harry followed. It was snowing again and Eva had her face covered with a ski mask and she had pulled the goggles down over her eyes. She was wearing black waterproof pants and the ragged black down jacket that was leaking feathers. Harry was wearing brown District Department of Public Works thermal coveralls with the DC stars and bars logo, the bounty of Eva's foraging expedition.

It was slow going in the snow. They had passed high above the Boulder Bridge that crossed the creek and then dropped down into the valley and hurried along the tarmac path under Military Road, which bisected the park on concrete stanchions from east to west, before climbing again to the Western Ridge Trail. Twice Harry had heard dogs barking in the distance.

They had come about two miles by Harry's reckoning and the Boundary Bridge that marked the edge of the District couldn't be more than another mile ahead.

She resolved to walk that far and no further. She would demand an explanation.

What are we doing?

They were close to the District line, squatting on a snow-covered sandbar beside the frozen creek. Harry had insisted that Eva put the battery back in her BlackBerry. In response, Eva had unfolded a map of DC and spread it out on the snow.

we hav 2 go 2 the lab

Her index finger with its bloody, grime-encrusted nail traced a line from the District, following the river on its meandering route north and then turning west, cutting under the Capital Beltway and around behind the National Institute of Health. The river would lead them directly to the lab. About four miles more.

Harry typed:

Why do we need to go there?

i hav 2 get something

What?

the rite kind ov sperm ;-)

What do you mean?

no time 2 xplain we hav 2 go!

The police will probably be watching the place

we can go in ^ the wall

Then what?

u can call yr contact & we can get out ov here

Eva reached out and gave Harry a reassuring squeeze.

itll be ok !!!

She stood up, folded the map again and stuck it inside her jacket. She pulled down the goggles over her eyes, turned and continued alongside the creek, scrambling from rock to rock.

Harry was left with two choices: refuse to go any further or follow Eva.

She chose to follow Eva.

SIXTY-ONE

'This is what comes of doing business with Americans.'

The light over the door of the interview room was green. Inside, Freeman and McCafferty sat on one side of the desk and Dr Alexander Markoff on the other. It was 8 a.m. on Thursday. Fifty-two hours since Harry Armstrong found Katja's body and called 911. They were in Police Headquarters. Dr Markoff was in custody and had waived his right to a lawyer.

'What do you mean?' Freeman asked.

'You don't know how to keep secrets. Your government leaks like a sieve. How else did the KGB know where to find me?'

'You mean the SVR?' McCafferty said.

Dr Markoff snorted derisively. 'Same animal, same spots. You can call them what you like.'

'You are saying that the men who invaded your house and ambushed the vehicle carrying your niece were working for the Russian intelligence services?'

'Of course. Only an idiot would think otherwise.'

'Why would the SVR be interested in attempting to kill you or abduct you?'

'Because of my work.'

'What is your work?'

'You must ask the Pentagon that question.'

'We have,' McCafferty said. 'They weren't so keen to share.'

Dr Markoff shrugged. 'Are you going to let me go?'

'We've spoken to the Customs and Border Protection Agency, Dr Markoff. There is no record of you entering this country. As far as we're concerned you're an illegal immigrant and we can keep you detained for as long as we want.'

'I have to find my niece.'

'Do you know where she is hiding?' Freeman asked.

'No.'

'Do you have any means of communicating with her?'

'No.'

'Let's run through the events of the evening again,' Freeman said. 'When did you last see your niece?'

'When I went to bed at about 10 p.m., she was in her room reading. I said goodnight.'

'Then what happened?'

'I've told you, I was woken by a call from my employee Harry Armstrong informing me that Eva had broken her curfew and was in a DC nightclub. I tell you, I was angry. I sent Yuri and the driver to collect her and bring her back immediately. I was waiting for her when the house came under attack. If I had been asleep maybe they would have taken me. Instead, I retreated to the panic room. They were unsuccessful in their attempt to break in. You found me there. That's it.'

'How long has Harriet Armstrong worked for you, Dr Markoff?' Freeman asked.

'Since yesterday morning.'

'Since she witnessed a woman's body being dumped in Rock Creek Park?'

'I don't know anything about that.'

Freeman opened the folder on the desk in front of him and removed a photo of Katja's barcode tattoo. He slid it across the top of the desk.

'Do you recognise this?'

'No.'

'I think you do.'

Dr Markoff shook his head furiously.

'Look at it,' Freeman insisted.

'I'm an expert in DNA barcodes, not commercial ones.'

'I think you recognise it. I think that when you came to this country you brought with you the young woman who had this tattoo.'

'I don't know what you are talking about.'

'I think you trafficked her and used her. You forced her to have sex with politicians and other influential people to secure funding for your work.' Freeman was aware of McCafferty openly staring at him. He didn't care. 'You pimped her out for your work.'

'You don't know anything,' Dr Markoff retorted.

'I know she called you Uncle.'

Dr Markoff flinched.

'Was she your niece also?' Freeman demanded.

'You don't understand,' Dr Markoff said.

'Somebody killed her,' Freeman said. 'They smashed her face to pieces and dumped her like a piece of trash in the woods.'

He slipped a photo of Katja's demolished face out of the folder and pushed it across the desk. Dr Markoff glanced at it and shuddered violently.

'Why have you shown me this?' Dr Markoff demanded.

'Because I think you know who killed her.'

'I have nothing further to say.'

'Did it make you angry when you found out what happened to her? Angry enough to kill anyone involved in her death?'

'I haven't killed anyone.'

'Not physically,' Freeman said. 'We've checked your prints against the crime scenes. They don't match. But I think you set it in motion. I think you spoke to Oleg Davidov not long after he dumped the body. We've got him on camera talking into his cell. I think he told you what happened and I think you sent someone to kill him and Byron Bastian, the driver. And I don't think it mattered to you or the killer if a lot of other people died along the way. Where is he? The killer, I mean. Have you got him in the basement of your laboratory?'

Dr Markoff snorted and then began to laugh. Soon he was laughing so hard he was crying.

'You stupid fucking guy,' he said.

SIXTY-TWO

The narrow, densely forested Klingle Valley ran right under the Connecticut Avenue Bridge, close to the site of the previous night's ambush. The asphalt road through the valley had been closed to cars since a storm in 1991 when a section three-quarters of a mile long collapsed into Klingle Creek.

Freeman parked the Impala by the chain-link fence at the north end with a large ROAD CLOSED sign on it. There were three cars there already. Patrol cars from Third District and the Park Police and Eli's silver Crown Vic. He recognised Kelly, who was standing by a gap in the fence. He was the overweight Park Police patrolman who had walked Freeman from the Park Road Bridge to the initial murder site on the first night. They were no more than a mile from Crestwood and the senator's house. He looked at his watch. It was 9.30 a.m. It had been snowing for more than twelve hours.

'They got you working that red ball,' Kelly said.

'They sure do,' Freeman replied.

He slipped through the gap and advanced up the broken tarmac road past dirty clumps of snow to where Eli was waiting with two uniforms.

'Follow me.'

Eli climbed down the bank, sinking to his knees in the snow, and crossed the creek with Freeman following. They headed into the closely packed firs and pines, where the snow had hardly penetrated, and the ground was thickly carpeted with pine needles. The light was dim, cathedral-like, with haphazard shafts of light piercing the thick canopy.

'Patrolman from Third District found it,' Eli said. He had

stopped in front of a deadfall of logs and branches that resembled a beaver's nest. Freeman squatted down by the dark hole that formed an entrance to the interior.

'Have you been in?' Freeman asked.

Eli nodded and passed him a torch. Freeman groaned. He got down on his hands and knees, and squeezed inside, crawling forward across a thick bed of pine needles to a hollow at the centre of the woodpile. A nest. There was a sleeping bag, some clothes and discarded takeout boxes. It was warmer than the outside and there was a stale smell of body odour and greasy food several days old.

'I reckon they holed up here for a few hours after the ambush and headed out at dawn,' Eli said, from the entrance. 'We'll know for sure once the techs are done.'

Freeman turned in the narrow space, the torch beam running across the low and ragged ceiling. There were several hairs caught in the jutting twigs; blonde ones and black ones. He shifted a bit further. He could feel something sticking into his lower back. From under the sleeping bag, he pulled out a brown paper bag. There was an iPhone in it with its battery missing. He crawled out of the nest and got to his feet.

Eli led him to the edge of the densely packed trees. There were footprints barely discernible in the snow, heading north into Rock Creek Park. They would soon be fully covered.

'K9 are out searching,' Eli said. 'I don't hold out much hope though. It's hard work for the dogs in this weather.'

'Come on,' Freeman said.

They walked back through the trees to the abandoned road and as they drew near Freeman called out, 'Any of you have an iPhone?'

'Sure,' Kelly said, hauling it out of his pocket.

'You ain't paying for that on your Park Police salary,' Eli said.

'Fuck you.'

Freeman snapped his fingers impatiently. 'Give me your battery.'

Kelly handed it over and Freeman fitted it to the iPhone he'd recovered from the brown paper bag and switched it on, hoping it wasn't password-protected. It was.

'Damn,' he said. He pocketed the iPhone and started walking back to his car.

'Hey, what the fuck?' Kelly shouted.

Freeman had just ducked through the gap in the fence when the iPhone began ringing. He snatched it out of his pocket. *Sonia calling.*

'Larry, where the hell have you been? The senator's furious . . .'

Larry Lumpe – Cannon's chief of staff.

'This is Freeman.'

There was a pause.

'Where's Larry?' she asked softly.

By the time Freeman and Eli arrived on the western side of Folger Park, patrol cars from First District had already blocked the street and set up a cordon. The Mobile Crime Lab's van and a Medical Examiner's Suburban as well as an engine from the Fire House on 8th Street were parked outside the row house and a uniform was standing by the door, which had been forced. They showed him their badges and entered.

'Damn,' Eli said.

The inside of the house had been extensively remodelled, walls had been knocked through, creating a loft-like space on the ground floor and a wide-open stairwell leading to the next level with a huge skylight in the roof above it.

Larry Lumpe's corpse was strung up in the stairwell and there were several firemen beneath him, discussing how to get him down. They were standing at the edges of a pool of crimson blood that had spilled down the wooden stairs and spread across the polished parquet floor. Marschalk, McCafferty and a woman, a red-haired Deputy Medical Examiner named Greenwald, were waiting with a couple of Crime Lab techs with cameras.

'He has visible injuries to his face, hands and genitalia,' Greenwald told Freeman. 'He's had his eyes gouged out. He was still alive when he was strung up.'

'How long has he been up there?' Freeman asked.

'Difficult to say,' Greenwald replied. 'At least seven or eight hours.'

'According to the cell phone company's tracking records Lumpe's phone was switched off at midnight last night,' Marschalk said and glanced at his watch. 'Just over ten hours ago.'

'Do you know what gibbeting is?' McCafferty said.

Freeman shook his head.

'It's an old English common law punishment,' McCafferty explained. 'The dead bodies of executed criminals were hung on public display.'

'Go on.'

'It's a message.'

'For us?' Maja said.

Freeman shook his head. 'No. Not us. For whoever killed Katja.'

'The injuries are the same as Davidov's,' McCafferty continued. 'And my guess is, it would have happened to Byron too if the killer had got to him before the SWAT team did. Mutilation is a commonplace characteristic with serial killers but it usually has some kind of broader meaning particular to the killer. In this case I'd say it's a punishment for what they did and what they saw. The rape and then murder of Katja. My guess is Lumpe's your third man.'

'If he is we've got probable cause to search the senator's house,' Freeman said. 'How quickly can you process a DNA sample?'

'Give me a swab I'll run it straight down to Quantico.'

Freeman glanced at the Deputy Medical Examiner.

'Get him down, I'll give you a swab,' she said.

'Lieutenant.'

Freeman turned to face the uniform in the doorway. 'Yes?'

'There's a woman out here. She says she works for the senator.'

Freeman pushed past him. Sonia Rojas was standing by a patrol car. She was wearing earmuffs and an ankle-length cashmere coat. She appeared to be on the brink of tears.

'He's dead, isn't he?'

Freeman nodded. She closed her eyes. When she opened them again they were full of tears.

'When did you last speak to him?' Freeman demanded.

'He called me last night,' she said. 'It must have been about eleven o'clock. He said there was something he had to tell me, something bad.' She hesitated. 'I told him I'd speak to him this morning.'

'Did he often call you that late?'

'Sometimes. Mostly when he was drunk.' She shrugged her shoulders. 'He had a puppy-dog crush on me.'

'I'm sure he did,' Freeman said coldly. 'Was he drunk last night?'

'I assumed so. He seemed distressed.'

'And you hung up on him?'

'Yes,' she replied.

'Come with me,' he said. He led her by the arm up the steps and through the front door.

'Quiet please!'

When she saw the body, he thought she might faint. She swayed on her feet and he tightened his grip on her arm.

'No . . .' she whispered.

SIXTY-THREE

She knows, Freeman thought. She's known all along.

They were sitting in a booth in Pete's Carry Out, just a block north of Folger Park. Eli and Kari were sitting in the next booth. Sonia Rojas had been crying.

It was 10.30 a.m.

'It's time you started levelling with me,' Freeman said.

She nodded, patting her red-rimmed eyes with the backs of her hands.

'Let's go back to the beginning,' he said, 'to the night of the murder. Lay out for me what happened.'

'I was with them,' she said, sniffing, 'until about 10 p.m.'

'At the senator's house?'

'Yes.'

'What were you doing?'

'They were horse-trading line items in the defence budget. The senator was taking calls from other members of the Armed Services Committee. The senior senator from Connecticut asked him to oppose a motion to kill an order for submarines that the Pentagon doesn't need or want. They build submarines in Connecticut, Lieutenant. They build tanks in Ohio, fighters in Georgia and aircraft carriers in Virginia. Everybody wants a piece of the pie.'

'And then you left?'

'Yes. I went home and took a shower and went to bed.'

'But he called you back.'

She nodded miserably. 'That's right. He woke me up and told me to get over there straight away. He said the Park Police had found a body by the fence. He said the situation needed managing.'

'How did he seem?'

'Subdued. Calm on the surface.'

'And underneath?'

'The senator is a complicated man. He keeps a lot hidden.'

'Even from you?'

She didn't like that. 'Even from me,' she said.

'And when you got to the house?'

'It was just Larry and the senator. The mayor didn't arrive for another five minutes or so.'

'What state of mind would you say that Larry Lumpe was in?'

'He was upset. More than upset. The senator told him to pull himself together. He was hard on him. Then the mayor arrived and after that the Chief of Police. They had a discussion about who to put in charge of the investigation. That's the first time I heard your name. The senator asked me to fix a flight up from Tennessee for his wife and stepdaughter. Then you showed up. We gave our statements. The senator insisted that we leave the house. I booked him a suite at the Mandarin Oriental. A room for Larry too. At first, I thought it was because of the press. But then when the killings began the senator seemed genuinely worried. He requested extra Secret Service protection and he wouldn't leave the hotel suite without them.'

'What about Larry Lumpe?'

'Cannon told me Larry was struggling with some personal issues. He instructed me not to discuss the events of that evening with Larry or anyone else. He said the police were pursuing a personal vendetta against him. I thought he was being paranoid.'

'And then Larry called you last night?'

'That's right.'

'How would you describe his state of mind when he talked to you?'

'He was drunk. He was freaking out. He kept talking about being punished. He'd walked out of the Oriental. He'd walked all the way home in the snow. He said he couldn't take it any more.'

'Did he tell you what happened that night?'

'He said the girl was in the house.'

'You're sure about that?'

'Absolutely. He said that he'd done something bad. He said that he didn't want to tell me what it was because he didn't want me to think he was a bad person. He said that he didn't kill her. He was emphatic about it. That's it. I told him to go to sleep. I ended the call.'

'Why?'

'Because I didn't want to know,' she said, and he heard the throttled sob in her voice. She was barely holding herself together. 'Does that satisfy you?'

'Why are you protecting Cannon?'

She hesitated. 'I'm not.'

'I don't believe you. What is the nature of your relationship with the senator?'

'I'm not having sex with him if that's what you mean. I'm not his type.'

'What does that mean?'

'Have you seen his wife, his ex-wives? They're of a type.'

'He's never touched you?'

She laughed bitterly. 'He doesn't like to touch.' She turned to look at him. 'The senator likes to watch.'

'What do you mean?'

'I used to stay at Cannon's house sometimes. If a group of us were working late and my ex-husband was looking after my daughter then I'd sleep in one of the guest rooms. I'd been doing it for a couple of months when I discovered a hidden camera in the room.'

'I see,' Freeman said, after a pause. 'What did you do?'

'I stopped staying over. Listen to me, Lieutenant, I have a very well-paid and satisfying job. If there is a downside, then I just suck it up. I'll tell you this, he's never laid a finger on me and he's never threatened me. Never!'

'What is it you're not telling me?'

She looked away from him. Outside, medics were wheeling the gurney carrying Lumpe's body from the house to the morgue wagon.

'Jesus Christ,' she breathed.

'Tell me.'

'All right,' she said. 'But it may be nothing.'

'Go on.'

'Back when I first started working for Cannon, he was getting frequent letters from an address in Arlington. It was weird. The letters were written by a young woman, a teenager, but the events that she referred to happened long before she was born. It turned out that an elderly man who didn't speak English was getting his granddaughter to write the letters. Eventually Cannon got a legal injunction, a restraining order, out on the man and the letters stopped.'

'What was in the letters?'

'Cannon said the old man was crazy, probably suffering from post-traumatic stress and we shouldn't pay any attention. He said he didn't blame the young woman. She was being manipulated. He told us not to read them.'

'But you did?'

'I only read one of them. And not at the time it was sent. This was maybe three years after the last letter and after I'd stopped staying over at the senator's house. I was clearing out his office. I found them. A bundle of the letters. I'd assumed that they'd been destroyed. I was curious, I suppose. It seemed so odd. I didn't understand why Cannon had kept them. I read one. The young woman claimed that her grandfather was in Vietnam with Cannon. She accused Cannon of killing a local girl. A prostitute. She said that he had smashed her face with a hammer. Yesterday morning, when you told me what had happened to the girl in the park, it made me think of the letter I saw.'

Sitting across from her, Freeman remembered the conversation that he had with McCafferty back at the Watergate when he'd asked him if Cannon had any enemies. McCafferty had told him about the restraining order but dismissed it as nothing out of the ordinary, a commonplace hazard of political life. Freeman struggled to remember the name on the paperwork.

'I didn't want to believe it,' Sonia Rojas said. 'I should have told you before. I realise that. I'm sorry.'

She bent her head in shame.

Freeman felt stirred in equal measure by anger and determination. Anger that he had had to wait so long to have his suspicions about Cannon confirmed, along with the determination to solve the mystery of Katja's death.

'What happens next?' she asked.

'One of my colleagues will take you down to headquarters and you'll give a statement.'

'And then?'

'I want you to go back to work for Cannon.'

'You're serious?'

'Yes.'

'I don't want to end up with my face smashed in.'

'I'll make sure that doesn't happen.'

'I've learned not to rely on the promises of men,' she told him coldly.

SIXTY-FOUR

Eva passed Harry the binoculars.

They were lying in the snow at the edge of the tree line, about a hundred feet from the back of the Germline BioSciences compound. It was 11 a.m. Harry studied the fence, which she judged to be about twelve foot high. There was an open field before it and a steep drop beyond it, with a frozen moat that was not visible from the road. It was the kind of moat that Harry had seen in the National Zoo that was designed to separate animals from the public. On the far side of the moat there was a large climbing frame with steel hawsers strung between wooden platforms: the bonobo enclosure. Through the binoculars Harry could make out the open steel hatch in the glass wall.

They had already completed a full circuit of the lab, staying well out of sight. Sure enough, the police were camped out at the entrance, two cruisers from Montgomery County Police Department blocking the gate.

The hatch was the only way in. Once inside they would have to contend with Raeburn security guards who were under orders to apprehend them on sight. It felt like the forces ranged against them – the police, Raeburn and the Russians – were too powerful for them to prevail against. But Eva didn't seem concerned. There didn't seem to be any option other than to face each challenge as it arose, and the first up was the fence.

Are you sure we can get over that?

piece of cake!!!

Eva stashed the binoculars back inside her duffel bag and the Curve in the pocket of her jacket. She rose to a crouch and showed five fingers, four, three, two . . .

She sprinted across the open space and was at the fence in seconds. She turned as she struck it, bracing herself against the chain link with her hands forming a stirrup on her knee for Harry's boot. Here goes, Harry thought, hopping into the stirrup. She felt herself gripped by the sole of her boot and then propelled effort-lessly upwards.

Eva took a few steps back while Harry balanced precariously on the top of the fence and then took a running jump that carried her up the vertical face of the fence and over the top, straight past Harry. She landed on the far side with her knees bent and her arms out, one hand gripping the duffel bag.

Harry dropped to the ground beside her.

They were in.

SIXTY-FIVE

Harry followed Eva down an all-white corridor.

They were on Level Three. At the end of the corridor was an airlock with a yellow and black bio-hazard symbol and a sign that said OBSTETRICS. Eva put her palm against a pad and the door hissed open.

Harry's jaw dropped.

Incubators.

Rows of incubators on cabinet stands, at least a hundred of them, stretching across a gleaming white space. Mottled pink shapes attached to tubes and monitors inside the clear glass boxes. About halfway across the room a woman in a white suit and face mask was leaning over one of the incubators. She looked up, startled, as they entered.

Eva grabbed Harry by the hand and pulled her along with her between two rows of incubators, heading for a door on the far side of the room. The woman was shouting, though it was impossible to hear what she was saying because her voice was muffled by the mask.

As they ran, Harry caught glimpses of individual babies: pale limbs, tufts of hair, eyes closed, tiny fists clenching and unclenching . . .

Eva reached the door and slapped her palm on the pad. The door hissed open.

They ran through a suite of labour, delivery and recovery rooms and into a laboratory area beyond. Eva stopped at a wall of stainless-steel refrigerators and opened one of the doors. It was stacked full of dewars, wide-mouthed steel Thermos flasks shaped like milk jugs, with Cyrillic markings stamped on the outside. Eva took one out and consulted the markings and then put it back. She did this several times before apparently settling on the right one. She shrugged off her backpack, stashed the dewar inside, zipped it up and slung the pack back over her shoulders.

A brief smile.

The right kind of sperm, Harry thought.

They set off again, running back the way they had come, Eva out in front and Harry following.

They were halfway across the room with the incubators when two Raeburn security guards carrying batons burst through the airlock and ran towards them.

Eva surged forward.

The baton thrust came low, aimed at Eva's legs. She shifted into a fighting stance and swept her right hand in a low, outward arc, sweeping the baton away from her body. Then she stepped in, grabbed the guard by the collar and pulled him down, pivoted, and slammed his head onto the painted concrete floor. She ducked under the baton that the second guard swung at her head. Eva sprang up and slammed the heel of her left palm into the guard's face, the other into his groin. Dropping her left hand, she locked the elbow of the arm holding the baton and straightened up. The arm snapped. The baton fell. She released the arm, spun around so that her back was to her attacker, and kicked out, driving her foot into the guard's solar plexus. He staggered backwards, collided with the nearest incubator and dropped to the ground.

Eva glanced back at Harry, who was standing, stunned by the ferocity of the attack. Across the room, the woman in the mask was cowering behind an incubator.

Eva summoned Harry with a gesture and set off again towards the door.

SIXTY-SIX

Freeman parked outside a detached bungalow on a half-acre plot situated in a quiet residential neighbourhood in Virginia between the Windy Run and Spout Run rivers. He got out of the car and walked up the freshly shovelled pathway to the front door. He knocked and waited. He glanced at his watch: twelve fifteen. A young Chinese-looking woman in jeans and a Georgetown sweatshirt opened the door. Freeman showed her his badge and said, 'I'm Lieutenant Michael Freeman, MPD. I'm looking for Colonel Moc A Pao.'

'My grandfather is expecting you.'

'He is?'

'This way please.'

She led him down a corridor adorned with framed photographs of groups of young men in army fatigues and into a sitting room with a crackling log fire and large flat-screen TV playing Fox News on mute. An old, frail-looking man was sitting in an armchair beside the fire with a blanket covering his legs and the remote in his liver-spotted hand.

'Please sit down,' the young woman said, indicating an empty chair beside the colonel's.

Freeman sat.

A breaking news strapline was running across the bottom of the television: 'Senator admits woman "may" have been at his house the night of the murder.'

The old man raised the remote and restored the sound: 'This morning's gruesome discovery of the body of one of Senator Cannon's key aides has prompted an extraordinary confession from the Tennessee lawmaker outside his Senate office,' the anchor was saying.

At the mention of the senator's name, the old man's nostrils had flared.

'The unknown woman whose body was found in Rock Creek Park early on Tuesday morning may ...' The anchor glanced down at his notes. 'I repeat, may have been at his house shortly before her murder. The senator's belated confession has already drawn sharp criticism from a former federal prosecutor who called the senator's two-day silence suspicious. At a hurriedly convened press conference, Abe Proust, the senator's attorney, defended his client's failure to disclose that the woman was on his property, saying that he has done all he can to help investigators. Here's what Abe Proust had to say when he was asked why the senator had not come forward sooner.'

Cut to Proust at the centre of a jostling crowd: 'He is not going to invade his and his family's private life,' he said, to a barrage of flashguns. 'He is a public figure who is holding onto his private life.'

The old man shook his head in disgust and muted the television again.

They sat in silence.

'My grandfather is fully compliant with the terms of the injunction against him,' the young woman said eventually.

'I understand,' Freeman said. 'I'm not here about the injunction. I'm here to talk about Vietnam and what happened there.'

She nodded. 'Then I'm sure he will be happy to speak with you.'

Freeman leaned forward. 'Sir, can you confirm that in March 1969 you were stationed at a Special Forces outpost near the Laotian border known as Old Rag?'

As he spoke the old man sank into his chair.

'Yes he was,' the young woman said.

'I'd like to hear it from him,' Freeman said.

'My grandfather's understanding of English is good but he does not speak it very well. I am familiar with his story.'

'Please ask him the question.'

The old man painfully rallied. He started speaking in a language that Freeman did not recognise. When he stopped the young woman translated his words: 'My grandfather says that Senator Cannon seemed very sympathetic and charming at first.'

'Can you confirm that you were at Old Rag when it was attacked by the North Vietnamese Army?'

The colonel began speaking again; he was much more animated, and every now and then his granddaughter gripped him by the arm and he paused while she translated. 'He says that he was at Old Rag twice. The first time it was in 1965 when it was just a small outpost used by Special Forces. It was safe and secure. When he returned in the autumn of 1968 the situation was very different. There was now a large compound, a helicopter landing pad and a company of just over a hundred soldiers from the ARVN – that is the South Vietnamese Army. He says that discipline was not good. He says that the American Special Forces had a separate hooch at the edge of the perimeter, a series of interconnected bunkers fortified with sandbags and a metal wall and surrounded by concertina wire. They did not like for the ARVN soldiers to go inside. He is saying that they were not social animals, the Americans that is. He is saying that they were animals but not social. My grandfather's job and that of his men, who were all Nung, not Vietnamese, was not just to protect the bunkers against the North Vietnamese Army but also to keep the ARVN out. There was also one bunker that even the Nung were not allowed to enter. This is where they kept the girl.'

'Tell me about the girl.'

'He says that the girl arrived a week before the new captain. When Captain Cannon arrived he was not very happy about the girl. The Americans had brought her with them by helicopter from Danang. She was Khmer not Nung, originally from Cambodia.'

The young woman explained that Cannon had a reputation in Special Forces. He was special. Even the Nung had heard of him. They knew he was special not just for his matinee idol looks and shrewd intelligence and the glow of his ridiculously wealthy father – perhaps it was because he was trying to get out from his father's shadow – he was special because he was willing to take risks that no one else would, to disappear with his men into the fiercest fighting for weeks on end. There had been some muttering among the Americans when they heard he was coming. The Nung over-heard Sergeant Skirving referring to him as a sightseer, a war tourist, neglectful of the safety of those under his command. The Nung understood the acquisition of the girl to be a kind of rebel-lion, a way for Skirving to assert that they would not be fodder for Cannon's ambition. Skirving had enough warning of his arrival to fly the girl up from the dogpatch in Danang on a re-supply flight and get her settled in before Cannon got there. It was presented as a fait accompli.

But Cannon was having none of it. He insisted that she would have to leave immediately. Skirving pointed out that the next scheduled flight was a week hence and there was no way they could justify an unscheduled flight to Command simply to remove a whore. Cannon responded by taking the unit out on an impromptu six-night patrol, leaving the girl in his bunk and order-ing the Nung to look out for her.

'My grandfather says that she was a typical girl from a very poor family,' the young woman said. 'She was a prostitute, of course. But they protected her as they had been instructed to do. Up to that point the Americans had been treating her with a measure of courtesy. But that changed when they returned. Everything was different when they came back from the patrol.'

'Go on,' Freeman urged.

The patrol had not gone well. Skirving and Cannon had argued over the placement of an ambush. Skirving had said that the site was too close to the compound and might lead the enemy to discover their operating base. Cannon insisted that it was a likely infiltration route with the real chance of surprising the enemy. The argument became heated and only when Cannon threatened to put Skirving on a charge of insubordination did Skirving relent. In the event, they were both right. An NVA unit walked straight into the ambush and was wiped out and a much larger NVA force subsequently attacked the compound. But not before tragedy struck. Two of the men, one of them Skirving, died on the way back to base, when they walked through a trip wire, initiating a fragmentation mine. Only five of the original seven Americans returned. They stumbled back into camp well after midnight and they were angry. Cannon was the angriest. The Nung saw a side of him that had not been revealed before. The Nung realised that they had mistaken Cannon's earlier insistence on the girl's departure as concern for her wellbeing, when in fact it became clear that he felt a profound contempt for her. That contempt had now turned to fury. There was no more talk of flying the girl out. Instead Cannon deliberately handed her over to the men. They took her into a bunker that the Nung were not allowed to enter. The Nung could hear what was going on, though, and they were not happy. The girl was calling out, pleading for someone to help her. Cannon was the last one to go in, this was about 3 a.m. on the 30th of March, and they were disturbed by the grim set of his features. After he emerged they did not hear the girl again.

'The Nung were divided between those who argued that they should go and check on the girl and those who argued that it was none of their business. My grandfather was torn. Eventually, he decided to go and check on the girl. As he was approaching the entrance to the bunker the outpost came under attack.'

The Battle of Old Rag was in the pouring rain. Colonel Moc shook his head and let out a soft tutting noise. His granddaughter explained that they were hopelessly outnumbered: two-thirds of the ARVN strike force was on leave and many of the remaining strikers fled, leaving only the five remaining Americans and the Nung. They fought for four hours. They called in airstrikes. But eventually it was too much. Burdened with casualties and running low on ammunition, they retreated.

Cannon arranged for the casevac of the wounded and then, despite facing a much larger enemy force and being the sole remaining American, he led the Nung in a counter-attack and succeeded in recapturing the position.

'My grandfather says that Cannon fought like a demon, like a man with no concern for his own safety. He showed no mercy. He says that his men were as filled with fury as Cannon. There were no wounded and they did not take prisoners. When it was done they were exhausted. They sat in the mud and waited for reinforcement. That is when my grandfather remembered the Cambodian girl. He went to look for her. He does not like to remember what he saw in that bunker but he cannot forget. The corpse was tied down to an old pool table that the Americans had brought up on one of the re-supply flights. She was naked. She had been raped. Beside her body there was a hammer. Cannon had used it to smash her face so that she was completely unrecognisable. My grandfather was very angry. You can say it was madness to be angry at one death in the middle of a war when they were surrounded by so many bodies but this was different. This was against everything that the Americans were supposed to represent. My grandfather confronted Cannon, he accused him of murder. Cannon laughed. His laughter was very frightening. He said that the girl was an animal, no better than a cow or a buffalo in a field and that it was his right as a man of power to decide whether she lived or died. My grandfather had to be restrained.'

The colonel's hand shot out and gripped Freeman to prevent him from rising and going. He said, in broken English, 'It happened again, yes?'

'Yes, it did,' Freeman said.

The colonel spoke to his granddaughter and she squeezed his arm in reassurance. 'My grandfather says that the bunker was destroyed and with it the evidence. It was not like these days, like Abu Ghraib. There were no photos to record what happened. The outpost was abandoned. He was not able to find the dead girl's family. The war was lost and he came here. He says that he loves America, for the chances that it gave to his children and his grand-children. But he thinks that Cannon and his family are a terrible stain on the character of this nation. They are not citizens, they are like ancient kings set above other men and they believe that they can do whatever they like. He says that you must make Cannon pay for what he has done.'

'Tell him that I will do my best,' Freeman said.

The colonel let go of him and Freeman rose, more exhausted than he could have imagined.

'Will you succeed?' the girl asked him as she walked him to the door.

'I don't know,' he told her. 'I really don't know. I'm going to try.'

'I've lived with this for most of my life,' she said, shivering on the porch. 'I'm ready to see it end.'

SIXTY-SEVEN

Freeman was driving east on Constitution Avenue when he got a call from an unfamiliar number with a 617 area code. Cambridge, Mass.

It was Kaplan.

'I'm in a pay-phone,' he said. 'Call me back from a pay-phone.'

Freeman pulled over in the forecourt of the Museum of Natural History, jumped out and ran inside holding up his badge. There was a pay-phone behind the big totem pole. He dialled the number. Kaplan answered immediately.

'Where the hell are you?' Freeman demanded.

'I'm at MIT. They have a genome sequencing machine up here.'

'Go on.'

'When Homeland Security showed up at the morgue and snatched the bodies, I knew something wasn't right. So I palmed some buccal swabs. I brought them up here and persuaded them to sequence the DNA. Y'all are gonna love this, Michael.'

'What?'

'A misbegotten and premature poke at re-engineering, that's what. Y'all know what a mule is? I don't mean a drug courier.'

'A cross between a horse and a donkey?'

'That's right. A mule is a hybrid: a sterile mix of two distinct species with different numbers of chromosomes. A horse has sixty-four chromosomes and a donkey has sixty-two. When they mate they produce a mule which has sixty-three.'

'OK.'

'The dead girl was a hybrid. Human cells have forty-six chromosomes. The girl had forty-five. Only one of her gametes was fully human.'

313

'And the other?'

'A bonobo, the most sexually promiscuous of all the primates. Somebody built a nymphomaniac in a petri dish.'

Katja.

Her hair fanned across the pillow, a knowing half-mocking expression on her face.

You think I'm a girl. I'm not. It would be better to think of me as a monster.

'Michael, are you there?'

He swallowed. 'I'm here.'

'I got a two-for-one deal,' Kaplan told him. 'I've persuaded them to analyse the killer's DNA recovered from Oleg Davidov's murder scene. It wasn't exactly difficult. They're doing it right now. As soon as the results come through I'll call you.'

SIXTY-EIGHT

Freeman checked in his weapon at the Capitol Police post on the Senate side and walked across Constitution Avenue to the public entrance to the Russell Office building where Eli Wrath and McCafferty were waiting with Dr Markoff, sheltering from the falling snow. It was just before 2 p.m.

Eli handed Freeman a folded piece of paper, which he slid into his notebook.

'We'll be waiting for you,' Eli said.

'Thanks.'

Eli walked back to his car.

McCafferty looked at Freeman. 'You ready?'

'Sure.'

Together they passed through the metal detectors and walked the length of a wide marble corridor with pools of meltwater.

Raised voices.

They turned a corner to find a committee staffer outside room 226, her features grimly set, barring the way to the press pack, a thick knot of cameramen, reporters and photographers.

The pack turned as one as they approached and surged towards them.

Shouting. Microphones thrust in their faces.

'Are you here to arrest Senator Cannon?'

'Did he do it?'

'Is Cannon the killer?'

Freeman and McCafferty elbowed their way forward, pulling Dr Markoff after them.

'We're escorting a subpoenaed witness,' Freeman shouted, showing his badge.

The staffer nodded and stepped aside long enough for them to drag a startled-looking Dr Markoff into the committee room.

The wood-panelled room was large, with a high ceiling and several chandeliers that were switched on because hardly any light was coming through the windows. The three tables were arranged in a triangle with the witness seating on one side and places for the Democrat and Republican committee members on the other two sides.

As chairman, Senator Elizabeth Oberstar sat facing the witnesses at the apex of the triangle with her fellow Democrats down one side.

Under normal circumstances she would be the focus of attention. But all eyes were on the Republican side. Senator James D. Cannon was sitting at the centre with empty seats beside him. For a man increasingly under suspicion, who appeared to have been abandoned by his own party and had a witness forced on him by his political foes, Cannon was looking remarkably unruffled.

He watched without visible expression as Freeman steered Dr Markoff to a witness chair with a card bearing the doctor's name on the table in front of it. Freeman sat in one of the last remaining seats in the public seating area and McCafferty sat in another. Freeman recognised some of the faces around him: a couple of print journalists and, he could have sworn, some of the protesters from outside Germline BioSciences.

'Let's get started,' Oberstar said in a businesslike manner, and when she had finished her introduction she laid out the ground rules for the hearing: 'Here's how we're going to do it. Dr Augusterfer, we'll hear from you first. Your written statement has been put in the records, but what I want you to do is take five or seven minutes and share with us your ideas and then we'll go to you, Dr Markoff, same thing, and then we'll get into some detailed questions if it is warranted and if we have time. Please begin.'

The contrast between the two witnesses could not have been starker. Dr Augusterfer was a small, neat man with soft, pink skin and blue plastic-framed spectacles. He was wearing a crisp white shirt with a pen in the breast pocket and a navy blue tie and there were several sheets of neatly arranged paper in front of him. He looked like a parody of an IBM technician from the 1950s. Beside him, Dr Markoff looked like he had been up all night. He was tieless, his jacket was creased and his hair was disordered. He had no papers. There were no signs of preparation. He stared around as if lost.

'Thank you, Madam Chairman and ranking member,' Dr Augusterfer began. 'It is always a great pleasure to come before this committee and I'd like to thank you for your support in our longstanding efforts. I've prepared a written statement for the record and I have a few minutes' oral testimony.'

'Please go ahead,' Oberstar urged him. 'We're a little pressed for time here.'

'Thank you, madam,' Dr Augusterfer replied. He glanced down at the papers in front of him and began to read. 'The Defense Advanced Projects Agency has occupied a special role and mission within the Department of Defense since the time of Sputnik. Our mission is to provide the research and development that bridges the gap between fundamental discoveries and their military use. The work we support is necessarily high-risk and high return because we are trying to fill that gap. We do not look at what a military commander wants today. Instead we look at what future commanders might want. We look beyond today's needs and requirements because none of the weapons that have transformed modern warfare – the airplane, tank, radar, jet engine, helicopter, computer, drone, stealth, not even the atomic bomb – owed its initial development to a specific request by the military. At DARPA we focus on radical innovation . . .'

While Augusterfer was talking, Sonia Rojas looked up and briefly met Freeman's gaze before hurriedly looking down again. She was sitting behind Senator Cannon's right shoulder, almost hidden from view, taking notes on a yellow legal pad.

'DARPA's investigations at the intersection of biology, information technology and the physical sciences,' Augusterfer continued, 'began with the realisation that the biological sciences, when coupled with the traditional strengths of DARPA in materials, information and microelectronics, could provide powerful approaches for addressing many of the most difficult challenges facing the Department of Defense in the next fifteen to twenty years. Chief among these challenges is preventing human performance from becoming the weakest link on the future battlefield. For example, we must be able to maintain the decision-making and fighting capability of the soldier in the face of asymmetric attack, stress and increasingly complex military operations.'

Freeman took out his own notebook, opened it and flicked through the pages, with its messy scrawl of names, bullet points, lines and arrows, exclamation marks and crossings out. He reached the piece of paper given to him by Eli and removed it. Unfolded it. A search warrant for Cannon's house. Now it was just a question of deciding when to deliver it. He settled into his chair and waited.

'A major thrust for DARPA's biological science and technology programme is to explore solutions to extending human performance. Solutions include extending physical and cognitive performance during the stress of military operations.

'Let me give you some examples. For instance, eliminating the need for sleep during an operation, while maintaining a high level of both cognitive and physical performance of the individual, would create a fundamental change in war fighting. I'm talking about a 24/7 soldier, who could easily navigate, communicate and make good decisions for a week without sleep. Small groups of sleep-free Special Forces soldiers could run rings around an enemy. We are therefore working on preventing or reversing changes in the brain caused by sleep deprivation, expanding available memory space within the brain and developing problem-solving circuits within the brain that are sleep resistant.

'Hunger, exhaustion and despondency also slow soldiers down. One of the things we know about war fighters is that we can't deliver enough calories into them to maintain high levels of strength and endurance over time. A Special Forces soldier working a twelve-hour day burns about six thousand calories. If we increase that soldier's working day to twenty-four hours he's going to need twelve thousand calories a day. That's the equivalent of forty-six power bars in a day. You simply can't get that much food into a person and they can't carry it. So the question is, if you can't get enough calories in, why put in any at all? We've all got stored calories. Why not access them? To achieve this we are working on improvements at the cellular level. Take mitochondria for instance. They produce the energy to power the cells. We can improve them so that they can utilise the stored energy that's available. Instead of deploying lean and mean soldiers you deploy them mean and plump. And by modifying the number of mitochondria in the cells and increasing their efficiency at creating energy, we are confident that we can take an individual who is capable of eighty press-ups before exhaustion and make him capable of three hundred. Not to mention being able to walk for great distances with a hundred-and-fifty-pound backpack.

'The other issue is how to keep soldiers in peak condition the whole time so that there's no degradation in their performance level. We know that when you get hypoglycaemic you start to get depressed. You lose focus, mental acuity, response time and you stop caring. That's a bad thing to happen on a battlefield. We know that twenty-four hours after they go into action Special Forces soldiers' physical levels are 40 per cent below where they were when they started. We want to get rid of that degradation in performance. When you look at why people die on the battlefield it is because they are weak, or hungry, or making bad decisions or simply too tired to continue. We want to remove that if we are going to put people in harm's way. Thank you.'

'Thank you, Dr Augusterfer for your illuminating words,' Senator Oberstar said smoothly. 'But I'm keen to get into the specifics of this. We've had a good explanation of the problem, and we've heard some talk of living off your own fat and boosting your mitochondria but what are we actually talking about here? I want to know what it is that we are proposing to do to living creatures with taxpayers' dollars. I want reassurance that we're not meddling where we shouldn't.'

'DARPA does no work which we would consider execution,' Dr

Augusterfer replied. 'The actual work products – the milestones, goals and objectives – are all done by independent investigators.'

'Your hands don't get dirty,' observed Oberstar coldly.

'That's right, ma'am. We have no laboratory space.'

'Which is exactly why I requested the presence of Dr Markoff. Back in Soviet times Dr Markoff was the Chief Scientist at the Scientific and Experimental Production Base of Stepnogorsk in Kazakhstan. Now, Dr Markoff, I believe you have some experience of working with – how do you call them? Living systems?'

'Must I remind you, Senator,' Cannon said, breaking his silence, 'that this is an open hearing?'

'Of course, Senator,' Oberstar replied. 'Dr Markoff, please, we're all looking forward to hearing from you.'

SIXTY-NINE

Dr Alexander Markoff sighed, scratched his stubbled chin and shrugged. 'I must apologise to the committee because I have not prepared a written statement.'

'Don't worry, Dr Markoff,' Oberstar replied, 'this hearing is being recorded and so anything you say will be available online shortly after the hearing is concluded.'

Dr Markoff seemed surprised. 'Please go on,' Oberstar urged.

'I am listening to my colleague Dr, uh . . .' – he appeared momentarily confused and glanced at the nameplate on the table – 'Augusterfer. And I believe it was a good explanation.' As he spoke, Dr Markoff began to unfold himself. He uncrossed his legs and pushed his arms forward across the table with his palms out. 'In order to make future warriors, we must increase their physical limits. This is evidently true. So how to do it? That is the question you want me to answer?'

'Yes,' Oberstar said.

'With gene manipulation, of course. For this, animals are our best teachers. But to learn from animals we must first acknowledge that the differences between us and other living creatures are less a result of genetic and physiological difference than of the cultural construct we make around us. Understanding this is a fundamental element in finding the larger meaning of the control of human genetics and reproduction. People forget how close is our kinship to our animal ancestors – 98 per cent of human gene sequences are the same as a chimpanzee's, 85 per cent are the same as a mouse and more than 50 per cent of fruit fly genes have human homologues. We are all multi-cellular creatures.' With a flourish, he banged his fist into his open palm;

the showman had replaced the introvert. His eyes darted around the room.

'So questions, questions. How come a tadpole can re-grow its tail but an adult frog cannot? If we can figure that out then maybe we can re-grow a blown-off hand or the leg of a soldier. How come whales and dolphins don't sleep? If they sleep they drown. How do they do it? They switch off parts of their brain. What about the infrared and ultraviolet vision of spiders and snakes, the detection of magnetism of birds, sonar of bats and the acute smell of dogs? How come? It's all because of genes. Sure, there are loads of genes and gene combinations we don't understand but some we do understand. We know that we can change a single gene in a worm – *caenorhabditis elegans* – and double its life span. One gene! We can take a vole gene and put it in lab mice and they completely change their behaviour. They are not promiscuous any more. It's simple. You snip it out of one place and attach it in another. Could it be done in humans? Of course! Will it always work? No! It can take maybe tens, hundreds of embryos to make one successful change. There is the technical problem of nuclear transfer. There is the problem of cloned embryos and unpredictable gene expression that can lead to foetal abnormalities. There is the problem of pericentric inversions. All true. But these are just technical problems. Not fundamental ones. Every day we are solving these problems. Frankly speaking, *Homo sapiens* is not the final word in human evolution.'

He looked around expectantly. The entire room was silent.

'Thank you, Dr Markoff,' Oberstar said, 'for your very individual and highly theoretical views. I'm sure that I speak for all present when I say that I am glad that we are still a long way from making decisions about the genetic manipulation of human life.'

Dr Markoff shook his head in irritation. 'You can't stick your head in the sand.'

Cannon tapped the table several times with his fist.

Oberstar raised her eyebrows. 'Senator?'

'I propose that we adjourn the session,' Cannon told her.

'I have questions for Dr Markoff,' insisted Senator Oberstar. 'And you don't have the votes.'

Cannon visibly seethed.

Oberstar glanced down at her notes and then fixed Dr Markoff with her stare. At the same time, Freeman raised a hand to attract the attention of the nearest staffer. He gave her the warrant and, speaking in a whisper, asked her to deliver it to Sonia Rojas.

'Dr Markoff, is it true that in an interview with *Proceedings of the Academy of Sciences*, the foremost scientific journal of Russia, you said that, and I quote: "If we could make stronger human beings by knowing how to add genes, why shouldn't we?"'

Dr Markoff shrugged. 'Sure. Do you think that scientists unlocked the human genome out of idle curiosity or because we wanted to improve our capabilities?'

'I want this article put into the record,' Oberstar said.

Sonia Rojas glanced at the warrant. Then, as arranged, she passed it forward to Cannon.

'Dr Markoff,' Oberstar continued, 'I put it to you that the genetic manipulation of mankind would be a social nightmare from which no one could escape.'

'We're human. We change things. Look at you, Senator. You dye your hair blonde, you've straightened your teeth, fixed your nose, sucked out your stomach fat and made your breasts bigger.'

A ripple of laughter in the public seating; several of her fellow Democrats smirked.

'I have not!'

Dr Markoff laughed dismissively. 'Are you telling me you don't want high IQ, strength, endurance for your kids? Bullshit! You want to give up United States technological dominance because you're scared of science?'

Cannon was staring at the warrant in his hand, in a kind of trance, oblivious to the proceedings around him. The diversion was working better than Freeman could have hoped. It was extraordinary really, the level of Cannon's arrogance – that he had assumed that his house would never be searched.

'It is my belief, Dr Markoff, that human life is sacrosanct,' Oberstar said. 'That we were placed on this earth by God and given dominion over all other living creatures. It seems to me that what you are proposing, by which I mean the mixing of human and animal genes, is an abomination. If you go down this route you will create monsters.'

'It's done.'

You could have heard a pin drop.

'Excuse me?'

'The genie is out of the bottle,' Dr Markoff said with an indifferent shrug. 'It's done.'

Oberstar had registered that Cannon wasn't listening. She saw her opportunity and turned on Dr Markoff again. 'Is that what you were doing in Russia, Dr Markoff? Mixing animal and human genes?'

Dr Markoff looked to Cannon but got no response.

'What do you want from me?' he demanded.

'I want the truth!'

'Very well, Senator, in the 1980s I succeeded in reversing the chromosome inversion in a chimpanzee ovum so that it matched those in a human and I created a viable foetus. I did what no one else before me had managed to do.'

'Let me get this straight, you crossed a human and a chimpanzee?'

'That's right. Not just one, though. I made hundreds of them.'

'Why?'

'What do you think? For military purposes, of course. You're not as naive as you pretend. I did it for them for the same reasons that I am doing it for you, so that you can find new ways of killing each other. Only in the Soviet Union they were better at keeping secrets. Nothing in this goddamned country is a secret.'

The room erupted. Abruptly, Cannon snapped out of his trance.

'Clear the room!' he shouted. 'Clear the room! Now!'

Dr Markoff was pointing at him. 'You wanted monsters. I gave you monsters. But the truth is you're the monster!'

Staffers were advancing on the public seating. A man had produced a banner from somewhere and was waving it. Journalists were shouting questions.

Cannon stormed out of the room and was met by a tide of

electronic flash. He flung up his arm to protect his eyes or hide his face.

That's not going to look good on the evening news, Freeman thought.

Sonia Rojas appeared at his side.

'Are you satisfied?'

'Not yet,' Freeman replied.

He looked across at McCafferty who was perched on the table beside Dr Markoff who had his head buried in his hands and was ignoring the questions being shouted at him.

'You better get him out of here,' Freeman said.

SEVENTY

Freeman was the first to climb the steps.

One of the Crime Lab techs had found it: a nondescript doorway at the end of an unused corridor; and behind it, a narrow wooden staircase leading to the attic space, with the stub of a candle in a pool of stiff wax on every other stair. He took out his torch and told the others to wait. It grew colder as he climbed. He passed a light-switch on his right, paused and decided not to flip it. He remembered that the circuit that tripped and killed the cameras and the lights at the back of the house on the night of the murder also cut the lights to the attic. It was dark up here that night. He emerged into a long, low room that ran the length of the house, with a pitched roof and bare floorboards with paintings stacked against the gable end wall and in the spaces between bay windows. Stray wisps of cobweb. A line of candles ran from the top of the stairs to an old wooden pool table at the centre of the room. Outside it had finally stopped snowing and a shaft of light came through one of the bay windows, illuminating the floating motes of dust and the faded green cloth. It looked like a sacrificial altar.

You brought her up here, he thought, you led her up here by candlelight. The closest you could get to recreating a bunker in a distant land.

He circled the pool table, sweeping the torch back and forth: there were nylon straps in a pile beside one of the solid maple legs. She had allowed herself to be tied down. Each of the legs was scuffed from where she had risen against her bonds, like a flower opening.

The heat of her desire raising the room's temperature degree on degree . . .

326

And just as you did, more than forty years before, in a remote outpost near the Laotian border, you invited your subordinates to come and have sex with her. Did they stand like schoolboys waiting to be summoned at the bottom of the stairs? You knew that they wouldn't refuse. They couldn't. You watched them one after the other – Oleg, Byron and Larry.

Did it give you a special thrill that you were the only person who could refuse? Not as great a thrill as the knowledge of what you were going to do next.

You told them to wait again at the bottom of the stairs.

They thought that you were going to have sex with her. She must have thought that you were going to have sex with her too. She'd been filled with anticipation all evening. Longer than that – she'd been fucking people on your behalf for months but always, in her mind, fucking her way towards you; it was in her nature always to desire the alpha male.

You had your back to her, didn't you?

Was she talking? Whispering smut?

You turned to face her, the hammer in your hand.

Freeman and Maja stood out of the way at one end of the room and watched the three techs at work. They had switched on the single overhead bulb and were covering the skylight and bay windows with brown paper and taping up the cracks in the doorway. When they were done with the preparations they gathered around the pool table like the Three Kings at the crib: one with an ultraviolet light, one with a video camera and one with a big black spray bottle full of Luminol.

'Go ahead,' Freeman said.

One of the techs reached up and switched off the bulb, plunging the room into darkness.

Black space. Five people breathing.

The hiss of the spray bottle.

Freeman heard Maja's sharp intake of breath. Luminol reacts with even the smallest amount of blood, making it glow. The table blazed blue-white with abstract patterns: spattered arcs where the blood had shot outwards; a blotch behind where her head had been; and swipes and scrub-marks where Cannon's desperate subordinates had tried to clean it afterwards.

You told them to stop, didn't you? Freeman guessed. You wanted it preserved as it was: a bloodstained altar. And you were confident that no one would get this far into your house. You had the mayor and the Chief of Police in your pocket. You believed then, as you have always believed, that you are invulnerable.

Again the hiss of the spray bottle.

The tech with black-light squatted down. The blood glowed like something radioactive, a fan of droplets and stark lines in the cracks between the floorboards.

Luminescent murder.

SEVENTY-ONE

Freeman was driving south on the Rock Creek Parkway when Kaplan called back.

'Find a different pay-phone.'

Freeman flipped on his blue-and-reds and accelerated through the traffic. He drove straight past the Watergate, and the wrong way up the exit ramp to the Kennedy Center. He abandoned the car outside the Hall of States entrance and ran inside. A startled usher pointed him in the direction of a pay-phone in response to his barked command.

He called the number. Kaplan answered immediately.

'Are you feeling copacetic, Michael?'

'I've had better days. What can you tell me?'

'They finished the sequence.'

'And?'

'You have something very fucking dangerous loose in the city, Michael. A genetically engineered sociopath.'

'Tell me!'

'Something beyond a simple hybrid, way beyond, we're talking about some kind of cut and splice creation, a human base with a gumbo-ya-ya of added bonobo, chimp and baboon genes. Not just any old baboon – the Hamadryas baboon, which is by far the most aggressive of all primates. You know they have a saying, if Hamadryas baboons had nuclear weapons they'd destroy the world inside a week. That's your killer.'

The Fury.

'I got another shock for you, though. Are you holding on to something tight?'

'Tell me,' Freeman said, as evenly as he could.

'Get this, it's a female.'

SEVENTY-TWO

'Is he there?' Freeman asked.

He was sitting behind the wheel of his Impala, with the heater wheezing out hot, stale air. He was still parked outside the Kennedy Center. It was 4.30 p.m. The sun was low in the sky.

'No,' Sonia Rojas answered.

'Do you know where he is?'

'Yes,' she said softly.

'Can you speak to him?'

'Yes.'

'Tell him that I know what it is that he is frightened of. Tell him I know what it is that's out there and that is coming to kill him. Tell him I want to talk to him. No lawyers. No recording devices.'

'I'll call you back,' she said.

He leaned back against the seat's headrest and rubbed his temples. Eva Markoff was the killer. He'd been within touching distance of her in the basement of Germline BioSciences less than twenty-four hours before. She had reached out and effortlessly stayed the hand of her bodyguard who was drawing his weapon on Freeman. The bodyguard was now dead and Harry and Eva were missing and his only hope of catching them was that Eva would try to finish what she had begun – that she would come for Cannon.

His cell rang. It was Sonia Rojas.

'He says he'll meet you at the Finnish Embassy in an hour.'

SEVENTY-THREE

They were back inside the District, sheltering in a shallow depression caused by a fallen tree, the upturned roots and packed earth forming an overhang above their heads.

Eva held out a pile of phones in her cupped hands. Harry picked out the one that Allegra had given her the night before. She inserted a battery.

Twenty-five missed calls.

She wrote a draft text and passed the phone to Eva.

> Explain the babies in the lab to me?
>
> theyr mine
>
> Your babies?
>
> my eggs frozen then thawed & carried by surrogates! i told u im a battery hen!
>
> I don't understand!
>
> call yr friend we need 2 get out ov here

'Is she there with you?' Allegra asked.

'She's right beside me,' Harry replied. Eva was watching her closely.

'She hasn't harmed you or in any way threatened you?'

'No, of course not,' Harry replied.

There was a palpable sense of relief in Allegra's voice. 'Good, I'm very glad to hear it. We've been very worried about you, Harry.'

'I'm all right.'

'Now, I don't want to alarm you unduly but a warrant has been issued for your arrest.'

It was hardly surprising but it was a shock to Harry all the same. 'We were attacked,' she said.

'I know,' Allegra replied in a soothing voice. 'Everybody is very glad that the attempt against you was unsuccessful. We know you played a key part in that. You were doing what you were trained to do. Now we have to get the two of you somewhere safe.'

'OK.'

'Can you tell me roughly where you are?'

'In Rock Creek Park.'

'Good. That's good. I'm going to organise a pick-up. It may take a little time. An hour or two. Can you keep yourselves safe and hidden until then?'

'Yes.'

'OK, Harry. I'm ringing off now. I'll call you back when it's all fixed. Stay warm. Goodbye.'

SEVENTY-FOUR

It was dark when Freeman announced himself at the embassy gate. He showed his badge and was escorted to the main building where a tall, blond man in a shiny slim-fit suit and a narrow tie was waiting. He introduced himself as Miikaa and led Freeman down three flights of stairs to the basement, past a sign on a door that read VAROITUS. LATTIA LIUKAS!

'Do you know for how long the senator intends to stay here?' Miikaa asked tentatively.

'I can ask,' Freeman told him.

'Obviously we are very honoured to have him here but it's not, well, usual.' He shrugged his shoulders. 'Not any more.'

The basement was decorated with brightly patterned cushions on wooden furniture, photos of fair-skinned Finns stretching out on rock beaches and a projector beaming Wolf Blitzer's *The Situation Room* onto the wall. A bottle of Finlandia vodka stood on a bar across from a buffet of red gravlax and white trout, shrimp and Finnish meatballs.

'So, help yourself,' Miikaa said. 'I'll leave you to it.'

Freeman stripped naked and hung his clothes on a wooden peg. He wrapped a towel around his waist, picked up a sauna seat mat and a bottle of water from an aluminium ice bucket that was packed with beer cans and water, and stepped into the sauna.

It was like walking into a furnace.

Cannon was there waiting for him. He was naked and Freeman saw that his body was tanned everywhere and except for his crotch nearly hairless. Perspiration ran off him in silvery lines. The sheer physical smoothness was intimidating.

Freeman sat on the wooden bench, careful to be just out of

reach, and tufts of steam enveloped him. An electric heater in the corner warmed a pile of igneous rocks and according to a thermometer on the wall the temperature was 190 degrees.

Cannon began talking before Freeman could say anything. He seemed relaxed and amiable. 'I hope you don't mind, Michael, but I thought it was a sensible precaution. Are you familiar with the Finnish Embassy? No prying ears or eyes. It has always been neutral territory. Back in the Cold War, opposite numbers from the KGB and the CIA used to meet in the basement sauna. It was an opportunity for both sides to let off steam.' He smiled at his own joke, reached forward and doused the rocks with water, causing an overwhelming wave of steam. 'That was at the old embassy, of course,' he said a disembodied voice in the steam, 'but the tradition continued when they built the new one. The Finns are very accommodating. If there are sensitive issues that need to be thrashed out, then here is a good place. Do you know anything about the Chinese, Michael?'

It was not lost on Freeman, the repeated use of his given name. He shrugged. 'Hardly anything.'

'Let me tell you about the Chinese, Michael. They are set to overtake us in scientific output in the next two years. I was in China last year. I visited an IVF clinic in Xi'an. It had a double containment entrance, state-of-the-art equipment. The lab looked like something off a sci-fi movie. You have to wonder why China, with its teeming population and its aggressive control of family size, its eugenics and sterilisation laws, its push for rapid economic growth, is so concerned about human fertility? There are more than forty IVF clinics in China, most of them built with military assistance. The first licensed gene therapy came out of China. I have seen intelligence that suggests that they are harvesting stem cells from human cloned embryos. China was the pre-eminent world power in 1500 and will be again soon, and the manipulation of genetics, the biological modification of human beings, is viewed as a necessary step on that path. Influential segments of the Chinese government and the military are committed to the technology. They have the resources, the predisposition and the self-reliance to pursue the new technologies and create a new breed of metabolically dominant soldiers. The Chinese are at the frontier, Michael, where the bonds of custom are broken and unrestraint is triumphant. What the Mediterranean Sea was to the ancient Greeks, breaking the bond of customs, offering new experiences and activities, the field of human enhancement is to the Chinese.

'It is my role as chairman of the Subcommittee on Emerging Threats to understand the challenges posed by these technologies and to ensure that America and not China is at the forefront of them. It is not an easy task. It calls for difficult choices. Morally questionable alliances. You have to understand the parlous state we find ourselves in. Americans have a shrinking interest in military prowess as a way of life. No one but dirt-poor fools from our inner cities and Appalachia want to be soldiers. Across the globe our young men and women in uniform find themselves fighting tooth and nail for causes they barely understand. What kind of chance do they have against genetically enhanced soldiers bred in labs in China?'

Freeman wasn't sure what to say. This was not a conversation; it was a monologue.

'Let me tell you, as a politician I have been fortunate enough to visit various former Soviet facilities. In 1995 I flew to Kazakhstan to tour the biological facilities at Stepnogorsk. I became aware of what they had done there. I was one of the first people to understand the possibility. So when Dr Markoff approached me I was quick to seize the opportunity offered, just as my predecessors at the end of the Second World War were swift to seize on the technological expertise of German scientists, to ensure that America remained technologically dominant in the nuclear arms race. They did not hesitate to put aside their qualms and enlist the help of their former enemies and nor did I. Unfortunately Dr Markoff has not proven to be a reliable partner. He is given to insensible rage and acts of vindictiveness. Sadly, the same is true of the test subjects that he has created. Reluctantly, I have decided that his research will be discontinued. The programme will be terminated.'

Cannon had come to the point.

'How will they be killed?' Freeman asked.

'Who?'

'The test subjects.'

'I see. I have no idea.' He turned to look at Freeman. 'Do you take a professional interest in everything, Michael?'

'You have to admit it's an interesting subject. Who is going to do it?'

'An approved contractor provides security to the containment facility and the Defense Science Office is able to call on the Pentagon's help to terminate the test subjects if necessity dictates.'

'Forgive me for saying this, Senator, but the approved contractor, by which I assume you mean Raeburn, hasn't done such a great job so far. I've got dead bodies all across the city.'

'I told you there was a problem with Dr Markoff's test subjects.'

'Not only with them,' Freeman said. 'I mean there is also a problem with Katja's killer. A beautiful young woman tied to a table and her face smashed to a pulp.'

In Cannon's eyes, he saw a tremor, a shiver of excitement.

Freeman took a breath; under better circumstances he would have preferred a confession. He found it difficult to order his thoughts when called on to articulate them verbally – he preferred the written word; when speaking, he often sounded like a child to himself, interrupting himself with details he initially forgot to put in. He could be articulate with his fellow detectives. But Cannon was a different story altogether. He must have sensed Freeman's nervousness.

'Go on,' he urged.

'There is a big difference between a man like me and a man like you, Senator Cannon,' Freeman began. 'Obviously there is. Any fool can see that. We come from very different backgrounds. You're a man of privilege. I'm just one of your dirt-poor inner-city blacks. I've struggled to understand why a man of status and prestige would bother to kill a pretty young woman like that. I must admit, I can't fathom it. Usually it's easier. The scene of the crime is a mess of blood, hair and fibres. The murder weapon is probably discarded nearby. The motive? Usually one gang member killing another over a corner, a piece of turf. So it's kind of a shock to come across a crime of daring and humour.'

'Humour?' Cannon was interested.

'Dark humour admittedly. But I mean, to invite three men, who let's not forget know exactly what she is, to have sex with her and then, when they're done, to kill her. That's genius. I mean they had no choice but to try to cover it up. No wonder the killer was laughing.'

Cannon smiled. 'I think you are letting your imagination get the better of you, Michael.'

Ignoring him, Freeman pressed on. 'If I could for one minute think not as a black man but as a man of privilege, perhaps it would be easier.'

'What do you mean?'

'What I want to know is the reason. Why? Why would an intelligent, successful, wealthy and extremely powerful man, why would he murder a young woman? If I could understand the man perhaps I could understand the crime. Could I understand?'

'I don't think so.'

'Was it a sexual thing?'

A flicker of irritation. 'That would be like having sex with an animal.'

'But he offered her to the others?'

The senator gave him a withering look. 'A black man, a Jew and a Mormon.'

'OK, we'll agree for the sake of argument it's not about sex.'

'That seems wise, Michael.'

'Which leaves us a crime without a motive.'

'Are you serious?' He laughed. 'That's your conclusion? A woman killed purely for a whim?'

'Yes.'

Cannon tutted. 'I don't think so, Michael. Not from a detective with your experience and training. I think you can do better than that.'

'Perhaps. I mean, if I could only put it in context. See it from a historical perspective, then perhaps it might make sense.'

'Now you're a student of history?'

'I'll give it a go, Senator. Let's assume someone who is sent as a young man to a war in a far-off country, and he is posted to a remote area of that country, a very primitive place. Mountains. Jungle. Relentless heat. Torrential rain. When he gets there he is expected to work with the locals. He grows fond of them. He befriends their leaders and he learns a few words of the local language. At the same time he is conscious of his superiority. He never forgets who he is and where he has come from. In fact, if he's honest with himself, for all his affection for the locals, he finds them ridiculous, beneath contempt.' Freeman spoke slowly, recalling the colonel's account of the Cambodian girl killed at Old Rag. 'At some point, in a fit of anger, he kills a native. This is wartime so he is not punished but rewarded. He is given a medal. And as time passes he comes to savour the memory of the act of murder the way another man enjoys recalling the details of how he lost his virginity. There is a magnetism in primitive society, don't you think?'

'A magnetism?'

'A powerful attraction. It is a revelation to this man. He discovers what his most powerful impulses are.'

He had Cannon's full attention now. He was leaning forward on the bench, with his face flushed and a distant, dilated look in his eyes.

'For all his civilised appearance I suspect he feels the same loathing for everyone,' Freeman said. 'It's only in certain circumstances that he is able to be open about it. After all, he's a public man. He is forced to wait many years before indulging his violent impulse again. But then it's handed to him on a plate. A girl, almost the same age as that native girl in Vietnam, a true primitive with primitive desires, only partly human – really she belongs in a zoo; he can do with her whatever he wants.'

'Yes,' Cannon said breathlessly, shifting his thighs on the bench.

'He has to wait, however, because although she is an ape, she is also a very valuable tool. Primitive yes, preternaturally lustful yes – but beautifully made. He needs her skills in order to neutralise

338

his political opponents and to secure control over the legislature, to ensure that nothing can stand in the way of his broader ambition. So he has to wait until she's no longer useful. Difficult to judge when that might be and perhaps he goes too early. No matter, the wait gives him time to plan. He wants it to be as close as possible to the previous crime. She must be tied down in a dark space. That's no problem. After all, she was bred to please . . .'

As he was speaking, Freeman became aware that Cannon had, without embarrassment, parted his legs to allow his erection to stand proud of his thighs.

'She must be enjoyed by his subordinates, one after the other, while he watches,' Freeman continued, feeling strangely light-headed. 'Same deal, no problem. They can't help themselves.'

'Yes, Michael.'

'And then, when they have finished with her, it is time for the finale.'

'Yes! Of course!'

'He takes a hammer and utterly destroys her face and in doing so, completely erases her.'

'Yes . . . !'

Cannon flung more water on the rocks and they were once again enfolded in billowing clouds of steam. Freeman paused and waited for the air to clear before continuing.

'If anything, he believes that he has improved on the crime,' he said, more slowly now. 'He knows that modern DNA evidence means that his subordinates will be so thoroughly compromised that they will have no choice but to cover up the crime. But planning can only go so far. It's unfair but there's always an element of chance. Byron, the driver, who for nearly two years now has been driving the girl from assignation to assignation exactly as instructed, acts unexpectedly. He runs back to the car and drives off. If Byron hadn't panicked; if your car hadn't been in the shop; if Davidov hadn't fallen and lost a shoe in the snow – unlucky events – if any of these things hadn't happened your chances of getting away with it would have been much improved, isn't that right, Senator?'

Cannon sneered. 'In my experience, Michael, life is full of unexpected events.'

'Of course, your real problem is that Dr Markoff responded in a manner that you did not expect. He unleashed his niece. Now she's on a killing spree and my guess is she's left the best until last.'

'I have security.'

'Do you really think they'll keep you safe? I think we both know what's coming for you. A death of your own making.'

'What do you want?'

'I want you to help me catch her. After all, we can't have a killer mutant loose on the streets of the capital of the nation with a high-powered rifle. Is mutant the right term? It trips off the tongue easier than, how do you say in your budgetary allocations, meta-bolically dominant?'

'How do you want me to help you?'

'Oh, I want you to act as bait.'

'You want me to act as bait in a trap?'

'Sure. Why not?'

'Are you insane?'

'Actually I think you're the one who is insane, Senator, but we'll put that aside, like the sex thing. What I'm offering you is a deal. You help me by acting as bait and I'll forget that I ever went to see Colonel Moc. I mean you don't want to see him on the stand, testifying against you as a prosecution witness, do you?'

Cannon shook his head. 'Moc's a fantasist. Face it, Michael: you don't have any evidence or any credible witnesses. They are all dead. You don't even have a body. It's been burned.'

'It doesn't matter though, does it? I'm the only person who understands what you are up against who hasn't given up on you. You need my help and the only way that you're going to get it is to agree to my plan.'

'I'll think about it.'

Freeman got up off the bench and paused with his hand on the door. 'I have one more question.'

'What is it?'

'The hammer? What is the significance of the hammer?'

Cannon smiled. 'You don't give up easily, do you? Because you want to know so much I'll tell you. I stole it from my father's toolbox.' He shook his head as if surprised at himself. 'We had a dog, you see, a retriever that I had named Scout. He was trusting but stupid, so stupid. I couldn't bear the way he looked at me. I made him lie down and I knelt on his chest. I hit him with the hammer. The first blow did it but I didn't stop hitting him.' He looked up at Freeman again. 'They imprisoned a Negro for stealing that hammer. When you're rich and powerful, Michael, you can always find a way to make something look like something else.'

SEVENTY-FIVE

Freeman arrived at Germline BioSciences at seven, just as the Pentagon Police SWAT team members were exiting the building and the Homeland Security Hazmat team was preparing to enter. The scientific staff had been evacuated and they were now huddled together in the brightly lit foyer. He could tell from the expressions on their faces that something appalling had happened

The man in charge of the civilian side of the operation was tall and muscular with a soul patch and a gold incisor. He was wearing a black beanie hat and a black jacket with RAEBURN stencilled on the back in white lettering and BUCK GROLIG written in red on his left breast.

'I'm going in to take a look,' Freeman told him.

'Nothing to see but corpses,' Grolig replied, handing him a mask. 'It should be fully cleared but there may still be pockets of gas.'

'What did they use?'

'Tear gas. It was a turkey shoot.'

Freeman descended an emergency stairwell.

The bonobos had been slaughtered. They had retreated to one corner of the habitat where they had been gunned down. Staring at the pathetic huddle of bodies through the round eyeholes of his mask, Freeman felt almost as strong a sense of moral outrage as when he discovered the bodies of the human victims.

He went down the stairs to Level Two.

The Hamadryas baboons had put up a fight. They had used the furniture to build a series of barricades across the habitat. Their bodies were floating in the scummy ankle-deep water from the overhead sprinklers that had flooded the level during the firefight. Each baboon had been shot several times.

The stairwell to Level Three was running with water. He met Axley, the SWAT team commander, on the way down; Axley had his gas mask pushed up on his forehead and his eyes were streaming. Freeman resisted the urge to punch him.

'Emergency Fire Protocol must have been to seal designated areas and then flood them,' Axley explained. He looked distraught. 'It was automatic. We had no idea what was down there until we blew a hole in the door and the water drained out. By then it was too late.'

He shook his head sorrowfully and trudged up the stairs.

Freeman continued down. Level Three was knee-deep in water.

In one of the bright-white corridors, he found the corpse of an obese orang-utan floating face down in the water.

Further along the same corridor a shaped charge had been used to blow a hole at waist height in an airlock door with OBSTE-TRICS written on it. Freeman ducked through the ragged opening and waded into the open space.

The incubators were bobbing in the water

The pale shapes inside were drained of all colour.

Freeman was standing outside half an hour later, smoking a cigarette, when the senator called.

'I agree to your terms,' Cannon told him.

Freeman didn't trust himself to reply. The sound of Cannon's voice made him feel like retching. He cut the connection.

SEVENTY-SIX

Through Eva's binoculars Harry could make out the unmistakable silhouette of Neil Trefoil, formerly First Secretary at the British Embassy in Islamabad and now Washington representative of the UK Joint Intelligence Committee, his considerable bulk squeezed behind the wheel of a Range Rover parked in the otherwise empty parking lot. Where the hell was Allegra Puck?

Harry slithered back down off the ridge, squeezed Eva's hand for reassurance and moved off into the darkness as agreed, scrambling across the rocks. Satisfied that she was far enough along not to give away Eva's position, she climbed the ridge again and muttered, 'Here goes.'

She stood up.

Nothing happened. No yelling. No spotlights. No police.

So far so good. She advanced slowly down through the trees, her feet sinking in the deep snow, crossed the salted apron of the parking lot and got in the passenger seat. It was hot inside and she pressed her frozen fingers to the air vents. She hadn't been warm since the ambush the night before.

Neil didn't seem particularly happy to see her.

'You've been shooting people again, Harry.'

'It was self-defence.'

'Tell it to the judge,' he said in a weary tone.

'Where's Allegra?'

'Organising safe passage for you and the girl. I have no idea why. As far as I'm concerned this is a little local difficulty between the Russians and our American cousins. We have no place getting involved.'

'It's a good job you're not in charge then, isn't it?'

He gave her a look that suggested that he had been chewing lemons.

'What now?' Harry demanded.

'Tell the girl to get in the car. Then I'm going to drive you to a helipad. Hopefully by the time we get there a helicopter will be waiting.'

'Where will it take us?'

'I don't know and I don't care. That's between Allegra and her counterparts at Langley. What I do know is you won't be coming back here any time soon. Not if you want to stay out of prison. I wouldn't recommend the US prison system, Harry. It's a tad overcrowded.'

'Thanks for the reassurance.'

'You're welcome.'

'Flash your lights,' Harry told him.

'I'm sorry?'

'Flash your headlights three times.'

'This isn't Checkpoint Charlie, Harry.'

'Just do it, Neil.'

Reluctantly, he reached forward and flicked the lever three times. On the ridge above them, a figure rose out of the shadows, cradling a familiar stick-like object.

'Is that a gun?' Neil demanded. 'Shit!'

He tried without much success to duck under the steering wheel.

The figure turned and dashed back down the far side of the ridge, disappearing into the trees. Seconds later, Harry's phone beeped.

wait 4 me! EVA :-)

'Damn,' Harry said.

'Where the hell has she gone?' Neil demanded, once he had stopped hyperventilating.

'I don't fucking know,' Harry snarled.

Allegra called. Harry had to explain what had happened.

'She's gone to kill Cannon,' Allegra said.

'What?' Harry said.

'Jesus, Harry, catch up! The girl's the killer. She's been on a bloody rampage right under your nose.'

It was like a blindfold being raised. Of course: Eva's spectacular bruises, the blood under her fingernails; her startling attack on the security guards at the lab.

'What should we do?' Harry asked, once she'd recovered enough to speak.

'I'm getting the hell out of here,' Neil said, starting the engine.

'I heard that,' Allegra said. 'Pass me to Neil.'

Harry handed over the phone and listened to the crackly sound of Allegra telling Neil to stay put.

'Fuck's sake!' Neil swore, under his breath. Harry switched on the radio. It was just after 10 p.m. An NPR meteorologist was announcing yet another severe weather warning.

SEVENTY-SEVEN

After the weather and the latest from the earthquake zone, a segment opened with Senator Elizabeth Oberstar calling on Cannon to resign.

'His improper conduct in the obstruction of justice in the murder investigation discredits the institution as a whole not just the individual offender. I have this evening written to the Standards of Official Conduct Committee invoking the Senate's inherent and constitutional right to protect its own integrity and reputation. Everyone in government service must uphold the constitution, laws and legal regulations of the United States and never be party to their evasion.'

Freeman and Maja were sitting listening to the radio in the Impala outside the senator's Crestwood house. It was the first time that they had been alone together since they shared a bed the night before. Two hours had passed since the senator agreed to move back in and Cannon's wife had just emerged from the front door, thrown them a contemptuous look, and climbed in the back of a black Suburban that was taking her to National Airport and a flight back to Tennessee.

'Rats off a sinking ship,' Maja said, trying her best to sound cheerful.

The SUV drove off down the front drive, past a lone Raeburn man armed with an assault rifle who was standing at the gate. There was another at the rear gate and two more in the woods. Kari was in the house and Eli was on the terrace. The pitiful few. There was a crisp and ominous clarity to the air: the calm before the approaching storm.

On the radio, a spokesman for the US Attorney's Office was

refusing to comment on rumours of a federal investigation of Senator Cannon. Next up, Chief of Police Thielen was denying suggestions that the DC police waited too long to search the senator's house.

Freeman reached forward and switched it off.

'Do you think she's going to come?' Maja asked.

'She'll come,' Freeman said, sounding more sure than he felt. 'It's unfinished business. Besides, Cannon wouldn't be here if he didn't think she was coming.'

'Do you think we can stop her?'

'I hope so.'

'This is no time for heroics,' Maja told him.

'I know.'

A slight breeze stirred the heavily laden branches of the nearest trees.

'Have you heard from Shawna?' Maja asked.

'No. I don't expect to.'

'Why not?'

'The way she did it. Emptying the apartment like that. It was well planned. She'd made her mind up. And once she's made her mind up about something she rarely changes it.'

'Perhaps this time she will,' Maja said.

'I doubt it.'

He smiled sorrowfully and she rubbed his forearm as she had done so many times before.

'I'm going to go in and take a look around,' he told her.

'You know there's nothing to worry about. Between you and me, I mean. I meant what I said before.'

'What do you mean?'

'I mean what happened. It was a one-time deal. I caught you on the rebound. Don't worry about it.'

He wished he could tell her that he wanted it to be more than just a one-off but he had no idea whether that was true. He didn't know what he wanted or what to think about what happened. He felt deeply grateful to her, but he was painfully aware that the comfort that she had given him was, more than anything, a way for him to forget his troubles. She reached out and touched his cheek with the fingers of her right hand.

It would have been so easy to kiss her and keep on kissing her.

'Whatever happens, stay put,' he told her.

He slipped out of the car and walked up to the door. He lifted the knocker and let it drop with a hollow thud. Sonia Rojas answered. She was wearing an expensive-looking black silk wrap dress and a string of pearls.

'You look well,' he said.

She offered him a brittle smile. Since the committee hearings she had found the time to visit a beauty parlour. The subtle red in her hair was perfect. To Freeman, it was an unfathomable response to her circumstances. A counter-voice retorted, *As unfathomable as sleeping with a friend and colleague on the night your wife leaves you?*

'Good evening, Lieutenant Freeman,' Sonia Rojas said.

'I wanted to thank you for your help with the investigation,' he said.

'Oh,' she said, and glanced nervously around, 'I did what I had to. That's all. I should have told you sooner.' She closed her eyes and opened them again. 'Look, it's bad here tonight. Nobody is returning his calls.'

'What's up with his wife?'

'She's threatening divorce.'

'Is that bad?'

'Once I might have welcomed it. Not any more.'

They went down the hall to the study. Cannon was in the same chair as he had been sitting in when Freeman called at the house on the night of Katja's murder, and he was wearing the same dressing gown, only this time he did not get up. He gave no sign that he was even aware of Freeman's presence. He stared at the logs in the fireplace with an intense and brooding look on his face. The other two people in the room were Kari Marschalk and Buck Grolig of Raeburn Security. Like Freeman, Kari and Grolig were wearing semi-rigid body armour with special-threat ceramic panels front and back. They both had hand-held radios in pockets on their tactical vests.

The landline rang.

'It's Nashville,' Sonia announced.

Cannon appeared to rally. His hands gripped the arms of his chair. 'I'll take it in the other room.'

'It's for Mr Grolig,' Sonia said, with a hint of spite in her voice.

Cannon reacted as if he had been slapped. He shot a look of pure malice at her.

'This way,' Sonia said and led Grolig from the room.

'Tell them you need more men,' Cannon called out after them. He finally acknowledged Freeman's presence. 'I should have sacked that *cubana* bitch long ago,' he said over his shoulder. 'Imagine, she wanted me to put a child in her spicy little box. I would not pollute myself.'

'I guess she's lucky you didn't kill her,' Freeman said.

Cannon turned to look at him. His eyes were shining like opals, his skin was flushed and he had never seemed more like a big animal. A flush of greed, of something predatory, came off the air about him. 'Yes, I thought of killing her.'

Grolig returned. 'We're being pulled out,' he said.

Cannon sneered. 'You don't have the balls for a fight.'

''S right,' Grolig replied. And to his radio, 'All call signs stand down.'

'Get out!' Cannon snarled. He fixed his glare on Freeman and Kari. 'What about you two? Are you going to go running like little pigs – eee, eee, eee – all the way home?'

'We're here to see this thing through,' Freeman told him, grim-faced.

'We're ready for anything,' Kari said. He gulped in a manner that suggested he was terrified.

'So am I,' Cannon replied.

Cannon got up out of his chair and went over to a mahogany cabinet that concealed a stainless-steel safe; he opened the safe door with a key from his pocket and produced a double-barrelled shotgun with a walnut-burl stock and gold wire scrollwork on the frame and lock plates.

'An LC Smith No 05,' Cannon said, stuffing the pockets of

his dressing gown with loose cartridges, '8 Gauge, Damascus steel barrels. It was my father's gun. He shot a hundred-and-fifty-pound Hamadryas baboon with it in East Africa. It will do the necessary.' He lifted the barrels and poked Freeman in the ribs with them. 'You know I didn't think you had the balls to solve this case.'

Freeman grabbed the shotgun and struck Cannon with the stock across the face so hard he staggered backwards and went down in a heap. Freeman almost struck him again but if he had it would have been again and again. He was in such a rage he would not have stopped; instead he threw the shotgun into the corner of the room, and went out through the door past Kari to the hall outside. He had almost made it to the front door when Sonia Rojas caught up with him. She grabbed him by the arm and he turned to meet her.

Her face was flushed and her eyes were shining brightly. She surged up at him and he found himself kissing her. Just as suddenly, she pushed him away and stepped back.

'Afterwards,' she said.

'Afterwards,' he agreed, taken aback.

Without saying anything further, she turned away from him and walked back to the library, her heels clicking on the flagstones. An immediate flutter of guilt: Maja was waiting patiently in the car; Christ knows where his wife was at. What was he thinking? More unfathomable responses. He felt like a pinball in a machine, careening out of control.

Then it began: a single muffled shot somewhere out on the perimeter followed by a panicky burst of automatic fire. Freeman drew his gun and pulled the slide, pumping a round in the chamber.

Eli Wrath's voice crackled on the radio: 'She's in the woods somewhere. I don't know where.'

Freeman rushed back into the study. Cannon was pulling himself up using one of the armchairs and Sonia Rojas was standing startled in the middle of the room, her hand over her mouth.

'Cut the lights,' he yelled at her. He opened the door onto the terrace and slipped outside, in time to see Kari drop down onto the hillside below. The house went dark behind him. There were more flashes of gunfire in the woods and the headlights of a car on the drive. He crept forward to the end of the terrace feeling for the drop that he knew was there.

He was lying on his belly, his head and shoulders overhanging the drop, trying to see what was going on in the woods. He heard Kari shouting. Now and then there were more shots. His radio was broadcasting permanent static. Eva was using the frequency disrupter. After lying still for a while, he switched off his radio, swung himself over the edge and dropped into the snow.

The shooting had stopped and it was quiet. Freeman moved from tree to tree. His breathing sounded terribly loud. Occasionally the wind brushed snow from a tree and it crashed into the ground, startling him. The fight seemed to have moved away.

Maybe she'd given up.

Halfway down the drive Grolig's car had rolled into a snow-bank with the lights on and the engine gently idling. The rear window had shattered and in the front seat Grolig sat upright with half his skull missing.

Then Freeman heard Maja calling from the direction of the house.

'Run,' Freeman yelled, turning back towards the house, following in someone else's tracks. He saw an abandoned baseball cap in the trail. A little further on he found Eli Wrath face down in the snow, dead. There was a rifle shot close by. No discernible flash. Where was she?

'Michael!' Maja cried.

'I'm coming.' The fear of death had come for him in the darkness but now all he wanted was to save Maja. 'I'm coming.'

There was a burst of automatic fire, spraying the snow and tree-trunks around him. A round thumped into his vest, knocking him flat. He rolled over and fired in the direction that the shots had come from and kept on firing until the magazine was empty. He changed position, lying sideways in the snow to re-load.

He was winded and his chest was on fire.

There was more gunfire, further away this time. Raising his head, Freeman saw two figures crashing through the trees behind him, heading downhill. The last of the Raeburn security men. He saw them cross Beach Drive and disappear into the darkness of the flat ground by the river. Painfully, he lifted himself up and crept forward, soaking wet, with the Glock shaking uncontrollably in his hands, expecting to be shot any second. He found Kari sitting slumped against a tree. He was still alive, and by the faint light of the terrace, Freeman could see where the bullet had torn through his shoulder and under his arm. He turned his head as Freeman approached and attempted to speak. Dark, frothing blood spilled from his mouth. Freeman knelt beside him.

'She's inside,' Kari whispered.

There was another burst of gunfire and suddenly the lights in the house came on, revealing Cannon in silhouette. He was backing out of the French windows with the shotgun in his hands.

'Die, bitch!'

He fired both barrels into the house. He broke open the shotgun and fed new slugs from his pockets into the breech-ends of the barrels. He was too slow. As he locked the barrels, a shadow fell across the doorway.

The Fury.

'No! No!'

Eva shot him three times. The first snapped Cannon's head back and the second and third struck him in the chest as he staggered backwards like a boxer taking blows. He collided with the terrace wall and slid down it to the floor.

For a few moments all was quiet and then the air was filled with the sound of approaching sirens.

Freeman scrambled up the hillside.

'Maja,' he shouted frantically. 'Maja!'

He climbed onto the terrace and rushed through the French windows into the library.

Inside it was carnage: bright crimson blood on the walls and furniture. Sonia Rojas was sprawled on a couch with her arms and legs outstretched, a bullet hole at the centre of her forehead. On the floor, Maja was trying to prop herself up and slipping in her own blood. She was bleeding copiously. She looked up at him, making a panicked, groaning noise in the back of her throat.

'No,' Freeman said, dropping to his knees beside her, 'no.'

Her face was very pale, a greyish-green hue and she was having trouble focusing. He took her in his arms and held her tightly.

The two of them were huddled in the same position, a few minutes later, when the first ambulance arrived.

PART TWO
GRAND TURK

SEVENTY-EIGHT

Ten forty-five p.m. Wailing sirens. Two police cars hurtled past at the bottom of the creek, heading south on Beach Drive. Then an ambulance and a fire engine.

'What the hell is going on?' Neil demanded.

'We'll know soon enough,' Harry told him.

Fifteen minutes later, Eva appeared over the top of the ridge-line with the rifle in her hands. She advanced down the slope, scanning left and right, and across the parking lot towards them.

'I don't like having guns pointed at me,' Neil said, his voice quavering.

'Just unlock the doors,' Harry snapped.

When she was almost at the car, Eva stopped. She looked around, lowered the rifle, and hurried the last few steps to the vehicle.

'Let's go,' Harry said.

Neil started the engine and switched on the lights.

Turned in her seat, Harry watched with grim fascination as Eva swiftly dismantled the rifle, removing the sound suppressor and the box magazine before breaking it down into two parts: the integral stock and grip, and the two-foot-long barrel and rail. Eva stashed the separate pieces in the backpack.

When she had finished, Eva looked up and stared back at Harry, her eyes refracting the passing streetlights, implacable, alien . . .

Harry was having trouble reconciling the girl that she'd met two days before, with this new cold-eyed and defiant Eva. It wasn't that she doubted her ability – she'd seen plenty of evidence of her strength and agility. But she'd been looking at her through the

357

prism of a young woman barely out of her teens, an equally impetuous version of herself at that age. This young woman was something else entirely.

She could not believe that she hadn't realised it sooner. She felt anger and self-recrimination in equal measure. Deliberately she turned away, and stared at the road ahead. The city was quiet. There was very little traffic and there were hardly any pedestrians. She wondered if they would make it out of the city before the weather struck.

They passed the site of last night's ambush. The CVS pharmacy had been boarded up and the damaged vehicles removed; the only clue as to what had happened were a few ragged lengths of incident tape. The snow had buried the rest. She could easily have died. In the last two days her life had completely unravelled and there was no telling where it would end, maybe in prison, or worse . . .

She didn't know who to trust. Not Neil Trefoil, that was for sure.

At Dupont Circle, he turned left on Massachusetts and north on New York at the Convention Center to Florida Avenue. He pulled up alongside an open tarmac space on the corner of Florida and North Capitol with a sign at the gate: METROPOLITAN COMPLEX HELIPORT.

Beyond the chain-link fence, a roaring helicopter.

Allegra Puck emerged from another car and hurried towards them, her frizzy greying hair buffeted by the rotor wash. Seconds later, Dr Markoff emerged from the same car and stared anxiously around him.

'This is as far as I go,' Neil said, and unlocked the doors.

Harry got out and opened the passenger door for Eva. She climbed out with the backpack in one hand. As soon as Dr Markoff saw her he stiffened.

In response, she cocked her head and held out her hands: *What?*

Then she dropped to her knees and opened her backpack. She took out the stainless-steel dewar and held it up for him to see. Dr Markoff broke into a smile. He turned to Allegra. 'With the right lab facilities we can do it tomorrow.'

'Let's not worry about that now,' Allegra said. From her bag she produced a set of prisoner transport chains, hand and leg cuffs connected by a thirty-two-inch chain. She gave them to Harry. 'Put these on her.'

Eva looked to Dr Markoff.

'If she won't agree to it we're not going anywhere,' Allegra said firmly. 'She can take her chances with the Pentagon. They're hunting high and low for her.'

Dr Markoff signed at Eva and after a few moments she shrugged and held out her hands, palms up. Harry fixed the cuffs on her wrists and ankles. She checked that they were secure but not too tight.

'Come on.'

Allegra ushered them through the gate and towards the helicopter. Harry led Eva at a shuffling pace, crouching under the whirling blades. Allegra was first in, then Dr Markoff and then Eva and Harry. They belted themselves in, Harry reaching across to tighten Eva's strap, and then the roaring sharpened and it was as if they had been lifted by a cable, hoisted aloft and swung across the city.

They crossed the Potomac and flew west alongside Interstate 66 before turning north towards the dark caps of the Blue Ridge Mountains, passing the lights of Dulles Airport to their left. Allegra, who was sitting beside the pilot, had a large grey headset clamped over her ears. She was pointing and saying something but Harry couldn't hear her above the sound of the engine.

Through the curved plastic window Harry saw that they were approaching an airstrip, a single runway maybe five thousand feet long, running north-west to south-east in the midst of a snow-covered field. The runway was lit up and was painted with approach markings. There were no hangars, just a small parking ramp with a limousine and beside it a single-prop Cessna Caravan aeroplane.

The helicopter halted in mid-air and then settled towards the tarmac.

As soon as they had landed, Allegra removed her headset and climbed out. Harry, Eva and Dr Markoff followed. Crouching low with the wind tearing at their eyes, they scrambled out from under the rotors. Behind them the pitch of the roaring changed and Harry turned in time to see the helicopter leaving, swinging out over the runway, then rising higher, receding against the grey sky.

In the sudden quiet, Harry asked, 'Where are we?'

'Upperville Airport,' Allegra told her. 'Ostensibly it's a private airstrip but we're only six miles from the Mount Weather presidential bunker. The government thought it would be useful to have a capacity to land fixed-wing aircraft nearby.'

A man got out of the limousine and walked towards them carrying a small camera.

'You're having your pictures taken,' Allegra said. 'So we can make you viable identity papers.' She took a packet of wet wipes and a hairbrush from her handbag and gave them to Harry. 'Make yourselves presentable.'

Harry cleaned her face and brushed her hair and then took the brush to Eva's hair, taking some satisfaction in tugging it fiercely through the tangles. She cleaned Eva's face with several wet wipes, rubbing hard at the skin to remove the blood and grime. If Eva sensed Harry's anger she gave no indication of it. When they were done, the man with the camera took head and shoulders shots of them and then returned to the car.

'Where are we going?' Dr Markoff asked.

'South,' Allegra told him. 'Under the radar. Private airfields. No airports. Come on.'

She went up the little stairway on wheels that led to the aeroplane and the rest of them followed. Inside there was a couch at the back and four swivel chairs in two rows behind the instrument-filled nose where the pilot was sitting. Allegra and Dr Markoff sat in the swivel chairs and Harry and Eva sat on the couch. The pilot climbed out of his seat and stretched, cracking his vertebrae and rolling his head from side to side. He was a large, dark-skinned and fearsome-looking Brit with a packet of Marlboro Red tucked in the sleeve of his rolled-up T-shirt.

'I'm Jonah, your pilot,' he said, in a polite tone that seemed at odds with his appearance. His accent was difficult to place. 'Fasten your seat belts. No smoking till we've landed.'

He got back in his seat, its springs groaning beneath his weight. Moments later the Cessna's propeller started to turn lazily and then sped up and they began to taxi. Harry checked that Eva's seat belt was properly fastened. Suddenly the plane rushed forward and leapt into the air. They climbed steeply. Harry looked out of the window and watched the lights of the airstrip recede behind them.

SEVENTY-NINE

Harry woke as the Cessna's wheels touched down.

They raced along the runway, the pitch of the engines changing. The plane slowed, taxiing. Eventually its propeller stopped. She sat up in sudden silence, blinking out at an avenue of palms draped with icicles and an expanse of frozen water and icy reed beds sparkling in the moonlight. She looked at her watch. They'd been flying for close to five hours. Dawn was still a couple of hours off.

'Where are we?' she asked.

'Florida,' Allegra told her, closing her laptop, 'just west of Lake Okeechobee.'

'Fag break,' Jonah announced, getting out of his seat. 'You've got time for a stretch and a pee.' He opened the door and cold air rushed in. 'All right,' he called out to someone unseen. 'Good to see you.'

He jumped out.

'Come on,' Allegra said, standing up and putting on her parka.

A short Hispanic man in bright yellow PVC oilskins had propped a short aluminium ladder against the door. Allegra climbed down and Harry followed. They stood shivering on the tarmac watching while Jonah and the man in oilskins unrolled a rubber hose from a reel on the back of a small tanker truck.

'It's the worst freeze in recorded history,' Allegra told her. 'I read that the fruit crop has been decimated . . .'

Harry shook her head. This was no time for small talk. 'Where are we going?'

'The next stop is Grand Turk in the Turks and Caicos,' Allegra explained with a sigh. 'A pliable member of the House of Lords

362

has loaned us his house. Eva can have the eggs removed and fertilised at a local clinic in Cockburn Town and we can work out what to do with you. You did the right thing, you know. We couldn't let her fall into the hands of the Russians.'

Harry looked back and watched Eva poke her head out of the door and then jump, with her knees bent, to the tarmac below. Dr Markoff followed her out, using the ladder. Eva shuffled a short distance from the plane and after a brief conversation in sign language Dr Markoff left her and went over to the edge of the runway and stood with his hands in his pockets.

Eva met Harry's eyes for a moment. Harry held her gaze. Eva shrugged and looked away.

'How many people has she killed?' Harry asked.

'In DC?'

'Yes.'

'At least eleven that we know of,' Allegra replied. 'A couple more we're not so sure about.'

'Why?'

'Maybe it was revenge,' Allegra said. 'That seems the most likely explanation. For whatever reason she lost control.'

Harry frowned. 'All right. But now she's calm?'

'Seems that way.'

'That doesn't make any sense to me.'

Allegra shrugged. 'Why should it?'

'What does that mean?'

'On a basic biochemical level she's not like you or me,' Allegra said. 'I know you can't tell from looking at her, but she's not fully human, is she?'

'No,' Harry said, her cheeks reddening. She felt like the last one let in on a cruel joke. 'I guess not.'

'According to Dr Markoff, both her gametes started out human but they were cut and spliced with a cocktail of chimp, bonobo and baboon genes,' Allegra explained. 'Down in the limbic lobe and the amygdalae and up into the orbitofrontal cortex she has hundreds, maybe thousands, of biochemical processes going on that we don't, processes governing behaviour and emotion. The brain is such a mysterious thing, a hothouse flower, who knows what is going on? On top of that she's fertile, the only fertile female that Dr Markoff ever produced. That's why her eggs are so valuable. Her children will be a whole different species. Not half of one thing and half of another like the hybrids. It's extraordinary when you think about it. Something profoundly new. Post-human. I think people will look back and say it was a technological breakthrough on a par with . . . I don't know – the first domestication of wheat from wild grasses eleven thousand years ago.'

As soon as Jonah attached the end of the hose to the plane, the man in the oilskins yanked a cord on the back of the truck, starting up the engine of a pump.

Allegra led Harry away from the reek of fuel.

'What will happen to her?' Harry asked.

'Eva? Provided she behaves, she'll get to enjoy a discreet beach holiday in a more agreeable environment than DC. Somewhere safely beyond the reach of the Russians and outside the scrutiny of Congress.' Allegra produced a bottle of mineral water from her bag. She swallowed a mouthful and passed it to Harry. 'She'll have to keep producing eggs but as I understand it she's been doing that since she first ovulated.'

Harry took a sip of the water and passed it back.

'What will happen to the eggs?' Harry asked.

'That's still to be negotiated. First, Langley and the Pentagon have to make up. The likelihood, the presumption, is that once things are straightened out between the two, we'll fly the eggs up to the US Army Medical Research Institute of Infectious Diseases in Fort Detrick, Maryland.'

'And what happens to them there?'

'Initially they will be kept in storage and then at some point the research and development programme will be reactivated. But under joint CIA/Department of Defense control this time.'

An image of the incubators in one of the basement levels at Germline BioSciences flashed through Harry's mind: row on row of mottled pink babies under fluorescent white lights. Eva's babies . . .

'I'd like to talk to her,' Harry said.

'Of course,' Allegra replied, producing a BlackBerry Storm from her bag. 'You can give this to her. Tell her the wireless has been disabled.'

Harry took the Storm, typed a hurried message in MemoPad and handed it to Eva.

why didn't you tell me?

Eva sneered.

hello im EVA im a MONKEY & a SOCIOPATH?

I should have known!

Why so angry? R u shocked? when I 1st met u - u said its not my job to be shocked! u said that!!! u LIED I think . . .

I'm not shocked! I'm disappointed.

who r u kidding?

Harry turned her back on Eva and walked away with the Storm gripped tightly in her hand. She got about five or six paces before turning back.

The girl whose body I found in the park. Who was she?

who or what was she?

Both

her name was KATJA she was a basic hybrid a BONBO/ HUMAN cross – a fuck monkey!

You killed all those people because of her?

sure! why not???

Harry turned away again to find that Dr Markoff had crossed the tarmac and was standing in front of her.

'I don't mean to give you any offence, Harry,' he said, 'but Eva doesn't like you any more than she likes me. She's not capable of that emotion. She finds you useful, that's all. You have brought us here, Harry.'

Conscious of how ridiculously strident all this marching back and forth must look but too angry to care, she ignored Dr Markoff and walked up to Allegra.

'Why did you even agree to this?' she demanded.

'Because we were asked to, Harry. Langley makes a request and we comply. That's the special relationship at work. It is not entirely one-sided. They are drafting up a Data Use and Reciprocal

Support Agreement, which means the research findings will be shared with our people at Porton Down. Eventually our biotech companies will be able to apply for a share of patents.'

'This is about patents?' Harry said incredulously.

'Forgive me, but that girl's the goose that lays the golden eggs . . .'

She felt like stamping her feet. 'I can't believe you just said that!'

'And I don't think you've grasped the scale of this yet, Harry. We're talking about a brand-new Manhattan Project. Think of the human form but weaponised. Think of what they could achieve in places like Afghanistan. Britain can't afford to be left behind in this. We have to be there in lock-step with the Americans.'

'She's a psychopath!'

'She's a prototype!'

Harry was shaking her head. 'How do you know she's not going to kill us?'

'That's why she's in restraints and right now it's in her interests to cooperate. If that situation changes we're ready to take appropriate action.'

'Christ!' Harry muttered.

When the plane's fuel-tank was full, Harry watched Jonah walk to the edge of the runway. He had the shambling gait of a bear. He stood with his back to them, urinating. After that he squatted down and lit a cigarette. In his T-shirt, he seemed oblivious to the cold. The man in the yellow oilskins fetched an envelope from the cab of the tanker and handed it to Allegra.

After a couple of minutes, Jonah returned to the plane and climbed up the steps, squeezed himself through the door. Allegra, Harry and the Markoffs followed.

'Your passports,' Allegra said. They were maroon with a gold crest. 'When we land at Cockburn customs officers will come on board. I'll give them the passports, they will open them, check the numbers against the flight plan we filed back in DC, and hand them back. That's it. They shouldn't ask any questions and don't behave as if you expect them to.'

'What about Eva's restraints?' Harry asked.

'Cover them up with a blanket. It's fine. All they want to do is check the paperwork.'

Harry looked out of the window at the frozen saw-grass prairie below. They had turned east and the plane was following a two-lane highway through the Everglades towards Miami. As far as Harry was concerned nothing that had happened in the last few days was fine. She was travelling further and further away from herself.

'They call it alligator alley,' Jonah called out, raising his voice to be heard above the engine. 'Poor bastards in this weather.'

From Miami they headed out across open water.

EIGHTY

Harry woke the following day to the sounds of the sea, of gently lapping waves, in a room flooded with sunlight.

She was in a large bed in a room with whitewashed plaster walls and an east-facing French window that opened out onto a verandah clad with crimson bougainvillea. She reached for her watch on the nightstand. It was 10 a.m. Her watch was out by an hour. It was 11 a.m.

Saturday morning. She'd found the body in the early hours of Tuesday morning, less than a week before.

She stared at the plain white ceiling. She realised that she couldn't be more than a hundred miles north of where Jack must be, surviving in utterly different circumstances. She wished that she could speak to him. She wanted to be the first to tell him that she was no longer welcome in the USA, that the little world they created in Washington had been torn apart. She supposed that it would fall to someone else to tell him, an embassy official perhaps. She imagined Neil Trefoil's wearisome expression: 'She wouldn't listen and now she's got herself and Her Majesty's Government in all kinds of trouble . . .'

She wondered how long it would be before Jack even noticed she was absent from DC, a day or two more, a week maybe; he was deep in a story. It could be that long.

Face it: she was all on her own.

She flung back the covers in exasperation. It was hard to be angry for long though. The view from the French window was of a rocky outcrop and beyond it azure-blue sea and in the distance white breakers on the reef. All of it framed by crimson flowers. It must be sixty degrees at least. She felt genuinely warm for the first time in days. Her father, who had considerable experience of lying shivering in ditches, had a saying that being warm was reward enough. So Trefoil might be right, she might be in all kinds of trouble, but at least she was warm. Warm and out of the District.

There was a pair of baggy shorts with cargo pockets and a pink T-shirt, both folded, waiting for her on a chair. A three-pack of black cotton panties. A pair of flip-flops. She dressed and ran her fingers through her unruly hair. In the en suite bathroom she found a travel pack complete with toothpaste and a toothbrush.

After wandering back and forth brushing her teeth, she left the room and went down the stairs. She heard them before she saw them. The clash of leather-bound bamboo canes. She stepped into the room and saw two figures in black robes with bamboo shinai in their hands. One large. One small. They were wearing masks with hardened wimples, lacquered body armour and padded gloves.

Kendo – *the way of the sword.*

They were not the only ones in room. A black man in navy blue shorts and a white polo shirt was sitting on a chair with a machine pistol resting on his knees. He nodded to Harry and returned his attention to the figures on the mat.

Harry watched them step up to each other, squat down and cross shinai. They paused, as if meditating and then straightened up so that they were standing facing each other, mask to mask, sword to sword. Eva was the smaller of the two and Harry guessed from his size that her opponent was Jonah. They backed away from each other and Eva raised her shinai above her head and danced back and forth in bare feet, looking for an opening. There followed a sudden flurry of cuts aimed at the head, wrist, waist and throat – on the face of it chaotic and noisy but in fact precise and targeted. Eva was incredibly fast and Jonah struggled to parry her blows. They locked swords several times and then broke away, resuming the dance before closing and striking again. Eva scored several hits. After five minutes or so, they squatted down again, bowed and made as if to sheathe their swords.

Eva stepped off the mat and untied her mask. Behind her, Jonah removed his mask. 'Hello, Harry.'

The man with the machine pistol had got up out of his chair and was watching warily as Eva stripped off her armour. Once she had finished, she stood expectantly with her arms hanging loosely by her sides.

'Eva's allowed an hour each morning for indoor exercise,' Jonah said, putting the transport chain back on her. He handed Harry the keys. 'But the restraints don't come off unless Colin here has got the gun on her. I know it's not sustainable in the long term. You can tell her we'll review the situation in a week or so. If she behaves the restraints can come off more often, maybe for good.' He gave a thumbs-up to the man with the machine pistol. 'Thanks. That will be all.'

Once he had gone, Eva shuffled over to Harry, reached up and kissed her on the cheek.

'T'aaank 'uuu,' she said.

Harry frowned and raised a questioning hand.

Eva went over to a chair and picked up her new BlackBerry. She passed it to Harry:

> 4 rescuing me from the RUSSIANS
> You're teasing me

Eva took her by the hand and led her down a corridor with Jonah following. The room was small with whitewashed walls and bars on the window. There was a bed and a nightstand with a stack of magazines, and an en suite bathroom. Eva swung herself up onto the bed. Harry sat beside her while Jonah watched from the doorway.

Eva typed a message:

> wat is going 2 happen 2 me?

Harry typed a reply:

> I'm not sure. I'll try to find out

Later in the kitchen, Jonah offered to make Harry an omelette. He took a Taser and a spare battery out of a drawer and slid them across the counter towards her. It was a multiple-shot X3 in waspish yellow and black moulded polymer, with a trigger and a pistol grip. It matched the one on Jonah's belt.

'It's fully charged,' he explained. 'It's the wildlife management model. They go crazy for them up in Alaska – brochure says it'll knock out a grizzly. If she gives you any trouble don't hesitate to use it.' He went over to the fridge and pulled out eggs and milk. There was something about the way he moved his head. Harry thought he might be blind in one eye.

'After this, I'll take you on a walk of the perimeter and you can meet the security team,' he told her. 'It's a four-man team, two on days and two on nights. They're local law enforcement from Cockburn Town, off-duty cops, the best we could scrape together at short notice. They've been told to maintain at all times at least fifteen feet between themselves and the girl, for the obvious reasons.' He started whisking the eggs in a bowl with a splash of milk and a twist of pepper. 'This afternoon we're down the clinic and she has the eggs removed and fertilised. We then wait for them to ripen.'

He stopped when he saw the expression on her face and looked down at the whisk in his hand, the egg dripping from it into the bowl.

'I guess you don't want eggs?'

Harry shook her head.

'Toast?'

She nodded.

He dumped the eggy mess in the trash and started again: bread in the toaster and jam from the fridge.

'I need to speak to my husband.'

'You'll have to talk to Allegra about that,' Jonah told her. 'She's at the governor's mansion using the secure phone. She took the doctor with her. They should be back this afternoon. You can ask her then.'

'I can't stay here forever.'

'You have my sympathy,' Jonah replied, buttering her toast. 'You know, I remember your father from Hereford. He was on the training team. I was twenty years old. He kicked me around the killing house like a football. You must have been young when he died?'

'I was.'

'That's tough.'

'I barely remember him.'

'He was hard as nails. I think he'd be proud of what you did in DC, Harry. You didn't hesitate, did you? Three dead. Most people bottle it.'

'It wasn't my first time.'

'Of course, you killed a jihadi in Pakistan. Didn't he have dynamite strapped to him?'

'I thought so. The Pakistani Army took the body away so there was no way of proving it.'

'You know what you saw,' Jonah said. 'I have no doubt you're up to the task here.' He put the toast on a plate and slid it across the kitchen counter towards her. 'Eat that.'

After he'd watched her take a couple of bites, Jonah leaned across the table and whispered in a conspiratorial tone, 'Is it true she's part monkey?'

'Ape and monkey,' Harry told him.

'She's handy with a stick, that's for sure.'

The house was situated on a rocky promontory strewn with fez cactus at one end of a mile-long horseshoe of powder-white sand. Their neighbour to the south was an exclusive holiday resort and from the rocks you could see the serried ranks of empty sun loungers and the lifeguard's tower. To the north further limestone outcrops and scrub forest.

On her tour of the grounds Jonah showed Harry the white Land Rover Discovery parked outside the front door and introduced her to the two middle-aged black men loitering under the shade of a mature Flame Cordia tree with broad, leathery leaves and scarlet flowers. She recognised Colin from earlier. The other one introduced himself as Henry. They were both wearing shorts and polo shirts and were carrying compact machine pistols. When she asked them for their patrol plan they called her young lady, which she didn't care for at all.

Next, Jonah walked her out to the end of the rocky outcrop. In a small cove, hidden from view, was a black Zodiac Hurricane sea rib with a small two-man cockpit and three jockey seats behind it. It was about twenty foot long with two large outboard engines. 'You ever driven one of these before, Harry?'

'No.'

'All four of the guards have. If anybody comes up the drive you bail out of the house, pull back here and the boys will run you out past the reef and across to South Caicos. It's twenty-five miles west. There's a runway there I can use. Either way, we'll meet up when we get back.'

'Can I ask you a question?'

He looked at her. 'Sure.'

'How come you're allowed to fly?'

He shrugged his broad shoulders. 'I cheated on the depth perception test.'

The route back took them past the end of the beach, about half a mile from the resort.

'Place has been quiet since the financial crash,' Jonah told her. 'There are a couple of security guards who have been paid a bit extra to stop anyone coming this far along the beach.'

As they were approaching the house they saw a black car in the distance on the tarmac road.

'The field of view is unobstructed,' Jonah told her. 'Nobody can sneak up on you here.'

The car reached the junction and turned up the track that led to the house, leaving a dusty plume in its wake. It pulled up alongside the Discovery. Allegra Puck and Dr Markoff got out. Jonah waved. Allegra and Dr Markoff waited.

'Getting acclimatised?' Allegra said with a smile when Harry reached them.

She shrugged. 'Something like that.'

'Well, come into the kitchen. We're going to put you on a daily contract and I'm going to make you sign a declaration under the Official Secrets Act.'

'Now you work for government again, Harry,' Dr Markoff added. 'No need to worry about right or wrong any more.'

EIGHTY-ONE

The Turks and Caicos Fertility Management Clinic inhabited a neat single-storey white building on Hospital Road at the north end of Cockburn Town, sheltered from the passing traffic by a row of manicured Flame Cordia trees. The tarmac parking lot had sharp white lines to encourage regimented parking and the flowering beds either side of the entrance glistened like freshly misted produce on a supermarket shelf.

A brochure in the airy, sunlit reception area proudly announced the clinic's affiliation to the Advanced Training and Research in Fertility Management Unit of the University of the West Indies in Jamaica and advertised a range of treatments including Blastocyst Transfer, egg and embryo freezing, Intra Cytoplasmic Sperm Injection, Intra Uterine Insemination, in vitro fertilisation and pre-implantation genetic diagnosis.

Jonah drove them there in the Defender and he waited in the reception area while Harry and Allegra accompanied Eva into the changing room. Harry removed Eva's cuffs and shackles and put them in a locker along with her clothes. Eva dressed in a backless blue gown. A cheery Jamaican nurse in pink scrubs showed them to a curtained enclosure in the prep room and spread a heated blanket across Eva's tummy.

Five minutes later, a Brahmin anaesthetist in blue scrubs, who introduced himself as Dr Chatterjee, appeared through the curtain and vigorously shook Allegra's and then Harry's hand. He was tall and slight with luxurious hair. He watched while the nurse inserted a catheter into a vein in the back of Eva's hand, fixed it in place with surgical tape, and attached a bag of fluid on a saline stand.

'Soon I'm going to give her some medicine that will make her feel drowsy,' Dr Chatterjee explained, opening the valve on the catheter.

He told Harry that as soon as the sedative had started working they would wheel Eva through to surgery and in a procedure called follicular aspiration Dr Markoff would insert a hollow needle through the wall of the vagina into the right and then the left ovary and retrieve the mature follicles, each of which contained an unfertilised egg. He reassured her that it would take no more than a few minutes and after half an hour in the recovery room Eva would be good to travel.

'She doesn't need to remember any part of this that she doesn't care to,' he said with a beneficent smile. 'She can remember only to forget and forget to remember.'

Harry turned to Eva.

He's going to take the eggs out. He says it will be quick and you'll be fine afterwards. Any questions?

Eva shook her head.

Tell him 2 hurry ^

'Let's go,' Harry said.

Dr Chatterjee administered the sedative and Harry gripped Eva's hand and watched while her face relaxed and her breathing became shallower and slower.

Afterwards, in the recovery room, Harry sat beside Eva and stroked her forehead while she gradually became aware of her surroundings again.

Dr Chatterjee popped his head around the curtain to check up on her. He had changed into tennis whites and was obviously on his way out the door.

'You can tell her that she is a very good patient,' he said. 'I'm sure that she will have strong and healthy babies.'

Once he had gone, Harry sat and listened through the curtain while Dr Markoff explained to Allegra what would happen next.

'We prepare the eggs by stripping away the surrounding cells and at the same time we wash the sperm to remove inactive cells and seminal fluid. Then we will inject a single sperm into each viable egg. Each fertilised embryo will be kept in a separate petri dish, in a special growth medium, and left until it has subdivided into a blastoma of somewhere between six and eight cells. Then they are ready for implantation or freezing.'

Shift change was at dusk. A police car drove up the long road from the south and delivered the nightshift and Harry and Jonah went out to meet them. Their names were Jake and Devon. They were younger and more talkative than their daytime counterparts. They spent much of the night chatting on their radio with the guards from the neighbouring resort.

Every hour until midnight Harry completed a circuit of the house reassuring herself that all the doors and windows were locked and that the guards were in place. Just after 8 p.m. they ate Chinese takeout from Captain Zheng's that was delivered by a young man on a moped. Nobody spoke much. After dinner, Harry locked Eva in her room and Jonah went outside and patrolled the perimeter.

Allegra worked on her laptop and Dr Markoff sat in front of the television watching an episode of the BBC Natural History series *Life in the Undergrowth* on DVD. Several times Harry noticed him glancing towards the windows. He had the same nervous, watchful quality as when he first interviewed her at the house in Chevy Chase. As if he were examining his options. Back then Katja had been dead for less than eighteen hours, murdered by Senator James Cannon, the family's supposed benefactor. Dr Markoff had reached out to Harry, believing her to be a member of the British intelligence services. He'd been lucky that the rift between the CIA and the Pentagon over the killings had created a role for MI6. Now she wondered what options he had left; surely there was nowhere to go from here?

But he was a chancer and a survivor.

He looked as if he were waiting for something to happen.

EIGHTY-TWO

A cell phone was ringing. It was Monday morning and they had returned to the clinic.

Dr Markoff frowned above the microscope.

'I'm so sorry, Doctor,' the nurse gasped. She rushed out of the lab clutching her cell, forcing Harry to step aside and let her pass. The interruption over, Dr Markoff returned his attention to the microscope. 'As I was saying, we have four viable blastoma. We either implant them or freeze them.'

'We freeze them,' Allegra said.

'There is always a risk with freezing,' Dr Markoff said.

'It's not open for discussion,' Allegra said.

There were four of them in the lab. Allegra and Dr Markoff were sitting at the workbench, Eva was on a stool in the corner and Harry was standing by the door as usual. The nurse came back with a confused look on her face. She held out the cell.

'It's for Dr Markoff.'

'Who is it?' Allegra demanded.

'He said his name was Mr Gogol.'

Allegra looked from the nurse to Dr Markoff.

'I'm so sorry, Allegra,' he said.

'I'll take it,' she said. She snatched the phone and held it to her ear and as she listened her eyes widened in surprise and dismay.

'I understand,' she said. She put her hand over the phone and whispered to Harry, 'Go and check outside.'

Harry slipped out through the door, drawing the Taser as she did so. She ran through the prep room past curtained-off cubicles and down the corridor past the toilets and the changing rooms and burst out into the reception area. It was empty. She edged up to the front door, careful to remain out of sight. She knelt down, took a deep breath, and risked a quick look.

Out in the parking lot, Jonah was kneeling in full view with his hands on his head and a man wearing sunglasses was standing above him with a gun pressed to the back of Jonah's head. Harry ducked back into cover.

'Shit!'

She scrambled back across the reception area and dashed down the corridor through the prep room to the lab.

'Put the Taser down, Harry,' Dr Markoff said.

He was holding the cell phone and beside him Eva had the chain wrapped twice around Allegra's neck.

'We don't want anyone to die here,' Dr Markoff said in a placatory tone.

'You bastard!'

'Put the Taser down on the floor and kick it over here.'

Harry didn't see that she had any choice but to do as she was told. Dr Markoff picked up the Taser and pointed it at her. 'Now lock the door please, Harry.'

She turned and locked the door behind her.

'Good. Very good,' Dr Markoff said. 'Now, I think we have about fifteen minutes before Gogol and his people break down the door. I'm sorry, Harry, but there is no future for me in dealing with the Americans or even the British, though I thank you for your hospitality. I must work with the Russians again. I don't see that I have any choice. I'll be frank with you, I'm not very happy about just handing the embryos over to them. I wasn't very happy about giving them to the Americans either but I did and look how they repaid me. So, rather than have the embryos sit for years in a deep freeze while the Kremlin fails to make a decision about what to do with them, I have decided to opt for implantation. I could put them in Eva but then she would be out of production for many months. Besides, as I've told you before, she lacks the maternal instinct. She's not ready for it. I'm short on options. Do you know what a Hail Mary Pass is, Harry?'

'No.'

'I didn't until I came to America and started watching sports on television. It is an American football term. It's a pass made in desperation with very little chance of success. Tell me where you are in your cycle?'

'What?'

'When did you last have a period?' He was aiming the Taser at her chest. 'Don't lie. Eva is very keen to kill Allegra and you must give her no encouragement to do so.'

Harry met Eva's eyes. What she saw in them terrified her.

'Twelve days ago.'

'Good. That's very good. Maybe there is a chance after all.'

'What are you talking about?' Harry snarled.

'It's simple. I'm going to put the eggs inside you.'

He pulled the trigger.

PART THREE

THE JETSONS VERSUS THE FLINTSTONES

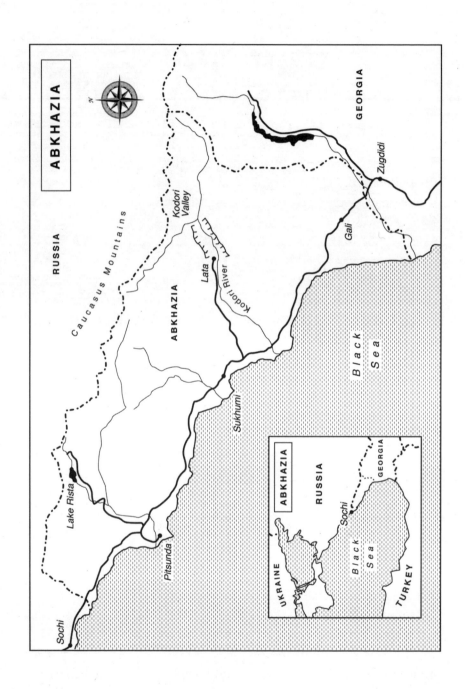

EIGHTY-THREE

The circuit breaker was thrown with a dull clang and the cell was flooded with light.

Freeman swung his bare feet off the bed and onto the cold floor. He was in a windowless white space somewhere inside the Marine Corps Brig at Quantico. It was a Special Quarter's two room: there was a bed that hung from the wall on a hinge and a steel sink and a steel toilet pan. The walls were concrete thickly covered in white paint. There was a metal door with a hatch for meals. It did not feel like a room that was bounded by a floor, walls and a ceiling. It felt like an air bubble in a cinder block.

They had taken his watch so he had no clear idea of the passage of time. Only the illusion of day and night created by the lights shutting on and off at irregular intervals and the Meals-Ready-to-Eat that were pushed through the hatch.

The door opened.

Two Marine Corps guards entered. One watched impassively while the other cuffed his wrists and ankles. They escorted him down a corridor of closed doors to an interrogation room with a metal table and chair that were bolted to the floor, facing a mirror on the wall. The guards made him sit and attached his handcuffs to an eyebolt on the desktop. They left and locked the door behind them.

He stared at his reflection in the mirror.

He listened to the sound of the bolt in the door clicking open. A tall, thin man of indeterminate age walked in carrying a chair. He was wearing a grey suit and his hair was iron-grey and his face was grey and he stank of cigarettes. He put the chair down on the opposite side of the table to Freeman and sat with his back to the mirror.

They stared at each other.

'Kaplan has told us everything,' the man said casually. He had yellow teeth and practically no gums.

'He has?'

'You conspired with Dr Alexander Markoff, the CIA traitor John Bohlayer, and the British double-agent Harriet Armstrong to abduct the genetic variant called Eva.'

'I have no idea what you are talking about.'

'Detectives Hadžiosmanagič, Wrath, Marschalk and Menendez and the Medical Examiner Kaplan were your unwitting accomplices in this endeavour. Hadžiosmanagič, Wrath, Marschalk and Menendez paid for it with their lives. Kaplan's career is finished.'

'Everything I have to say is in the report that I submitted to Assistant Chief of Police Streeks.'

'We aren't interested in your report. We want to know what you've done with Eva.'

Freeman was accused of conspiring with the fraudster Dr Alexander Markoff aka Uncle Sasha to kill Senator James Cannon and with rogue elements within the CIA and the British intelligence services to arrange for the doctor and his murderous niece to escape overseas; his marriage break-up was cited as proof of mental instability; destroying evidence including Oleg Davidov's hard drive was bitterness at his lack of promotion; his assault on Gideon Wu and his use of an unregistered firearm were proof of his violent, lawless nature: to sum it up, they knew him better than he did and it was time to start cooperating.

They took him back to the cell. Time passed. A meal was delivered. He wolfed it down. The lights clicked off and on again. They escorted him back to the interrogation room. The same grey-faced man made the same accusations and the same demand. They took him back to the cell. They did it four more times while the intervals between day and night seemed to get shorter and shorter. To every accusation he told the man to read his report.

'You're going to prison for a very long time,' the grey-faced man told him.

* * *

The guards came for him again and escorted him to the same interrogation room with the mirror on the wall. They shackled him to the table.

'I can't stay.'

Chief of Police Michelle Thielen was sitting on a plastic chair though she had not been there when they brought Freeman in and he couldn't recall her coming in. He realised that they had drugged his food. The walls were glistening with mauve patches like algae.

Thielen produced an envelope from thin air. 'I came with these for you to sign.'

Inside the envelope were two copies of a letter of resignation from the police. It made him feel sad; after all, he'd only been trying to uncover the truth.

'You're giving them a hard time, aren't you?' Thielen said. 'It's not easy to interrogate an interrogator?'

'I guess not.'

He signed. He couldn't help himself.

'You're a clever man, Michael, but obstinate. It's my fault; I should never have listened to Jim Cannon and all that band of brothers' bullshit. Why he thought you'd be any more pliable because you'd worn the same uniform I'll never know.'

Freeman felt depressed and tired, so tired he felt that if he closed his eyes he'd sleep for hours. He was grateful that the Chief was taking the time to stay and chat. She was now perched on the table though Freeman couldn't recall seeing her move.

'Anything I can do to help, you just ask,' Thielen suggested in a sympathetic tone. 'Go on and ask.'

'Maja . . .'

'There's nothing you can do for her, Michael. I'm so sorry. She died of her wounds. The whole thing was a bloody mess. On top of that the killer's gone missing. We need to know where she is. What have you done with Eva?'

It was difficult for Freeman to concentrate.

'What you need now is a friend,' Thielen said in a soothing voice. 'Someone to confide in.'

'Baba John . . .'

'Baba John is no friend of yours. You can't trust those guys at Langley.'

'Why did I have to resign?' Freeman asked, careful to speak slowly and distinctly.

'You didn't really look at what you signed, did you?' Thielen opened the envelope and handed him the letters. 'See what I mean?'

Struggling to focus, Freeman read the letters again. They were confessions to all the crimes that he had been accused of since they locked him up in the Pentagon. 'That's not what I signed,' he said.

'I saw you sign them,' Thielen told him. 'It doesn't matter. They're not going to bring charges.' She leaned forward and whispered softly in Freeman's ear. 'If you can't help them they're going to have to take you out in the woods and kill you. What choice do they have? And no one is even going to notice you're gone. Certainly not your wife.'

Freeman looked at the mirror on the wall. Its gleaming, over-bright surface was a facade for the murderous people on the other side.

'It'll be like you never existed.'

'My report . . .' he managed with a gasp.

'It's been deleted. The only way to spare yourself now is to tell us where you've hidden Eva.'

There was no doubt they were going to kill him; Freeman saw that.

'I'm your friend,' Thielen said. 'Your only friend.'

He was running with sweat, it was coming out of every pore. He wanted to talk; to confess to anything while there was still a chance it might save him. But he pressed his fists to his mouth. He clamped his knees together and closed his eyes. If he weakened for even a moment, any old words would force their way out through his fists in a tumult, so he thought about Maja instead. He thought of her slipping and sliding in her own blood on the senator's carpet. It made him angry and hungry for revenge against her killer.

He opened his eyes and saw Thielen – not this friendly Thielen, but the Thielen of before: the ruthlessly ambitious Thielen who had manoeuvred her way to the top, who had sacrificed all around her to become the Chief of Police; the ruthless Thielen who had conspired with the Pentagon to close down the investigation. The same Thielen was telling him that she was the only person in the world he could trust.

It was a lie. It was all a lie.

Freeman brought his hands down from his mouth. He was crying but he felt a wave of fury – the same wave of fury that had followed on from the 9/11 attacks and carried him across the world from the US to Afghanistan. He whistled and made the sound of an explosion. He was back in Afghanistan. He was fighting the Taliban. He was a Jetson up against the Flintstones. He had immense powers at his fingertips.

'I'm your friend,' Thielen said.

'Pickle, pickle, pickle,' Freeman whispered.

He guided another bomb from the bays. He whistled as it fell. He made the sound of a massive explosion. A deep-throaty rumble. Something of his fury unnerved her. Recoiling from the sound, she backed away from the table and banged on the door to be let out.

They moved him across the base to an out-of-the-way house. Quantico was spread out over a hundred square miles and the house they put him in was on the furthest edge of the training area. It was an old, wooden two-storey hunting lodge surrounded by a chain-link fence that was patrolled by men with dogs. He was free to wander in the grounds as long as he returned for meals.

They didn't make any further attempt to interrogate him. Why should they bother? He was a condemned man.

After lunch on the second day he found his wife Shawna alone on a bench. He was surprised. He sat beside her, and stared at the distant mountains.

'I've lost my job,' she told him, after the silence had stretched to breaking point.

'I'm sorry.'

'You're sorry?' She was outraged. 'Look what you've done to me. You've ruined my life.'

'Why did you come?'

'Do you think it was my idea to come here?'

'No,' he conceded.

'Why can't you just tell them what they want to hear?'

'Because it would be a lie. I've no idea where Eva is or why she was taken.'

After another silence, she moved towards him on the bench and held his arm. 'Look, we've had some difficulties. It's my fault. I know that now. I wasn't understanding enough of the pressure on you. We could start again.'

'No.'

'I could stay tonight.'

'Don't!' Freeman pried her fingers off.

'You fucking bastard.' She slapped his face.

They drove her away.

Something had changed. They weren't going to kill him after all.

He realised that eventually they'd have to let him go.

He sat on the bench and repeated the names of his dead colleagues: Hector Menendez, Elias Wrath, Kari Marschalk and Maja Hadžiosmanagič.

He wouldn't be satisfied until he'd avenged their deaths.

EIGHTY-FOUR

She could feel it in the tenderness of her breasts and in the dull ache in her belly.

She knew it was too early to tell. The physical symptoms were probably just a consequence of the Prometrium injections administered each morning by Dr Markoff. But she could feel it nonetheless. Growing hour by hour. Cells multiplying as fast as cancer and burrowing into the walls of her uterus: last year's miscarriage had left her feeling that there was an empty and repellent space in her belly, but this new sensation of unchecked growth was even more repellent.

The clock was ticking with a particular force and fury. She was cradling something monstrous in her womb. She could feel it. She wanted to scream.

'Russia cannot be understood by ordinary measures,' Gogol told her as they drove south alongside the Don River, its churning grey waters echoing the drab and overcast sky. Gogol had been in a much better mood since they touched down in Moscow, almost cheery. 'Russia is larger than the full moon. It's true. I'm telling you. Isn't that right, Alexander Ilyanovich?'

Dr Markoff stared sullenly into the footwell. His two black eyes made him look like a melancholy owl. His assumption that by switching sides he would earn himself good will had proven to be a miscalculation. It turned out that Gogol wasn't an employee of the Russian state; instead he was a freelancer working with a small, mobile team and a minimum of baggage. He'd freaked out when he discovered that Harry had been impregnated with the embryos. He'd knocked Dr Markoff to the floor of the lab and stamped on his head while his men wrestled Eva to the ground.

'You'll have to come with us,' Gogol had spat at her when he'd finished with Dr Markoff. 'I can't afford to leave you behind.'

To Harry, it felt like they were travelling into a void, a feeling compounded by hunger, light-headedness and an eight-hour time difference on the back of a twelve-hour flight from Havana with a two-hour fuel stop in Guinea Bissau.

It was Wednesday morning.

She was curled up in the back of the Mercedes with her face pressed to the glass, trying not to think about the ache in her belly, watching the dismal landscape drift by: the concrete bus shelters and stacks of abandoned fifty-gallon oil barrels, the thickets of weeds and the weathered grey villages, one after the other on the endless road. Trying not to think about her swollen breasts. Instead watching the skinny, long-legged cows with muddy shins that grazed alongside the road and the old women in rubber boots and trousers under their skirts who sold milk and butter from roadside stalls.

They drove beside railroad tracks and past slowly rolling trains of blackened oil tanks and sea containers.

'Russia is subject to the same centrifugal forces as the old Soviet Union,' Gogol declared, using a cloth to clean his round, wire-framed spectacles, 'worse even; the more uncontrolled it is, the faster it travels, the more its peripheral parts want to break off and spin away. Not just peoples – Chechens, Ingush, Tartars, etc. – but ideas too. Not just ideas. Also secrets: chemical, biological and nuclear. Our most precious possessions. We have a saying in Russia: "If something has spilled from somewhere, then that must mean that something has poured into somewhere else." Somebody has to get it back. You understand that is what I do, Harry? I perform a public service, for money of course. I am a business-man, after all. I recover assets that have been misplaced, sold off or stolen. Like the perfidious Dr Markoff and his feral niece. Like the embryos in your womb. All Russian state property. I grab them back with violence if necessary. I get well paid for it.'

There were six of them. Gogol and his driver who was a swarthy Kalmyk with a pot belly and scuffed leather shoes. They travelled in the Mercedes with Harry and Dr Markoff. The other four were Ossetians, tall, gym-built henchmen with leather coats, sparse hair and the acne scars of steroid abuse on their chins. Gogol called them his big game hunters. They travelled in the second vehicle, a black Range Rover with Eva trussed up in the trunk.

Both vehicles had blue flashing lights and registration plates with white characters on black backgrounds and a numeric code that Gogol explained denoted the Ministry of Emergency Situations.

He laughed. 'You're pregnant. Is emergency, right?'

The road stretched and contracted, narrowed and widened; at times it was a four-lane highway with advertising hoardings and speeding trucks throwing up huge fantails of spray, at other times a ribbon of tarmac crumbling at the edges. The worst section was between Voronezh and Rostov, one lane each way divided by an erratic white line, giving way to stretches of gravel with enormous potholes that slowed their progress to a crawl.

They passed a ruined church with the onion domes broken off.

They filled up at a gas station that was no more than a gravel apron with a single pump and a battered sheet-metal kiosk with glass so old and opaque that you could hardly make out the person behind it. Everywhere there were broken-down cars with men under the hoods, hammering at the innards.

They stopped at an ad hoc picnic site, a roadside expanse of mud and gravel and crusted snow with felled tree-trunks for benches and trash everywhere. The Ossetians lifted Eva out of the Range Rover's trunk and marched her in her chains over to a concrete post. Her head was covered in a sandbag and steam rose out of the pointy ends like horns. They attached her to the post and removed the sandbag. Underneath she was wearing an obscene-looking red ball-gag.

'In the brothel Tiraspol they used to tie up the fuck monkeys between clients,' Gogol said.

'She's not a fuck monkey,' Dr Markoff said softly.

'What's that, Alexander Ilyanovich? She's not a fuck monkey? That's right, she's not. She's your little secret. The proof of your success.'

They ate a lunch of cold chicken and boiled eggs, served on aluminium foil spread out on the ground. One of the Ossetians removed Eva's ball-gag and threw some pieces of chicken and an egg at her feet. Squatting down, she shovelled them into her mouth. Harry could hardly bear to look at her. She had no means of communicating with her and no wish to do so.

Gogol sat on one of the fallen trees and watched, sipping at juice through a straw. 'I took two bullets in the stomach in Baghdad back in 2003,' he explained, when he realised Harry was watching him. 'They cut out half my intestines. I live on soup and juice. How are you, Harry? Can you feel it inside you?'

Harry shrugged. 'I'm not sure. It's too early.'

Gogol returned his attention to Dr Markoff. 'Hey, Alexander Ilyanovich, when are you going to tell her who the father is?'

Dr Markoff, who was standing staring down the road, turned to face them.

'I'll tell you, Harry,' Gogol continued. 'He was a Russian. A monkey, admittedly, but a Russian monkey – a Hero of the Revolution. Tell us what scientific marvels you performed, Doctor. Illuminate us with your wisdom!'

'Our work in the breeding programme concentrated on increasing the number of spindle cells in the subjects' brains and improving the articulation of the thumbs,' Dr Markoff explained in a defensive tone. 'We tried to make them more human.'

'But you are being too modest,' Gogol sneered. 'Tell her what else you did.'

Dr Markoff stared at him.

Gogol drew his Makarov and pointed it at Dr Markoff. 'Tell her, you cunt!'

'We also subjected them to different kinds of stress.'

'You tortured them! You went to Africa and you brought back to Kazakhstan only the biggest, meanest monkeys and you locked them in a cell and starved them and forced them to fight each other for food. Only the fittest of those who survived were allowed to breed. And so it went on, over several generations. You understand, Harry, on the one hand he made them smarter and more dexterous, he fundamentally changed their nature, and on the other hand he nurtured their basest instincts. He made them into rapacious predators. *Homo rapiens.* That's progress, Harry, the summit of his achievement. That's what you've got inside you.'

She spat a half-eaten piece of chicken on the floor and began heaving; seconds later the rest of her lunch came up. She spewed on the trash-covered ground.

Gogol found it hilarious. He holstered his gun and began clapping.

They drove through the night and into the dawn.

Harry first caught sight of the dark waters of the Black Sea above the town of Dzugba, the jagged mountains falling hundreds of feet to the sea. They drove the final stretch on the Mountain Highway and skirted the edge of Sochi. The city was being transformed for the Winter Olympics. Everything was under construction. They drove through endless avenues of traffic cones surrounded by gigantic diggers cropping up mud and earth like dinosaurs.

It was early Thursday afternoon when they crossed the border into the disputed territory of Abkhazia, a narrow strip of coastline squeezed between the Caucasus Mountains on one side and the Black Sea on the other.

'They called it the Soviet Riviera,' Gogol told her.

It was like travelling into some kind of alternate reality, a dystopian vision; it reminded Harry of a novel she had once read – an abandoned beach resort after a near-apocalyptic disaster, with a few listless survivors poking about among the rubble.

On the empty highway they passed abandoned houses, fields overgrown with vegetation, minefield warning signs and several geysers of steam from ruptured pipes, leaks in a barely functioning Soviet-era heating system that Gogol told Harry stretched for hundreds of miles underground.

'The Abkhaz and the Georgians hated each other in a special way,' Gogol explained, 'like brothers who know each other well but hate each other all the same. It was Stalin, who thought nothing of moving entire populations from one place to another, who gave Abkhazia to Georgia and trucked the Georgians in en masse. They swanned about like they owned the place. Of course, the Abkhaz seethed with resentment. And then the Soviet Union collapsed. Georgia declared independence and immediately fractured into civil war. The Abkhaz saw their opportunity for revenge. With the help of the Russians, the Abkhaz rose up and kicked the Georgians out. A quarter of a million of them fled. Many died along the way. Almost two decades later, a Georgian return is prevented by a Russian peacekeeping force and so far only four countries, Russia, Nicaragua, Venezuela and Nauru, have recognised Abkhazia as a sovereign nation. The Abkhaz survive by stripping their buildings and bridges and piers and selling them to Turkey for scrap. Soon there will be nothing left to sell. They would sell their organs if they could but no one in their right mind would buy them.'

In the ruins of a town called Pitsunda, they turned off the highway and drove past a concrete bus stop in the shape of a huge scallop shell and headed north into the mountains. They drove through a forested gorge alongside a tumultuous river and into a narrow canyon with trailing beards of red and green moss hanging from rock walls.

They spent Thursday night in a large single-storey wooden dacha painted an institutional forest green. Hidden in the dense forest, and impossible to see from the opposite shore, it sat at one end of a deep glacial lake that gleamed like ice and was surrounded by dark mountains with snow-packed ravines.

'Stalin had five dachas in Abkhazia,' Gogol told Harry. 'They are almost invisible. He would never say which one he was going to stay in so each time he came they prepared all five for his arrival. This one is my favourite. I have a treat for you, Harry. You are an honoured guest. Tonight you will sleep in Stalin's bed.'

The bedroom was large and functional with a hard parquet floor and the bathroom was enormous and tiled like a public bath.

Harry lay on a mass-murderer's bed with monsters in her womb.

She imagined herself as a character in a horror movie, outstretched like a crucifix, the creatures bursting out of her . . .

EIGHTY-FIVE

The handover took place on a neglected stretch of road in Spotsylvania County with woodland on either side. Freeman got out of the car and shuffled down the road in transport chains, heading towards two Suburbans with blackened windows that were waiting with their engines idling about a hundred feet away. Before he was halfway, the front passenger door on the lead Suburban opened and Walter Streeks got out. He was wearing the neatly pressed uniform of the DC Chief of Police.

'It looks good on you,' Freeman said tersely.

'I'm sorry we couldn't get you out before,' Streeks told him.

McCafferty got out of the second Suburban. He went past Streeks and taking Freeman by the arm steered him back to his vehicle. He knelt down and unlocked Freeman's leg cuffs, straightened up and did the same for his handcuffs.

'Where is she?' Freeman demanded. 'Eva Markoff. The Fury. Where is she?'

'Easy, tiger,' McCafferty said.

'Well?'

'She's gone. The Russians have taken her.'

It defied belief. 'You stupid fucks!'

'We're going to straighten this out, I promise you that,' McCafferty said, holding the car door open for him. 'Come on. Let's get you out of here.'

Behind him, Chief Streeks cleared his throat. Freeman glanced back at him.

'I guess this is goodbye, Michael,' Streeks said, refusing to meet his eye.

Freeman shrugged. 'What can I say? I'm glad that you made the most of my misfortune.'

In the back of the Suburban, fatigue overtook him and he slept.

The joint CIA/FBI taskforce had taken over a modest house with bars on the windows in a quiet Georgetown neighbourhood of the District. There was direct access to the house from the garage and as soon as the roll-up door had fully closed Freeman was smuggled out of the car and into the house. John Bohlayer was waiting in a thickly carpeted hallway that smelled of fresh paint.

'I'm glad you made it, buddy.' He escorted him upstairs to a bedroom with an en suite bathroom and a wardrobe with clothes hanging in it.

'Take a shower. Get yourself cleaned up. The clothes should fit.'

The view from the window was of a small garden with a magnolia tree. There was a man in a hooded parka jacket with fur trim standing beneath the tree, presumably to prevent Freeman from attempting to escape.

'Make sure you're down in the basement for a briefing in half an hour.'

'The Markoffs were abducted on Monday from a fertility clinic in the Turks and Caicos,' Bohlayer explained. 'We believe that they were taken off the island to a waiting yacht owned by a Russian oligarch. From there they travelled by seaplane to Cuba and from there by private jet to Moscow. The man behind the operation is Yevgeny Gogol, a former KGB officer turned private contractor who has been known to act as a go-between in transactions between the Russian Kremlin and various non-states actors and terrorist groups, as well as certain business interests including the Russian mafia. He's a self-employed repo man. His speciality is Cold War-era asset recovery.'

They were in a dining room in the converted basement. Bohlayer was standing in front of a collage taped on the wall. It was a mish-mash of satellite photos, mug shots, flight plans, emails, transcripts of phone intercepts, frame-grabs from security cameras and relief maps of the Caucasus Mountains. McCafferty and Freeman were sitting beside each other at the dining table. McCafferty was in shirtsleeves.

'So where are they?' Freeman demanded.

'According to Georgian intelligence, who maintain watchers on the border, a small party matching their description crossed from Russia into the disputed territory of Abkhazia just a few hours ago. That's Thursday afternoon local time.'

'Where are they heading?'

Bohlayer unpeeled a series of satellite photos from the wall and laid them out on the table.

'The Upper Kodori. At least that's what we think. It's a lawless, mountainous area of the Caucasus that borders Russia; the Abkhaz and the Georgians contest it and it is inhabited by a tribal people called the Svans. It's a breakaway fragment of a breakaway region of a breakaway state.'

'It's also where we think the gang known as the Furies is located,' McCafferty added. 'They've been hiding out up there since the KGB programme Progress fell apart in the nineties.'

Freeman studied the photos: a scarred and fractured glacier muscling its way through jagged, snow-capped mountains; fields of boulders and broad alpine meadows; deep gorges carved by ancient run-off and old growth forest; a meandering road.

'There's only one road in and it comes from the Abkhaz side,' Bohlayer explained. 'In the summer of 2008 during the Russia-Georgia war, the Russians sent an expeditionary force up it to bring the Upper Kodori to heel.'

'It didn't go so well,' McCafferty said.

'The expeditionary force was never heard from again,' Bohlayer added.

'Which is the point at which we assume that someone in authority over there woke up to the fact that there was a surviving colony of genetic variants in the mountains,' McCafferty explained. 'Rather than pass the information to the Kremlin they must have sold it to Gogol and he has been hot on the trail of Markoff and his creations ever since. Here in the US and in the Kodori Valley.

Now he's heading up into the mountains and he's taken the Markoffs with him, probably as hostages. Perhaps he thinks they will offer him a measure of safety in his dealings with the Furies.'

'Will it?' Freeman demanded.

'I'm sorry?' McCafferty said.

'What do we really know about the Furies?'

McCafferty glanced at Bohlayer who shrugged. 'Practically nothing. We think the gang is made up of the surviving remnants of the test subjects of the KGB Directorate S programme Progress, human-primate hybrids bred for strength, agility and aggression and trained in languages, covert operating and combat skills. When Progress fell apart they escaped and they've been holed up in the Caucasus Mountains ever since. The KGB seems to have believed that the test subjects were all destroyed in a laboratory fire. And anyway, the reports that we've seen from that time suggest that they had already concluded that the test subjects were too crude and unreliable to form an effective fighting force and their genetic traits were untransferable. We're guessing that they didn't know about the girl.'

'Eva Markoff?' Freeman said.

'That's right. The fact that she's fertile changes everything. It raises the possibility for further refinement over successive generations, by which I mean a proper breeding programme with tailor-made outcomes. It also raises the possibility of cutting and splicing selected genes from existing genetic variants, i.e. the Furies, into Eva's embryos. The Kremlin will want control of the test subjects, for their own special weapons programmes and for the export market. The Chinese for instance would pay big money for access to the technology. Gogol is looking at a sizeable reward. For our side, we have the prospect of a whole new arms race. I don't mind telling you, Michael, it's a nightmare with no prospect of waking up.'

'Unless? I mean you got me here for a reason, right?'

'We did,' Bohlayer agreed. He nodded to McCafferty.

'The Georgian authorities are as eager as we are to prevent the Russians reasserting ownership over the genetic variants,'

McCafferty explained. 'To that end they have stated that they're willing to send a police unit up there to take the Furies into custody before Gogol does.'

'Are you serious?'

'What?'

'I got my entire squad wiped out by just one of them!' Freeman said. 'You think they're going to come quietly?'

'What do you suggest we do?'

'There's only one way to solve this mess.'

'What's that?' McCafferty said.

'Kill them all. Every last one of them.' Freeman didn't just want the Furies dead, he wanted them obliterated off the face of the earth – burned to a few handfuls of ash. 'Send me over there and let me call in an airstrike.'

'You'd do that?' Bohlayer asked, after a pause.

Comprehension dawned on Freeman. This was what they'd been hoping for. He started to laugh. A strange and ugly sound full of bitterness and irony.

'Why didn't you just ask?'

'We had to know whether you still had it in you,' Bohlayer said.

'I have it in me,' he said grimly. He wasn't interested in any fancy notions of justice. He wanted revenge. Simple as that. For Hector, Eli and Kari and most of all for Maja. *You betcha I do . . .*

'Give me a B-52,' he said. 'I'll wipe them off the face of the earth.'

Later that night, asleep on a plane over the Atlantic, he found himself walking in the mountains after an airstrike. All around him were smoking bunkers and bodies in grotesque positions. Just as he thought he was the last person alive, a naked young woman with long hair and a pale face joined him.

It was Katja. She called him by the name the Taliban gave him: '*bor-buka*', which means black or devil or whirlwind.

She took him by the hand and led him down into a cave.

EIGHTY-SIX

He remembered the flight to Incirlik airbase in Turkey in November 2001, just a few weeks after 9/11. The feeling of nervous and fearful anticipation that gripped him and that was replaced by a kind of grim resolve for the next leg from Incirlik to Karshi-Khanabad airbase in Uzbekistan. This time he flew commercial, from Dulles to Heathrow and from Heathrow to Tbilisi, arriving on Friday night. He experienced a similar progression of emotions. By the time he reached Tbilisi, he felt the same determination to see the task through to completion.

The plane touched down, a teeth-jarring impact, followed by the roar of deceleration.

By the time the plane was taxiing to the terminal the aisle was full of pushing and shoving Georgians dressed in black, pulling down suitcases, bundles of gifts and large red-and-white-check plastic bags. They exited the plane in a rush through a covered walkway at the front of the plane.

When all the other passengers had gone, Freeman sat and waited as he had been instructed to, watching the door to see who would come for him. He was startled when a man came up behind him and tapped him on the shoulder. The man was short with pale, unshaven cheeks and black brushed-back hair and he was wearing a black leather jacket over a black polo neck. There was a pistol in a holster at his belt.

'I'm David Vashadze,' he said enthusiastically. 'Call me Dato.'

It was the Homicide cop who'd reached out to Freeman during the investigation, who'd made the link between the DC killings and the Russian gang known as the Furies.

'Michael Freeman.'

Dato led Freeman, clutching his single piece of luggage, down the service steps at the rear of the plane to a black Mercedes with AAA plates, waiting on the tarmac. They didn't pass through customs and nobody looked at Freeman's passport. The car drove them directly to an exit and out onto a highway.

'We have an agreement with your people,' Dato said, settling into the rear seat alongside Freeman. 'You're not here legally and you're not here illegally either.'

'My people?'

'The CIA.'

'I'm not with the CIA,' Freeman told him.

'That's very funny. The CIA says you're not with them too. It's what we expect them to say.'

The highway was a strip of light in the midst of vast concrete, Khrushchev-era housing blocks and mountains either side.

'What is the agreement that you have with the CIA?' Freeman asked.

'The agreement is that this will be a Georgian police operation. Nothing to link it with the CIA.'

'And you think I'm with the CIA because they say I'm not.'

'What else would they say?'

Freeman sat in silence and stared out of the window. Maybe Dato was right. He certainly wasn't a cop any more. He was doing the bidding of the CIA. That made him one of them whether he liked it or not.

The old part of the city was a maze of narrow streets, wooden balconies, small basement stores, brightly lit bars, cobbled court-yards and hidden, briefly glimpsed atriums. They passed the presidential palace with its massive glass dome and the gleaming new Iveria Hotel that Dato told him used to be full of refugees from the war in Abkhazia.

The car parked outside a hotel at the foot of a thickly forested mountain with a radio tower on top. Dato handed Freeman a key with a large leather fob. 'I will see you tomorrow morning.'

Freeman got out of the car. He pushed open the glass doors. The hotel lobby had red walls, marble floors and richly patterned

Armenian carpets. A large man rose from a sofa as he entered and waved a newspaper at the Mercedes outside. He tapped his chest and said, 'Bezik.'

He pointed at the elevator before sitting down again and returning to his newspaper.

Freeman rode alone up to the fourth floor. His room was at the end of a hall. Without switching on the light he put his bag on the bed and went to the window. Looking out, he saw that the black Mercedes was still parked outside.

It was difficult to remember what it had been like back before he was constantly under observation. In less than two weeks his life had been turned upside down: he had lost his job and his wife, his colleagues and friends were all dead and it seemed there was a good chance he wouldn't survive the next few days.

All because he'd tried to solve Katja's murder . . .

Just after 8 a.m., the door burst open and Dato Vashadze staggered backwards into the room propelled by a hand.

'This man is under police protection,' Dato protested.

'I got to check you got the right tommy tank, mate.'

A large black man barged into the room, brushing Dato aside.

'Hello,' said Freeman from by the window.

'This is a Georgian police operation,' Dato warned.

'Don't make me laugh,' the man said. He was bulky like a lineman with a shaved head and sleeves rolled up high on his biceps. He clapped his hands together. 'You're Freeman, right?'

'I am.'

Dato was speaking in Georgian on his cell phone.

'Fifth Special Forces Group?'

'I was once.'

'I don't want your enthusiasm getting the better of you. I know what you lot can be like.'

'My lot?'

'I don't want Harry ending up in Gitmo.' He shook his head, surveying the room. 'She's not a Uighur.'

'What are you talking about?'

403

'The rendition. You're going to freight the Furies to Guantanamo. I don't want Harry on that plane.'

'Rendition? Is that what they told you?' Freeman shook his head.

'What are you talking about?' Jonah demanded.

Bezik and another man that Freeman hadn't seen before rushed into the room and together with Dato they manhandled Jonah out into the hallway. Freeman was too busy shaking with laughter to stop them.

'We got everything you asked for.' Special Agent Syverson from the embassy's legal attaché office put a black waterproof tote bag on the bedspread and handed Freeman a folder containing tactical air cards with up-to-date directions on how to call in a drone strike. 'I've been told that you've done this kind of thing before?'

Syverson was a tall, blond Minnesotan with a prominent Adam's apple and a cheerful disposition.

'I have,' Freeman confirmed. 'Though with a bomber not a drone.'

Syverson's smile broadened. 'I'm sure it'll be no problem. The Reaper is flying out of Incirlik in Turkey and the pilot is in Creech Air Force Base in Nevada. Georgian police will get you as close as possible to the terrorists.'

'Terrorists?'

Syverson's bonhomie was unassailable. 'It's a budgetary issue. We have funds for counter-terrorism so terrorism it is. Once you've confirmed that they are where we think they are, you call the number on the card and speak to the control centre. You get four Hellfire missiles. Don't miss.'

Alone in the room, Freeman unpacked the bag and set the things out on the bedspread: five sharpened pencils, a notebook, a Thuraya satellite phone and car charger, a military-spec corrected GPS, a prismatic compass, a pair of laser range-finding binoculars and four six-by-two-inch infrared flashing beacons.

It felt like he had come full circle, from the general to the particular to the general again, impersonal to personal to impersonal, from committing state-sanctioned homicide on a massive scale in Afghanistan to solving homicides case by case on behalf of the state, and now – here he was again, with the means and the motive to unleash hell on earth.

EIGHTY-SEVEN

'We're going to make sure everything gets straightened out back here for you,' Bohlayer told him.

Freeman didn't know whether to believe him or not. He was standing on the roof of the hotel with the Thuraya clamped to his ear. It was Saturday evening. Dato was standing about twenty feet away, keeping an eye on him.

'I gotta tell you, it's getting pretty hairy on the home front. Leaked cell phone footage from the Germline labs is all over the web. Some very human-looking drowned babies on display. There are a lot of senior people at Langley and the Pentagon who want this to go away.'

'There's a Brit here,' Freeman said. 'He says his name is Jonah Said.'

'Yes. He's some kind of washed-up ex-undercover guy with a drink problem. He's come across Gogol before, though. Which could be useful to you, yes?'

'He says he's looking for Harry Armstrong.'

'I've spoken to the Interior Ministry there in Tbilisi and we've agreed to let him go up there with you.'

'You think she's being held against her will?'

'Listen, just so we're clear, your mission takes precedence over any kind of rescue attempt, if the British woman is even there.'

'I see. You don't mind, for instance, if she ends up as collateral damage?'

'You gotta do what you gotta do, Michael. That's all I'm saying.'

Freeman was finding it increasingly difficult to believe that he and Bohlayer had ever been friends.

★ ★ ★

Jonah found them at dinner with the Criminal Police. They were in a restaurant that resembled a grotto, somewhere in the old town. There were large stone fireplaces and textured concrete columns and the walls were covered in murals of rustic life. The owner, who was a friend or relative of Dato, showed them to a table in a private alcove laid out with plates of shashlik on skewers, grilled eggplant and Khachapuri, a cheese-filled bread. They hadn't been there long when Jonah barged in, scooped up a chair and set it down alongside them. He ordered a beer. He had obviously drunk several already.

'She's not a spy,' Jonah said, helping himself to a slice of Khachapuri.

'What are you talking about?'

'Harry. Harry Armstrong,' he said. 'I know you think she's a spy. She's not. She's just a bloody civilian. She was in the wrong place at the wrong time. She doesn't deserve to die.' When his beer arrived he took a long swig on it and said emphatically, 'I won't let you kill her.'

Freeman sighed. 'How do you know she's even with them?'

'They didn't tell you?'

'What didn't they tell me?'

'She's been forcibly impregnated. She's got six modified embryos inside her womb.'

'How do you know that?'

'One of my colleagues witnessed it. That's why Gogol kidnapped her along with Markoff and his niece.'

Freeman realised that Bohlayer deliberately hadn't told him. 'You think he'll keep her with him?'

'Definitely. Gogol's a private contractor. He works on commission and his resources are finite. So when he's working with high-value assets he's going to keep them close to hand, especially in enemy territory. On top of that he's famously paranoid, and rightly so. He wouldn't trust them in someone else's custody even temporarily – there's too much risk that they might be seized by his commercial rivals.'

'What about Gogol?' Freeman asked. 'What more can you tell me?'

Jonah finished his beer and called for another. 'He's a typical Russian self-hater. He loves all things American. He wears black Levis and smokes Marlboro Red. I was kidnapped by him once. That was in Iraq back in '03, just before the war kicked off. I was there on a WMD hunt that went awry. Gogol scooped me up and a colleague along with me.'

'What happened?'

'One of your fellow countrymen rode to our rescue.'

The owner delivered a bottle of vodka. Dato rose with a glass in his hand and spoke in English.

'We are here to welcome new friends. I welcome Michael and Jonah, our guests from America and England, who have come to rid us of the Furies. We are friends and friendship begins with a glass and a toast. *Gamarjos!*'

They drained their glasses and thumped them down on the table. One of the policemen stood up as soon as the glasses were re-filled and began speaking in Georgian. From the broad grin on Dato's face it seemed that he was describing his virtues. Next Bezik spoke and then another policeman. The owner joined them for a toast. Even Jonah had a go.

'I'm a dogged sort of a fellow,' he muttered before tossing back another shot. He wouldn't meet anyone's eye. 'Once I've got my teeth in something I don't let go.'

Freeman decided that Georgian drinking was a kind of aggression, like a prizefight, round after round with the winner as the last one standing.

They were swaying back and forth, butting shoulders beneath a sagging wooden balcony in an alley somewhere in the tilting maze of the old town. It was 3 a.m., it was raining, and they had fought themselves to a standstill. Freeman could taste blood in his mouth. It didn't seem to matter how hard or how many times Freeman hit Jonah, he couldn't put him down.

It wasn't clear in Freeman's mind how the fight had begun, or who threw the first punch; maybe he just got fed up with Jonah's hectoring tone and his oh-so-British sense of self-righteousness.

Come to think of it he might have told Jonah that if he'd done a better job of protecting Harry in the first place they might not be in this mess.

Jonah swung his arm in slow-motion imitation of a roundhouse punch that under normal circumstances might have knocked Freeman unconscious, but before it could connect Freeman had staggered backwards a couple of steps. With nothing to lean on Jonah fell flat on his face on the cobblestones.

Surprised to find himself victorious, Freeman lifted his arm above his head and raised his face to the rain, letting it wash the blood out of his mouth. He looked around for an audience. Dato and Bezik were sheltering in a nearby doorway, watching with consternation on their faces.

'Let's go,' he said. He stumbled and tripped over Jonah, landing beside him on the cobbles. He shook him by the shoulder.

'Come on, let's go rescue Harry.'

EIGHTY-EIGHT

From the railway station, now a dilapidated ruin covered in weeds, Harry climbed a crumbling concrete stairway through palms and oleander trees to a jumble of buildings, many pocked with bullet holes or collapsed by bombs.

Sitting on a plinth at the entrance to the Primate Institute there was a dog-faced bronze baboon with a massive chest and a neck ruff that resembled a set of ear-muffs. On the side of the plinth was an inscription in Cyrillic. 'Polio, yellow fever, typhus, encephalitis, smallpox, hepatitis and many other human diseases were eradicated thanks to tests on primates,' Gogol translated for her. 'You know they sent six monkeys into space from here. That's not all they did. Come on.'

The first thing that assaulted them was the putrid smell of animal faeces, then from inside one of the buildings there came a primal screaming that sounded like a child being tortured. Cage after cage of frenzied-looking monkeys came into view, hundreds of them running around the enclosures and then throwing themselves at the chain-link as they passed, shaking it before leaping down and running again.

'This is where it all began,' Gogol said, wincing against the noise. 'Here in Abkhazia. Isn't that right, Alexander Ilyanovich? Stalin was on a crusade to turn the whole world upside down, to build it new. He said to the doctor's grandfather, "I want a living war machine, a new and invincible human being, insensitive to pain and indifferent to the quality of food."'

An octogenarian in a white lab coat had appeared in the doorway of a nearby building. There was a twist of smoke rising from a hole in the roof. The man was unshaven and reeked of alcohol. When he saw Dr Markoff he rushed over and started pumping his hand and speaking animatedly.

'Grandpa Ivanov fucked it up though,' Gogol said. 'He had chimps and orangs and beautiful Natashas from the Pioneers. But he couldn't get the monkey sperm and the Natasha eggs to fuse. His monkeys died and he ran out of options. He should have stuck to breeding horses. Stalin was pissed. If Grandpa had done a better job maybe Alexander Ilyanovich here wouldn't have had to grow up in Kazakhstan in the ass end of nowhere.'

'What do you want me to do?' Dr Markoff said.

Ignoring him, Gogol continued talking to Harry. 'The father and the son never got anywhere. They didn't have the technology. But the grandson, Uncle Sasha, Alexander Ilyanovich Markoff, succeeded where they had failed. He solved the problem of peri-centric inversions. He used specially adapted viruses to insert combinations of human genes into ape embryos and vice versa. By mixing them up he managed to make them compatible. He gave the world human-ape hybrids just like Stalin ordered – baboon/humans and bonobo/humans. War machines and fuck machines! The Furies and the Peaceful. *Homo rapiens* and *Homo ludens!* The Kremlin thought he was on the point of mass produc-tion. They had big dreams. Thousands of cloned bonobo variants for the People's Pleasure Palaces and hundreds of thousands of cloned baboon variants for the People's Army. Can you imagine a horde of Furies come raging through the Fulda Gap? We could have overrun Western Europe. It was all bullshit, of course. Like everything else in the Soviet Union, they were badly made. Alexander Ilyanovich was cutting and splicing genes with no clear idea what the results would be. The variants were full of defects and prone to disease: liver and bone marrow cancer, Parkinson's, you name it. Very few of the variants made it through their child-hood training. By the time the Soviet Union collapsed nobody gave a shit. The money ran out and everything fell apart. The Kremlin thought the last of the variants were destroyed in a fire in the training facility.'

Gogol pulled the sandbag off Eva's head. He circled around her and she stared defiantly at him, her lips curled back, her teeth biting down on the ball-gag.

'It's ironic really. It's a classic Soviet tale. Just when things fell apart the breakthrough came. Alexander Ilyanovich produced a fertile female. And because nobody gave a shit any more he managed to keep it a secret. For a long time he kept her hidden in the mountains. She's beautiful, yes? And deadly too! Not perfect of course, she can't hear a word of what I'm saying. But her children, with the right genes in the mix, could be close to perfect. The Kremlin could build that army, maybe not as big as the Soviets would have done, but still big enough to make Russia truly great again. Can you imagine it? We are part of something very big, Harry.'

Gogol's cell phone beeped. He lifted his spectacles and peered at it.

'The general will see me now. Let's go.'

While Gogol met with the Russian general who commanded the peacekeeping forces, the Ossetians took their captives to the beach. They drove past the bombed-out shell of a hotel and parked on the crumbling concrete promenade.

It looked like a tide of rust had washed up from the Black Sea bearing anything made of iron on it: hulks of ships, locomotives and pieces of machinery, all scattered across the pebble beach; everywhere the rusting debris of the Soviets. The husk of an empire. Also pebbles, stones and rocks. Earlier Gogol had told her that the Abkhaz had their own unique creation myth: that when the world was formed God had walked across their land carrying a basket of rocks and by accident dropped it, spilling them everywhere.

The Ossetians drank beer and smoked cigarettes and Eva sat in her chains with the ball-gag in her mouth; Dr Markoff sat beside her. Harry did her best to ignore them all. She walked down to the water's edge and skimmed stones – God's inadvertent gift – across the surface of the sea. The water was dark with an oily, unhealthy sheen.

She supposed that she should be frightened but more than

anything she was angry, angry with Gogol and the Ossetians, at Allegra Puck and Jonah for not protecting her, at Jack for abandoning her for a story and above all the Markoffs for impregnating her. She felt like screaming. Instead, she threw stones with renewed vigour.

'I loved them as if they were my own daughters.'

Harry felt her neck stiffen with anger. Dr Markoff had joined her at the water's edge.

'The girls were easier than the boys,' he explained tentatively. 'It was in their nature to please. Until Eva, of course. She has always been difficult. I couldn't trust her with the eggs. That's why I did what I did, Harry.'

Without looking at him, Harry moved further down the beach.

After an hour or so, Gogol's Mercedes pulled up on the promenade and he leapt out.

'Come on,' he shouted, 'we are going to the top of the world.'

A platoon of thirty or so soldiers with three eight-wheeled BTR armoured personnel carriers escorted them north into the Kodori Valley, an unconquered fastness that was the Furies' hideout but also home to a fiercely independent people named the Svans.

'The Svans are a wild and wicked people,' Gogol told Harry. 'They are much known for banditry, blood feuds, inbreeding and stupidity.'

'They will not welcome us,' Dr Markoff said.

Apparently the Svans had also been known to leave crude improvised explosive devices buried in the road and rather than risk the inside of the BTRs the soldiers huddled together for warmth on the top. They were Russian Airborne Troops wearing light blue berets, eager volunteers from dirt-poor families beyond the Ural Mountains, seconded to 'special corporate duties', which seemed to mean any activity that would put money in the general's pocket. They had wide, gap-toothed grins, bad skin and none of them was over twenty.

As the convoy climbed into the mountains on the crumbling, potholed road, past towering peaks with scree-covered slopes, they passed through several regular army checkpoints – sand-bagged, cinder-block pill-boxes manned by skinny Russian conscripts who looked like they had been abandoned to their fate. The Airborne Troops threw them cigarettes and in return the conscripts wished them luck.

It was late afternoon when they reached Lata, the main village in the Lower Kodori. A heavy mist hung in the air and everything was clammy and wet. The atmosphere was menacing. Young Svan men dressed in filthy camouflage loitered idly in the doorways of weather-beaten shacks, smoking cigarettes.

'If I understand these people correctly,' Gogol said, 'they should be more hostile to the Furies than to us.'

While the Russian officer went off to speak with someone, the young men surrounded the vehicles. They did not smile or say hello.

Gogol wound down his window and spoke to them and when Harry asked him what they had said, he told her that the Svans wanted to know what they were doing here and he had told them that they were here to meet with Ras Serditye, the Furies.

'What did they say to that?' Harry asked.

Gogol shrugged. 'They said that all life is cheap to the Furies. They said that they are crazy fuckers.'

'They said the Furies are going to kill us,' Dr Markoff added.

'They know nothing,' Gogol snapped.

At that moment the officer returned and the young men backed off.

'Let's go,' Gogol said.

They continued north into the upper reaches of the valley.

The convoy halted in twilight, in the muddy courtyard of an abandoned hamlet of stone cottages beside a five-storey stone tower. Dr Markoff told Harry that the stone towers of Svanetia dated back to the eleventh century, when they provided defence for families against marauders and avalanches.

On arrival, the BTRs formed a laager with their gun turrets facing outwards and the soldiers dragged weapons and packs into the cottages. They put out trip wires and directional fragmentation mines on the perimeter.

Harry was on the top floor of the tower, looking down the length of the valley when she saw the approaching helicopter. It was a Mi-24 Hind helicopter gunship, with distinctive double air intakes, bulbous glass cockpits one behind the other and short stubby wings loaded with missile pylons. It circled the tower and then settled in a nearby field.

When Harry emerged from the narrow entrance to the tower fifteen minutes later, she found that the soldiers had put up a tent in the courtyard and Gogol, Dr Markoff, the Russian Airborne officer, and the pilot were huddled around a laptop looking at a montage of aerial views taken by a camera mounted on the helicopter gunship. Gogol summoned Harry over to have a look. The images showed a collection of stone buildings and three stone towers on the edge of an alpine meadow nestled between mountains with a deep ravine on one side, and the jumbled tip of a glacier on the other.

'This is where they are hiding,' Dr Markoff told them. 'A few hours north of here. When I left there were only twelve of them alive, eleven male variants from Clade B and a female variant from Clade A. They were dying at a rate of one or two a year.'

'What are you going to do with them if you capture them?' Harry asked.

'If she's still alive I'll sell the girl to recoup some of my costs,' Gogol replied in a matter-of-fact tone. 'There will always be work for a fuck monkey. As for the boys, the war monkeys, I'll sell them to the state. I imagine the state will extract their DNA, either voluntarily or by force. After that, who knows? Maybe they will be put to work. There are opportunities for them in Chechnya and Dagestan, pockets of resistance that must be eliminated. They could kill, and kill, and kill.'

'Why should they agree to that?' Harry asked.

'Because if they don't I'll exterminate them.'

'And what about me?' she demanded. 'What are you going to do with me?'

'You shouldn't worry so much,' Gogol told her. 'If you're not pregnant you can go. If you are, then you have to stay but only until you have the babies. After that you can go. I'm not an unreasonable man.'

'I want to speak to my husband.'

'Later, Harry,' he told her. 'When we know for sure whether you are pregnant.'

After dinner, Dr Markoff spoke with one of the Furies on the HF radio from the back of a BTR. Harry sat beside him with Gogol and listened to the crackling radio waves and the deep bass rumble of a man's disembodied voice, speaking slowly in Russian.

'It is Aslan,' Gogol told her. 'The alpha male. He is their leader.'

'What is he saying?'

Gogol frowned. 'He is not speaking clearly. He is saying that the Furies were born in pain and incomprehension and they don't fear death. He is drunk, I think.'

EIGHTY-NINE

Freeman remembered the drive west from Tbilisi as a series of jumbled vignettes observed through the lens of his hangover: a sixth-century monastery commanding the heights above the road; an abandoned Soviet factory as large and as desolate as the Packard Motor Plant in Detroit; gypsies selling puppies by the side of the road near the town that was Stalin's birthplace; Dato playing chicken with the oncoming traffic and proudly informing them that he had removed the seat belts.

Jonah slept most of the way, snoring gently beside him, sometimes with his head lolling on Freeman's shoulder. He had a spectacular black eye and a thick lip from hitting the pavement the night before. They spent Sunday night in Zugdidi, at Bezik's father-in-law's house. Another banquet: more rough red wine and vodka; more boastful toasts to Harry's inevitable rescue. They slept fitfully. Bezik left ahead of them at dawn in an old Soviet Uaz Jeep. Dato, Jonah and Freeman followed on in the Mercedes a couple of hours later. They drove north from Zugdidi into the high western Caucasus, following the line of the Inguri River that marked the boundary between Georgia proper and the breakaway region of Abkhazia, heading towards Svanetia.

'Svanetia is the most beautiful place on earth and the most dangerous,' Dato told Freeman. 'Svans are Georgians but they are a different kind of Georgian. They have something but they are mad too.'

They drove through a muddy village surrounded by steep mountains; beside many of the houses there were ancient stone towers with narrow arrow slits. People stared sullenly at them from doorways.

'They were the only Georgians who were never conquered,' Dato said. 'It's too far, too high, too easily defended, too many crazy people.'

Bezik was waiting for them at the end of the road, dressed for combat in forest-green fatigues with a Dragunov sniper rifle slung over his shoulder. He had parked his Jeep at the edge of a pine forest with a trail leading through it and he was accompanied by a Svan, a sombre red-faced man wearing a sweater with holes at the elbows and black rubber boots. He was holding a machete and beside him stood his moon-faced son. Nearby were seven shaggy, thin-legged horses tied to pickets.

'You're not serious,' Freeman swore.

Dato eased the Mercedes over the pine needles and parked beside the Uaz.

'What's the matter?' he asked.

'You're not expecting me to get on a horse?'

'Of course,' Dato said. 'The trail is too narrow for cars. The only road in is on the other side of the mountains.'

'I don't believe this.'

Freeman got out of the car and walked some way down the road muttering, 'Fuck! Fuck! Fuck!' He had vowed when he left Afghanistan that he'd never get back on a horse. Almost ten years ago. Eva Markoff was somewhere up in those mountains though, which meant that he didn't have any choice if he was going to see this through.

It's just a horse, he told himself.

When he walked back again he saw that Dato had opened the truck and taken out a short-barrelled assault rifle with a folding metal stock, an AKS-74. He handed it to Jonah, together with a couple of banana-shaped plastic magazines and a metal can full of ammunition. There was one for Freeman too. They sat on the pine needles and filled the magazines with bullets from the can while the Svan and his son looked on without expression and Bezik busied himself loading one of the animals with camping gear and food and a fuel can full of wine.

'Last time I rode a horse was in Afghanistan,' Jonah told him.

'Me too,' Freeman said, putting on his daypack and slinging the AKS across his chest.

'We're not so different, you and me,' Jonah said.

'I guess not,' Freeman conceded.

'Let's go,' Dato said, crushing a cigarette beneath his heel.

The moon-faced boy gave Freeman the reins of one of the horses. It had a white star on its roan forehead and prominent yellow teeth. It resembled the horses that he remembered from Afghanistan, barely larger than ponies, with rough-haired legs, knobby knees, thin ankles and cracked, unshod hooves. It was short enough that he could look directly into its eyes and engage with the malice lurking there.

'I'll shoot you,' he told it, without hesitation.

'Then I think maybe our guide will cut off your head,' Dato told him with a smile. He had swung himself up into the saddle of his horse and was sitting, gripping its mane with one hand and the reins with the other. The Svan was on the largest of the horses, with the machete resting across its neck. It seemed possible that Dato might be right.

With a sinking feeling, Freeman considered the saddle of his horse. It was made of wood, with a stained and rancid-smelling blanket spread over it. The stirrups were iron rings hanging down on short pieces of leather with no means of lengthening them. There was no getting away from it: it was going to be a painful experience.

'Here goes,' he said.

He put his left hand on the saddle seat and his right hand on the edge of the wooden board, slotted his foot in the stirrup and, just as he expected, the horse started circling, leaving him hopping after it. After the third hop, he kicked up and swung across. He landed in the saddle with a groan.

Beside him, Jonah was also hopscotching after his circling horse. After several attempts he managed to scramble up. They were all mounted.

Freeman kicked his horse in the flanks. It lurched and started

419

towards the others. Soon they were lined up at the trailhead behind the Svan.

'You better keep up,' Dato shouted over his shoulder.

They spurred their horses and rode into the forest.

NINETY

It had been an uneventful Monday morning, grey and overcast.

Harry was woken at dawn by the roaring of the V8 engines of the BTRs and the smell of diesel in the frigid morning air. She rolled out of the sleeping bag and reached the narrow slit of a window in time to see the helicopter gunship take off and fly north to scout the route ahead.

After a swift breakfast, the Russian officer had led his men in a brief prayer in the muddy yard. The soldiers took off their helmets and bowed their heads while Gogol watched from the doorway of the tower with an incredulous look on his face.

'These guys think they're on a crusade to rid the world of demons,' he said, shaking his head. 'In the old days we didn't need God. Besides, it was forbidden.'

The prayer finished, the soldiers clambered back on top of their vehicles.

The Mercedes stayed behind with the driver and so Harry and Dr Markoff were put in the back of the Range Rover. Eva remained in the trunk. Gogol got in the front and reached across the driver and banged several times on the horn. The convoy moved off, headlights glaring in the grey morning light, driving on the rocky track that ran north into the mountains.

It was early afternoon and they were driving through a steep-sided, thickly forested ravine when they became aware of shapes moving in the sparser trees on the ridgeline far above them. They were keeping pace with the slow-moving convoy as it negotiated the rutted track. The Russian officer called a halt over the radio and instructed them to turn off their engines.

There was something ominous in the silence that followed. The soldiers on the BTRs gripped their weapons tightly. Several clutched the crucifixes at their necks and kissed them. The officer stood among them like Rommel, and scanned the ridgeline with binoculars.

Then the howling began: a strange and haunting call that echoed throughout the valley.

'It is the Furies,' Dr Markoff said.

'Shut the fuck up,' Gogol told him.

The howling continued. When one voice died down another picked up, so that it seemed that there were many voices in the forest around them. Harry caught a fleeting glimpse of something that might be a man loping between two trees.

It was too much for one of the Russian soldiers who opened fire, shooting at the ridgeline. After a few moments, they were all firing, spraying the hillside with small arms fire. But the shapes were plunging down the slope into the densest forest.

The Russian officer was shouting, yelling at his men to stop firing. Eventually he got them under control. Silence. There was no sign of movement on the hillside.

'What are they doing?' Harry asked.

'Choosing their moment,' Dr Markoff said.

Crack!

A single shot. It took off the top of the Russian officer's head.

Gogol banged his fist on the car window.

The BTRs opened up with their turret-mounted heavy machine guns, scything tracer across the hillside. Pine trees thrashed and toppled and black smoke billowed.

'No,' Markoff shouted. It was over in five minutes. When the smoke cleared a swathe of the forest now resembled clear-cut. The senior sergeant, who had stepped in to replace the officer, dispatched a ten-man section to investigate. They advanced up the hillside under the watchful eye of the turret-gunners and came back down ten minutes later carrying a body between them. They dumped it by the side of the road.

Markoff jumped out of the car and dropped to his knees beside the body before gathering it up in his arms. Gogol wandered over more slowly and Harry tentatively followed.

Markoff was holding the corpse of a man, partially shredded by gunfire. He had broad shoulders and a massive bony forehead, long and powerful arms, large hands with calloused knuckles and a jaw full of uneven, yellow teeth.

'I don't think they want peace,' Gogol told Harry. 'You only have to look at them to see that.'

'They want to be left alone,' Dr Markoff told him.

'You should have thought of that before you went off to America and sold your secrets,' Gogol told him.

From there on in Harry and Dr Markoff and Eva were sealed inside the jolting, sweat-smelling belly of one of the BTRs with the soldiers, hanging on to each other for balance and staring out at the passing mountains through the ball-swivel firing ports. The condition of the track deteriorated the further north they went and they moved ever more slowly.

Several more times they heard the strange and unworldly howling.

They have forced us inside the vehicles, Harry thought, and then she asked herself, Why have they done that?

NINETY-ONE

The trail rose steeply into a pine forest and Freeman rocked back and forth on the horse. From the moment they started to climb he began to experience a curious kind of elation. As they struggled up through the trees he felt it more and more strongly: a sense of anticipation, of fear and excitement in equal measure. There was nothing for him back in America. Chief Thielen had been right about that. He'd been cut adrift. There was only the smell of pine sap, the cool wind on his face and the trail ahead. He didn't even mind that he was on a horse again. He was ready for battle.

Further up they came to a hardwood forest and the angle of the slope grew gentler. Dato called for a rest and they dismounted. Bezik spoke to the Svan, who pointed to a distant ridgeline.

'He's saying the Furies are beyond that hill,' Dato explained. 'They live in some old stone towers in an abandoned village. Bezik's asking him how many of them there are.'

The Svan shrugged and showed his palms.

'This man is not very helpful,' Dato complained.

Suddenly, Bezik pointed his Kalashnikov in the Svan's face and snarled at him.

'Take it easy,' Jonah said, pushing the barrel of the gun down.

The Svan shrugged again and said a few words in a low voice.

'He says there are not so many. Some of them have weapons.' Dato shook his head. 'You like it? I don't like it.'

Bezik and the Svan walked in front, leading their horses by the reins. At the top of the ridge there was a jumble of rocks and beyond it a meadow with patches of snow and small clusters of crocuses. As they reached the top of the rocks they came in sight of a rock pinnacle looming out of the trees on the far side of the meadow.

The Svan pointed to the rock pinnacle. His legs were trembling.

'We're going to be pretty exposed when we cross that field,' Jonah said. He took the binoculars from Freeman and surveyed everything around. He passed them back to Freeman who did the same, scanning the rocks for signs of movement.

'I don't see anything,' Jonah said. 'What about you?'

Freeman shrugged, unwilling to commit himself. There could be anything out there watching them and the field was a perfectly constructed killing zone.

Eventually they decided to proceed, but one at a time. Bezik was the first. He led his horse across the meadow and stopped at the edge of the wood on the far side. The Svan was next, then Jonah, Freeman, Dato and the boy. They crossed without incident.

The Svan undid the straps on the saddle of his horse and removed it.

'He says the trail is too narrow and the horses must stay here with the boy,' Dato told them.

They unloaded their equipment onto their backs and followed the Svan into the woods, Freeman cradling his gun across a forearm, Jonah carrying his pointed at the ground. It was colder in the shadow of the trees.

At a turn in the trail, they disturbed a mass of crows that took sudden flight. Jonah froze and then crouched down. Freeman went down with him.

'Look at that.'

'It's a wolf,' Dato said. He walked forward and looked at it. The animal was strung between two trees, with the glistening, ice-crusted loops of its entrails spilling on the forest floor. There was barely any smell.

'There's another one,' Jonah said, pointing through the trees. There were several frozen mutilated carcasses in the forest. He and Freeman got up.

The Svan stood still. Freeman watched him swallow.

Bezik spoke harshly to him and the Svan replied without taking his eyes off the nearest wolf.

'What did he say?' Freeman demanded.

'He says they are warnings.'

'For Christ's sake,' Jonah said.

Dato looked at them apprehensively.

'Do you think they know we're coming?' Dato said.

'Probably,' Jonah said.

They walked warily among the carcasses. It was only when you got close that you could detect the sickly-sweet smell of death. They went on, more cautious now, with their weapons raised, scanning the shadows.

The trail dipped into a hollow. It was dark and cold.

As he climbed up out of the shadows and reached the edge of the hollow, Freeman heard the Svan draw breath. Suddenly he sprang into the bushes in front of them. Bezik surged after him and went crashing through the bushes yelling. He returned soon after. There was no sign of the Svan.

'Do you think he's gone to warn them?' Dato asked.

'Let's see where he went,' Jonah said, grim-faced.

The brush was much thicker and it was difficult to see ahead. Jonah went first, forcing his way through the grasping branches that closed in on the trail. At the first turn he shouldered his way through a brake, shielding his eyes with his elbow and abruptly disappeared from sight. They heard a panicked shout.

Suddenly there was a ledge before them and Jonah was rolling down a grassy slope below them; the slope ended at a cliff and a sheer drop. Jonah stopped rolling just short of the edge. He sprang up on his hands and knees, his face pale, staring down into the chasm.

'Fuck!' he said, furiously rubbing his face with his palms. 'Did you see that? Did you?'

'Yes,' said Freeman.

Across five hundred yards of ravine, on another side of the mountain, there was a meadow and the top of a stone tower. Looming above it a distant glacier.

Freeman looked left and right. The ravine extended as far as the eye could see in both directions, an impassable barrier. There was no sign of a track that the Svan might have taken. Jonah scrambled back up the slope and they lay down in the brush where they could look across the ravine at the tower.

'What do you think?' Dato asked.

'I don't know,' Freeman said.

'It's the Furies' hideout,' Dato said.

'You think there's anyone home?' Jonah said.

Freeman consulted the GPS and saved the latitude and longitude for their current location in its memory as a waypoint. Then he used the compass and rangefinder to give him the bearing and distance to the tower on the far side of the ravine. He entered these into the GPS projection facility and it gave him back a lat/long for the tower. He saved it as a second waypoint. He carefully wrote down both readings in his notebook.

'Can you destroy it?' Dato asked.

'Not unless I know what I'm hitting.'

'We need to find the route over there,' Jonah said.

Freeman nodded in agreement. Together, they went back into the woods and searched among the trees for a while, trying to find where the Svan had gone. After ten minutes or so they gave up and followed a path at the edge of the woods, following the line of the cliff.

'Let's have another look across,' Jonah suggested.

They pushed through the brush. Just below them was another ledge with an outcrop of rock to provide cover. From this vantage point they could see that there were two more towers and a cluster of single-storey stone houses around them. Through the binoculars, Freeman spotted the Svan darting between two buildings. There was no sign of anyone else.

'There must be a route over there,' he said.

'I'm going to go and scout around.' Jonah went crouching back into the brush. Freeman made another couple of projections and recorded the results as waypoints. He drew a sketch-map from what he could see. He was reasonably certain he could take out all three towers. Dato and Bezik sat on rocks and smoked cigarettes.

Twenty minutes later, Jonah returned. 'I think I've found the way down.'

It was a dark hole concealed by rocks and surrounded by packed earth. A slight breeze ruffled the ragged cobwebs at the mouth of the hole.

'Wait till you see this,' Jonah said, getting down on his hands and knees and crawling in with his rifle in front of him. Freeman crawled in after him. A few more feet and they were able to sit up. The tunnel opened into a small chamber high enough to stand up in. Jonah switched on his torch. At the centre of the chamber was a man-sized hole with the top of a wooden ladder sticking up out of it.

Jonah pointed the torch into the hole and it lit up the ladder's rungs to the limit of its reach.

'I don't know how far down it goes,' he said. 'At least forty feet.'

The route in.

'How long will you give me?' Jonah asked.

'I'm coming with you,' Freeman said. 'I told you we'd rescue Harry together.'

NINETY-TWO

Freeman spoke to a businesslike young woman at the 42 Attack Squadron Control Centre at Creech Air Force Base in Nevada and gave her the projected lat/longs for the three towers and a 'no strike before' time of 0800 hours on Tuesday, just before dawn tomorrow. That gave them all night to rescue Harry or return and cancel the airstrike if it turned out that the settlement was empty.

Next he handed the satellite phone to Dato. Dato and Bezik had agreed to remain at the rocky outcrop.

'Wait until an hour after the strike then fall back to where the cars are parked at the road end,' Freeman told them. 'If we don't show up by sunset tomorrow call the legal attaché's office in Tbilisi and tell Agent Syverson that we're missing or dead. Got that?'

Dato nodded.

Freeman glanced at Jonah. 'Are you ready?'

'I'm ready.'

They descended rung by rung into the chamber and when they pointed their torches at the walls they revealed the solid stone of the mountain covered in white hands.

'Another warning,' Jonah said.

Everywhere they turned their torches there were handprints, pressed into the stone with bright pigment. They reminded Freeman of Eva's bloody hand on the doorframe in Byron and Renee Bastian's row house back in DC, a world away.

Soon, they reached the packed earth at the bottom of the ladder. The walls of the chamber narrowed to a tunnel through which they moved in a crouch. It was a long way before they observed the first faint suggestion of light. They turned off their torches and went more slowly, feeling the ground ahead. It seemed to Freeman that by some trick of acoustics he could hear a woman singing far off. The faint white glow resolved into a point of light that grew larger as they approached it. They emerged onto a platform ten feet or so above the sandy floor of the ravine. There were handholds in the rock and they swung themselves over the edge and climbed down. A narrow trail followed the foot of the cliff before turning into the ravine, between walls of rock that widened into a pine glade. They could hear running water not that far away. Beyond the glade was a stand of hornbeams beside a stream. They could both hear the woman singing.

They followed the stream downhill to a rock pool in a meander in the river. A woman was washing laundry in the pool, drying clothes spread out on the rocks around her. She was wearing black rubber boots and a long sheepskin coat and her head was covered with a scarf. She looked up as they approached with a wide-open smile on her face.

Freeman was pinned by the force of it.

For a jarring, telescoping moment he thought he was seeing a ghost. It was Katja, her beautiful face raised towards him; it was the dead girl in the snow. The woman in his dreams. He heard a roaring noise in his ears. A split second later the roaring ceased, the world righted itself and he realised what he was seeing.

She stood up.

'You've met one of my sisters,' she said in English before Freeman had a chance to speak. Her voice was husky, and free of any accent; just listening to it caused a lump in his throat.

'You can tell?' he managed.

'I can see it in your face. You're an American.'

He nodded. 'I'm Freeman.'

She considered his companion and said, 'And you?'

'I'm Jonah,' he said breathlessly. She was obviously having the same effect on him.

'Welcome. I am Katarina,' she replied, with a playful gleam in her smile that suggested she found them amusing. 'I am one of the Peaceful. Come on, I will take you to Aslan.'

They crossed the stream and followed Katarina across the bottom of the ravine to the foot of the cliffs. Concealed from view by a stand of trees, there was a stairway hacked in the rock that led, via a series of switchbacks, to the top of the ravine.

Katarina climbed nimbly ahead of them, the coat clinging to her swaying hips. Freeman noticed that the back of her neck was covered in bruises that looked like bite marks.

'Who is Aslan?' Freeman called out.

'One of the not-so-peaceful,' she said, smiling over her shoulder at him. 'He is the leader of the Ras Serditye.'

At the top of the stairs there was an arched doorway, large enough for a crouching man to walk through, and beyond it a pretty alpine meadow with scattered clumps of snow. A paved stone path led along the top of the cliff. Beside it a low stone wall that was covered in lichen cut across the meadow towards the towers. From the cliff edge, Freeman could see the narrow ravine and the clifftop on the other side where Dato and Bezik were sheltering.

'It's quite a place,' Jonah said.

'It's nothing like it was,' Katarina told him. 'It used to be full of people.'

'What happened?' Freeman asked.

'Most of them died. Some left for your country.'

At the edge of the meadow furthest from the cliff were several low brick buildings and the three ancient stone towers standing amid churned-up mud; beyond them was the vertical face of the glacier and a succession of ridges and jagged piebald mountains with snow on their flanks. Freeman noticed that a high frequency dipole antenna was strung between two of the towers.

As they approached the nearest tower a very large, hunched man with a broad, bony forehead and thick black hair squeezed out of the narrow opening at its base. Freeman had thought that Jonah was big but this man dwarfed him. He walked slowly and stiffly towards them. He was wearing a dark cloak of uncured animal pelts that trailed in the mud behind him. His most striking features were his hands: they were huge, like spades, crisscrossed with scars and calloused patches and with ragged, grime-encrusted nails as hard as rhino-horn. They were shaking, with anger or illness, Freeman could not tell.

'You found us,' he said in the same accent-free English as Katarina, his voice a deep and threatening rumble.

Katarina joined him and he rested one of his massive hands on her shoulder. She ran her hand across his chest and kissed his neck.

'I am Aslan,' he said. He raised a shaking fist and pointed it at the tower. 'Go in. Leave your weapons at the door.'

Freeman and Jonah exchanged a look. It was obvious that the same thought had crossed their minds: if they went in they might never make it out again.

'Don't worry, I've already eaten,' Aslan said.

'He's kidding you,' Katarina said.

'It's very funny,' Jonah said.

They set down their rifles and went through the narrow entrance into a large straw-covered room that took up the whole bottom floor of the tower. There was a single arrow-slit opening about twenty foot up, close to the wooden ceiling, and on the far side of the room a ladder leading up to the next storey. The only other light was from a candle on an upturned crate and the flashing red and green pin-lights on an HF radio rigged to a truck battery on a bench in the corner. Aslan squeezed in after them and sat down on a stack of wooden ammunition boxes and Jonah and Freeman sat on upturned crates opposite him.

In the time that it took for Freeman's eyes to adapt he realised that the guide, the Svan who had brought them here from the road end, was sitting on the straw against one of the walls. He was watching them with an unreadable expression on his face.

From a stone shelf Katarina took down four glasses and a grimy soda bottle. She filled the glasses and handed them to Freeman, Jonah, Aslan and the Svan. Jonah sniffed the contents of his glass.

'What is this?'

'It's cha-cha,' she said, setting the bottle on the crate.

'To sentience,' Aslan said, raising a glass in his trembling hand. 'Long may it endure . . .'

'Are you OK?' Freeman asked.

'He has Parkinson's,' Katarina said.

The blow knocked her to the straw; Aslan's fist moved so fast that none of them had time to react.

'Nobody asked you,' he told her. At rest again, his fist resumed shaking. 'Go and finish your work.'

After stealing a glance at Freeman, Katarina went out of the door.

Aslan returned his attention to them and smiled menacingly. His mouth was crowded with teeth. Hunched over the crate, with the candle lighting up the deep furrows in his skin, he was within a couple of feet of them. He was close enough that he could have reached out and grabbed them.

'The rain in Spain falls mainly on the plain.' He started laughing, his whole body shaking. 'All those hours of lessons. They wanted us to understand you. Understand your enemy, they said. Study his ground, his capabilities and his modes of communication. We were going to reduce America to rubble. We could have done it too. You should have seen us. In our day, we were magnificent. Almost like gods. It didn't last though. There were unforeseen consequences. How old do you think I am?'

Jonah and Freeman exchanged a look. It was impossible to tell. His face was ravaged.

'I'm twenty-seven years old. I've shocked you, haven't I? I'm the oldest surviving member of Progress Clade B.'

He drained his glass. He wiped his mouth with the back of his hand. He bared his teeth.

'I envy your lifespan. So what can I do for you? Why have you come here?'

'We're looking for a woman named Harry,' Jonah told him. 'We think that she is with the girl, Eva.'

'More.' He held out his empty glass and Jonah filled it for him.

'As you can see, Eva is not here,' Aslan said. 'She has not been here for more than two years. Not since Uncle Sasha stole her and took her with him to America.'

'Do you know where Eva is now?' Freeman asked.

'The Russians have her,' Aslan told them. 'They are coming

433

here and bringing her with them; perhaps they also have your friend. We'll know soon enough. I've sent a raiding party to meet them.'

'Why are the Russians coming?' Freeman asked.

'The Russians thought that we were extinct. But they were wrong. They have realised their error.' He drained the glass and held it out to be refilled. 'Now they think that they can harvest our genes. Not the junk. Just the good stuff. And they have Eva's eggs. They think that with some cutting and splicing they can excise our defects. Uncle warned us it would be like this. He argued that we must secure a future for ourselves somewhere far away from the Russians. He said it was impossible to remain hidden even here in the mountains.'

'But you stayed?'

Aslan shrugged. 'He believed in America. We did not.'

He climbed unsteadily to his feet and staggered to the entrance. He squeezed through it. The Svan got up and followed him out.

The settlement was empty. They had no idea where Aslan or the others had gone. They decided to explore the buildings and their immediate surroundings and in one of the towers they found a sizeable store of weapons and ammunition. There were stacks of crates with Cyrillic writing containing brand-new AK-107 assault rifles with under-slung grenade launchers and infrared night-sights, five to a crate, cradled in foam. There were crates of RPG-22s, one-shot anti-tank rocket launchers; and beside them wooden boxes filled with plastic-wrapped bricks of plastic explosive. In one corner there were five metal cases, each one containing a Grinch surface-to-air missile.

'They have enough weapons and they have the terrain on their side. They could hold off an army,' Jonah said.

Behind the settlement, in the direction of the glacier, they found a burial ground with eighteen graves, each one marked with piles of stones and beyond it a field of debris, including boulders as large as Metro buses that had been pushed down the mountain by the advancing glacier.

'Time is against them,' Freeman said. 'They're dying off.'

He went from tower to tower and checked the actual GPS readings against the projections he had made from the far side of the ravine. He was within a couple of metres in each case. Close enough for the pilot at his console in Nevada to bring the missiles directly onto them.

It was just a question of waiting for the Furies to return and deploying the beacons to confirm the targets.

At sunset, Freeman decided to wash in the river. He left Jonah cleaning his weapon and went back across the meadow and down the stone steps into the ravine with a towel under his arm. He dropped his sour-smelling clothes on the river bank and jumped in. The bottom was covered in pebbles and the water was freezing. He ducked his head under and came up feeling scalded.

Katarina was sitting on a rock a few yards upstream. She waved to him.

'Want some soap?' she called to him.

'Please.'

She threw him a square of lye-smelling home-made soap. He soaped himself while Katarina looked on, rinsed and dried himself. He wrapped the towel around himself like a sarong and put his Parka on over it. He stuck his bare feet back inside his boots.

'Is that better?' she asked him.

'Sure.'

He walked over to her and sat down on the bank beside her. He saw the barcode tattoo on her wrist and it was impossible for him not to think of Katja, impossible also not to feel a frisson of sexual excitement. Like Katja, this young woman was designed for sex.

'How long have you been here?' he asked.

'Almost five years now,' Katarina replied. 'Before that I was an indentured worker in Tiraspol along with Katja. We escaped and came here.'

Freeman watched the water tumbling over the rocks.

'How is Katja?' she asked.

'Katja is dead,' he told her, after an agonising pause. 'I was the detective who investigated her death.'

'Then I am the last of my kind,' she said calmly.

'I'm sorry.'

She smiled sadly. 'It's OK to want to fuck me.'

He didn't dare respond.

'I want to get out of this place,' she told him. 'Will you take me with you?'

'If I can.'

NINETY-THREE

At dusk, the convoy entered a narrow, tapering valley that was scattered with the wreckage of the previous expedition. When they stopped and got out to look, Harry counted the rusting hulks of two tanks and four armoured personnel carriers. They were buried up to the top of their tracks in the snow. One of the tanks had lost its turret completely, it was hanging off the body like a hinge, and the other had a gaping hole in it caused by an explosively formed penetrator.

Harry noticed that the vehicles were all pointing in one direction, back the way they had come.

'They were retreating,' Dr Markoff said, as if reading her thoughts. He glanced at Gogol and then scanned the ridgeline above. 'Where's your helicopter?'

'It's re-fuelling,' Gogol told him. 'It'll be back soon. What happened here?'

'You are not the first to have come this way,' Dr Markoff said.

'I know that,' Gogol snapped. 'During the August 2008 war with Georgia a mechanised unit was sent up here. We lost communication with them.'

'Half of them were dead by the time they turned back,' Dr Markoff said. 'The Furies picked them off one by one.'

'You don't scare me, old man.'

Dr Markoff wasn't listening. 'Once they turned back the intensity of the attacks increased. It ended here in an ambush. The Furies blew massive charges at either end of the valley, blocking the road with a rockslide. The remnants of the force were stuck, like fish in a barrel.' He sighed and eyed the nearest BTR. 'What's the thickness of the armour on these?'

Harry was looking along the length of the road, to the valley entrance where the rock-strewn hillsides converged.

'If the roads were blocked,' Harry said, 'who cleared them?'

Gogol spun around to look at her.

Dr Markoff smiled. 'The Furies.'

'Why?'

It was the same smile as when he last switched sides. 'So that they could do it again.'

Gogol was running and shouting. Seeing her chance, Harry started sprinting towards the nearest hillside.

The first massive detonation demolished the lead BTR. They must have used a shaped charge buried in the road. It punched a hole through the bottom of the hull and the whole vehicle swelled up like a blood-gorged tick. Harry was bowled over and showered with rocks and dirt. There were five or six more huge detonations in the road and the rear BTR was flipped on its back.

Smoke billowed across the valley.

Then the firing began: the crack and thump of small arms fire all around; the distinctive champagne cork pop of rocket-propelled grenades fired from the hillside and the industrial rattle of the remaining BTR's heavy machine guns returning fire. A further ripple of explosions. A near miss rocked the BTR on its chassis. It stopped firing. Smoke canisters spun out of the turret dispensers. The rear hatch hinged open with a thud and for a moment harsh, high-altitude sunlight lit up the vehicle's interior. The first Russian soldier out was struck in the chest and the rest tumbled out after him into a hail of gunfire and expanding tendrils of white smoke.

Lying flat on her front in the icy mud and slush, Harry moved her head to the left and the right. She looked back under her arm. There was no sign of Dr Markoff or Eva. As far as she could tell the Furies were firing at the convoy from concealed positions in the rocks on the hillside ahead of her. She had been running directly into their fire.

Soon the smoke was so thick it was impossible to see more than a few feet. She decided her best chance was to turn around and crawl back through the wreckage and then run up the opposite hillside to the ridge above.

Bullets kicked up the earth nearby. It occurred to her that if the Furies were using infrared sights then she was probably in full view. She shimmied around and started crawling towards where she judged the nearest hulk to be.

The heavy machine gun on the BTR started up again, a thunderous noise right on top of her.

She had misjudged the direction she was crawling in and had returned to the one functioning BTR. She scrambled around the back wheels into cover and a searing cascade of shell cases tumbling down the vehicle's armoured flanks.

She crouched down beside one of the wheels. Next to her, a soldier who was apparently a medic was giving rudimentary aid to another. Other men were beyond help, lying dead or dying.

Eva was squatting two wheels back. She had lost the sandbag and someone had removed the ball-gag. She grinned at Harry, a grin that was more like the baring of teeth. Harry shuddered and looked away. Through the drifting smoke, she caught a glimpse of brilliant sky and the hillside rising beyond the rusting tank hulks. From about halfway up and to just short of the ridgeline there was a dark mass of trees that offered cover.

It was now or never.

Her escape route was directly in front of her.

Harry jumped up and ran, staggering through the snow. She had reached the first tank hulk when she heard the distinctive *thudda thudda thudda* of the returning helicopter gunship and the *whoosh* of the missiles leaving its pylons.

The hillside behind her erupted: a wall of flame roared up like a tsunami and the shockwave bowled her over. She could feel it scorch her skin and singe her hair. She was lying on her back with sooty flakes falling on her face and a rolling, surging noise in her ears like surf. She spat dirt out of her mouth and rubbed it from her eyes.

It seemed to take an unbearably long time to roll over onto her hands and knees. She scrambled to her feet and staggered forward again, leaving the tank hulks behind her.

As she began to climb, the helicopter swept overhead, skimming the tops of the trees. Dense black smoke rolled down the valley. She dodged between boulders.

The firing was more sporadic now. It seemed difficult to believe that any of the Furies could have survived the gunship's attack.

She felt a brief surge of elation – she was going to make it.

Then she was tackled to the ground.

One of the Ossetians pounced on her. He started punching her and tearing at her clothes. A blow to the side of her head made her see double. Then abruptly he stopped. He was lifted, hands clutching at his neck, a steel chain tightening there, gagging the life out of him. He toppled sideways and Harry backed out from under him. She watched Eva rummaging in his pockets and coming up with the key to her chains.

Harry rolled over and pulled herself hand over hand across the meadow. She had to get away from the Russians, from Eva. She didn't want to die here in this place. Her feet found purchase and she pushed upwards.

She was running again. Within seconds she was in the trees.

She ran uphill between trees on a soft carpet of pine needles while further explosions echoed the length of the valley below. Suddenly the trees came to an end and she stumbled out onto a ridgeline of shifting, silvery scree and jumbled snow-clad rocks that seemed to overlook the entire Caucasus. Deep gorges and jagged ridges stretched away to the horizon.

There was no cover and so when the helicopter rose out of the smoke-filled valley below, passing her on its way up, she had no alternative but to stop and wait. The gunship circled her, before sheering away and coming back around to hover a few feet above the ridgeline.

Gogol and the remaining Ossetians jumped out, plunging into the scree in an explosion of dust and tumbling down as the whole hillside shifted around them. When they reached the top again they were dust-caked and as pale as wraiths.

★ ★ ★

The last light of the sun was fading and the darkness was fast approaching. The remnants of the expeditionary force huddled beside the remaining BTR. There were only twelve of the original thirty Airborne Troops still alive and three of them were seriously wounded.

'They will probably wait until after midnight before they attack again,' Dr Markoff said.

Harry was sitting against the wheel of the BTR and Dr Markoff was beside her. They both had their hands bound together with cable ties.

Eva was gone. She had escaped during the ambush.

The helicopter was circling overhead and Gogol was striding back and forth, smoking a Marlboro Red.

Ignoring Gogol, Dr Markoff continued speaking. 'We identified the gene for a tissue layer called the tapetum lucidum in the back of the eye. It's common in nocturnal animals. It reflects light back through the retina. It's why the Furies can see so well at night and it's why their eyes shine in the dark. You don't stand a chance.'

Gogol kicked Dr Markoff in the ribs and he folded over on himself, groaning. Gogol kept on kicking him.

'Stop it!' Harry yelled, struggling onto her knees and launching herself at Gogol. He knocked her back onto the ground and starting kicking her too. Part of her wanted him to go on kicking her until the things inside her were destroyed. Eventually, one of the Russian soldiers pulled him away.

'We're not going to wait for them to come and pick us off,' Gogol said, struggling to contain himself. 'We'll take the fight to them. We're going to get in that helicopter and we're going to fly to where they're hiding out and we're going to exterminate every last one of them! You got that?'

It was like being drawn into a whirlwind, a vortex of anger. Harry did not think they would survive.

NINETY-FOUR

The raiding party returned six hours before the airstrike was due.

T minus six hours.

Freeman was sitting with Katarina in front of a bonfire on which a blackened pig had been roasting for several hours, drips of fat hissing as they struck the burning embers. They were at the centre of the settlement, in a ring of stones. The first thing Freeman felt was a deep prickling sense of being watched and he sat up rigid. A few moments later, he caught a glimpse of eye-shine out among the glacial debris. He heard the quick sound of feet and hands scrambling in the icy mud of the burial ground.

'Don't make any sudden movements,' Katarina told him. 'Don't reach for your weapon.'

The sound was all through the settlement, rising and falling, drawing closer on every side. Out beyond the tower something growled, a raw primordial sound. The hairs rose on the back of Freeman's neck. He wanted to grab his rifle and run, to throw himself into the nearest doorway.

The darkness around him was shifting, shapes flitting between the towers; creatures with matted hair and filthy, blood-slicked limbs clutching weapons camouflaged with rags.

Animated scarecrows. The last of the genetic code variants bred in the Progress labs.

Somewhere in the flickering shadows on the far side of the fire something was breathing, something big. Freeman clenched and unclenched his fists. His breath came in jagged bursts.

There was a sudden rush of bodies; helot faces with bloodshot eyes and mouths crammed with teeth as sharp as tusks; an explosion of sparks and then the pig was pulled from the fire and dragged away into the darkness.

Aslan advanced slowly towards them, shambling into the firelight with his hand on Eva's shoulder. He towered over her, like the Beast and Beauty. She seemed shy at first, her head bowed. But then she looked up. Her face was bloody and stained with mud and black powder burns. She was wearing the same defiant look as when he first met her in the basement of Dr Markoff's laboratory. He felt such a rush of anger that if it had been him, instead of Jonah, hidden on top of one of the towers with a brand-new assault rifle and a night-scope he would have pulled the trigger there and then. And kept firing until the magazine was empty. No hesitation.

'Where's your friend?' Aslan demanded.

'He left,' Freeman lied.

Aslan lowered himself to the ground, a slow toppling that gathered speed and momentum. He crashed into the mud. He licked his lips and looked away into the darkness.

'He won't get far.'

'Where are the Russians?' Freeman asked.

Aslan sneered. 'They got into their little helicopter and flew away.'

'Where's Harry?'

Standing at Aslan's shoulder, Eva signed at Katarina.

'She says that after the ambush they didn't find Uncle's body or your friend's,' Katarina said. 'She thinks that they may still be alive. She thinks the Russians have them.'

Eva raised her chin in Freeman's direction.

'She says that she recognises you,' Katarina said. 'She is asking why you came here?'

'Because she killed a friend of mine,' Freeman replied.

'She says that if you have friends she doesn't know them,' Katarina said. 'Who did she kill?'

'She shot a woman called Maja, a police officer, when she attacked Senator Cannon's house. She shot her and she died.'

'Were you in love with her?'

He refused to answer.

'She says it was a firefight,' Katarina told him. 'It wasn't personal. Cannon had to die. She says you know what he did.' Eva looked away into the darkness where the Furies were feeding. 'She says that you shouldn't have come . . .'

Aslan nodded to someone behind him and before Freeman had time to react several hands had grabbed him by the arms and shoulders and dragged him through the mud into the darkness.

He was imprisoned in one of the towers.

Freeman sat on the straw in the cool, dark, cave-like space that was lit by a single spear-shaft of light from an unreachable arrow slit far above. He listened to the sound of the Furies calling to each other and the monotonous beating of drums that filled the air, each muffled shock an outbreak of pent-up frenzy. He reflected on the likelihood that if the Furies didn't kill him in the next few hours the airstrike probably would. He had been haunted for so long by airstrikes; to die by one now seemed a fitting end. Death from above; it was said that you never heard the one that got you. He hoped that it would be painless.

He wondered what had happened to Jonah.

He closed his eyes. The drums were having a strange narcotic effect on him. He was so tired. He waited for the beautiful young woman of his dreams to come to him through smouldering ruins.

The sound of gunfire woke him. He looked at his watch.

Five a.m. T minus three hours.

The Furies were still drumming.

The bolt was thrown. Aslan filled the doorway, his face a mask of wrath. He flung a hessian sack onto the straw by Freeman's feet. It was sticky to the touch and the blood was black by moonlight. Inside were the crushed remnants of the Thuraya phone and two severed heads.

Dato and Bezik.

Freeman recoiled violently and scrambled back against the icy wall, filled with horror.

★ ★ ★

Again the bolt. T minus one hour.

Katarina's voice in the darkness: 'Quickly! The Russians are here.'

Freeman climbed to his feet and went out through the door. He emerged in time to hear the thudding rotors of the approaching helicopter. Its searchlight flicked on, lighting up the nearest ridgeline.

'Time to make a swift exit,' Jonah said, his voice soft and thick. He was kneeling beside the body of one of the Furies with its limbs splayed. It was wearing a hooded cloak of animal pelts and its head was at an unnatural angle, its neck broken.

'Have you got the beacons?' Freeman demanded.

'In my pack.' Slowly, painfully, Jonah put down his rifle and slid the pack off his shoulder.

'You're injured,' Freeman said.

'I had an angry exchange with a furious fellow,' Jonah managed. He tried to laugh but ended up coughing; a bubble of spit and blood rising in his throat. The whole left side of his body was soaked with blood.

As they were speaking, Furies had begun to tumble out of the buildings and were spreading out across the settlement.

The helicopter was almost upon them.

'Get him out to the glacier,' Freeman told Katarina. 'I'll join you there.'

'Take the rifle,' Jonah told him. 'Good luck.'

Flailing lines of tracer from anti-aircraft guns arced up into the sky from the tops of the furthest towers as the helicopter swept overhead.

Freeman removed the first of the infrared beacons from the pack, switched it on and threw it down beside the base of the tower. He then removed the Fury's cloak and wrapped it around himself, pulling the hood over his head to disguise his face. He picked up the AK and cocked it. He ran towards the centre of the settlement heading for the nearest tower. Several times he dodged between buildings or ducked into the shadows to avoid Furies, but their attention was focused on the sky and no one tried to stop him.

Behind him, the helicopter banked and came around for a second pass.

Missiles streaked out of its pylons.

The tower that Freeman had been imprisoned in was hit and toppled. Then firing began from the nearest ridgeline, bullets nicking the wall beside him, peppering him with stone fragments. Freeman realised that instead of retreating the Russians must have used the helicopter in the night to ferry the troops forward to a position from which they could now attack the settlement.

Hissing flares, falling and swaying under their chutes, lit up the buildings and the spaces between. Freeman watched as several of the Furies were cut down. With each death he felt a surge of grim satisfaction.

He set off again, hugging the ragged, slanting shadows. Two more times he threw a beacon into the muddy yard beside a tower; he was determined that whatever the Russians failed to destroy would be annihilated by the Predator's missiles.

As the helicopter came around for a third pass, he saw Eva emerge from the tower that held the weapons store with a large rectangular case. She dashed between two buildings and he ran after her. He followed her as she cut across the burial ground to the field of debris. The fractured edge of the glacier towered above her.

In the shadow of a massive boulder, she set the case down on the ground and opened it. Freeman took cover by the nearest rock. He raised the AK and looked at her down the night-sight. A burning white cross with broken arms: a voice in his head yelling, *Kill her!* But as she lifted the launch tube onto her shoulder, Freeman saw what had been in the case: one of the man-portable surface-to-air missiles – a Russian Grinch with a high-explosive warhead.

He paused with his finger on the trigger.

Let her kill the Russians first. Then kill her.

Ahead of him, Eva was kneeling with the weapon's grip-stock in her hands and as the helicopter swung out over the forest on the far side of the meadow she took aim and pulled the trigger. The missile sliced through the air and struck the helicopter's fuselage.

It broke apart mid-air.

The tail dropped away in flames and the cockpit tumbled forward and came crashing down through the forest canopy with its rotor blades spinning, throwing up a blizzard of splintered trees, earth and fractured rock.

Before Freeman had time to react, Eva had flung away the launch tube and was running towards the crash site with a knife in her hand. He jumped to his feet, slung the rifle across his back and continued to pursue her, scrambling across rocks and squeezing between boulders. She was quick and agile among the rocks and he feared he might lose her but once they reached the meadow his longer legs allowed him to keep her within sight.

She never once looked back.

She reached the wood line and darted between trees with Freeman close on her heels. She climbed into the helicopter's fuselage, and across the canted deck to the shattered cockpits, where the bodies of the pilot and his co-pilot were wedged, one above the other. She dragged them from their seats onto the ground and stabbed them again and again with the knife.

When she finally stopped and looked up, Freeman was kneeling waiting for her at the edge of the swathe of broken foliage cut by the helicopter's descent. He had the AK braced against his shoulder and the fire selector was on semi-automatic fire.

She was crouching, poised on folded haunches like a predator about to leap. Her forearms were covered in blood and rivulets of blood were running down her face. Freeman could hear gunshots close by and voices calling his name. Eva cocked her head and rolled her shoulders. She could see him but she didn't seem to be in any hurry.

Freeman wasn't afraid. The strangest thing was that he wasn't really all that angry. He felt a huge, weary irritation – he just wanted this finished.

'For Maja,' he said.

Eva pounced, leaping at him with her hands out like claws.

Freeman squeezed the trigger. She slammed into him and he tumbled backwards, hitting the ground hard enough to knock the air out of him. He was momentarily paralysed. He expected Eva's jaws to clamp down on his neck or his face.

Instead someone was calling his name.

He rolled over to see Eva on her back with her arms and legs making a kind of paddling motion, clawing at the air. Her chest riddled with bullet holes. Standing above her were two figures, Jonah and beside him Katarina. They had come looking for him. Katarina was holding his rifle. At their feet Eva was making a kind of soft sighing sound, and Freeman finally saw her for what she was or what she should have been, a teenage girl.

A dying teenage girl.

Katarina lowered the AK's barrel and pressed it to Eva's forehead.

'I'm sorry,' she said, and pulled the trigger.

Freeman rose to his feet. Eva was motionless now. A spray of blood on the pine needles. Katarina passed the rifle back to Freeman.

'Are you OK?'

Freeman realised that he was shaking violently. He nodded.

'The Russians are in the village,' Jonah said. 'They've got Harry with them.'

Freeman looked at his watch.

T minus eight minutes.

NINETY-FIVE

The Russian troops advanced nervously through the settlement with glowing cinders swirling around them like fireflies. They were shouting to each other for reassurance and occasionally one of them dropped to his knees and fired a shot. Answering fire was sporadic. Flares continued to drift lazily across the sky and by the light of them Harry saw the folded-over corpses of dead Furies among the rubble.

Gogol was dragging her along with him, just behind the advancing troops. He was shouting at them in Russian, goading them on. The attack had proved to be the last straw for Dr Markoff, who was wandering amid his dead creations, shell-shocked and oblivious to the danger.

There was a sudden roaring sound, a deep bass rumble that seemed to come from all directions at once, and then a huge black shape lunged out of the shadows at the nearest soldiers, swinging its massive fists. It was the largest Fury that Harry had seen. Gogol reacted by pulling her into the narrow, dark entrance of a tower and a draught of cold air broke across her face. He threw her down on the straw.

Outside the gunfire intensified.

A shadow fell across the door and Gogol looked up with a startled expression, flare light flashing on the lenses of his spectacles.

'You,' he said in an incredulous tone.

Jonah was standing silhouetted in the doorway. He raised the barrel of his rifle and shot Gogol in the chest. Gogol fell back against the wall and slid down to the straw. Freeman squeezed past Jonah and knelt beside Harry. He cut the bonds at her wrists with a knife.

'Aslan's coming,' Jonah said.

'Come on,' Freeman said, helping Harry to her feet. 'We've got less than two minutes.'

'Until what?'

'Airstrike.'

Freeman hurried her out through the entrance. He imagined that the Predator was already overhead, its pilot staring at them on a console half the world away: fleeting white shapes on the infrared and the pulsing beacons at the base of the towers. Ahead of him, beyond the settlement, the glacier rose out of the darkness and behind him, when he glanced back, he saw Aslan limping towards them.

T minus one minute.

'This way,' Jonah yelled. 'Run.'

They ran between stone huts and out across the churned earth of the burial ground to where Katarina was waiting.

T minus thirty seconds.

Katarina led them through the maze of boulders and up the slope of a hill to the edge of the glacier.

Five ... Four ... Three ... Two ... One

Freeman looked back in time to see the first missile strike its target.

It lit up Aslan so that it appeared as if he was at the centre of an explosion, a beast in flames.

PART FOUR

THE EAST END

NINETY-SIX

An hour before dawn, Harry pushed back the bed covers and swung her feet onto the polished hardwood floorboards. She sat with the weight of her belly on her thighs, aware of Jack softly breathing beside her and the orange streetlight leaking in at the edges of the window blinds. The bedside clock read four thirty. This far into the pregnancy she struggled to find a position comfortable for sleeping; she didn't feel tired though, despite the hour, in fact she was fully awake.

It was a big day. She was due at the hospital later that morning for her twenty-week ultrasound.

She rose to her feet and shuffled to the nearest window, raised the blind so as not to wake Jack. She stared out at the narrow street with its Georgian houses, many of them occupied by traditional Bengali families, and a few by gay couples filled with restorative zeal, the vanguard of gentrification, with only the East London Mosque at the end of the street as a bulwark against them. Waves of immigrants had come through here: Jews, Irish, Huguenots – most of them fleeing persecution of some kind or another.

The alarm wasn't due to go off for another hour and a half. When it did, Jack would roll out of bed with a familiar groan and stagger to the shower before becoming fully conscious. He had a new album to listen to – *Heligoland*.

She decided to make herself a cup of tea.

The August edition of Jack's magazine was lying on the butcher's block in the kitchen, together with a pile of books and papers. It had a distinctive cover, a chiaroscuro screen print of a chimp's glowering, heavy-browed face and beneath it a barcode and the title: 'Metabolically Dominant?'.

Harry couldn't resist flicking through it again while the kettle boiled. Inside the magazine and accompanying the text, there were several photographs: the burned-out facade of Germline BioSciences; the long derelict breeding labs of Progress in Stepnogorsk, Kazakhstan; Cannon's widow in black at his grave-side; and, as a last-minute addition, Senator Elizabeth Oberstar at a press conference with her co-sponsors announcing the new human hybridisation and cloning bill.

'Never again must this be allowed to happen,' she declared.

Jack had pieced together events including the murder of the human-bonobo variant Katja at the hands of Senator Cannon, Eva's vengeful killing spree, the botched Pentagon cover-up including the termination of the metabolically dominant soldier programme and the CIA operation that led to the destruction of the genetic code variants in a remote outpost in the Caucasus Mountains, using a range of named and unnamed sources within the law enforcement and intelligence communities on both sides of the Atlantic. Detective Lieutenant Michael Freeman was portrayed as a good cop struggling to uncover the truth in the face of insurmountable odds and neither Harry nor Katarina, the one surviving variant were mentioned at all.

Harry ran a hand across the taut dome of her belly and smiled; it was like being in on a joke.

Jack called her his ghost in the machine.

There would be no new variants.

Markoff had been right when he'd described it as a Hail Mary Pass. Harry was in Tbilisi, two days after she was rescued, when she finally got hold of a pregnancy testing kit. She remembered the lurching sense of fear in the seconds after she peed while she waited on the result, and then the overwhelming sense of relief at the sight of a single blue line.

'I'm not pregnant,' she'd shouted at the hotel walls, crying because she was so damn happy.

And Jack was on his way.

He'd scooped her up and bullied the British Embassy into issuing her a brand-new passport in record time and whisked her away to a Greek island, where she'd told him the whole story from beginning to end and over again while he took notes, and when they weren't talking or eating or drinking they were making love. And two months later when she'd consulted a different kit in a different frame of mind and saw the two parallel blue lines she'd shouted out loud again, only this time: 'I'm pregnant!'

For inspiration: Edwin Black *War Against the Weak*, Joel Garreau *Radical Evolution*, John Gray *Straw Dogs*, Ray Kurzweil *The Singularity Is Near*, Paul McAuley *Fairyland*, Richard Morgan *Black Man*, Doug Stanton *Horse Soldiers*, Gregory Stock *Redesigning Humans* and Martin Cruz Smith *Gorky Park*.